S0-AXT-765

TIME OF ATTACK

TIME OF ATTACK

MARC CAMERON

PINNACLE BOOKS
Kensington Publishing Corp.
www.kensingtonbooks.com

PINNACLE BOOKS are published by

Kensington Publishing Corp.
119 West 40th Street
New York, NY 10018

Copyright © 2014 Marc Cameron

All rights reserved. No part of this book may be reproduced in any form or by any means without the prior written consent of the publisher, excepting brief quotes used in reviews.

If you purchased this book without a cover, you should be aware that this book is stolen property. It was reported as "unsold and destroyed" to the publisher, and neither the author nor the publisher has received any payment for this "stripped book."

All Kensington titles, imprints, and distributed lines are available at special quantity discounts for bulk purchases for sales promotions, premiums, fund-raising, educational, or institutional use. Special book excerpts or customized printings can also be created to fit specific needs. For details, write or phone the office of the Kensington special sales manager: Kensington Publishing Corp., 119 West 40th Street, New York, NY 10018, attn: Special Sales Department; phone 1-800-221-2647.

This book is a work of fiction. Names, characters, businesses, organizations, places, events, and incidents either are the product of the author's imagination or are used fictitiously. Any resemblance to actual persons, living or dead, events, or locales is entirely coincidental.

PINNACLE BOOKS and the Pinnacle logo are Reg. U.S. Pat. & TM Off.

ISBN-13: 978-0-7860-3182-5
ISBN-10: 0-7860-3182-4

First printing: February 2014

10 9 8 7 6 5 4 3

Printed in the United States of America

First electronic edition: February 2014

ISBN-13: 978-0-7860-3183-2
ISBN-10: 0-7860-3183-2

*For
Catelyn,
our beautiful, wild flower*

And they took ashes of the furnace . . . and Moses did sprinkle it up toward heaven and it became a boil breaking forth with blains on man, and on beast.

—EXODUS 9:10

PROLOGUE

Early October
Yodok Internment Camp 15
North Korea

Qasim Ranjhani had not come to buy a bomb, though the regime had plenty for sale. He wanted something far more deadly.

Though he detested the squalor of Yodok prison, such an isolated place was the perfect laboratory for what he'd come to purchase.

The portion of Camp 15 where the hospital was located was dubbed the Total Control Zone, tucked deep in a dry river valley of one of the seemingly endless waves of mountain ranges that had caused early European visitors to describe the northern part of Korea as "a sea in a heavy gale."

Ali Kadir, Ranjhani's heavily bearded assistant, looked a decade older than his boss, but was the same age at thirty-nine. On the ride in, he had stared out the dusty window of the military van with an intrigued grin, studying the prisoners as if they were animals in a zoo.

Guard towers bristled every hundred meters among row after row of slumping concrete buildings. The entire camp, set at the base of a windswept mountain face, was surrounded and crisscrossed with barbed wire and rolled concertina, much of it electrified. Sharp-eyed guards, hunched and angry against the bitter cold, stood post, patrolled, and smoked here and there among the rabbit warren of dilapidated buildings.

Apart from the red points of their green wool DPRK uniforms and hats, gray ruled the day at Yodok, as if color had been bled from wood and paint and sallow faces, so all melded into the surrounding rock and snow.

Some of the prisoners, new arrivals, had been arrested with as many as three generations of their family. Their faces still held the look of mouth-gaping astonishment, having only vague guesses as to what had brought them, their children, and even their aging parents to such a hell on earth. Others, the old-timers, clad in whatever rags they could stitch together against the high mountain cold, trudged along at their daily chores like the walking dead that they were. For in Yodok internment camp, *life* was the only sentence.

Inside the hospital, Ranjhani took shallow breaths, as if he might somehow avoid particular aspects of the squalid air.

The unsettling scratch of tiny claws on tile jerked the Pakistani's attention away from a babbling DPRK colonel. He watched a skinny black rat scuttle along the baseboard, then dart across the chipped floor of the hospital's front office. There was no waiting room. It was not that kind of hospital.

A gaunt cleaning woman wearing a threadbare prison

smock and patched gray pants looked up at the sound. Hawk-like, she turned her head toward the rat. A deft flick of her straw broom sent the animal slamming against the block wall. Pinching the unconscious beast by the tail, she let it drop into a plastic paint bucket with a rattling thud. Like the rat, the woman was little more than a bag of bones. Her chopped, utilitarian hair hung lifeless and sparse. Brown eyes sagged over hollow cheeks, absent even the memory of a smile.

Ranjhani paid particular attention to the skin of her left arm. It was pink and puckered well above her gnarled hand, as if by a chemical burn. She moved to resume her sweeping, but the Pakistani grabbed her arm above the elbow, as one might pick up a stone to examine it. He was careful to avoid contamination from the seeping scar at her wrist. The woman went limp at his touch.

Ranjhani was not tall. Most would have considered him on the slender side, but compared to the stooping woman, he was a well-fed giant. A smartly trimmed goatee, flecked with gray, framed full lips that pursed when he thought about anything very hard—as they did now while he studied the prisoner. In her hollow eyes there twitched the same sense of desperation he heard from the snick of tiny claws as the rat tried to escape the plastic bucket.

Ranjhani perused the wounded flesh with great interest. It was recent, still weeping clear fluid. The simple act of handling a broom must have been excruciating for the woman.

Colonel Pak of the North Korean National Security Agency bent at the waist, peering down at the bucket, nose crinkled.

"That is astonishing!" He stood under a life-size picture of Kim Jong-Un, the Dear Leader.

"Astonishing?" Ranjhani raised a black eyebrow, letting the woman's arm fall away. "How so? What could possibly be so astonishing about a rat?"

Colonel Pak gave a detached shrug. "We do not see many rats around the camp. The filthy prisoners have eaten most of them." He laughed, the chuckle turning into a phlegm-rattled cough. "They eat snakes, snails, even kernels of corn they dig from plops of cow dung. They are dogs, I tell you, Doctor Ranjhani. Not even human."

Ranjhani had known hunger, but never bad enough to dig his food from cow dung. It was, he thought, easy to imagine this half-wild woman doing just that. There was a quiet panic about her and the hundreds like her inside this forlorn mountain prison. He'd seen the look before, in the eyes of a girl he had drowned for snubbing his advances.

Most of the girls he'd known considered Qasim Ranjhani handsome—or at least they had told him so. A Pakistani national, he'd inherited his father's dark skin and thinnish features. He was given to precise haircuts, face lotions, and strong cologne—a metrosexual, if such a term had existed in Lahore.

He raised a scented handkerchief to his nose and looked up at the colonel. "Perhaps we might take a look at our objective?"

"Of course," Colonel Pak said, sticking out his bottom lip in an odd, chimpanzee-like way he didn't seem to realize he was doing. He shot a withering stare at the woman with the broom, a stare that held the power of life or death. "Get out of here, bitch!" he barked. "Go clean the guards' dispensary!"

"Yes, Comrade Colonel," the woman answered robotically as if numb to his tone. She grabbed the rat bucket and slipped out the door without looking back.

Pak picked up the desk phone outside the door and barked something in Korean. All Ranjhani understood was "Doctor Khong," the name of the man he'd actually come to see.

While they waited, the colonel produced a little notebook from the pocket of his uniform. He looked up from under the bill of the round military hat that sat on his head like an overly large platter. His bottom lip crept out again. "I must have the guards remember to cut that woman's corn ration since she has found herself a rat. Full bellies breed a sense of entitlement—"

The metal door swung open without warning, and a harried man that had to be Doctor Khong stepped out. Sweat covered his high forehead. His hair was mostly hidden under a white surgeon's cap that matched his lab coat. Flitting eyes, like those of a nervous prey animal, flicked around the room.

"Oh. You are already here," he said, panting as if he'd run a block to meet them rather than just coming from the back hall.

"I gave you plenty of notice." The colonel's face darkened, bottom lip curling.

"Of course, of course." Doctor Khong's head bobbed in an automatic nod. He spoke in short choppy sentences, as if he had to breathe between every two or three words. "It is fine. Really. Some minor issues, but I will explain."

"Issues can earn a man a bullet in the back of his head," the colonel said. "You would do well to remember that, Doctor."

Khong pulled open the door. "Not to worry, Comrade Colonel. Really. Please, follow me."

Ali balked outside the door, having an idea what was on the other side. "Should we not put on some sort of protection, a breathing apparatus perhaps?"

"A surgical mask is sufficient," Khong said. "Really."

Colonel Pak gave a withering glare. "I was led to believe what you have is suitable for Doctor Ranjhani's needs."

"Please, please, please." Khong waved his hand, motioning the men through the open door. "Come and see for yourselves."

Doctor Khong walked like he spoke and led the little entourage haltingly down a narrow corridor. Naked incandescent bulbs spaced along the mildewed ceiling struggled to emit any light at all. Unmarked doors, like those in a cheap hotel, ran down either side of the hall. There were no windows and, Ranjhani noticed, no sound but the electric whir of unseen fans. The smell of mothballs and, oddly enough, boiling fish hung on the air. Khong paused at the sixth door on the right, produced four surgical cloth masks from the pocket of his lab coat. He passed them to the men.

Donning one himself, he waited a moment for everyone to stretch the elastic over their ears, then shouldered his way into the room before the colonel could chastise him again.

Ali stopped in his tracks on the hallway side of the door, a low moan escaping his chest. In spite of himself, Qasim Ranjhani held the scented kerchief to his nose. The colonel gagged a bit, quickly turning it into a cough so as not to appear weak.

"As you see," Doctor Khong said, "the virus is virulent, just as I told you." He pointed with an open hand to four hospital tables lined up on the other side of a head-high glass partition. The lab was glaringly bright in comparison to the dim hallway, like an operating room or dentist's office. "Weak outside the body, but really, the virus runs wild once it finds a home."

Ranjhani noticed a metal drain grate in the center of the floor, for easy cleaning. The colonel had bragged on the ride in how North Korean surgeons saved a great deal of money during their training by using Yodok prisoners to practice their craft. With an endless supply of patients, they could practice unneeded appendectomies and all manner of operations and experiments, generally without the benefit of costly anesthesia. It was a gruesome notion, but one Ranjhani could understand as long as the surgeries were for a scientific purpose.

On the far side of the glass partition, two women and two men occupied the four tables. Two lay faceup, two were facedown, illustrating the full effects of Doctor Khong's project. All four were completely nude, their swollen bodies exposed to the bright light and chilly air of the laboratory. Wide leather straps secured their ankles to each individual table. Eruptions of angry red boils covered the patients, draining in horrific gore on the dingy sheets beneath them. Even the soles of their feet were not immune from the pustules.

"As you can see, the disease manifests outwardly through the formation of boils," Doctor Khong said, waving a hand at the glass. The partition did not go all the way to the ceiling and proved to be more for appearance than any real quarantining effect.

The colonel stuck out his lip, feeling it necessary to prove he was in charge by giving at least some of the briefing, though he was just getting most of the information himself. "Everyone has likely had a boil at some point in his life," he said. "It is easy to understand the intense pain this virus would cause."

"Quite so, Dear Colonel," Khong said. If he was upset at the interruption, he didn't show it. "The boils are painful. Extremely so. But they are only a symptom. Death occurs due to acute respiratory distress. The Americans call it ARDS. In my studies with prisoners it has proven one hundred percent fatal."

"Ah," Ranjhani observed. "But these prisoners are half starved already."

"That is correct," Khong said. "But I feel certain that mortality would reach well over ninety percent, even in healthy Americans."

"Let us now ask the real question," Ranjhani said. "Is it contagious?"

"Very much so," Khong said, "given the right set of circumstances." His head bounced as if on a spring. His eyes began to dart again, as if he expected the bullet Colonel Pak had promised. "The virus must enter the bloodstream to be communicable."

Pak sputtered in angry protest, obviously seeing a sale slip away.

Ranjhani raised a hand to calm him. "Interesting," he said, leaning closer to the glass to get a look at the woman on the nearest table. "How old is this one?"

"Seventeen." Doctor Khong spoke clinically, detached, as if the girl wasn't another human being. "She is pregnant, nearing full term."

"Hmm, I know this little bitch," Pak said, lip inching out again. "Jeong Gyo. Her father spoke ill of the Dear Leader during one of his university lectures. A family of dogs."

The pregnant girl's head lolled to one side, facing them. A clear oxygen tube ran from her nose. Cracked lips parted, but she did not speak. Her left eye was swollen closed from a pustulent boil on the lower lid. A distended belly was knobby and red as if she'd been branded with a hot poker. One arm was thrown back above her head, exposing a nest of weeping boils that infested her armpit like wasp stings. Straining lungs filled with fluid. Her breath already impeded by the press of the baby against her diaphragm, she took short, shuddering gasps, drowning in the air.

Ranjhani found it difficult to look at but impossible to tear his eyes away.

A smile twitched across Doctor Khong's face. "I am allowing the virus to run its course in the others. No intervention." He was obviously pleased with himself. "However, I have sedated this one and put her on supplemental oxygen to ensure that she does not go into shock before the birth. It will be most interesting to see if the virus has passed to the fetus in utero."

"Quite." Colonel Pak nodded.

"Tell me, Doctor," Ranjhani said, taking a breath through his mouth before he spoke, like the up-note of a snore. "Have you identified the disease?"

"That is the issue," Khong said, his facial tics returning in full force. "We are not certain. We first saw it manifest last winter in a prisoner from the bachelor quarters. They huddle together at night for warmth, leaving their clothes outside in an attempt to freeze the lice. Blood, fecal matter, and other bodily fluids are in great supply in such places. A wonderful environment for such a virus. I've done a myriad of tests over the last year—"

The colonel's lip curled out again, nearly as far as the plate-like brim of his hat. His face screwed into a disgusted sneer. "These prisoners keep company with pigs. They eat all manner of garbage. It is no wonder they catch some disease unknown to civilized man."

"Quite so, Dear Colonel," Khong nodded. "Pigs and other animals play a vital role. The exact host from which it sprang is still a mystery. In some ways it resembles smallpox. In other ways, it is closer to respiratory flu. The boils are interesting. Most such sores are full of bacterium from an infected hair follicle or minor cut. These teem with virus. Think of each and every boil as a swollen pocket of extremely potent influenza." Dark eyes flitted over the lab tables. "No one has ever identified the particular disease that caused the plague of boils in the Judeo-Christian Bible. Perhaps this could be it."

"What do you know of the Bible, Doctor?" the colonel snapped.

"Nothing more than scientific perusal, Colonel," Khong said. "I assure you."

"I am curious, Doctor." Ranjhani took another long, thinking breath behind the surgical mask. "How much of the virus needs to enter the bloodstream in order to affect the host?"

Khong raised his forefinger, grinning. "That, sir, is

the most wonderful thing. I have personally induced it with dirty needles, a small nick with an infected razor, even a dentist's drill—all with a hundred percent success. Both these women contracted the disease through sexual contact with infected men."

"Still." Colonel Pak stared at the prisoners, his lip nearly touching the glass partition. "It proves useless as a biological weapon if it cannot be transmitted more easily. An infestation of boils would even thwart a rutting American's desire for sex."

"It may still prove useful," Ranjhani said, his mind racing with ideas. Envisioning the possible had always been his strong suit.

"Whatever you say," the colonel grunted. "You know better than I. Rest assured, my country is an ally in whatever you decide . . . as long as it is used against the West."

"And I can *assure* you, Colonel," Ranjhani said, "that will be the endgame." He turned again to the doctor. "I would require a sample for transport as early as possible."

"Of course." Doctor Khong sighed. The look of relief on his face said he knew that this deal would not only bring valuable cash to his country but might also avert the possibility of his getting shot in the back of the head.

The colonel had grown twitchy from loitering so long among the moaning patients. He motioned for everyone to follow him out of the room and back down the hall. Ranjhani stopped at the door, turning before he left the lab.

He cleared his throat to summon Khong's attention.

"There was a female prisoner sweeping when we first arrived—"

"Why?" Khong's face pinched in a look of worry and guilt. "What did she tell you? One cannot trust the word of a prisoner. Really . . ."

"She said nothing." Ranjhani shook his head. "But I wonder if you might know what caused the wound on her hand."

"Oh, that." Khong breathed easier. "She came in contact with some mold . . . in one of the storerooms."

Ranjhani nodded toward Khong's right hand, which showed similar signs of burning, though not nearly so severe. "Did you also find yourself in that storeroom?"

Khong shot a worried glance at Colonel Pak. "I merely cleaned the prisoner's wound so she could complete her chores. Some of the mold must have gotten on me."

Ranjhani narrowed his eyes, studying Khong's blistered hand. "A potent mycotoxin to cause so much damage in its natural form. Would it be possible to get a sample of this mold? I will add fifty percent to our agreed-upon price." He looked at the colonel. "Off the books."

Ten minutes later, Qasim Ranjhani and his assistant stood in the colonel's office, sipping weak coffee while they waited for the truck to be brought around. Ever attentive for listening devices, Ranjhani leaned sideways, whispering the basics of his plan in Ali's ear.

Ali turned up his nose. "If the sickness does not jump from one person to another, how can it do us any good? Would we not do better to focus on attaining a significant bomb to blast away the American swagger?"

"With a little orchestration and the will of Allah, this will prove better than any bomb." Ranjhani inhaled deeply, a smile slowly infecting his face. He put a hand on Ali's shoulder. "Surely you have seen how a brood of small chicks will peck and peck at a bit of red fuzz on a fellow chick, thinking it to be blood? Over and over they collectively worry the spot until it soon becomes an open sore. The wounded chick is eventually pecked to death over nothing more than a misunderstanding . . ."

The squeaking military truck rumbled up outside.

Ranjhani walked out a few steps behind Ali.

"Forgive me, my friend, but I must make a call. I will join you shortly." Ranjhani listened to his cell phone ring, stamping his feet against the cold. He slowed, allowing Ali to get well ahead and out of earshot before he answered.

It was difficult enough to explain the concept for the plague of boils. Ranjhani hadn't even mentioned the mold. If it was the sort of toxin he believed it to be, it would provide the ultimate weapon. The virus would just be the beginning.

Pyongyang
Seventy miles southwest of Yodok Prison

Governor Lee McKeon sat in his assigned seat in the sprawling grandstands, five vacant chairs away and one row below the North Korean president. Two female aides sat on the other side of McKeon, heads bowed in boredom, crunched close together against the chilly air. A retinue of groveling yes-men surrounded the Dear Leader, each in the full uniform of some high-ranking general. There was no shortage of beautiful, immaculately dressed people, ready to bring coffee or answer any other whim of the boyish North Korean president.

Rank after goose-stepping rank of North Korean soldiers marched by, falling boots vibrating the parade ground below. All were gaunt with frowning faces, as if someone had just eaten their favorite pet and hadn't given them a bite. The governor couldn't help wondering what the endless row of youth thought of their supreme leader. The look in their angry young eyes reminded him of the old proverb: *When the great lord passes, the wise peasant bows deeply and silently farts.*

McKeon had a perfect view of the parade below but had to turn half around in his plastic stadium seat to see if the president happened to be looking at him. Dennis Rodman had warranted a spot next to the Dear Leader on his visit, but the governor of Oregon was an official from the United States—the lowest of pariah in the mind of the North Korean president. A statement had to be made—loud and clear. Even if McKeon wasn't from the federal government—the Dear Leader's disgust for all things American earned anyone even remotely connected with Washington, D.C., far less respect than he'd afforded the retired basketball star.

McKeon was a self-proclaimed *Chindian*—of Chinese and Indian descent—with an Scottish surname. What could be more American than that? He was a lanky man, nearly six and a half feet tall, with narrow, somewhat sloping shoulders that drew many to compare him with Abraham Lincoln. These were traits that didn't hurt him in the election, considering the fact that he was actually Pakistani—not Indian—and Chinese with mahogany skin and thin, horse-like features.

Below, endless ranks of artillery, tanks, and missiles followed the troops—and then, more soldiers. Always, there were more soldiers. North Korea might not have enough food, but it was important for the world to know that they possessed an endless supply of angry-looking young men and women to throw at any threat.

McKeon leaned sideways to rest his back from so much sitting. He turned to smile and let the Dear Leader see how truly impressed he was by this show of force.

The governor's reasons for even being in the Democratic People's Republic of Korea set his nerves on edge. He jumped when his cell phone began to buzz in the pocket of his jacket.

It would be bad manners to answer, but the Dear Leader seemed enthralled with the spectacle of his own presentation, so McKeon picked up, half-thankful for the break from watching the never-ending river of grumpy young soldiers.

"Yes?" McKeon cupped his hand over his mouth in an effort to mask the blaring parade music pouring from the loudspeakers above. There was, of course, the remote chance that NSA or some other obscure U.S. intelligence agency would be listening in, but both men spoke on disposable devices that had been purchased in North Korea. Far from the smartphones the governor was accustomed to, the piece of junk he held to his ear didn't even qualify as a dumb phone. It was, however, theoretically untraceable.

"I have it, my friend." Qasim Ranjhani's voice clicked with a Pakistani-infused English, thick with Punjabi influence. Both men shared a *Chindian* heritage—among other things.

"There was never any doubt." McKeon snugged his

jacket up around his neck as a chill racked his spine. He'd hoped, but not dared to believe, this could actually happen.

"It will take coordination," Ranjhani said. "And we are so few."

McKeon glanced up at the Dear Leader, who thankfully was still watching the spectacle of his might and power. "We are few," he agreed. "But we have help."

"If that same help does not murder us," Ranjhani said.

"I will advise him you have it so he can make the necessary acquisitions." McKeon felt an electric jolt at the possibilities.

"Very well," Ranjhani said. "There is something else, but I will tell you about it in person." He ended the call without another word.

McKeon was used to such abrupt behavior from his friend, especially when he was excited. He returned the phone to his pocket, glad to keep the conversation short. The president of North Korea had decided to look up at that very moment and now stared down from the row above with a dyspeptic frown.

If the Dear Leader had known what McKeon had been talking about, or the havoc he was about to unleash on the United States, that frown would have been a smile— and McKeon would have been given a better seat.

Three months later, Saturday
Bagram Air Base
Afghanistan

First Sergeant Rick Bedford hung plastic reading glasses on the collar of a gray ARMY T-shirt and tossed the tattered copy of *Sports Illustrated* on the seat next to him. He tried to force a pleasant smile as he sat down in the worn barber chair. With high cheekbones and a thick mustache to match his dark hair, he was a known smiler among his men, but the days, weeks, and months in Afghanistan, so far away from his wife, had started to pile up on him. It was easy to see why the Russians always looked so angry during the '80s.

"Where's Aina today?" He did his best to grin at the girl who stood wide-eyed behind the barber chair, holding a pair of scissors. She looked so young, from Kyrgyzstan like most of the other barbers. He wondered why she was cutting hair and not in school.

"Aina has taken ill," the girl said. Her command of English was excellent—probably what got her the job. "My name is Macha. I have not work here for some months, but they call me back because it is so busy. Everyone wants a haircut before they go home to their sweethearts."

"That is so, Macha." Rick Bedford sighed, closing his eyes. "Gotta look nice for our sweethearts."

"You have been in Afghanistan for some time?"

"Long enough." Bedford knew better than to talk specifics with the hired help. But rather than go secret squirrel, he usually tried to joke his way out of such conversations. "I'll have to throw a handful of dirt in my sheets when I get home just to be able to go to sleep."

Macha gave a strained laugh, yammering on about the weather, the dirt, even the horrible Bagram traffic. He could feel her hand tremble as she clipped his hair. She'd probably gap him up something terrible, just in time to go home and see Marta.

"Aina is very pretty, no?" the girl said, adjusting Bedford's head with both hands. "You know her well over these months, I suppose."

"She was a good barber, that's all." Bedford shrugged. He didn't have any particular loyalty toward Aina. She just knew how to cut his hair. Some of the soldiers managed to hook up with the Kyrgyz women who worked in many of the service jobs on base. Even absent General Order #1, which prohibited such intimate behavior, Bedford wanted no part of such an affair. He'd lived and worked in this hellhole for nearly a year with his only thought to get back home to his wife. The fact that she was the sheriff's daughter and a very accurate shot had only a little to do with his fidelity.

"Ah, you work with the Desert Rats," the girl said, coming to a realization. Her scissors snipped away around his ears. "You all go home tomorrow."

Bedford groaned. It wasn't a question. She already knew. He made a mental note to remind his guys about Operational Security. Flagrant disregard for op sec could give the enemy enough intelligence to plant an improvised explosive or set up a sniper. Even so, Bedford found himself in a forgiving mood. The thought of returning home made him feel ten pounds lighter. Images of Marta flooded his mind.

"Tomorrow," Bedford whispered without thinking. He stifled a yawn. Hell, almost everyone was going home. They shouldn't talk about it, but by now, it was national news.

"Good for you," the barber said. "You should be home tomorrow night."

"Takes a bit longer than that." Bedford chuckled. Aina had never bothered him with such small talk.

"Still, you are going," the woman said. In her exuberance, she nicked him with her scissors.

He brought a hand to his ear and came back with a drop of blood.

"Please forgive me," the girl said, eyes down, glistening with tears. "It is nothing but a tiny scratch, I assure you."

Sergeant Bedford took a deep breath, biting his tongue. But, if he was anything, he was a nice guy. "Patient to a fault," his last performance rating had said. He just wanted to get home in one piece and see his wife before some overzealous barber cut his head off.

"It's all right," he said. "A little scratch won't kill me."

"It is done," Ali said, pressing the cell phone to his ear. A fierce wind blew down from the Hindu Kush, whipping the black beard across his face and pressing loose robes against his body.

"Excellent," Ranjhani said. "I will alert the others."

Eight days later
Sunday, 2:10 PM
Kanab, Utah

It took two days from the time they left Bagram for the members of Bedford's U.S. Army Reserve Civil Affairs 405th Battalion to plant their boots back on U.S. soil in Fort Dix, New Jersey—where they spent the better part of a week filling out paperwork and talking to shrinks. Military brass conducted mandatory training to assist returning war-fighters in their demobilization and reentry into civilian life—even going so far as to give a class on remembering to kiss their wife before trying for any other "end state."

First Sergeant Bedford and members of his reserve unit made it out at the head of their group and boarded a military hop to Nellis Air Force Base outside Las Vegas late Saturday evening—nearly a week after they'd left Afghanistan.

Two weeks before they returned to the United States, Sergeant R. J. Howard's wife had told him during a pouty Skype session that she'd decided to split the sheets in favor of a fellow professor at Southern Utah State. The young sergeant had bought a brand-new Ford F250 on the Internet that same night in an effort to salve his wounds.

Understandably, Howard was in no great rush to get back to Cedar City and decided to stop off and visit a sister in Kanab. Bedford hitched a ride with him.

Both men were feeling achy by the time they picked up the truck at the dealership in Las Vegas early Sunday morning but chalked it up to jet lag and deployment fatigue.

Seven days after his C-130 had gone wheels-up from the hellhole of Afghanistan, Rick Bedford found himself standing on the familiar concrete front porch of his modest red brick house—the thing that contained all he'd been missing and fighting for over the last year. His throat hurt and his butt was sore from endless hours of sitting, but he was home.

Marta answered the door, blond hair loose around her shoulders. It was just the way he liked it, but after a year's separation, he wouldn't have cared if she wore a Mohawk. She was the most beautiful thing he'd ever seen.

Her neck flushed red over the collar of a white blouse when she saw him. Her jeans were tight, oh boy were they tight. Red lips parted and hung there a moment before she spoke.

"I thought you weren't coming home for another day . . ." She fanned her face with an open hand in a futile attempt to keep from crying. "The girls went to Kendra's after church. They're doing homework over there."

"Well, you know I miss them," Bedford said, "but it's not such a bad thing for us to have the house to ourselves right now." He let his daypack and heavy canvas duffel fall to the porch. The change in weight made him sway on his feet. For a moment, he thought he might pass out. It was to be expected, he supposed, after being awake for so many hours. He winced when Marta reached back and grabbed him over both hip pockets, drawing him to her. Sitting for hours in airplanes and pickups had given him some kind of sore at the base of his spine.

Bedford was a soldier, a father, and a husband. The soldiering had taken up all his time for the last three hundred and thirty-six days. The fatherly stuff he'd get to later, when the girls came home. He wasn't about to let a little jet lag and a pimple on his butt keep him from the pressing husbandly duties before him. Any thought of discomfort or sleep or Afghanistan bled from his mind as he gathered his wife in his arms and pushed her back inside the door.

The governor of Oregon stepped away from a budget meeting at his office in Salem and answered his second cell phone, the one his aides were not allowed to touch.

"Yes?"

"Peace be unto you," Qasim Ranjhani said, a strange lilt in his voice.

"And to you," McKeon said.

Ranjhani's voice buzzed with excitement. "It has begun."

"Excellent." With over seven hundred fifty thousand people of interest on the government's terrorist watch lists, McKeon didn't waste much time with worry over whether or not anyone was listening to his phone. "Our friend has his people in place. He will be ready."

"I have to tell you"—Ranjhani's breath whistled through his nose—"this man we do business with is a cause for grave concern to me."

"Focus on the possibilities ahead," McKeon said, glancing around to see that he was alone. "We will prevail, Allah willing." He ended the call, preferring not to discuss the specifics of mercenary help in a holy war. In truth, he was as concerned as Ranjhani. Allowing outsiders to assist with their plan could have deadly consequences. But most of the assets his father had worked so hard to put in place had been hunted down and killed—a fact that a certain American agent would very shortly come to regret.

PART ONE

The wicked flee when no man pursueth, but the
righteous are as bold as a lion.

—PROVERBS 28:1

CHAPTER 1

Jericho Quinn wished he was on a motorcycle. The mess dress uniform, the tie, the crowds of wedding guests he didn't know, all left him with the urge to step away for air. He could put on a good face for a short time, socialize, tell polite stories. He was, after all, an officer and a gentleman trained on the very grounds of this hallowed institution. But it didn't take long before such talk grew thin and he found himself longing for that quiet place inside his helmet—on a long ride. It really didn't matter where.

Gunnery Sergeant Jacques Thibodaux stepped up beside him, dipping a Marine Corps high-and-tight toward Quinn's ex-wife's date. Air Force Captain Gary Lavin strutted around like a peacock, giving advice to anyone who would listen about all on which he was an expert, which, according to him, was everything under the Colorado sun. Kim appeared to agree.

Jericho couldn't help wincing every time the man opened his mouth.

"You know, 'Because he needed killin' ain't a valid defense in court," Thibodaux grunted. His voice was steeped in a gumbo-thick Cajun rhythm. Huge shoulders threw Quinn and much of the real estate around him into shadows. A black patch covered an injured eye, courtesy of flying shrapnel from a gunfight in a Bolivian jungle just weeks before.

Both men were OGAs—Other Governmental Agents, detailed from their regular assignments to report directly to the president's national security advisor. Quinn with Air Force OSI, Jacques from the Marine Corps.

Quinn chuckled. "Whatever. He's Kim's business." He nodded at Thibodaux's patch to move the subject away from his ex-wife's love life. "How's the eye?"

"It is what it is." Thibodaux shrugged. "Doc says getting my vision back is still touch and go. I don't really mind, though." He gave Quinn a sly wink with his good eye. "Camille likes it when I wear the patch to bed. She says it's like wrestlin' with a James Bond villain."

"You've been waiting all day to tell me that, haven't you?" Quinn said.

"Maybe." The big man laughed. "Speakin' of wrestling with villains, how's your baby brother? Is our pretty little Russian friend still takin' care of him?"

"He'll be in the hospital for the next week or so." Quinn's younger brother, Bo, had been wounded in the same gunfight where Jacques injured his eye. "And yes, the boss worked it out with State so she can stay in the States for a while. But, her allegiance is to mother Russia. She'll likely slip away someday soon when Bo's heart is healthy enough to break."

Prone to fits of pensive philosophy, the big Cajun

turned to gaze across the concrete deck at the bride and groom. He shook his head. "Damn women, they get us all, later or sooner. If you're single, they sneak up at you when you ain't lookin' and convince you you'll just die if you don't marry 'em. If you are married, then one comes along, sneaks up at you, and does her level best to make you single. They do it just for giggles, I expect."

Quinn scoffed, looking at the Marine's raven-haired wife, where she sat on the concrete wall with a blanket across her shoulder, nursing her baby, Henry—which Jacques pronounced closer to *Ornery*. Somehow, between Thibodaux's repeated deployments to the Middle East, he'd found the time to father seven sons. Each of the older six now wore a black eye patch to show solidarity for his daddy.

"I don't know," Quinn said, "you seem pretty settled."

"Oh, I am, l'ami." Jacques gave a somber nod. "And Camille's pretty good with a knife, if I ever decide I ain't."

"So," Quinn mused, half interested, half placating his friend's desire to philosophize about females. "You think a woman will be the end of me?"

The Cajun smacked Quinn on the back with a roaring laugh. "You kiddin' me, beb? You're here with the hottest *jolie fille* at the party, meantime you still broodin' over your ex. You're damn right it'll be a woman to bring you down."

A thousand meters to the west, the sweet hint of peppermint and gun oil hung in a deadly cloud among the shadowed boughs of a thick juniper. Not so tall as to stand out from its surrounding neighbors, the tree stood on a swell of earth across Academy Drive, with a perfect firing lane to the concrete deck in front of the cadet chapel.

A young Japanese woman settled among the branches, her almond eye behind a powerful Leupold scope. Strong legs entwined gnarled limbs, boots against the peeling bark of the trunk. Braced but relaxed, she melded into the lines and shadows of the tree like a leopardess in the relative comfort of her hide. Thick black hair hung across the oval features of her face like a sniper veil, parting to fall around each side of the .338 Lapua rifle. She was still years from thirty, but the flint-hard look in her eyes overshadowed her youthfulness. She'd learned to mask the hardness, but if anyone with discernment looked at her long enough, the age of her experience showed through. Two men had questioned her—each during an intimate moment when she'd let her guard down. She'd answered each in turn with a dagger to the throat.

She was dressed as a tourist, and her green long-sleeve T-shirt and dark jeans were tight enough that anyone from the Security Police would not think to look at anything else. An hour before, she'd batted her eyes at the baby-faced airman as she'd come through the North Gate of the Academy, shoulders relaxed with the full knowledge that if he tried to search her vehicle she'd kill him before he got to the trunk.

Of course, he had smiled and waved her through.

Once on base, she'd parked in the lot at the Academy Visitors Center beside a van belonging to a group of elderly tourists. She'd carried the three pieces of the custom rifle—barrel and action, Kevlar stock, and 3X12 mil-dot scope—in a flowered green case meant for a tennis racket. It was the weekend, and, for all anyone on campus knew, she was a female cadet out to enjoy the warm weather. Once off the trail, the earth tones of her clothing made it easy to disappear into the leafy undergrowth that surrounded the Academy.

If anyone happened on her now that she had the rifle assembled, there would be no doubt as to what she was and what she intended to do. But that would not happen. She was well hidden. Her mission would be over in a matter of moments. She would pull the trigger and then melt into the traffic on Interstate 25 before the echo of the gunshot died against the mountains.

The young woman sucked on the peppermint, letting it click against her teeth as she played the scope's graduated crosshairs across the wedding party. She let them rest on the gaunt lines of Quinn's jaw, just forward of his ear. He was handsome enough, with the rugged, predatory look she preferred in her men. The scope was strong enough she could tell that he needed to shave. His movements were smooth, as if every one had been choreographed and practiced many times. It would be such a shame to kill him.

She let the crosshairs drop to settle over his bow tie. From this distance the 250-grain spitzer ballistic-tip bullet would drop enough to hit him center chest. But, it was not yet time for that. She nudged the scope to the left. There were other ways to destroy a man's heart.

Quinn's seven-year-old daughter, Mattie, skipped across the concrete deck, rescuing him from further philosophy discussions with Thibodaux. He leaned forward, shoulder locked so she could hang on his forearm and do pull-ups. Despite acting as human jungle gym, the dark blue lines of Quinn's mess dress uniform were straight and razor creased. His shoulder boards—bearing the silver bars of a captain—his jump wings, and the three rows of miniature service medals on his chest were all perfect. Even the blue satin bow tie remained neat and snug, though he longed to rip the damned thing off and would at the first opportunity. Sometimes he thought he might hate neckties more than he hated terrorists.

The apple of Quinn's eye, Mattie had the face of her mother but with his dark hair. She'd also been cursed with his boundless energy and lust for adventure. From the time the wedding ceremony ended hardly a moment had gone by before she started begging to carry his ceremonial Air Force saber. He'd been able to calm the little dynamo for the time being with gymnastics and prevent her from hacking away at the guests with the sword.

Kim, Mattie's mother and Quinn's ex-wife, looked on with pursed lips, as if she had a bug trapped behind her teeth. It was warm for January in Colorado and a slight breeze tousled her blond hair. She was beautiful when she wasn't angry, which sadly was seldom the case. Her date didn't seem to make her happy. He was an Air Force Academy classmate of Quinn's. It stood to reason she'd end up with the guy. Gary Lavin had been sniffing around her since Quinn had taken her to the ring dance their junior year at USAFA. Apart from being a world-class know-it-all, Lavin was dull as uncooked oatmeal by Quinn's standards. Maybe that's what Kim was looking for all along—dullness—something Quinn had never been able to give her.

Jericho couldn't really blame her for bringing a date. They'd been divorced for years. She could see whoever she wanted to see. He certainly did. Jacques was right. He was with the most beautiful woman at the wedding— a fact that probably had a great deal to do with Kim's sour expression.

Veronica "Ronnie" Garcia had received permission to take a long weekend break from CIA training at Camp Peary to attend the wedding with him. Of Cuban and Russian descent, she was a tall but rounded woman— as her father had put it, on the athletic side of *zaftig*. The curves and swells of her coffee-and-cream skin filled her bright yellow dress with a sort of snug innocence, as if she was unaware of how alluring she actually was.

"I think you and your papa could go on like this all day," Garcia said, laughing an honest, abandoned laugh at Mattie and her pull-ups.

"That we could," Quinn said. He glanced over his shoulder at the steps leading from the angular white spires of the cadet chapel where Steve and Connie Brun stood in mess-dress tux and radiant white gown for their last few photographs. Other wedding guests, including Major Brett Moore—the B-1 bomber pilot who'd rescued Quinn from the Bolivian jungle just weeks before—mingled at the base of the steps behind the photographer. Some wore civilian clothes, but enough were in uniform to leave no doubt that Connie had entered not only the Brun family, but the United States Air Force family as well. Everyone chatted and laughed, watching the couple in the sunshine. The weather along Colorado's Front Range had given the bride a perfect wedding gift with unseasonable temperatures in the high fifties.

Quinn was glad for the warmth but wished they would hurry with the photos so he could go somewhere and get rid of his tie.

Kim took a step closer, clearing her throat the way she did when she was about to lay down one of her immutable laws. For a small woman, she could pronounce edicts like Queen Victoria.

"You're rumpling your clothes, Mattie." She put a hand out to take the little girl by the arm. "Come on. Let's get you straightened up." Both wore soft, robin's-egg blue dresses that reminded Quinn of photos from all the Easters he'd missed.

Ronnie sidled up to pull on the ends of Quinn's bow tie while Kim helped Mattie with the sash on her dress. Gary Lavin stood by, fidgeting. He'd chased away all the guests and could find no more victims to share in his vast knowledge.

Thibodaux sauntered back up with two of his seven boys, complete with their eye patches, swinging on a massive arm.

"Y'all go play with your brothers." He shook them off, grinning at Quinn. "Hey, l'ami," he said in an easy Louisiana drawl. "I'll deny it if you quote me to another Marine, but you Chair Force boys manage to be pretty STRAC here at the Wild Blue U."

Ronnie Garcia nodded, fluttering thick lashes that shone in the light like a hummingbird's wing. She ran the tip of a long finger over Quinn's shoulder boards. "*Strategic, Tough, and Ready Around the Clock*, that's Jericho."

"Is that what STRAC stands for?" Thibodaux snorted. He kept his voice low so Mattie couldn't hear him. "I thought it meant *Shit, The Russians Are Comin'* . . ."

The Japanese woman behind the rifle was tempted to shoot the big Cajun in his good eye. He was Quinn's friend, so his death would suit the purposes of her employer nicely. On the other hand, the new bride made a tempting target, fairly glowing in her white dress under the midwinter sun. A splash of red might make for a nice complement.

The woman swung the rifle a fraction of an inch. *Perhaps the ex-wife.* All reports indicated Quinn still worshipped the woman, though she would have little to do with him. That fact alone made her a less than desirable choice. Such a woman was better left alive to add to his misery.

The crosshairs hovered over Garcia—beautiful Veronica, with her curvy hips and full breasts. Her body alone was enough to make her a target. The sniper allowed herself the hint of a smile. *I ought to send you a bullet,* she thought. *If only to get you out of the way. It would be a favor to all others of our sex.* But no, that was not quite right, either. She and Quinn were a couple, but girlfriends came and went. Garcia's death might not cause the magnitude of emotion that was needed . . .

She'd saved the most likely for last.

Godlike, the sniper watched little Mattie swing on her papa's outstretched arm. There was an undeniable bond between a father and his precious daughter. The woman holding the rifle knew that from experience. Her own father had taught her how to kill a man when she was much younger than Mattie Quinn.

Target acquired, she took note of a light crosswind coming from her left, estimating it at less than five knots. She adjusted her windage and elevation for the drift and drop that would affect the 250-grain bullet during its quick journey of 3,900 feet. She parked the peppermint next to her back teeth and slowed her breathing—allowing her mind to clear. Buddhists called it *mu-shin* or *no thought*. Inhaling slowly, she released half, then held it. The picture in the scope came into crisp focus. All else around her fell away.

Jericho Quinn and his precious little girl threw their heads back in laughter as the trigger broke with a crisp snap. The powerful rifle bucked in the woman's hands. Quinn would live for a few hours more, but in the space of his next heartbeat, he would be done with such laughter forever.

CHAPTER 2

"It really is time to go," Kim said, her voice an exasperated sigh.

Mattie gathered the hem of her dress for another giant leap into her father's arms.

"Listen to Mom, kiddo," Quinn said, his arms still outstretched, ready for Mattie's last leap. "I'll see you back at the hotel."

Kim moved closer, ready to snatch her out of the air in midjump. "Guess I have to be the bad guy—"

Quinn heard the crack of a supersonic bullet as it hissed past. He was all too familiar with the downrange pop of gunfire. Time seemed to unhinge and slow as if he were moving through life a half step faster than everyone around him. Voices, screams, the sound of running footsteps became muffled and low.

A lock of his daughter's dark ponytail lay on the concrete walk at his feet, neatly clipped by the passing bullet while she clung to his neck.

Forcing himself to exhale, Quinn grabbed Mattie by the face with both hands, scanning her for wounds. He was rougher than he should have been. Startled, she began to cry but was otherwise fine. He shot a quick

glance over his shoulder at Garcia, who nodded immediately that she was unharmed. Behind her and nearer
the steps, Steve Brun had his new bride and everyone
around them moving toward the opposite side of the
chapel, out of the line of fire. An Air Force Special Op-
erator like Quinn, Steve knew the drill.

Thibodaux was also well accustomed to the unique
sound of bullets flying in his direction and shooed his
wife and boys toward the relative safety of the cadet
chapel's lower level.

The distant pop of a rifle moaned in on the breeze,
and Quinn made a subconscious mental note of the
time between the bullet's passing and the report.

He handed Mattie off to Garcia, shouting for them
both to run toward the stairs as he reached for Kim's
hand. She'd dropped at the shot and lay blinking up at
him as if dumbfounded. Gary Lavin stood over her,
staring cow-like, still with no idea what all the fuss was
about.

Quinn tried to pull Kim to her feet but she resisted.

"Jericho . . ." Her face had gone pale.

Quinn's breath caught hard in his throat when he realized her leg was bent at an impossible angle, crooked
at midthigh. A crimson stain crept from beneath the
perfect blue fabric of her dress, blossoming against the
concrete beneath her.

"Oh . . . Jer . . ." The words caught in her throat,
strangled. "I'm . . . shot . . ."

Lavin offered all the help of a blank stare.

Fearful of a follow-up attack, Quinn scooped Kim
up in his arms to run toward the chapel. He kept her leg
as immobile as he could to keep from causing further
damage, but the most important thing was to move to

cover. She was so much lighter than he remembered. Blood soaked his white shirt from bow tie to cummerbund by the time they reached the cover of the concrete buttresses surrounding the lower chapel. Kim's head and shoulders shook from fear and shock.

Thibodaux had drawn his pistol and stood at the end of the lower walkway outside the chapel, alert for secondary threats. He subscribed to Quinn's motto of *See One, Think Two.*

Camille Thibodaux adopted Mattie into her little clan for the moment, shielding her along with all her boys.

Major Brett Moore called base security with his calm, pilot-in-command voice to let them know about the attack and to get an ambulance rolling. Claxons sounded seconds later, warning USAFA cadets to shelter in place or move into the nearest building if they happened to be outside.

"I need your help here," Quinn said to Garcia, forcing himself to stay calm, though he felt as if his heart was about to explode.

She nodded, returning a small Kahr pistol to the holster suspended below her bra. She knelt on the concrete and pressed the palm of her hand where Quinn directed, high on Kim's thigh, next to her groin, putting pressure on the femoral artery.

Pushing back a rising panic, Quinn peeled off his uniform waistcoat and stuffed it under Kim's legs. She moaned, her head falling to one side on the cold concrete walk.

"Her pulse is over the top," Garcia whispered.

"Stay with me, Kimmie." Quinn yanked up the hem of her dress, tracing the arcing fountain of blood back to its source midway up her thigh. The entry wound was relatively small, roughly the size of his thumb, but high-speed bullets are made to tumble when they hit bone, and this one had done its job perfectly. Striking Kim's femur roughly four inches above the knee, it had bounced end over end in an upward line, literally mowing away bone and muscle. Much of her thigh was an unrecognizable piece of burger.

Fumbling through blood, bone, and flesh, Quinn pushed the fact that he was working on his high school sweetheart out of his mind. The femoral artery was fairly easy to locate. It was the diameter of a wooden pencil and arcing fountains of blood at each pulse of Kim's weakening heart. But getting a hold on it amid the mess of snot-slick gore so he could stop the bleeding was another matter entirely. Had it been completely severed, she might have bled out before he'd gotten her to cover. Even nicked as it was, her life expectancy could be measured in seconds.

Quinn moved Ronnie's hand down to the wound and used a wadded piece of Kim's dress to apply direct pressure over the bleeder. He yanked off his tie with bloody hands and ripped away his shirt. Using his teeth, he tore away a long strip of cloth to use as a tourniquet, smearing his face in red during the process. Field medicine was a grisly business. Looping the cloth around her thigh, he pulled it snug well above the wound, remembering the tactical medic's mantra *High or Die*.

Kim gave a rattling cough. Wincing. Pain had finally worked its way through the initial shock. "You're welcome." She forced a grin, peering at him through dazed eyes. "You've wanted to get out of that tie all day."

"Good girl," Jericho said. His heart was a stone in

his throat. "Keep talking to me." He pulled the cloth tight, knotting it, and then glanced at Lavin, who stood over them wringing his hands.

"Get me a stick or something to tighten this."

Lavin looked up and down the concrete walkway but didn't move. "I . . . I don't see any sticks."

Quinn spied a cheap fountain pen in the man's breast pocket and stood long enough to snatch it away. Lavin flinched, apparently thinking Quinn had meant to hit him.

Using the pen as a windlass, Quinn twisted the tourniquet as tight as he dared before tucking it under the knot to hold in place. He cursed for not having the pocket trauma kit he carried with him ninety-nine percent of the time. The trim lines of the mess dress tuxedo left him little room to conceal a pistol, let alone the wallet of QuickClot and bandages. Out of habit, he noted the time he'd applied the tourniquet.

Ronnie stayed where she was, leaning over Kim with both hands pressing the blood-soaked cloth into the wound cavity.

Brett Moore's comforting voice came from behind him.

"Ambulance is three minutes out," he said, taking off his jacket and motioning to Lavin to do the same so Quinn could use them as blankets for Kim, who now shook uncontrollably.

Three minutes. Quinn's eyes flashed up at Moore. He wondered if she had that long.

"No more shots," Moore offered. "That's good."

"Jer," Kim moaned, licking her lips. "You would not believe how thirsty I am . . ."

Quinn put two fingers to her neck. Her pulse was

rapid and shallow as her heart struggled to send what blood she had left to her brain.

Steve Brun trotted up with his wife. They'd been on the other side of the cadet chapel when the sniper fired, and it had taken them a few moments to find out Kim was a casualty. Steve had continued as a Combat Rescue Officer, or CRO, after Quinn had moved on to OSI. Connie was an ER nurse. It was natural for them to come running when they found out Kim was wounded, no matter the danger.

Connie smoothed the skirts of her wedding gown beneath her knees and knelt next to Quinn while Steve made his way to the opposite side.

"Should I move?" Ronnie asked. A line of blood ran down her chin.

"No, sweetie," Connie said, calm as if she was up to her elbows in bloody messes every day. "Go ahead and keep that pressure on for now." She touched the knotted cloth squeezing the flesh of Kim's thigh. "Tourniquet looks good," she said, seemingly oblivious to the red line wicking up the white taffeta of her dress as she assessed the wound. It was good to have friends that didn't run off screaming at the sight of such trauma.

She put a hand to Kim's neck, feeling for a pulse. Avoiding Quinn's eyes, she looked at her husband with a flash of pity.

Kim coughed again, weaker now. "Mattie . . ."

Quinn patted the back of her hand, nodding back tears.

Veins in his neck knotted in anger and sorrow. "You're going to be fine." The words caught hard in his throat. "Just hang on. The ambulance will be here in a few seconds."

Kim's eyes fluttered. She seemed to gather herself up, focusing all the will she had left on this single demand. "Let me talk to Mattie." Her head fell back against the folded uniforms with an audible thud. Her breathing slowed.

Quinn waved at Camille, who watched from halfway down the chapel walkway. The Thibodaux boys and Mattie were gathered around her like a brood of chicks. Mattie broke away as if released from the starting block. She was young, but even at the tender age of seven she had a tougher constitution than many men Quinn knew.

She knelt beside her mother without an apparent second thought over all the blood. Kim kissed her cheek, straining to whisper something in her ear. Mattie nodded. Tears dripped down on her mother's face.

Across Academy Drive, the young Japanese woman had settled back into position quickly after the concussion of the shot. She flicked at the peppermint with the tip of her tongue as she watched Quinn's ex-wife collapse through the reticle of her scope. She shrugged. That was the way of things. Much could happen in the 1.3 seconds it took for the 250-grain bullet to travel from the muzzle to its intended target. She'd heard accounts of birds flying into the path of oncoming projectiles, of strange winds, and targets bending to tie their shoe or pick a flower at exactly the right moment to prolong their miserable lives.

It did not matter that Kimberly Quinn was not her original objective. The choice had been left up to her, so no one need ever know. The death of his ex-wife would move Quinn in the direction he needed to go. That's what was important.

While Quinn and his friends flapped around like headless geese, the sniper was already on the move. She left the rifle resting in the crook of the tree. Though not the most common caliber, .338 Lapua rifles were well known in the community of professional shooters. Trying to trace this one would send the authorities down a dozen different rabbit trails. The serial numbers had been removed and the woman had taken great care to see there was nothing that could be used to obtain her fingerprints or DNA. They would think the rifle was a grand evidence coup and waste time comparing ballistics to hundreds of other shootings in FBI and Interpol databases. In truth, the rifle's maiden voyage had been this one. While the authorities racked their brains for a connection to other crimes, the woman who pulled the trigger would melt back into the black mist from which she had emerged.

Dropping lithely from the branches of the juniper, she brushed off her hands and took one last look at her surroundings to be sure she hadn't left anything unintentional behind. A group of German couples touring the Academy met her on the paved trail when she stepped out of the brush. It couldn't be helped. None of them were under sixty. If they were questioned, they would describe her as a cute little Asian girl, out for a walk in the woods.

Two minutes later saw her at the North Gate. She threw a wide smile at the security police officer, who waved her on as he tried to decipher all the traffic on his radio.

She crossed the bridge over Interstate 25, then turned

north, toward the Denver airport. There was a certain liquid nature to things such as this. She would have to hurry if she wanted to stay ahead of the torrent without getting washed away.

Three uniformed paramedics hustled down the steps with a folded stretcher. Heavy boots echoed off the concrete tunnel, but they looked like angels backlit by the bright sunlight at the mouth of the stairs.

Only then did Ronnie and Quinn step back.

Quinn held Mattie's hand while Ronnie knelt beside the sobbing child. Camille swooped in and took the little girl in strong arms.

"I've got this one," she whispered to Jericho. "Don't you worry about her."

The lead paramedic, grim-faced and quiet, used a plastic injection gun to insert a thick needle into the bone below the knee on Kim's good leg. Once he had the needle set, he started IO fluids while the others strapped Kim to the expanded stretcher. None of them smiled.

Quinn trotted up the steps beside the rescue personnel, holding Kim's hand. Her skin was cold now, her fingers slack. A red stain soaked the sheet at the site of her wound, but her chest still rose and fell. Quinn focused on that.

Thibodaux, Garcia, and the Bruns surrounded them in a mobile perimeter, eyes scanning the surrounding buildings and rolling hills.

Panting with emotion, Quinn held up his hand, knifelike, and pointed across Academy Drive while the paramedics got Kim situated in the waiting ambulance.

His voice was frayed with despair. He needed something to do, anything besides thinking about Kim's chances. He'd seen too many wounds like this.

"Jacques," he said. "Let the SPs know the shot came from over there. I'd say less than fifteen hundred meters from the sound of the report. I want to know when they find anything."

"You got it, l'ami," the big Cajun said.

Garcia touched his shoulder, letting her fingers slide off slowly. "You go take care of her. We'll check it out over there."

"We're ready to go, sir." A burley paramedic with slicked black hair waved Quinn inside. "It's a good idea if you ride along."

Quinn looked out the window of the ambulance as they pulled away, watching the thick line of cedar trees on the hills across Academy Drive. He ground his teeth. The trauma of working on Kim had knocked his tactics for a loop.

He pulled the cell phone from his pocket and pushed Thibodaux's number.

The big Cajun picked up immediately. "Talk to me, beb."

"It's only been minutes, Jacques," Quinn said. "There's a good chance the shooter hasn't made it off the campus."

"Way ahead of you," the Cajun said. "Security Police just arrived. They're lockin' down the gates as we speak."

Quinn hung up, torn between the urge to run down the person who'd shot Kim and the responsibility to stay by her side. He took her hand and gave it a squeeze. Her eyes were closed and the oxygen mask covered her face, but he felt her give him a weak squeeze in return.

"Dammit!" The heavyset paramedic watching the monitor wiped the sweat off his brow with the back of an arm.

"What?" Quinn held his breath.

Kim's hand fell away.

CHAPTER 3

Kanab, Utah

Rick Bedford's eyes snapped open. He groaned and smacked his lips, trying to figure out where he was. The sheets were soft and free of dirt, and the room was a comfortable temperature—sensations he found completely foreign to recent experience. It took a few seconds for reality to seep back into his addled brain and bring the realization that there was a naked woman clinging to him under those soft sheets.

He sighed, letting his body relax again. The smell of his bride so close now after such a long absence was balm for his wounded soul.

His arm tingled from the weight of her head on his shoulder. Muscles cramped in his leg where her thigh draped across his, damp, sweating from skin-to-skin contact. He didn't care and would have happily drifted back to blissful sleep. Still, he didn't want to have his arm amputated.

"Sorry," he whispered, lifting Marta's hand. He sighed again as her body slid away from his.

"It's all right." From the sound of her voice, Bedford

could tell she'd been awake for some time—probably never even gone to sleep. "The girls will be home from Kendra's anytime now." She smiled, hair mussed from the nap—and other things. "They're pretty smart teenagers, so I should have a shower before they get home."

"I've been gone the better part of a year." Rick laughed. "If they're all that smart, having a shower won't hide much from them."

Marta batted her eyes. A sure sign that she wanted him to stay in bed a few minutes longer.

"I hired a new girl at work," she said.

"Do I know her?" Bedford asked, as much to hear his wife's voice as to learn about any new employee. He'd never really thought about it, but these little "afterward" talks were something he'd missed.

"Not unless you've had a pedicure in China." Marta yawned. She threw her arms above her head in a shuddering stretch. "She just arrived in the U.S. and needed a job. Her name's Haifa."

"Haifa doesn't sound Chinese." Bedford took a long look at his wife across the pillow. He had to pee but couldn't quite bring himself to leave her.

"She's something else besides Chinese." Marta shrugged. "Anyway, customers are eating up these pedicures. You should try one."

"I thought you warned me about letting foreign women touch my feet." Bedford swung his feet to the floor, wincing as his hip brushed across the sheets. Naked, he craned his neck to try to see what was causing him so much pain. "Whew!" he gasped, swaying like he might pass out as he moved to the closet mirror. It felt as if something had stung him right above his tailbone. "Take a look at this, sweetie. I can't really see what it is." He flipped on the overhead light, then turned so Marta, too, could see.

She sat up in bed, letting the sheets slide off.

"Oh, my heck, Richard." She whispered the strongest language that ever came out of her mouth. "That's the biggest boil I've ever seen. You should have Doctor Todd take a look at it."

"Hmmm," Bedford said, still craning to look for himself. "First you want some Chinese woman to touch my feet and now you want the man that married your sister to check out my butt."

"This is serious, Rick." Marta put on her best pouty face. "Abraham Lincoln's son died from a boil."

"It was his grandson," Bedford corrected. "And the poor kid died from complications after doctors lanced his boil—which is exactly what your cutthroat brother-in-law will do if I go to see him."

"You can't see it, but I can," Marta said. "I'm making you an appointment for tomorrow morning." She pooched out her bottom lip as a sign that any further argument would be futile.

"Okay, okay," he said, hobbling to the bathroom, appalled that he was beginning to move like his dairyman father. He cleared his throat to hide a cough. "Set it up. This is probably just all the crap I absorbed in Afghanistan working its way out of my system."

He coughed again. This time it was a rattling, phlegm-filled cough that he was unable to hide. Maybe a visit to the doc wasn't such a bad idea.

CHAPTER 4

Colorado

Kim's heart stopped twice on the frantic ride between the Academy and the hospital. The paramedic at the wheel of the ambulance bypassed the closer St. Francis in favor of the Level II trauma center at Penrose Hospital just off I-25, south of the Academy. By the time they crashed through the ER doors with her strapped to the gurney, Kim had lost roughly a third of the blood in her body.

Emergency room staff had pushed her straight through to surgery. Quinn found himself scraped off as she went through the stark double doors. He couldn't help wondering if that was the last look he'd ever have of her, covered with bloody sheets and surrounded by stone-faced medical personnel.

She'd been in there for hours and Quinn had yet to bring himself to sit down. Instead, he paced, staring out the windows and beating himself up, oblivious to the fact that he wore only his dress blue slacks and a blood-soaked T-shirt that made him look like he'd been on the receiving end of a messy appendectomy. He could focus on nothing.

An orderly brought him a towel, and Quinn did the best he could to wipe Kim's blood off his hands and face. There was little he could do about the sodden T-shirt.

At the far end of the room, a young couple huddled together under the buzzing television, waiting for their child to get out of some procedure. The woman shot furtive glances at Quinn and whispered repeatedly to her husband. After a short time, the man walked slowly toward Quinn.

Breathing heavily, with no intention of getting into a long conversation over his present circumstances, Quinn wheeled with the beginnings of a snarling grimace.

The man stopped, then held out his jacket on tentative hands. "Here," he said simply. "Take this. You need it more than I do."

Quinn forced a half smile as he accepted the fleece. No matter how much he'd scrubbed with the towel, Kim's blood still rimmed his fingernails and stained the back of his hands.

"Thank you," he said.

"No worries," the man said over his shoulder, already retreating toward the safety of his wife.

Quinn shrugged on the jacket and zipped it up to cover the blood. He was thankful that he'd met one of the rare, decent people in the world who didn't feel compelled to dish out advice. He looked up at the sound of a chime. Measured relief washed over him as Thibodaux and Ronnie got off the elevator with two men. OSI was a relatively small organization, especially when it came to officers. Quinn knew the detachment commander at the Academy but wasn't familiar with either of these agents. One, an African American man in his mid-twenties, wore 5.11 khakis, a blue OSI polo, and a light cotton jacket. The other, older by a decade, had a blond goatee and wore pressed jeans. The senior man's sport coat was tailored too close to hide the fact that he was wearing a pistol on his left side.

Garcia snaked her arm around Quinn, oblivious to the blood. They'd all been close enough to the action that each looked as though someone had taken a red paintbrush to their clothes. The stains stood out starkly against Garcia's bright yellow dress. She snuggled next to Quinn, offering physical and moral support. He returned the gesture, arm around her waist, hand on the swell of her hip, to draw her even closer. Thibodaux raised the brow over his functional eye. Like a good partner, he said nothing, waiting instead for Quinn to fill them in about Kim's condition on his own time.

The African American agent extended his hand. He looked fresh out of the OSI Basic in Glynco. "Mr. Quinn," he said, shaking Jericho's hand. The formal title of *Mister* when addressing an agent who was an officer allowed OSI personnel, whether they were enlisted, officers, or civilian, to leave everyone's rank a mystery in the event their investigation led them to question a superior. "I'm Special Agent Torrance, Field Investigations Squadron here at the Academy. This is—"

"Mike DeKirk, FBI," the agent in the sport coat said, cutting him off. He had a strong Texas accent, which put a frown on Thibodaux's face as soon as he heard it. Texans had a way of ruffling the Cajun's feathers.

Jericho shook their hands. "Thanks for coming so fast." He glanced up at Thibodaux, filling him in.

"They've had her in surgery for a while now. I'm still not sure what's going on. Is Camille still okay to watch Mattie?"

"No worries, l'ami," the Cajun said. "She can drop off the boys with the Bruns and bring Mattie over when you give the word."

Jericho nodded. "I'm sure Kim will want to see her as soon as she wakes up." *If she wakes up* . . . He pushed the thought out of his mind.

DeKirk cleared his throat. "I hate to interrupt, but as you know, time is of the essence in these cases. Is there anything you can tell us that might help find who did this?"

Quinn took a deep breath, started to say something, then changed his mind. "I really wish I could."

"Nothing at all?" DeKirk pressed—as any good investigator would. "Does your wife have anyone that might want to hurt her?"

Quinn shook his head.

"I know it's difficult," DeKirk shrugged. "But I need you to think. Anyone at all, jealous boyfriends—maybe any of your old girlfriends—"

Agent Torrance shook his head. "Might not be the best time to worry with that," he said, nudging DeKirk.

"And how about you, Mr. Quinn?" DeKirk said. For some reason, *Mister* sounded much less polite when it came from the FBI agent's mouth. "You have any enemies?"

"I'm sure I have a few," Quinn said.

"Care to go into any detail?" DeKirk shrugged. "This shooter was a professional. You need to tell me what you know."

"Listen," Quinn said evenly, keeping his voice low

so the young couple across the room couldn't hear. "I know you're just doing your job, DeKirk. Believe me, I want to catch whoever did this worse than you—"

"Do you, Quinn?" DeKirk's eyes narrowed. "Because it seems like you're holding something back. It looks to me like you don't give a shit if your ex-wife's shooter gets away."

Quinn took a deep breath, held it, gritting his teeth. Ronnie touched his arm, surely feeling he was about to explode.

"Come on." Agent Torrance put up a hand again. "This isn't the time or place."

DeKirk glared at the young agent. "Don't tell me about time and place."

Thibodaux took a half step forward, closing on DeKirk with his intimidating height. "We all get the good cop bad cop thing," he said, voice flat. "But you press this now, while it's still touch and go with Kim's surgery, and it'll be good cop, flat-on-his-ass cop."

Quinn counted to ten before speaking.

"I will tell you everything I know, but I'll have to get you cleared first. Then I'll need everything you have on this."

"Not the way it works, Quinn," DeKirk said, dispensing with the *Mister.* "You know that. In situations of terrorism, the Bureau has the ball. Somebody shot your ex. I feel for you, I honestly do, but you're way too close to this. OSI can do a joint investigation if they want, but I seriously doubt your command will let you be part of it. Now calm down and tell me what you know."

Quinn's nostrils flared. The man was only doing his job. And yet Quinn felt the pressing need to hit someone, so it might as well be DeKirk.

Thibodaux snatched up a *Sports Afield* magazine from the lobby chair and borrowed a pen from Agent Torrance. Scrawling something quickly on the back cover, he held it up toward the FBI agent in a hand the size of a pie pan, trying to mediate. "Little suggestion here, DeKirk, why don't you get ahold of your boss's boss's boss and have him give this number a call. They will verify that you should cooperate with us. That way, we won't all have to pee on everything to mark our territory." The big Marine gave a smug grin. "How 'bout that?"

"Whose number is this?" DeKirk eyed the magazine.

Thibodaux shrugged. "Ask your boss."

"I thought you were just Air Force OSI," DeKirk scoffed.

"I am," Quinn said.

Fuming, the agent whipped out his cell phone as if it were a weapon. He ripped the back page off the magazine and stepped away to make his call just as a tall man in green hospital scrubs walked through the double doors from surgery.

He wore a black cloth surgeon's cap imprinted with red chili peppers. A mask hung around his neck and paper booties from the OR still covered his shoes.

Quinn felt his heart in his throat when the surgeon smiled a noncommittal smile. It was closemouthed, but hopeful—certainly not the smile of someone with horrific news.

Ronnie Garcia reached to take Quinn's hand in hers, squeezing it tight.

"She's stable," the doctor said. "It'll be a few minutes before they get her settled in recovery. She'll be groggy but you can see her."

Relief and guilt washed over Quinn. "Thank you, Doctor," he said.

"There are some issues we need to discuss." The surgeon folded long fingers together at his lap. "She lost a lot of blood." His eyes shot sideways, almost imperceptibly. It was just for a moment, but Quinn saw it and braced himself for what was about to come next.

"The bullet was moving extremely fast when it hit her," the surgeon continued. "There was a massive amount of hydrostatic damage to the nerves and surrounding tissue. Rounds like this tend to tumble." He shook his head as if recalling the damage—impassive, clinical. "We tried our best, but there was no way to save her leg."

Quinn's mouth hung open, stunned. He nodded stupidly but said nothing. What could he say? Kim's nightmares for him had now fallen on her.

"If it helps," the surgeon went on, his voice calm and earnest without a hint of condescension, "I'm an old Air Force surgeon and I've seen hundreds of wounds like this one. I could have had an OR table set up right beside her when she was shot and we still wouldn't have been able to save that leg."

He put a hand on Quinn's shoulder. "Son, you had about three minutes out there to keep her from bleeding to death. You did a hell of a job. I'll get her set up with a good rehab and prosthetics guy, a friend of mine. He can work miracles."

Special Agent Torrance cleared his throat as the surgeon walked away. DeKirk stood next to him, seething like a smoldering coal. Apparently the phone call had done the trick, but he wasn't happy about it.

Agent Torrance spoke first. "We don't have much yet, sir, but you get all we have."

Quinn said nothing. The last thing he wanted to do was turn this into a turf war.

"The shooter abandoned the rifle in a tree that looks like the shooting platform," Torrance went on. "A heavy-barreled Remington 700 MLR in .338 Lapua."

"Hmmm." Quinn mulled the information over. It was no wonder Kim had lost her leg. MLR stood for Medium Long Range rifle. The .338 Lapua had been purpose-built as a sniper round, capable of sending a 250-grain bullet downrange at a thousand meters per second.

"Looks to have some custom work done on it," the young OSI agent said. "But nothing outside the realm of what a neighborhood gunsmith could do."

"I'm sure you won't find any prints," Quinn said. "It takes a professional to make a shot like that."

"My thoughts exactly," DeKirk said, finally calm enough to join the conversation. "We interviewed a bunch of German tourists at the Visitors Center who said they saw an Asian woman walk down the trail from the woods near where we found the sniper rifle. They describe her as small but strong looking, maybe in her mid-twenties. One guy said she had"—he consulted his notebook—"*den bösen Blick.*"

Torrance nodded. "I did a Google search. It means 'evil eye.' Anyway, a quick review of the security tapes looks like she knew where the cameras were. We have her walking down the trail and through the Visitors Center lot, but she never lets us get a view of her face.

She must have parked in a spot without a camera, because we lose track of her after that."

"What about cameras at the exits?" Quinn asked.

Torrance smiled. "That's where we got something. Seven minutes after Major Moore called in the shooting, a white Hyundai Santa Fe left through the North Gate with an Asian female behind the wheel. She had a ball cap pulled down low so we didn't get much of a shot of her face, but the LP comes back to a rental company out of Colorado Springs. The clerk there says it was rented by someone named"—he consulted his notes—"Roku Yamamoto."

"Hmmph." Thibodaux scoffed. "That's fittin'. Isoroku Yamamoto planned the attack on Pearl Harbor."

"Anyway," DeKirk said, unimpressed by the Cajun's knowledge of history. "I put a BOLO out on the car. I have Colorado State Patrol scouring the highways north and south of here. Denver and Cheyenne airports are on alert as well. But I gotta tell you, trying to locate someone when our only description is 'Asian female' gives us pretty grim odds." He narrowed his eyes at Quinn. "So, what I really hope is that you can give me something else to go on. You know of any Japanese women who'd want to hurt you?"

Quinn shook his head. "No," he said honestly, but stopped there.

"Look," DeKirk forced a tight smile. "Believe me, I understand the whole 'need to know' thing. Hell, I'm with the FBI. The Bureau practically invented the shutout. But I'm not one of the counterintel spooks. Someone attempts to assassinate a civilian on a military installation, so it falls to me to investigate. I happen to be a damn good investigator—and all I want to do is catch this person. Here's my card. If you find yourself in a spot where you can help me do it, give me a call. Otherwise . . . these guys can fill you in on the damn little we know." He shrugged. "I hope your ex gets better soon."

Torrance gave Quinn his card as well, noting his cell number written on the back. "Call if you need anything, sir. I'll have my reports in I2MS today, so you'll have access to everything I do."

Quinn shook hands with both men. They were just doing their jobs. DeKirk, keeping up the FBI tradition of trying to run the entire show, and Torrance, the dutiful subordinate.

Quinn turned to Garcia and Thibodaux after the elevator doors closed on the other two agents. The Marine's dark uniform hid most of his stains, but Garcia's sunshine yellow dress showed broad swatches of red, like a Jackson Pollock painting.

Quinn closed his eyes, trying to gather his thoughts. "What else did you see out there?"

"No tracks good enough to follow," Thibodaux said, shooting a glance at Garcia. "The kid here noticed something, though."

"It's probably nothing." Ronnie shrugged. "But I could have sworn I smelled peppermint around the tree where the shooter left the rifle."

"Peppermint," Quinn mused, making a mental note. "Sucking on a breath mint's not like a professional assassin . . ."

Thibodaux's eyebrow crawled above his black patch. "Maybe she was aimin' at you and missed. That ain't very professional."

Quinn's head spun at a sudden realization, remembering how Mattie jumped just before Kim fell, how her ponytail had been neatly clipped away by the bullet. "The shot wasn't for Kim. It was for Mattie." Quinn reached in the pocket of his uniform slacks and pulled out the lock of dark hair. He swayed on his feet, dizzy, letting adrenaline overwhelm him for the first time since the attack. He fell back, collapsing in one of the waiting-room chairs.

Ronnie sat beside him. Strong thigh pressed alongside his, she stroked the back of his hand.

Thibodaux hunkered down in front of him so they were face-to-face. "Who would do that? Who's out there that would kill your little girl but leave you alive?"

Quinn sat very still, remembering his confrontation with a handful of Japanese punks while he'd been following Hartman Drake. A plan began to form in his mind. With every breath, his strength and resolve returned. At length he stood, letting Garcia's hand slide away.

"I don't know," he said, his voice a hoarse whisper. "But the Speaker of the House will. I've been wanting to talk to him for some time now."

"What are you thinking, l'ami?" Thibodaux stood as well.

"I'm going to call Palmer and find out where Hartman Drake is, then I'll book the first flight there after I get Kim settled."

"We'll come with." Thibodaux gave a somber nod. "You better change clothes first. You look like you been choppin' off zombie heads."

"It's better if I do this alone."

"The hell you say." Thibodaux frowned. "You were half a breath away from ripping that FBI guy's head off—and, it pains me to say it, but he's one of us. The way you're feelin', ain't nobody gonna blame you for showing some emotion. But the last thing you ought to do is go in by yourself. You need a wingman." He looked at Garcia. "And woman."

"This is liable to be bad," Quinn said. "I can't risk getting you two involved."

"For a guy who speaks umpteen languages you can be pretty dense, Chair Force. It's because things might get bad that you need us along."

"No," Quinn said.

He took a tight breath through his nose, staring into space. In defensive tactics they called it a thousand-yard stare. It was almost always the precursor to a fight.

"Okay." Jacques threw up his hands. "I've seen that look before. You get like this and you can't even get out of your own way. There's no arguing with you. Even if I happen to be right and you happen to know it . . ."

A redheaded nurse with a soft smile and a voice to match came in to tell them Kim was awake enough for Jericho to see her. He followed her through the swinging doors.

Left behind, Ronnie Garcia's heart tightened as if gripped by a fist. She found it difficult to draw a full breath as Quinn disappeared through the double doors toward the recovery room. She cursed herself for what she was thinking—blaming Kim for getting shot and ruining a perfectly good weekend. Garcia knew it was moronic to wish that she had been the one to take the bullet so Quinn would be worried about her instead. But that was the way her mind worked. Love sucked.

She turned to Thibodaux, who'd become a great confidant. His jaw was still set from the run-in with Jericho. He was right to be upset, too. Quinn was out of his head with worry and guilt, but too bullheaded to accept help, even from his closest friends. For all his gruff, gunnery sergeant exterior, Thibodaux had a wife and flock of small boys who made certain he kept a nurturing side alive.

"You know," Ronnie whispered, "right after the wedding, Kim swore to me she would fight to get Jericho back."

"That's weird," Thibodaux said, raising his good eye and nodding slowly as if he knew it was not weird at all. "I thought she wanted to be shed of him and his danger-man lifestyle for good. Maybe this latest little *fais do do* will clinch her mind."

"It'll clinch her mind all right." Ronnie sniffed, feeling a good cry coming on. "And Jericho's, too." She breathed through her mouth in a vain attempt to hold back tears. Her Cuban accent came on stronger when she got emotional. "Oh, Jacques, you know this is probably the one and only thing she could do that would get him to choose her over me. She'll need him. There's no way he can resist that."

Thibodaux put a hand on her shoulder and drew her into his chest, dwarfing her in a big, brotherly squeeze. "He's acting the stupid SOB right now, cher," he said. "But let's have a little faith in our man Jericho. He'll do the right thing."

Garcia let herself go, sobbing in the safety of Jacques's massive embrace. "That's what I'm afraid of."

CHAPTER 5

The stress of having her mother shot was bad enough, but Quinn suspected there was more to Mattie's tears than that. She was a smart girl, well beyond her seven years. When she replayed the events in her mind, it would not be too much for her to figure out that the bullet that took her mother's leg was really meant for her.

Quinn longed to stay with them, to hold Mattie in his lap and pat her back and tell her everything would be all right. But that was a lie. Nothing would be all right unless he went out and made it so.

Kim motioned him closer. He put a hand on her forehead, smoothing her hair, then bent down with his ear to her lips.

"You need to get out of here," she whispered. The oxygen cannulas gave her already soft voice a pitiful, nasal tone that twisted a knife in Quinn's gut.

He stood up, trying to gauge her emotion from the look on her face. It was impossible.

"Just try and get some sleep," he said. "We'll make some decisions soon enough."

Kim's chest began to jerk with sobs, oblivious to Mattie's crying.

"Jer . . . icho." Her voice caught in her throat between breaths. "They . . . shot me . . ."

Quinn caressed the top of her head.

"And I'll find out who, Kim—"

"You . . . need to get . . . out of here," she groaned.

"I will," he said, trying to soothe her with his voice though he was anything but calm inside. "Soon enough."

She gave a minute shake of her head. "You don't understand, Jer . . ." She swallowed hard, panting to catch her breath. Her voice climbed with each word. "I'm not giving you permission . . . I'm telling you to go. I . . . don't want you here!"

He would have rather she'd shot him.

Nodding, he hugged a weeping Mattie.

Kim reached and caught the tail of the borrowed fleece jacket as he turned to go.

"Jericho."

"Yes?"

Oddly, Kim, who had boiled over with fear and anger just moments before, smiled.

"I don't know . . . exactly what it is you do." She sighed. "But whatever it is, I trust you to go do it well."

She gave his hand a squeeze. It was the worst possible thing she could say, the thing that would cut him the most. He'd grown used to angry. He could prepare himself for angry. Trust was too much to handle.

Quinn left a cadre of a half dozen OSI agents from Buckley, Peterson, and the Denver Joint Terrorism Task Force to look after Mattie and Kim. All of them appeared happy to help, closing the protective ranks around the OSI family.

Quinn called Winfield Palmer in the car on the drive back to the Marriott. Still on the books with OSI at the Headquarters Detachment in Quantico, his detail as an OGA gave him certain access to the highest levels of government, but it had also made his family a target.

Palmer answered on the second ring.

"I heard," he said, not waiting for Quinn to brief him. With the national security advisor, conversations often leaned heavily toward the one-sided if he had all the information he wanted. "How's Kim?"

"Minus a leg," Jericho said through clenched teeth. "But she'll live. I'm pretty sure the shooter was trying to kill my daughter."

"Reports say an Asian female?"

Quinn could hear computer keys clicking in the background over the car's speaker. He didn't believe in multitasking, but you didn't get to Palmer's level without being a champion at rapid transitioning back and forth between several tasks.

"Yeah, I'm thinking Japanese," Quinn said, glancing over his shoulder to take the right lane as his exit approached. "And that's about all we have. Remember I told you I followed Hartman Drake to that meeting with a woman at the docks in Old Town?"

"How could I forget?" Palmer scoffed. "You brought me a couple of severed fingers as a memento."

"That's right," Quinn said. "Japanese fingers." Quinn had cut them off during a fight with the guards standing between him and the clandestine meeting—and broken Yawaraka-te, his ancient Japanese killing dagger, in the process. "Drake is a part of this. He has to be."

"Maybe." Palmer tapped away at his computer. "I

really should relieve you. You know that, don't you, Quinn?"

Quinn's jaw clenched. "You'll have to put me in prison to keep me off of this," he said.

"I know." Palmer sighed. His keyboard still clicked in the background. "That's why I'm not even trying. It would just piss us both off. Listen, I smell something bigger than a simple vendetta."

"Me too." Quinn took the exit to Garden of the Gods Road, toward his hotel. "No organization is going to waste a well-placed asset like Drake on some little operation."

"Interesting connection," Palmer said. "If we're right and Drake was working with Doctor Badeeb—"

"I'm sure of it," Quinn said, cutting Palmer off.

"At any rate," Palmer went on, "PSIA says they're catching an inordinate amount of chatter linked to several terrorist groups in Pakistan." PSIA or *kōanchōsachō*—the Public Security Intelligence Agency—was one of the agencies within the Japanese government that dealt with counterespionage and threats to national security. "Not much of a leap to connect Drake to the Japanese woman to this chatter with Lashkar i Taiba and other bad actors."

"You get no argument from me," Quinn said, nodding to himself as he pulled into the parking lot and turned off the ignition. "I thought I was going to have to convince you."

"We need to make a plan on this, Jericho," Palmer said. "I know you're going to talk to Drake, but let's do it the right way."

"Understood."

"My version of the right way. Not yours."

Quinn ignored the counsel. "Congress is on a recess, isn't it?"

"It is," Palmer said. "Drake is in Las Vegas, presumably blowing off some steam after all the budget debates. Capitol Police say he's staying at Caesars Palace for one more night but will be back in his office tomorrow."

No sir, Quinn thought, taking a deep breath. *He won't.*

CHAPTER 6

Munakata, Japan

Shimoyama Takako sat on a flat cushion with her stockinged feet dangling near the heat lamp in the small, pit-like cutout under a low Japanese table. Her home was spacious by Japanese standards, with a full sixteen tatami mats in her living room alone—nearly five hundred square feet.

It was here that she conducted her business, dressed in a traditional cotton *yukata* robe of gray and white, and seated at the traditional warming table with an embroidered quilt draped over her lap. A black Beretta pistol lay at the top corner of the table, angled just so, always within easy reach. Directly in front of her, a small notebook was held open by a delicate ivory fountain pen. Shimoyama pushed gold-framed reading glasses back on her nose, large for a Japanese woman, and pushed SEND on her cell phone.

She was tall, with hips that had grown somewhat broader than she would have liked over the years. Strong, almost mannish shoulders from decades of physical training made it difficult to find a yukata that fit correctly. She had all her clothing custom tailored, preferring the older methods and styles that pleased the man she loved, or at least had pleased him at one time.

Now, with graying hair dyed black, a powdered face, and the hydraulic maladies of age wrenching at her joints, she doubted there was much she could do that would please him.

Still, such things couldn't be helped, and it was not in her nature to let him go without some sort of a fight.

Breathing deeply, rhythmically, she took up the ivory pen and consulted the notebook, while the phone rang.

"Yes," the voice on the other end answered. There was no polite hello in the greeting, only demands.

She introduced herself, using her best Arabic.

"*As-salam alaykum.*" Peace be unto you.

"Do not even try," he snapped. "It is not given for a believer to answer such a greeting by an infidel. Your pronunciation is so bad you could be wishing me death."

Shimoyama sighed to herself. So much for pleasantries.

"Why do I not deal with your superior?" The voice clicked and popped with educated Punjabi English. It was the voice Shimoyama heard in her mind when she'd read Rudyard Kipling in school—before her life had turned so upside down.

"He has asked that I keep you informed," she said. Accustomed to a more formal structure in matters with superiors, subordinates, and even victims, Shimoyama grimaced at the abrupt nature of this man. She much preferred dealing with others who understood the niceties of simply being Japanese. Even feudal samurai had been polite in their brutality when they struck down someone of lower class.

Kiri-sute-gomen, they would say: *I kill you, I discard you, I am sorry.*

Had it been up to Shimoyama, she would not have accepted this assignment—no matter how much it paid. These men were devils, erratic in their behavior, completely unrefined.

Nevertheless, the job had been accepted, and now honor demanded it be done well. Honor—reputation—was everything.

"We are on schedule," she said.

"Good." The voice on the other end had an aggravated whine to it, like a gearbox winding down. "And, the business in Colorado?"

"The first phase is complete," Shimoyama said. She placed a small check in the column of her notebook. It was important to keep track of the items on which she'd briefed her superiors and clients. "Our friend is on the way to see to the next portion of her assignment."

"Very well," the man said. The voice grew more distant, as if he was engaged in something else as he spoke.

"I must point out." Shimoyama hesitated. "This does not come without some degree of risk . . ."

"We are aware of the risk." The man inhaled sharply. "You would do well to focus on your own tasks rather than worry over something you know little about."

"Of course," Shimoyama demurred. "I only hope to be of the most assistance possible. If you will recall, we have more than one asset in place. That alone makes for—"

"Recall?" the man said, taking a long, nasal breath. "I will tell you what I *recall*. I recall hearing of some nonsense in Virginia that very nearly brought the Black Mist into the light of day."

Shimoyama recoiled at the mention of the organization's name. Black Mist. *Kuroi kiri*, in Japanese. No one associated with it would ever dare speak the title aloud and certainly not on the phone.

"I remember that incident very well." She glanced down at the inflamed nub on her left hand, where her pinkie finger should have been. The skin was raw and just beginning to heal over the bone at her first joint. Her right hand bore a similar nubbin, though this one was well healed and from long ago. She had run out of little fingers. The next time, penance would be nonexistent.

The three bodyguards she had taken with her to the United States—her only son and his friends—had been sorely lacking for such a task. It was she who had underestimated the possibility for conflict during her meeting with Hartman Drake. She knew full well that her son could be erratic, but she'd not comprehended how bizarre he could be and how such behavior would come so close to ruining everything. He'd paid the ultimate price. It was fortunate indeed that she had escaped such an error with her own life.

"I am sure you do remember it," the man said, his words clicking like a train on a track. "And I do not particularly care. Frankly, the only thing that interests me is Jericho Quinn's death. Is that too difficult to understand?"

"No, but I must—"

"See to it then." The man cut her off, apparently bored with her report. "Call again when you have more information."

Shimoyama dropped the cell phone on the table. She knew the line was dead. Qasim Ranjhani was not a man for good-byes.

CHAPTER 7

Quinn showered quickly at the hotel, taking just enough time to scrub Kim's blood from his hands and chest where it had soaked through his shirt. He'd shaved for the wedding, but his black beard had already started to form a shadow over his copper complexion—a look that, along with his flawless Arabic, allowed him to blend in in many areas of the world without anyone suspecting he was an American agent.

He pulled on a dark blue polo, khakis, and a pair of well-worn Lowa Renegades that fit more like sneakers than boots. He wanted to be ready in the event he had to run. Press-checking his Kimber 10mm out of habit to make certain he had a round in the chamber, he slid it into the Comp-Tac holster inside the waistband of his slacks and snugged down his belt. A small .22-caliber Beretta with a micro suppressor hung in a leather shoulder holster under his left armpit. Light for any serious work, the diminutive .22 had a specific niche in the world of deadly weapons—it was extremely quiet. Quieter still was the seven-inch blade of the CRKT Hissatsu fighting knife he carried.

His Aerostich Transit Leather motorcycle jacket did

double duty, covering the weapons and adding a layer of ballistic armor installed by the national security advisor's special team at DARPA known as the Shop.

Quinn threw the rest of his clothes and gear in a bag for Garcia to pick up, and made it to the Denver airport in time to hop the afternoon Southwest flight to Las Vegas. He wasn't allowed to sleep on the plane since he was armed, but wouldn't have been able to anyway. Closing his eyes when surrounded by a hundred strangers had never been something Quinn could bring himself to do. Reading was out of the question since the shooting, so he sat and stared at the seatback in front of him, letting his mind drift and his body metabolize the residual adrenaline.

The flight squawked onto the tarmac at Las Vegas McCarran International Airport just under two hours later. Quinn's cabbie was a talkative Romanian named Tiberius who gabbed about his large family and the tremendous opportunities offered by the "U.S. of A." nonstop during the fifteen-minute ride to the Strip. Quinn gave him a good tip, which, of course the patriotic jabbering had been intended to induce, and got out of the cab in front of the Bellagio, down the boulevard from Caesars Palace so there would be no record of him being dropped off there.

Once Tiberius was safely on his way, Quinn walked into the Bellagio's spacious lobby and turned right under the kaleidoscope of flowers that hung like an inverted glass garden from the ceiling. Walking easily but with purpose, he could feel the eyes of countless security cameras on his back as he cut this way and that to make his way through the maze of tourists. He counted at least a half dozen different languages from all nationalities—many of them Chinese. Glancing up at one of the small black domes on the ceiling above, he remembered the line from the movie *Ocean's Eleven*—someone was "always watching" at the Bellagio.

He popped out to flashing neon lights on the north side of the casino and breathed a sigh of relief to be back outside again, even if it meant leaving the crowded hotel for a crowded street.

It was warm, even for Vegas in the winter, though the sun had been down for nearly an hour. Taillights flashed and dimmed on stop-and-go traffic that backed up Flamingo Road all the way to the Las Vegas Strip. Quinn was able to trot between a bumper-to-bumper phalanx of two black stretch limos, a canary yellow Ferrari, and a pearl white Hummer to reach the great cluster of bone white buildings that made up Caesars Palace Casino and Forum Shops.

Looking for any one guest who happened to be staying at a hotel as large as Caesars Palace would normally require a good deal of time and a large surveillance team, but Quinn had an inside man—Adam Norton, of Drake's Capitol Police protective detail the year before. Officer Norton had pulled Drake's dead wife from the Potomac River and had a strong suspicion that she'd been murdered. He knew the Speaker's tastes along with his secrets. Of course, he'd been summarily kicked off the detail shortly after the incident, but Quinn had kept in contact with him for just this sort of event.

As Speaker of the House of Representatives, Hartman Drake was allocated a small protective detail of Capitol Police officers when he traveled. According to Norton, he liked to keep them at a distance during his visits to Vegas so he could spend time with a certain Puerto Rican escort he'd taken up with since his wife had been killed. In the world of dignitary protection, there was often a sort of cat-and-mouse game played by the protector and protectee. People wanted and needed space—but it was that space that could get them killed. It was the detail leader's job to figure out just how much space was possible to give and still keep the protectee safe from harm or embarrassment.

Quinn made his way through the entry off Flamingo Road, past the bellmen and row of perky clerks at the Diamond VIP check-in desk. He strolled through the Palace casino like a tourist, eyes peeled for Drake. Norton had said the Speaker had a thing for blackjack, and since this was his last evening in Vegas, Quinn assumed that he'd be at the high-stakes tables.

Failing to find Drake anywhere in the Palace section of the enormous gambling complex, Quinn ducked down a narrow, dimly lit hall of dark paneling and crushed velvet cocktail tables, passing under the bulbous wooden breasts of Cleopatra's barge that hung over the walkway. The din of the crowds and rattling ping of slot machines grew louder as he neared the Forum casino floor.

Quinn's gut knotted when he finally saw the Speaker. He thought of Kim, of all the blood, and of Mattie, the sniper's intended target. Pausing to take a slow breath, he pushed any notion of instant revenge to the back of his mind and studied the situation. Palmer was right. There was much more to this than a simple assassination. Otherwise, Quinn knew he would have been the target.

Hartman Drake was seated at the nearest blackjack

table, a fat cigar clenched between his teeth. Extremely fit, the Speaker spent several hours each day in the House gym and picked his clothing to show off broad shoulders and a narrow waist. He wore faded blue jeans and a tailored white shirt. Absent his trademark bow tie, it was open at the collar. A gold Rolex hung from the cuff of a navy blue blazer. Behind a cloud of cigar smoke, a derisive smile smeared across his mouth. He was winning.

Quinn kept walking toward the sports book lounge. He ordered a Bacardi and Coke from a roving waitress and watched the Hispanic woman pressed in close beside Drake. She was young, maybe twenty-two, with expressively dark eyes and a wide mouth, heavily covered in crimson lipstick. Gray tights clung like a second skin to slender legs. A bloodred minidress hung off petite shoulders. Her manicured hand, matching her lipstick and the dress, rested on a cocked hip.

Twenty feet away a blond Capitol Police officer with the earnest look of an Iowa farm boy loitered beside the bank of slot machines. A light golf jacket and khaki slacks helped him blend in some with the crowd of gamblers, but the flesh-tone earpiece and clear pigtail radio wire that disappeared at the back of his collar were dead giveaways. The slight bulge on the right side of his jacket would be his Glock. Pale blue eyes looked over the casino floor with mixture of boredom and disgust.

A second agent, older, with an air of experience, sat at a small table near the Forum entrance, nursing a cup of coffee while he watched the crowd.

Quinn's source said no one on the detail cared much for Drake. They were, however, honor bound to protect him and would give their lives to do so. But in order for them to do that, the protectee had to cooperate in at least some respects.

The Hispanic escort's hand moved across Drake's shoulder, caressing, but urging him to hurry. He gave an annoyed shrug, brushing her away. She let her hand drop and dug her toe into the carpet. The four-inch stiletto heel arced impatiently back and forth.

She was getting bored.

Quinn smiled within himself. This was going to be easier than he'd imagined. He knew Drake was staying in the Augustus Tower, but had no idea which floor or what room. He couldn't very well ask the protective detail, and that same detail would make it nearly impossible to follow the Speaker without hurting one of the good guys.

But now he wouldn't have to follow the Speaker. He could follow the escort. It was a good bet the call girl had a room nearby, probably on a different floor, so he could sneak away from his detail without having to go very far. She'd leave first—and since Drake was winning, he'd let her.

CHAPTER 8

Quinn left the rum and Coke untouched along with a ten-dollar bill and a nod at the waitress. Wanting to stay ahead of Drake's date, he walked quickly back under Cleopatra's wooden cleavage, through the Palace casino, and around the corner to Diamond VIP registration. Thankfully, there was no line. He badged the girl with a Croatian accent behind the desk, explaining that he was conducting a routine advance for a protective operation on an Air Force three-star general. She was professional enough that she didn't mention the Capitol Police detail already on site.

"The general is very averse to the media," Quinn said, hoping she'd afford him the same restraint when she spoke with any other protective agents.

"Of course, sir." The girl, whose name was Cetina, gave a conspiratorial nod and pointed to a map on the marble counter. "We have three vacant suites at the moment. I can get security to show you any or all of them if you wish."

Quinn took a deep breath, feeling a twinge of guilt for lying to this sweet girl. "That won't be necessary," he said. "I just need to take a few photos of stairwells, fire escapes, and whatnot. We're still in early stages."

"Very well." Cetina slid a key card across the counter. "This will give you access to the elevators around the corner." She smiled, a splash of freckles accenting the pink skin of a button nose. "Be careful taking photos of our guests. Like your general, most are not very fond of publicity."

Quinn made it around to catch the elevator in time to see a flash of red as Drake's buxom escort passed the restrooms down the hall, coming toward him. She was alone.

Quinn got on the elevator without looking back and punched the button for the twenty-seventh and the forty-sixth floors to make certain the car would continue up when he got back on. He stepped off immediately at twenty-five, but held the door and watched the floor numbers above the adjacent elevator, which surely contained Drake's date. They flashed past him and on to thirty-nine before stopping. Quinn stepped back on and inserted the card again. He made it to thirty-nine as the red dress disappeared into her room, four doors down from the elevator.

What happened in Vegas did indeed stay in Vegas, often for a great length of time, recorded digitally on cameras in virtually every casino, lobby, and hallway. Thankfully, guest floors were not places where the casinos lost money, so Quinn knew it was unlikely a live set of eyes would be focused on the particular cameras watching the thirty-ninth floor.

Quinn smiled broadly as he gave a knock on the door. The woman opened almost immediately, tilting her head sideways when she saw it wasn't Hartman Drake.

Quinn held up his room key. "I think you dropped this," he said. When she turned instinctively to look at the desk where she'd put her own key, he shouldered his way in, pinning her arms and putting a hand over her mouth before she could scream. The door clicked shut behind them as she began to rake his shins with her feet.

Over the years Quinn had dealt with more than a handful of women involved in prostitution. The reasons they got into such work were as varied as their hair color and descriptions. Some were sad sacks. Some did it because they wanted to make a lot of money fast, but nearly all of them shared at least one particular trait. They were almost impossible to intimidate. Unlike most men in modern America, the vast majority of hookers had been punched in the face, many times. They knew what it felt like, and they also knew it took more than a smack to kill them.

"Police!" Quinn hissed in the woman's ear. He arched his back to make it harder for her to get at his legs with the hard edges of her pedaling high heels.

Her body arched with him, trying to get away, but she stopped kicking.

Quinn moved his hand away from her mouth, careful not to let her bite him. He prepared to slap it back down if she began to scream.

"I knew it. Secret Service," she spat. "That bastard told me it was okay. He said I wouldn't get in any trouble."

Quinn didn't correct her. In the minds of the American public, the Secret Service protected everyone. For all he knew, Drake had told her just that. Instead, he took a pair of handcuffs from his back pocket and snapped them around the woman's wrists, behind her back. Knowing Drake could arrive at any moment, he gave her a quick pat-down for hidden weapons. The tight dress left little room to hide anything, but Quinn had seen firsthand how Veronica Garcia could secret a pistol away under some pretty flimsy bits of cloth.

The call girl's mouth hung open when he spun her around and set her on the bed. A flicker of terror sparked in her brown eyes. Her lower lip trembled slightly. The handcuffs and the dawning reality of her situation had finally staggered her confidence.

"You don't look like no Secret Service agent I ever saw."

"How well do you know your client?" Quinn said.

Apparently satisfied Quinn didn't mean to rape her or beat her to death, the woman fell back onto the bed, looking up at the ceiling with a tired groan. "I don't know, seven, eight months. My friend says to me, 'Dolores, you should meet this guy. He's some big shot in politics and he pays very well.' "

"Does he talk to you?" Quinn kept an eye on the door.

"Hell, yes he talks to me," Dolores said. "He won't shut up. Mostly about himself and how buff he looks. I think he only hires me so he's got somebody to brag to."

"Anything else?"

"Every man I know gonna brag some." She rolled sideways a little to take the pressure off her wrists. Her face remained passive as if she was used to being handcuffed and thrown on a bed. "Drake, he brags a hell of a lot more than most. Like he can't help himself, you know. Says he's gonna be the most powerful man in the world someday. He's always going on about how he could save the world or destroy it if he wanted to, just like God himself." She blinked up at Quinn. "No shit, I ain't lyin'. He actually says stuff like that."

Quinn took her by the arm and helped situate her in a more comfortable position against the headboard. "Did he say how he might save or destroy the world?"

She batted her eyelashes and stuck out her bottom lip, pouting. "I don't suppose you could loosen these cuffs a little?"

"Maybe in a minute," Quinn said. "Did Drake ever give you any specifics?"

The pout vanished. "To be honest, I usually just tuned him out. If you guys knew the things that go through a woman's mind while you're breathing in our ears—"

"But you heard something."

"He talked about the Bible all the time," Dolores said. "You know, all that whirlwind, fire, and pestilence crap and how he would be a modern-day Moses."

"What else," Quinn prodded every time she fell silent.

"No kidding, I really did tune him out." She shrugged, eyes wandering around the room trying to find something more interesting than this conversation. "You can ask him. My meter's running and he don't like to pay me to just sit here in the room, if you know what I mean. He'll sneak away from his agents pretty soon." She looked up at Quinn, dark eyes shifting to the pistol that was now visible under his open jacket. Her voice was strangely detached, as if she'd seen this sort of thing many times before. "Are you gonna kill him?"

Quinn shook his head. "No," he said.

Not right away, he thought.

CHAPTER 9

Dolores said she had no great love lost for Drake. She swore she would cooperate but didn't have much else to give in the way of helpful information.

The far end of the suite was a sunken living area with plush sectional couches to match gold drapes. A glass coffee table and long oak chest of drawers with a big-screen television rounded out the décor. Quinn left Dolores in handcuffs and sat her on the far couch so she could lean against the corner with her back to the door.

"You know what they call handcuffs in Spanish?" she asked, settling in against the cushions.

"No idea," Quinn said. He spoke five languages but Spanish wasn't one of them.

"Esposas." She winked thick, heavily mascaraed lashes. "It is the same word for wife. Fitting, don't you think?"

Quinn didn't answer. He'd have to check that one with Garcia. He set the television to a home shopping channel and turned up the volume.

"You don't have to worry about the noise, baby,"

Dolores said. "The ladies who clean on this floor are used to me making a lot of racket. I give them a nice tip when I leave."

"Good to know," Quinn said, stuffing half a wadded washcloth in the hooker's mouth. She accepted it with little more than a roll of her eyes.

A sudden rattle at the door, followed by the electronic whir of the lock, sent Quinn around the corner between the wall and the plush king bed. From here he had a clear view of Dolores and would be in the perfect spot to ambush Drake when he walked down the small entry hall past the bathroom.

He popped his neck from side to side, letting his shoulders hang loose and ready to move. He'd waited over a year for a chance to have a few minutes alone with Hartman Drake. The picture of Kim, lying on the concrete covered with blood, flashed before his eyes. Quinn pushed thoughts of revenge down in the dark recesses of his gut. It would be so easy to end this man here and now. Beating him to death would bring a certain closure if not real satisfaction, but there were still too many questions that had to be answered.

Quinn held his breath.

"Honey, I'm home!" Drake clapped his hands, stepping out of his shoes as he came through the door. Quinn heard the jingle of a belt buckle before the man even made it down the short hallway. "Let's get this show on the—"

Fighting was rarely something Quinn took lightly. Underestimating an opponent could cost the battle, or worse, your life. But in this case Drake did half the work for him. His arms were occupied with shrugging off his sport jacket when he came around the corner, while his ankles were effectively hobbled by the puddle of loose slacks at his feet.

Well muscled, Hartman Drake was no one to toy with even when hampered by his pants. A snap-kick to his unprotected groin bent him double and put his chin in a perfect line with Quinn's uppercut. Quinn was on him in an instant, slapping him hard across the ear to keep him stunned.

Pressing the advantage of momentum, Quinn rushed in, pummeling Drake with blow after blow to the ribs, driving the wind from his body and shocking his heart. With no time to collect his thoughts or regain his bearings, Drake could do little but give a halfhearted attempt to ward off the assault. Ten seconds from the time he'd walked into the room, warm in the knowledge he would have some quality time with sweet little Dolores, Hartman Drake found himself nauseated, dizzy, and half-deaf.

Quinn caught the Speaker's wrist and wrenched it backward, feeling a satisfying crunch as tendons stretched and tore. Dolores half turned on the couch to watch the show and looked on with an interested sparkle in her eye. Quinn used three zip cuffs from the lining of his jacket to hog-tie Drake and leave him lolling, face-down, on the bed. With his target incapacitated for the moment, Quinn took the protesting Dolores by the arm and dragged her into the bathroom. She managed to spit out the washrag on the way.

"Whoa!" she said, wide-eyed. "You're pretty damn good at what you do. Can I please watch? I'll be quiet as a mouse, I swear."

"Safer for you if you don't hear this," Quinn said,

checking her cuffs. He took another zip tie from his jacket and fastened her to the sink before turning on the faucet in the tub for background noise. Stuffing the washcloth back in her mouth, he shut the door.

With Dolores stowed out of the way, Quinn sat on the bed beside a blinking, wide-eyed Drake. "Now," he whispered, "you and I have some things to talk about."

"Do you even know who I am?" Drake mumbled, his face smashed against the bed linens.

Quinn grabbed him by the hair and lifted his head. He looked the man over, as if considering how to carve a piece of meat, then let his head fall back to the mattress. "Let's see what I know . . . I know you're the kind of trash that kicked out three of your wife's teeth and then held her underwater until she drowned. Yeah, I'd say I'm probably one of the handful of people in this country who actually does know who you are. What I need to know is who is pulling your strings."

A flash of panic crossed Drake's eyes. "There are a bunch of Capitol Police guys looking for me right now . . ." His words slurred against the bed with a line of drool.

"I'm going to ask you this once." Quinn's voice was barely audible above Drake's whimpering. "Who shot at my family?"

Drake began to sob uncontrollably, flinging his head from side to side. "I don't know what you're talking about. Seriously . . . I am . . ." He panted, as if trying to catch his breath. "I am the Speaker of the U.S. House of Representatives. My name is Hartman Dra—"

Quinn slipped into Arabic. "Who is the Japanese woman that was sent to shoot at me?"

Drake rolled his lips, pressing them together in a

tight line as if to keep himself from talking. "Mister," he finally said, trying to regain some of his bravado, "you have no idea what a shitload of troub—"

Quinn cuffed him on the back of the head, then drew the suppressed .22 from the shoulder holster under his Transit jacket. "As you wish," he said, pressing the weapon to Drake's temple. Without another word he turned the pistol slightly and fired a round into the mattress. Drake flinched at the shot. The spent casing ejected and landed in his ear, causing him to howl as if he'd been splashed with molten lava.

"I know you worked for Doctor Badeeb," Quinn said, still in Arabic. He leaned in for effect. "And I know you tried to kill my little girl."

"Please, I can't understand what you're saying," Drake yowled. "I don't speak Arabic . . ."

Quinn sighed. His voice grew calmer, almost sweet. "Perhaps you will not mind if I shoot you in your foot."

Drake flinched at the words, doing the best he could to move his trussed feet out of the line of fire.

"You understand me perfectly," Quinn spat. He flicked the pistol a fraction of an inch to put a round in the sole of Drake's foot.

The .22-caliber bullet punched completely through, snapping tiny bones and spraying the sheets with a fine mist of blood.

"Okay! Okay! Stop!" Spittle spewed from Drake's mouth. "Don't shoot me anymore! But stop speaking Arabic. Badeeb was Pakistani. I barely understand Arabic." He turned his head sideways, cheek against the mattress, sobbing through clenched eyelids. He nodded in defeat. "What do you want to know?"

Quinn leaned in, whispering. "What was killing her

supposed to do to me, exactly? Make me lay down and die?"

"Seriously . . ." He panted, trying to catch his breath. "I don't know anything about that . . ."

"I need a name, Drake," Quinn said, his voice an acid whisper. "I don't care about you or your failed attempt at the White House. I want to know who shot at my daughter."

Drake looked up, puzzled. "Shot at?" He panted. "She missed?"

"Who is *she*?" Quinn aimed the little .22 at Drake's other foot.

"Wait, wait, wait!" Drake screamed, wincing at the pain it brought his battered ribs. "What'll you do with me if I tell you?"

Quinn jerked him sideways to get his full attention. "You should be more worried about what I'll do if you don't."

"You don't understand . . ." Drake began to hyperventilate. "These people are cruel. Capable of things you can't even imagine."

"Oh, I can imagine a lot."

Drake started to sob again. "I have to have assurances."

"You—"

Quinn froze as an electronic whir came from down the hall. Someone else with a key was at the door.

"Ahhh." Drake sniffed, then rolled up on his side with his ear toward the door. His conceited swagger bloomed across his slobbering mouth along with the courage of a man who thought he was about to be rescued. "That'll be my Capitol Police guys coming to shoot you in the face."

Quinn grabbed Drake by his collar and dragged him off the mattress to the floor. At that same moment a slender man wearing a gray hooded sweatshirt popped around the corner from the hallway, blazing away as if he had unlimited ammunition. At least two rounds hit Drake as Quinn pulled him down.

At first, Quinn thought the newcomer might be Dolores's pimp, but the Browning pistol the newcomer carried was nearly a thousand bucks without the suppressor—much too professional for a man lording over a string of prostitutes, even in Vegas. The man took another shot at Drake's bare feet where they trailed past the end of the bed, obliterating a big toe in the process.

Quinn fired back with the Beretta, sending the attacker into retreat down the hallway. He got a fleeting glimpse of a face under the gray hood and guessed the man to be Pakistani.

Firing with the suppressed .22 didn't exactly provide a show of overwhelming force, so Quinn swapped the diminutive Beretta for the Kimber 10mm tucked inside his waistband. During the heat of battle, people hit with a silenced weapon often didn't realize they'd been shot. The big bang provided the signal to drive that point home.

Kimber in hand, Quinn prepared himself for the onslaught of police and federal agents that would rain down on him as soon as he fired the booming gun with no suppressor. No amount of tipping would keep the housekeepers from calling security once he started shooting.

A sudden thud, followed by a surprised grunt, came from the hallway. The door slammed and Dolores's husky voice came tentatively down the hall.

"It's me, baby," she whispered. "Don't shoot, okay. You good in there?"

"I'm good," Quinn said. He kept the Kimber trained toward the voice. "What happened?"

"He's run off." Dolores peeked her head around the corner. Her hands were still cuffed behind her back. "I smacked him with the bathroom door. He didn't know I was in there so I think it scared him."

"Just curious," Quinn said, standing, but still eyeing the door, "how'd you get out of the flex cuffs hooked to the sink?"

"Oh." Dolores shrugged. "You gotta learn to loosen up when you search women. Be a little more thorough. We got . . . places, you know."

Drake moaned at Quinn's feet. "That son of a bitch tried to kill me . . ."

Dolores sat on the bed, bouncing on the edge of the mattress while she stared down at the bloody mess that had been her date. "I think he did more than try," she said.

Drake looked up at Quinn, anger flashing in his eyes. "You have no idea what hell I'm going to unleash on you . . ."

"Apparently, I'm not the only enemy you have." Quinn leaned in closer to make sure Drake heard correctly. "But I'm the one close enough to kill you. Now, who is the Japanese woman?"

Drake smiled through his pain. Blood smeared his teeth. He coughed. ". . . I'm the most powerful man in the world . . ."

"The woman." Quinn patted his face to keep him focused.

Drake gave a rattling chuckle. "Powerful . . . until

they killed me . . ." His head lolled, eyes rolling back to show their whites.

Quinn jumped to his feet and pushed his way past a dumbfounded Dolores. "I'll leave the handcuffs on you so the police will know you weren't involved in this. Stay with him."

"What do I tell them?" she shouted down the hallway.

Quinn yelled over his shoulder as he ran. "Tell them I'm going after the man who killed the Speaker of the House."

CHAPTER 10

Quinn slid the Kimber back in the holster under his jacket as he sprinted toward the elevators, ready to draw again at the first sign of a threat. He took the first elevator going down to the lobby, smiling at an elderly couple who were already on board. They stood well back from him, as if plastered to the wall, wanting to be as far away as possible during their ride. It wasn't until he caught a glimpse of himself in the mirror that Quinn realized a smear of Drake's blood was splashed across his cheek and ran down like a tear under his left eye.

Assuming he was on camera anyway, Quinn shrugged it off and stepped into the Augustus Tower lobby when the doors finally opened. He scanned the knots of milling hotel guests that stood here and there, looking for some sign of irregularity.

Frightened or violent people left a sort of wake behind them when they ran. Not everyone recognized it for what it was, but some did, even if subconsciously. Quinn saw two older men, each wearing Vietnam Veteran caps, staring down the hallway toward the casino. Veterans, men who had seen close conflict, would sense people who were out of the ordinary. Following their gaze, Quinn trotted past the two men, nodding in salute as he went by.

By the time he reached the Palace casino floor, the man in the hoodie had gone. But the invisible wake remained. Most of the hotel patrons were ambivalent, happy to stay blissfully unaware. But a handful of people here and there craned their heads to look toward the door. A bellman stood by his stand, his back to the casino, gazing out the window as if watching something. Two uniformed security guards walked toward the front exit, intent on making sure someone had left the premises.

Very likely a man in a gray hoodie.

Quinn picked up his pace, leaving his own wake of watchers. He ran past the bellman and pushed his way out the front door into the covered portico and valet parking.

The blast of chilly night air was a pleasant reprieve from the stuffy, bottled atmosphere of the casino. The sun had long since set, but the lights of the Vegas Strip danced and exploded in a blinding rainbow of colors and hues. Quinn had to slow for a moment and let his eyes adjust. There was always a chance the man would be waiting for him outside, behind a potted shrub or around any corner. He had the smell of a runner though, so Quinn chased, hoping his instincts were correct. By the time he knew better, it would be too late.

Quinn jogged past the line of sparkling black limousines and assorted Prius cabs parked along the circular drive. The man in the hoodie was nowhere to be seen, but a turbaned Sikh beside the lead cab brushed the seat of his pants as if he'd been knocked over before

Quinn came on the scene and was just regaining his feet. The Sikh stared past the fountains and statuary, muttering angry words under his breath.

Quinn followed the cabbie's gaze and broke into a full run, sprinting across the concrete plaza under heroic statues of muscular horses and Roman gods. Arms pumping, he slid to a stop as he reached the pedestrian bridge that crossed above Las Vegas Boulevard. He scanned the rivers of people flowing north and south, leaning over the bolstered concrete edge to check both sides of the Strip. He'd nearly given up when he caught a glimpse of gray, heading north between the palms and boxwood hedges in front of the garishly lit Flamingo casino. The hoodie bounced with a particular bobbing walk and moved a half step faster than the crowd.

Quinn bolted across the bridge, dodging and ducking his way through tourists, beggars, and con men. Half sliding, half running down the escalator to the street below, he sprinted north the moment his feet hit the pavement.

Evening brought a heightened activity to the Strip. Tourists stood and gawked at the lights, the buildings, and each other. Huge parties of all ethnicities and nationalities moved in great herds, blocking sidewalks in search of the perfect cheap buffet. Greasy men and sad-looking women wearing matching T-shirts lurked at every corner and chokepoint, snapping business cards for strip clubs to everyone who met their tired eyes. Bands of motorcycles, from Harleys to Hayabusas, blatted and growled at each stoplight. Stretch limos, Hummers, and every sports car conceivable jammed Las Vegas Boulevard, bumper to expensive bumper.

About the time Quinn got to the Imperial, he saw the hooded man flag down a cab. Though traffic was stop-and-go, if the cab took the left lane, the hooded man would be gone before Quinn could sprint to it and drag him out. Two college-age boys slouched on the curb in front of the Rockhouse Bar. One wore a green Windbreaker, the other, a mustachioed UNLV sweatshirt. The objects of their attention were a couple of working girls. The boys were trying to convince the ladies they were old enough not to be jailbait. A Ducati Hypermotard and a Kawasaki Ninja stood parked along the curb behind them.

Thankfully, the boy in the sweatshirt was brain-addled by the short skirt and long legs of the two hookers. He'd backed his Ducati into the curb and left the keys in the ignition.

Quinn took one last look at the bobbing gray head of the hooded shooter as the cab rolled passed Harrah's a block away. Quinn was fast, but the shooter had too much of a lead. Following on foot was not going to work.

Without slowing his stride, Quinn threw a leg over the red Ducati and brought the engine roaring to life. Bikes rumbled by incessantly on the Strip, and by the time the kid in the UNLV shirt tore his eyes away from the girls to look behind him, Quinn was halfway down the block.

Quinn bent low, leaning in over the handlebars, coaxing as many of the 110 horses from the Duc's Testastretta engine as he dared without spilling into traffic. Rolling on the throttle, he split the lanes, shooting between an idling panel truck that advertised HOT BABES ON CALL and a low-rider Silverado pickup.

The Hypermotard, Ducati's version of a dirt bike for the street, was built for speed and maneuverability in all terrains, perfect for Quinn's needs at the moment. He caught sight of the gray hoodie's head through the back window of the cab, craning backward to see if he was being followed. Quinn pulled to the side of the road, in the shadow of a Hummer limousine.

The hoodie jumped out of the cab after less than a block and began walking again. Quinn often used the same trick to see if anyone was following him. The short ride made the drivers mad, but a good tip got them over it in a hurry.

Quinn slowed the bike to a rumbling putt, falling in with the flow of stop-and-go traffic while he watched the hoodie bob its way north with the sidewalk crowd. This man had shot Hartman Drake, likely to shut him up before he could tell Quinn anything useful. He'd had enough resources to find out what room Drake was in and the juice to get a key to that room. Had Dolores not assisted by plowing into the guy, Quinn might have thought she was involved.

Quinn veered right, nearly forced into a line of palm trees by a big-haired redhead paying more attention to her cell phone than the path of her shiny Coupe de Ville. The mere act of riding a motorcycle in such traffic brought an extra level of awareness that only added to the intensity of the chase. Not only did he have to worry about keeping the man in the hoodie in sight, or that same man turning to shoot him, but half the vehicles crammed onto the Strip seemed hell-bent on grinding him into the pavement.

"Where are you headed?" Quinn mused to himself as he leaned on the handlebars and watched the gray hoodie bob across the small service street on the other side of Denny's and Casino Royale. The shooter continued walking in front of the Venetian, answering his cell in the flickering green glow cast by the outdoor gondola canals.

Quinn knew that phone would contain a wealth of information.

Still moving, the man in the hoodie turned to look over his shoulder while he spoke, his bob becoming more animated. Turning again, he scanned the pedestrian bridge that crossed Las Vegas Boulevard to Treasure Island, then back over his shoulder. His head on a swivel, the man's eyes shot back and forth, looking behind him, then up at the bridge. Twenty meters back, partially hidden by the *Hot Babes* panel truck that had caught up with him in traffic, Quinn couldn't hear the conversation. But he didn't need to. Someone was telling the shooter that he was being followed, warning him.

Instinctively, Quinn began to scan the area, eyes combing the windows above. When he looked back, the man in the gray hoodie hunched his shoulders—and ran.

CHAPTER 11

Rolling on the throttle, Quinn shot around the *Hot Babes* panel van, squirting between traffic. His knee was just inches from the wrought-iron fence along the curb. The light changed on the street somewhere up ahead, and Quinn felt the wind from a passing side mirror graze him as a Hummer sped by.

The man in the hoodie shot a glance over his shoulder as Quinn bore down on him under the Palazzo portico. Spying the oncoming bike and certainly the look of death on Quinn's face, the man redoubled his efforts and sprinted toward the open double doors to the hotel. Less than ten meters behind, Quinn held his breath as he sailed through the same doors and into the lobby of the Palazzo.

Crowds of milling hotel patrons scattered like quail at the machine-gun blat of the oncoming bike. The marble interior of the huge, columned rotunda seemed to shake with the captive roar.

Quinn's target slid along the floor, squatting low to regain his traction on the slick marble.

Behind him, Quinn fared little better. He planted a

foot and let off the gas to maintain some semblance of control on the torquing bike.

The man in the hoodie darted left to keep from becoming trapped by an oncoming group of Chinese tourists. Quinn gunned the throttle, drifting the rear tire in a squalling rooster tail of smoke to get the bike pointed in the right direction. Hotel patrons turned to watch what many thought was some incredible Las Vegas attraction. Some had to scramble out of the way as Quinn followed his target straight into the casino.

The shooter cut left, yanking an older man off a stool at the champagne bar before darting up the middle of the casino floor. The Ducati's tires found easier traction on the carpet, and Quinn flicked the bike easily back and forth between casino patrons. He gained quickly on the runner, nearly catching him at the high-stakes blackjack tables. Feeling Quinn behind him, the man grabbed a cigarette girl and shoved, sending her flying into a cursing tangle of cigar tray, tiny dress, and boobs, directly into the path of the oncoming motorcycle.

Quinn jagged to the right to avoid the spitting girl, narrowly missing a row of roulette players with his knee as he fought to keep the bike on two wheels. Men in dark suits began to materialize from every pit and shadow of the casino. Some identified the man in the hoodie as part of the problem, but most converged on Quinn.

Quinn poured on the gas to keep out of the grasp of a particularly large, baldheaded pit boss who vaulted over a craps table after him.

Speeding up on a straightaway between the tables,

he watched the man in the hoodie flee the casino for the lobby and jump on the escalator beside a huge, floor-to-ceiling waterfall. He bounded upward, jerking other riders to the side as he bulldozed his way past. He reached the top at the same time Quinn reached the bottom.

With a virtual army of security behind him, some in suits, some in the comically loose Italian gendarmerie blues worn by hotel security, Quinn yanked up slightly on the handlebars and goosed the Ducati into a low wheelie.

No motorcycle was purpose-built for climbing escalators, but the Hypermotard came close, making the tooth-jarring journey to the top in time for Quinn to see the runner shove his way through the protesting crowds. He brutally yanked a young girl to the ground as he ducked under the arch into the adjoining Venetian Canal Shoppes.

Quinn rolled off the gas again at the top of the stairs, planted a foot to turn the bike toward the Shoppes, then accelerated smoothly on the slick marble. It looked as though he would make it until he hit a puddle of melted milkshake, part of the wake of shoppers and food left by the fleeing man in the hoodie.

The front wheel flipped sharply left, handlebars slapping the tank. The Ducati went down hard, bucking wildly and throwing Quinn over the front. He landed on his shoulder, rolling like a bowling ball through a crowd of gawking onlookers to send them scattering in all directions.

The armor in the Transit jacket took the brunt of the impact and Quinn was on his feet in an instant, running. He reached instinctively for his waist, touching the butt of his Kimber to make certain it had survived the crash.

Humidity and the swimming-pool smell of the indoor gondola ride hit him in the face as he rounded the corner. The man with the hoodie had cut to the left of the canal, darting between the milling crowds that stood at the rail, watching the singing gondoliers and waiting for their turns for a boat ride.

Quinn scanned the area ahead, spotting an approaching wedding party that blocked the runner's path. He cut to the right of the canal. The man in the hoodie, realizing he'd been cut off, tried to cross the small footbridge that arched over the water. Quinn met him halfway across.

Wanting to buy time away from the approaching security, Quinn crashed into the hooded gunman, hips low and rising like a football player off the line. He used the man's energy to spin him, driving him sideways, then backward over the concrete railing of the bridge to land with a splash in the clear blue water of the gondola canal ten feet below.

The man in the hoodie hit the surface flat on his back, catching the brunt of the force. Quinn landed on top of him, hands at the throat of the hoodie. Kicking as hard as he could, he drove the man down to the bottom of the shallow water. A cloud of silver bubbles erupted from the man's mouth as Quinn kept pushing, forcing the air from his lungs. Aware that his opponent had a gun, Quinn kept the pressure up, squeezing the man's throat and hoping the desire to breathe would outweigh any ability to shoot.

Quinn held him under for a full minute, writhing on

the bottom of the crystal blue water and surely giving the crowd above a good Vegas spectacle. They broke the surface together, the man in the hoodie choking and spewing water, gasping for air. A ring of security stood along the railing above, shouting orders but unwilling to get themselves wet now that their quarry was contained.

Quinn twisted the shooter's arm behind his back, wrenching upward, not caring how much damage he caused. He spun the man around so he was facing away and Quinn could talk directly into his ear.

"Who sent you?" he hissed, water spraying from his mouth.

The man, a Pakistani from his accent, rattled off a vehement oath. Although Quinn didn't understand completely, the gist of the words was clear. He wrenched the arm higher against the man's back. Sidestepping, Quinn bent at the waist, using the man's arm to shove his head underwater.

Along the railing, some people clapped, still thinking it was a show.

The Pakistani struggled as Quinn held him under, ignoring the shouts from the security men above. "I need a name," Quinn said, lifting him back to a standing position.

Sputtering, the Pakistani looked up as if to speak. His body suddenly tensed, as if hit with a bolt of electricity.

"The Foo Dog," he said under his breath, mouth hanging open. He backpedaled furiously, trying to get away.

"What?" Quinn jerked the man upright again.

A series of muffled *woompf*s from a suppressed pistol popped in the humid air. Quinn felt a splash across his face. The Pakistani convulsed and then went limp in his hands, a gaping wound where his forehead had been. Quinn held the body up as a shield, spinning slightly to make sure he kept the dead Pakistani between him and the shooter. Four more shots came in quick succession, riddling the Pakistani but obviously meant for Quinn.

He caught a glimpse of dark hair beyond the Venetian railing above, tucked back in a small recess beside the stone support column that led from the escalator to the Canal Shoppes.

"Hands in the air!" a voice barked from the gondola docks. Quinn looked up to see a Las Vegas Metro police officer, pistol pointed directly at him.

He let the dead man fall and raised his hands, not bothering to mention he was a federal agent. They would find that out soon enough. For a split second, he got a clear view of the woman beyond the railing. A uniformed Palazzo guard stood immediately beside her, not realizing that she was the shooter.

The law enforcement and casino security chasing Quinn had run right past. They'd left her virtually alone long enough to fire several rounds from her suppressed pistol, which was obviously now tucked under her brown leather jacket. She was compactly built, with narrow hips and long hair that hung like a thick mask over much of her perfectly oval face. Black eyes stared out from beneath the curtain of hair. An exasperated sneer hung on her small mouth.

Quinn looked away long enough to follow orders from the Vegas Metro officer, who was shouting at him to walk backward to the side of the canal.

Quinn's heart sank when he realized how little he had to go on. Drake had told him nothing, and the Pakistani shooter had given him only two words.

Foo Dog.

These ferocious lion dogs guarded virtually every temple and shrine in Asia. The words had something to do with the woman in the archway.

When Quinn glanced back, she was gone.

CHAPTER 12

Two days later
Tuesday
Kanab, Utah

Marta Bedford woke at three in the morning to Rick's snores. Between his frequent training with the Army and the sheriff's office and now his deployment, she had grown accustomed to being unaccustomed to him each time he returned. If he was gone more than a month it took her several days to get used to his movements beside her in bed and the little noises he made in his sleep.

But this time was different. He'd never been a snorer, and, though she could overlook even that, the way he moaned hurt her heart. The first night after he'd gone to see her brother to take care of the boil, she'd shaken him to make sure he was all right. Of course, he'd said he was fine. Rick Bedford wouldn't admit pain if he drank a glass of molten lava.

She slipped out from under the covers and went into the bathroom, waiting to turn on the light until she'd pulled the door shut behind her.

Staring into the mirror, she grabbed a handful of straw-blond hair and pulled it toward the ceiling, shrunken-head fashion. Blue eyes, normally bright, stared dully back beneath drooping lids. Her face was beginning to break out like a teenager, and she was getting a sty that would soon turn her into a squinty cyclops. The girls would really get a kick out of teasing her for that. Thankfully, her mother had agreed to take her granddaughters for a few nights while Rick tried to shake whatever this was that had him down.

She grabbed two aspirin from the medicine cabinet and swallowed them with a cup of water, grimacing at the pain in her throat. If this kept up Marta would have to ask her mother to watch the shop as well as the girls.

She looked at her watch—3:15—and mulled over the idea of going to the clinic. She knew she should—but nobody, least of all a wife and working mom of two teenagers, had time for that. Besides, she'd just had her forty-year checkup and been deemed, as her brother-in-law the doc joked, fit as a thirty-nine-year-old.

What she needed was a good, long sleep.

She saw the first sore when she reached to put the aspirin back in the cabinet. Gritting her teeth, she raised her arm to look in the mirror. A swollen red boil stared back like an angry eye. Two more bumps, red but in earlier stages, dotted her armpit.

"This is going to suck," she muttered as she dabbed at the boils, feeling the fevered tenderness and tight pink skin. She hadn't gone in the room with Rick when he'd had his treated the day before. The whole process of lancing a boil was just too medieval for her. She'd had her own experience with it shortly after the girls were born. That one had been much lower and more intimate than Rick's. It involved an extremely painful and incredibly embarrassing procedure she'd hoped never to repeat—lying naked from the waist down, facedown on the table, while the doctor lanced and pinched her butt cheek to drain the awful thing. She remembered vividly the dull ache in her jaw from gritting her teeth and the perfect sweat imprint of her body on the paper cover of the exam table.

By the time Marta made it back to bed, Rick sounded as if he was trying to breathe through a clogged snorkel. She rolled up next to him, ignoring her own pain, and put an ear against his chest. Something wasn't right. She'd never heard of boils being catchy like this—but they both had them. It sounded like Rick was getting pneumonia. And now, her throat was killing her.

CHAPTER 13

Munakata, Japan

Shimoyama Takako took great pleasure in the simple, Zen-like design of the things that surrounded her. She had few friends, but at least two of the girls she knew as a child had mothers who practiced ikebana, the art of flower arrangement. That was well and good, but Shimoyama had found such an art constraining. There was so much more to arrange in the world than flowers.

She knelt in front of the low table in her spacious room, palms flat against the cool lacquered top. Her notebook was open, the ivory pen forming a perfect diagonal across its pages. Her metallic cell phone case and dangling fuzzy charm lay at the tip of her fingers, faceup. The design of it all was a work of *wabi sabi*— art and beauty in the mundane—and set Shimoyama's heart at ease.

Taking a quick breath, she pressed a number into the phone. Someone of less focus might be tempted to toy with the gun when they were forced to make such a nerve-racking call. Shimoyama took comfort in the simple focus of looking at the weapon.

"Ah, Auntie," the man said on the other end of the line. Her superior was exceedingly polite, if not actually kind. He'd once called her his lover. Now, it was auntie, if only to prove she no longer held her previous position. "I hope you have good news."

"If you have a moment," Shimoyama said, willing her voice not to crack—from sorrow more than nerves.

"Of course, Auntie," the man said. She imagined him as a huge spider, beckoning with one of eight whiskered legs while he grinned at her from a dark corner. "Please, go ahead."

Shimoyama licked her lips.

"The business with our mutual friend in Las Vegas did not go as planned."

Though the man said nothing for some time, she could feel his mood darken over the phone.

"Yes," he said, "I have heard that very thing."

"The Pakistani was late in his arrival," Shimoyama said. She took some solace in the fact that the blame did not rest entirely with her people. Her employer would surely have required more than a finger if that had been the case. "I fear Quinn had a very short window of time to speak with the American." Shimoyama crossed off another note in her book with a perfectly straight line of black ink.

"What do you intend to do about him?"

"The Pakistani?" Shimoyama nodded to herself.

"Not the Pakistani," her employer snapped. "I am speaking of Quinn. It will please me greatly, Auntie, if he were dead before nightfall."

"These matters are fluid," Shimoyama said, sound-

ing more sure of herself than she was. "But I have another contact working on that as we speak."

"I hope so, Takako-chan," he said. "For your sake."

Shimoyama's heart leaped in her breast. Not because of the threat, but because he had called her by
her given name, something he had not done since he
had loved her, so many years before.

CHAPTER 14

Alexandria, Virginia

Quinn stood beside a squat Japanese lamp carved of gray stone, watching. The contest, or more correctly, the spanking that Emiko Miyagi was giving Jacques Thibodaux, did little to take his mind off Kim.

Palmer had summoned him back to D.C. after the incident in Las Vegas with the curt order to go to Miyagi's and wait for his call. Quinn hated waiting more than he hated neckties. It made him feel like a racehorse trapped in the gates. But wait he did, at Palmer's order, and while he waited, he trained.

They'd already run several miles as a warm-up that morning. Chasing the sun, Miyagi called it, trying to run a prescribed course through the Mount Vernon neighborhoods before the sun peaked over the tree line to the east. Quinn was in excellent shape but never turned down the opportunity to rest during one of Mrs. Miyagi's killer workouts. Apart from being entertained by the big Cajun's swordplay, it gave him time to breathe—and think.

Kim wouldn't be able to travel for several more

days, so she and Mattie had stayed behind in Colorado. Before he left, Jericho made certain a full complement of security from OSI and the El Paso County Sheriff's Department surrounded them in concentric circles of security, each layer going outward bristling with progressively heavy weapons.

Quinn's parents had flown in and that was what really calmed him. His mother had raised two of the wildest sons in Alaska and knew how to handle herself. In truth, she'd never been a huge Kim fan, but Mattie had won her over from the first moment she saw her in the hospital. Quinn's father, a commercial fisherman, was an aloof, quiet man. He felt the good Lord had given him a finite number of words, so he did his best not to waste any of them. He was also the toughest human being Quinn had ever met. Even tough men could be killed, but it did Quinn's heart good to know that his father was there, watching over things.

A rattling clash of wood on wood drew Quinn's attention back to the moment. He watched as Miyagi chased the big Marine in a tight circle over the frosted grass.

The fact that Jacques only had one good eye made no difference to Emiko or the Marine. In battle, weakness had to be overcome or it brought defeat—and both of them knew it.

It would have been a mistake to call what Miyagi taught *defensive* tactics. Tactics they were, but due to the nature of their jobs, much of what she taught was offensive in nature—and no one Quinn had ever met was better than taking the battle to the enemy than Emiko Miyagi.

She'd dispensed with the more traditional martial

arts uniforms, reasoning that they needed to learn to fight in the same clothing they wore in everyday life. In this case, that meant khaki slacks and polo shirts. Miyagi wore a long-sleeve Under Armour shirt beneath her polo, black to match the hair she kept pulled back in a high ponytail like some sort of medieval Mongol warrior. Thibodaux's khakis, like Quinn's, were stained at the knees and butt from repeated contact with the ground over the last half hour. The birds were just waking up in the surrounding oaks and sycamore trees and there was enough sun to give them light, but not nearly enough to chase away the clammy cold of a Potomac morning.

The big Cajun moved forward in his attack, feet sliding through the brown grass with a lightness that belied his mountainous size. Shouting a chilling war cry that was combination Marine Corps charge and martial arts *ki-ai*, Thibodaux brought the wooden sword crashing down toward the tip of Emiko Miyagi's head.

Most anyone else would have wilted at such a ferocious attack, but Miyagi turned deftly to the side. Barely five feet tall, she was a mouse to the six-foot-four Cajun. In that same instant, she raised her own wooden sword so both hands were high above her head, letting the tip fall so her blade ran diagonally down her arm and shoulder, deflecting Thibodaux's sword along its length toward the ground. Her movements were small, no greater than they needed to be, but were filled with such surety and force that her thick ponytail swung back and forth, brushing either side of her face as she moved.

Thibodaux leaned forward a hair farther than he should have as his sword hissed downward. Quinn grimaced, feeling pity for the big Cajun. He saw what was about to happen.

Keeping a high grip, Miyagi wheeled her sword in a great arc, bringing it up, then down, directly into Thibodaux's centerline, before he could raise his again. She stopped an inch above his forehead.

"Shit!" Jacques said, freezing in place, his sword still pointed at the ground.

"Do not fret," Miyagi said. "You would have felt little pain had it been a live blade instead of a *bokken*."

"Yeah," Thibodaux said. "That's just what I wanted to hear. I know it's supposed to help our footwork, but this Louisiana boy just don't do swords."

"You fight mixed martial arts." Miyagi stepped back, sword held high and back at her shoulder like a baseball player in the batting box. "Add blade work to the mix."

Thibodaux was in fact an MMA champion, fighting under the name Daux Boy.

He bowed, conceding defeat. "Thank you for the lesson."

Miyagi's agate-brown eyes shifted toward Quinn. It was the only cue that it was his turn to receive more instruction. They might rest. She never did.

"Do me a favor and kick her ass," Thibodaux said under his breath as the two men passed. The Cajun slouched beside the stone lantern, nursing his wounded pride.

"Yes, Quinn-san," Miyagi said. "Please. Show Mr. Muscleman how it is done." The mysterious Japanese woman had taken to Quinn right off, but for some unknown reason, she had no love lost for Jacques.

Wooden bokken in hand, Quinn circled slowly, eyes intent on Emiko Miyagi.

"The objective," Miyagi said, always teaching, "is to *feel* exactly where your blade is in relation to your body at all times."

She strode forward, cutting down at Quinn. He used the same hands-high, tip-down technique she'd employed on Jacques to deflect the blade, first from an attack to his right, then immediate follow-up cuts to his left and then his right again. Wood cracked against wood, echoing off naked trees that surrounded the training area in Miyagi's five-acre backyard, just a stone's throw from Mount Vernon.

Apparently satisfied that he understood that particular block and the footwork that went with it, she retreated a few steps.

"When you scratch an itch," she continued, her breath calm though she'd just tried to beat him to death with a stick, "you do not pause to think where your hand is located. You simply know. This is what you want with the blade. Notice I do not say the handle of your sword. I speak specifically of the blade. When you know where it is at all times, you may use it more effectively."

She held her bokken low now in one hand and to her side so it trailed behind as if she was dragging it. She stood straight, hips loose and ready to move.

Quinn held his blade upward, a mirror image of hers. It was a technique she'd taught them called *tsuki no kage* or *moon shadow*, where the opponents mimic each other's movements, looking for an opening.

Eyes fixed on each other, the two circled slowly, feet

shuffling in the dead grass of winter in Miyagi's walled retreat. She'd been training both men for a year and a half now, knocking off rough edges and filling in blanks left by traditional instructors.

The life of a hunter-killer had taught Quinn to be a natural skeptic, but he'd learned enough from this five-foot-tall, 115-pound enigma that if she said she could teach him how to fly, he would put his faith in her and jump off the roof. He had, of course, been beaten over the course of his fighting career, but not nearly so often and with as much consistency as Miyagi had been able to do it.

Thibodaux pointed out after one of their sessions that a hundred pounds of the woman was badass muscle—and fifteen was fighting heart.

Miyagi advanced without warning, bringing her sword around to thrust at his belly.

Quinn stepped to the side, seizing the opportunity to bring his blade down in an attack of his own now that she had committed herself.

Instead of countering, Miyagi continued her forward attack, striding past so she was directly behind Quinn. His sword hissed by her, missing by a fraction of an inch. He raised his arms to attack again as he turned, but he felt her spin behind him, grabbing his shoulders with both hands to swing her feet and legs upward and under his raised armpit. Her thighs clamped around his neck, muscular buttocks in the air. Her body hung straight down in front of him. He tried to raise his blade, but she swatted it away. With Miyagi inside his guard, there was little he could do with the cumbersome long sword. She bore down with her thighs, squeezing as he spun to throw her before she cut off all the blood to his brain. A half breath later, her wooden dagger touched the ribs under his heart.

He tapped her back to let her know he realized she had won. Her rump would have been more convenient, but he thought she might have used the dagger to greater effect had he tapped her there. She relaxed her legs and dropped to the grass, rolling to her feet with her wooden sword still in one hand, a wooden dagger in the other.

"Please remember," she said as she stood, "just because you hold a sword, does not mean it is the only weapon you can use to win the battle." Her voice was calm, absent the breathlessness even Quinn felt after such a bout.

Quinn bowed and walked over to Thibodaux to grab a drink from his water bottle.

"I told you to kick her ass"—the Cajun frowned— "not let her strangle you with it."

The morning held on to its chill but Miyagi and both men were bathed in sweat.

She kept them going from the moment they arrived back at her house. Most of the training occurred on the five acres of traditional Japanese garden that was tucked in the hardwood forests behind the house, all of it surrounded by high walls of imposing gray stone.

After sparring and prior to yoga, Miyagi had changed into black tights and long-sleeve leotard of the same color. The men wore loose T-shirts and running shorts.

Inverted now in a yoga headstand, Miyagi craned her neck to look up at her two charges, brown eyes glinting in approval when they landed on Quinn but going dark when they fell on Thibodaux. Neither man was sure how old she was. She had the force of will common to mature women, a teacher who'd learned much in all her years, but her smooth complexion and physical vigor suggested she was much younger. When they sparred, Quinn guessed she was in her mid-thirties. When she spoke of strategy and combat philosophy, he thought she might very well have been a contemporary of Miyamoto Musashi, the sixteenth-century Japanese swordsman.

Emiko Miyagi had a way of tailoring each workout to coax out the last drop of sweat. Swimming, running, sparring, more running, and more sparring generally took up at least two hours before she settled in to her favorite pastime of contorting their bodies into complicated and often painful yoga positions.

It would, she assured them, train their bodies and minds to be more resilient and aware. Quinn had to admit that he seemed to heal a little faster since he'd taken up the training.

Generally, the yoga portion of their morning saw her leading them through a *vinyasa*—or series of poses that flowed from one to the other on measured breaths. But, above all other poses, Miyagi preferred a variation on *sirsasana*, a headstand on her forearms with her back arched and knees bent so her feet were poised directly above her head. Thibodaux called it the Evil Scorpion and groused about it to no end, coming close, but never quite getting it right.

Inverted like Miyagi and Thibodaux, Quinn should have been clearing his mind. Instead, he let it wander.

So far, Winfield Palmer had avoided talking to him.

There was no doubt the national security advisor was upset. Quinn had screwed up and become embroiled with local authorities. The Speaker of the House was in serious condition—though his wounds were far less serious than Quinn had supposed—and Palmer had been forced to call Vegas Metro PD and the governor of Nevada in order to smooth their seriously ruffled feathers.

"Very well," Miyagi whispered, pulling Quinn out of his thoughts and signaling the end to the morning torture.

Bending gracefully at the waist, she lowered her feet to the grass and stood before the two men, waiting for them to do the same. She arched her back, looking up toward the sky so the dark corner of a hidden tattoo peeked above the scoop neck of her leotard. The mysterious ink had been at the center of many a discussion led by Thibodaux in late-night camps in various corners of the world. Neither man could tell what it was, only catching glimpses during workouts—and neither wanted to be caught staring at this badass woman's chest. Quinn never would hazard a guess. Thibodaux, keeping his thought process streamlined, decided it was an evil scorpion—just like the yoga pose he couldn't do.

"Thank you for your work." She bowed deeply in turn to each man. Her voice held only the slightest hint of a Japanese accent. "Quinn-san," she added, turning toward him. "Mr. Palmer would like to have a word with you on the telephone, but he won't be available for another twenty minutes. May I suggest you both take advantage of the traditional bath while you wait."

"I got a school thing with the kids," Thibodaux said,

situating his eye patch. "Camille insists I go when I'm anywhere near home."

"As you wish," Miyagi said.

Quinn sighed at the thought of a long soak. The prospect of a traditional Japanese bath sounded inviting. Mrs. Miyagi had allowed him to use it before, and he found the wood-fired cedar tub a cure-all for many ills physical and mental. What he did not look forward to was the talk with Palmer. The national security advisor had been unavailable since the incident in Las Vegas. Quinn, accustomed to direct access to his boss, had felt cut off and even a little betrayed at the isolation. Now, after the emotional dust had settled and he was able to see what a scene he'd made on who knew how many cameras, he was certain the conversation would be even more one-sided than usual.

CHAPTER 15

Both Quinn and Thibodaux had lived at Emiko Mi-yagi's home for a time when they'd first been tapped by Winfield Palmer to work as Other Governmental Agents. Quinn was familiar with the layout as well as the woman's love for the austere when it came to furnishings. Though the outer brick façade of the home had changed little over the two centuries since it had been built, the interior had been completely gutted and replaced with tatami grass mats, white pine beams, and sliding paper doors.

The bath area was off to the side of the rear patio and—as all traditional baths—located far from the toilet. It was enclosed in a ten-by-ten cedar room with benches and hooks along the inside wall like a pool house. A sliding cedar door led from a lower alcove that contained a shelf stacked with folded white towels used to both wash and dry. Quinn left his running shoes in a small wooden cubby above the floor.

Japanese baths were often social locations, a place to share gossip as well as to clean oneself. Two cedar stools were situated under a row of water spigots, low and easy to reach when seated. The round tub beside the spigots was built from cedar slats and resembled an oversize barrel that had been cut in half. At nearly six feet across, it dominated the steamy room.

Stripping naked, Quinn left his sweats and T-shirt on a cedar shelf over one of the benches inside the sliding door. The faint hint of smoke from an oak fire drifted through the humid air, mingling with the smells of soap and scorched minerals from pipes that heated the near scalding water. Quinn sat in front of the spigots with a bar of soap and a wooden bowl. The stool was small, like something meant for a child, but it got the job done. Though a long soak was traditional, it was customary to scrub until your skin was pink before entering the tub, leaving the water clean enough for the next person to use as well.

Quinn finished washing and fed a length of split oak into the wood-fired heater box. He'd just slipped into the steaming water when his phone rang on the bleached wooden table next to the tub.

Winfield Palmer began talking as soon as Quinn picked up the call.

"I gotta ask," Palmer began his rant. "Do you have any idea what kind of a shit storm you've ignited with your little stunt? Every news outlet in the country is filing Freedom of Information Act requests for the casino security camera footage that shows you trying to drown a man before someone else blows his brains out."

"As far as they know it was a man who shot the Speaker of the House," Quinn said, half to himself. He was not the type to try very hard to explain his actions. He slid down so only his head and the shoulders were above the surface.

"*One* of the men who shot Drake," Palmer said, as if he had the winning card. "And a lot of good you did. Thanks to you, Drake is back at his residence and demanding answers."

"He's out of the hospital?" Quinn sat back up in the water, wiping beads of perspiration out of his face. This was news.

"Yes," Palmer said. "Shot twice in the chest, but neither bullet got close to anything vital. He did lose a toe in the shootout and, oddly enough, he also had a small-caliber wound through the bottom of his foot. You wouldn't know anything about that, would you?"

Quinn chose his words carefully. "Do you remember when we met?" he asked.

"Of course," Palmer said, momentarily stumped by the sudden question during his tongue-lashing.

"Your sister's boy had been kidnapped in Iraq. I was sent in to get him back and . . . take care of things."

"I said I remember," Palmer snapped. "What's your point?"

"You and I both know Hartman Drake murdered his wife. We know he was intimately connected to a terrorist organization that tried to kill the president and the VP. Someone connected to this man tried to shoot my little girl and ended up nearly killing my wife. You said it yourself before I went to Vegas. There is something bigger than an attempt on my family going on here. You are strategy, I'm tactics. I get that. But if all this had happened to someone else, you would have sent me." Quinn plowed ahead, not giving Palmer a chance to speak.

"Point taken," Palmer said.

"What are we going to do about Drake?"

"I'm working on that," Palmer said. "He's become a media darling again—attacked twice by terrorists and survived. The conspiracy blogs have fuzzy photos of you in Vegas from a half dozen tourists' smartphones. Some call you a government agent; others have branded you one of the terrorists."

"I can't help that now," Quinn said. "But I can find this Japanese girl and get some answers from her." He kept the Foo Dog information to himself for the moment.

"All right," Palmer snapped. "Just do us all a favor and keep your head down. Listen, I've got to go. We have some kind of plague outbreak in southern Utah. That's not too far from Vegas. You don't have anything to do with it, do you?"

"I do not," Quinn said, feeling worse than he had before the call. "I'd better let you get to it."

He reached over the edge of the tub and dropped the phone on the wooden table beside his towel before letting his back slide down the slick cedar boards of the tub. The slightest movement brought prickling pain in the near scalding water. He welcomed the feeling, hoping the heat and sweat would purge his body and his mind.

He closed his eyes and breathed in the heavy scent of the oak fire and mineral odor of steam. A whisper-like rustling at the sliding door caused them to flick open.

He sat up straighter, ignoring the burn at his movement, and wiped a hand across his face when he saw the form of Emiko Miyagi through the cloudy haze. She stood in front of the curtains that blocked the doorway as if waiting for permission to enter her own bath.

Quinn wasn't uncomfortable with his own nudity. Miyagi had seen him naked before, when she and Thibodaux had rescued him from three of Doctor Badeeb's men. But there was something oddly out of place about this visit. Japanese baths were often communal, but in the year and a half since he'd known her, Miyagi had drawn a strict line between teacher and student, remaining ever aloof and distinct.

She tilted her head to one side, studying the situation before she committed herself by stepping fully into the room. Dark hair fell in damp strands, dripping against the indigo cloth of a cotton summer kimono, known as a *yukata*. It was printed with large white chrysanthemums as big as a fist. A bright red sash wrapped around her narrow waist. Her face was flushed, presumably from a hot shower of her own before she was to enter the bath.

"I apologize." Quinn grabbed his towel from the nearby table and started to get out of the tub. "You expected me to be finished with my bath by now."

Miyagi raised her hand to stop him.

"It is quite all right, Quinn-san," she said. Her voice was soft and matter of fact, as if she did not want to mar the contemplative mood of the bath. "Please, wait a moment longer if you do not mind."

Jericho settled back into the water.

"I . . ." She paused, taking a tiny step forward, her hands clasped at her waist. The wet hair and bright kimono made her look girlish, more feminine and fragile than he knew her to actually be. "In light of all that has happened . . ." She nodded, moving forward again. Her steps were small, constrained by the tight kimono. ". . . I feel that I must tell you a story."

She stood a mere two feet from the tub now, close enough that Quinn could see the slight tremor in her lips.

"I believe it will explain much that you need to know." Her hands moved behind her back. "But it will also produce many questions. It is a story of youth and heartbreak—of violence and death."

Quinn, who was surprised by little in the world, let his mouth fall open when Miyagi drew away the red sash and let the kimono slip from her shoulders and fall to the floor.

Completely nude, she gave a shuddering sigh, fragile, and completely out of her normal character.

"It is a story of my tattoo."

CHAPTER 16

Salem, Oregon

The cell phone in the breast pocket of Governor Lee McKeon's camelhair blazer began to vibrate the moment he cut into his French toast at the Sassy Onion. He considered ignoring it. His breakfast mate, the president of Willamette University, had a lot of powerful and, more important, wealthy friends who were potential political backers. It wouldn't do to snub him by answering a cell phone.

"Go ahead and take that, Lee," the bow tie–wearing academic said around a mouthful of bread and syrup. "I'm sure it's important gubernatorial business." It was he who'd insisted they have the French toast. What else would one order for breakfast at the Sassy Onion?

McKeon thanked him for his understanding and answered without getting up, though he knew that would severely hamper his side of the conversation. Since the call was international, it would likely be monitored by one of the alphabet-soup government agencies anyway. The phone was a burner, purchased at a convenience store in Portland. Ranjhani would have a similar device that he'd picked up in Lahore. Everyone expected a governor to have more than one phone, so even his aides didn't give him a second look.

"Yes," McKeon said.

"Peace be unto you," Qasim Ranjhani said.

"And to you," McKeon said in English.

"Can you talk?"

"Yes, for a moment," McKeon said.

"Very well," Ranjhani gave a long nasal breath. "I believe we should meet to discuss a few options."

"I'm not sure that is advisable," the governor said. "There are a lot of delicate issues with that project." Though it was no secret that his biological father hailed from the subcontinent, the last thing McKeon needed was for some photo of him with an unknown Pakistani to end up on the Internet. Americans loved to showcase their minority candidates as long as they associated with the correct sort of people.

"As you wish," Ranjhani said. "Your father would be very proud of you, you know. We are going to change the course of history."

"I look forward to it."

Governor McKeon ended the call. His hand shook as he cut into the French toast. He tried to keep up his side of the conversation with the university president, but all he could think about were the words Qasim Ranjhani had spoken. The course of history would indeed make a sharp bend and he, Lee McKeon, would be at the forefront. McKeon smiled as he swallowed the sweet toast and syrup. He would be a good son, and, Allah willing, see his father's plan to the glorious finish.

CHAPTER 17

Kanab, Utah

Doctor Todd Elton peeled off blue nitrile gloves, using the thumb of one to pull off the other so they ended up in a neat, self-contained ball without the outside of either ever touching his skin. He let them fall into the red infectious-materials bag lining the bin in the corner, then scrubbed his hands in the exam room sink.

A serious runner with seven marathons under his belt, Elton was slender with a mischievous glint in his eyes and the deep dimples of someone who smiled in his sleep.

He did not remove his protective glasses—meant to keep any errant fluids out of his eyes—and spoke over his shoulder while he washed. His scrubbing and speaking were more animated than usual.

"Well, okay, Mrs. Johnson," he said, working the Betadine soap into a thick lather all the way up to his elbows. "Sorry about causing you so much pain there." He pushed his glasses back with his shoulder, hoping his patient didn't notice the sweat beading on his forehead.

Draining a boil on an elderly woman's neck was not unknown to him in his nineteen years of medical practice—but treating so many people for the same such sores in one day was like something out of a horror movie. Surely this was a record. And no boil he'd ever treated had a sore throat associated with it. He had already lanced three boils for his brother-in-law and then sent him home with a prescription for a steroid inhaler that the doctor hoped would ease his labored breathing. A half hour before Mrs. Johnson arrived, Bedford's army buddy, R.J., had come in with six of the cursed little boils. And that had just been the beginning.

"It's okay, Doctor Todd." The sweet little woman coughed into a crumpled white tissue. She weighed less than a hundred pounds and couldn't have been five feet tall from her bunioned feet to the top of her perfectly quaffed silver-blue hair. "I've felt worse pains, I suppose." She gave a tremulous chuckle. "Though I can't remember when at this very moment."

Elton dried his hands on a paper towel and then looked down at the red bag filled with medical lances and gauze covered with blood and gore. It was a struggle to resist the urge to keep scrubbing his hands until they were raw.

He turned to face his patient, keeping a good distance between them. "We'll get you a prescription for some antibiotics. I'm going to go ahead and treat you for MRSA, just in case you've got one of the nastier bugs. The culture will take about three—"

Brandy, his PA, knocked on the door and then opened it without waiting for an answer. Her purple scrubs were visible through the narrow crack.

"Can I see you a moment, Doctor?"

Elton forced a smile, relieved to have an excuse to escape the confines of the exam room. "I'll just be a minute, Mrs. Johnson."

The old woman gave a polite nod and he pulled the door shut behind him.

Brandy's round face was ashen. "There are two more in the waiting room now."

"Seriously?" Elton stared blankly at the wall. "That makes—"

"Your brother-in-law came in yesterday. You've done nine already since we opened. Four more have come in over the last twenty minutes." Brandy rolled full lips into a white line. "This is just too weird."

The doctor gave an exhausted sigh. "I'll give Public Health a call . . ." As lead physician at both the Kane County Hospital and Clinic it was his responsibility to ensure all necessary protocols were followed when it came to the outbreak of a contagious disease—something he'd never had to face in his small, southern Utah town.

Brandy followed close behind as Elton made his way down the bright hall to his office, as if she were afraid to be left alone. Donita, the records clerk, glanced up as they passed her office. A worried half grin crossed her face. Everyone could tell this was no ordinary day at the clinic.

The public health hotline picked up on the second ring. Instead of helping him with his problem, the harried woman on the other end said she would need to transfer him. A half second later, someone from the Centers for Disease Control answered.

He put his hand over the receiver and looked at Brandy. "Odd," he whispered. "They've transferred me to the CDC." He turned back to his conversation. "Yes, this is Todd Elton in Kanab, Utah . . . No, K . . . *A* . . . N . . . Yes, Kanab. Anyway, I'm a family practice physician and . . ." He took a deep breath. "We have a bit of a situation I'd like to run by you—" He nodded, though talking on the phone and the woman on the other end had no idea he was nodding. She asked a series of questions, callback numbers, physical address, number of people involved, all likely off a predetermined checklist kept beside the hotline telephone.

"Yes," Elton answered at length. "Well, it's an acute outbreak of feverish boils around the groin, armpit, and neck. There's been one male patient but it generally appears to be affecting women . . . Yes, fourteen total so far . . . Yes, I'm running cultures—"

He sat silently for a moment, listening, perfectly still but for his eyes that kept darting between Brandy and his desk.

Elton shook his head, grimacing at Brandy as if he'd just heard something odd. "Yes," he said. "As a matter of fact one of the patients is a soldier. All right, I understand."

He hung up. "Get this," he said, taking a deep breath, "they were already working on it."

"How'd they know about us?" Brandy crinkled her forehead.

"Not us," Elton said. "I guess there are cases popping up in other places."

Brandy caught her breath. "What other places?"

"I was talking to a government agency." Elton chuckled, trying to relieve the tension he felt in his gut. "She was not extremely forthcoming with that information."

"What are we supposed to do?"

Elton toyed with the notepad where he'd written the number for CDC. "The lady said she'd call right back. But I get the feeling they are sending someone to take over."

CHAPTER 18

Virginia

The tiny edge of the hidden tattoo that had plagued Quinn and Thibodaux for the last year and a half was actually the beginning of a design that covered virtually every inch of Miyagi's torso.

Brilliant splashes of black, orange, pink, and green started at her shoulders like cap sleeves and worked their way down. An orange carp, or koi, covered much of her back, swimming beneath fallen pink cherry blossoms. The image of a gaudily made-up courtesan adorned the ribs and hip of her left side, completely covering her buttock and thigh. The opposite side of her body was graced by the goddess Kwannon, who faced inward, as if staring into her soul.

Her upper chest around her collarbone and a four-inch line of flesh running down the center of her body remained un-inked, making it possible for her to wear shirts open at the neck and even her workout leotards without revealing the presence of a tattoo. Only the tiniest black outline of a cherry blossom sometimes peeked out on the swell of her breast.

Her head bowed demurely, chin pressed against her chest, Emiko brought her leg over the side of the tub in a movement that reminded Quinn of ballet. The steam parted as her foot pierced the surface. Water shimmered like quicksilver, lapping at the taut muscles of her belly, just below her navel.

She stood perfectly still.

The musky scent of her body drifting over the superheated water made Quinn feel as though he'd been drugged. He found it impossible to tear his eyes away. Apparently wanting him to look, she kept her hands at her waist, turning in a slow revolution before she settled into the bath. Only her head and shoulders were left exposed.

Her body was the canvas for an incredibly intricate work of art. The fact that Quinn had known her for so long without any idea such a thing was there only added to the mystery.

Miyagi kept her face down, toward the water. Her wet hair hung in a sort of protective curtain, concealing her eyes but not her emotions.

"Many servicemen get tattoos," she said, finally breaking the silence. "I have often wondered at the fact that you do not have any."

"I've thought about it," Quinn said, surprised at how dry his mouth was. "But I started working outside the wire, posing as an Arab, early in my career, so it seemed advisable to keep my skin unidentifiable."

"That is a good choice," she said. "One that will hopefully keep your skin intact as well." Her chest shook with a nervous chuckle. "I think Americans would consider my tattoo hideous, no?"

"It doesn't matter what anyone thinks," Quinn said.

His voice was throaty and hoarse. He opened his mouth, but could not think of another worthwhile word to say.

Miyagi looked up, her eyes probing to know what *he* thought of her. "Do you know how we begin a tale of long ago in Japan?"

Quinn gave a quiet nod. "Of course. *Mukashi, mukashi*—once upon a time . . ."

The tiniest of smiles parted Miyagi's lips. She was close enough that Quinn could almost feel her breath across the water. She trembled slightly as she spoke. Her shoulders, which had always been so powerful during their lessons, softened and seemed to melt into the water. She tilted her head, ebony hair trailing the surface of the bath.

"Well then," she whispered. Steam swirled around her face. "*Mukashi, mukashi*, when I was a little girl, my father was a yakuza underboss, second only to the *oyabun*. My father was a powerful man, respected by his peers and the many men who worked for him. His name was Yamada Senzo and he was an expert at kendo and *tameshigiri*." She looked at Quinn to see if he understood. "Do you know *tameshigiri*?"

Quinn nodded. He'd practiced the art of cutting with a functional Japanese sword—some of his targets considerably more realistic than others.

Miyagi continued her story. "You may know that the yakuza were originally gamblers. Even the name ya-ku-za comes from the term for eight-nine-three, a losing hand in a Japanese card game. Some call them rogues and thieves, but to my father's mind, the yakuza had an ancient samurai ethic. He trained me in all things according to the martial way from the time I was old enough to walk. We were very close, he and I.

"Unfortunately, when I was thirteen years of age, he became very ill. Wicked men, men who had sworn oaths to support him, schemed instead behind his back and took everything he had. In his weakness, he could not fight them. He died a broken man, leaving my mother overwhelmed with crushing debt. There was nothing she could do but take up house with another yakuza lieutenant."

Miyagi looked up suddenly, pained eyes locked on Quinn. Tendons knotted along her delicate neck. The tip of her tongue quivered against her lips. "It is here, when I began life on the street, that my story, the story that is relevant to you, begins . . ."

CHAPTER 19

April 2, 1983
Saturday, 2:00 AM
Fukuoka, Japan

Yamada Emiko had the stomped look of a girl with a broken heart—but she knew how to fight.

"Choke! Choke! Choke!" The chant rose from the darkness in the deserted train tracks behind the vacant box factory. The empty shell of broken windows was a precursor of the economic slump that would soon strike Japan's industry and powerful markets, but the fighting youth knew nothing of that. To them, the vacant building offered a place to hide from the crushing conformity society tried to push on them.

Locked on the gravel in a deadly embrace with her opponent, Emiko puffed her hollow cheeks and reared back, catching the other girl's throat in the V of her bent arm. Chiyo was new to the group. Still well fed from her parent's table, she had Emiko by thirty pounds—but that didn't matter.

Emiko grasped her own forearm with the opposite hand, pulling tighter, her body settling in next to her opponent. Each time Chiyo moved, Emiko adjusted her grip, squeezing the life out of her like a constricting snake. One leg entwined the other girl's ankles, keeping her from kicking free or turning around.

Chiyo gurgled, struggling to draw a breath. Her hands clawed at the arm that wrapped around her neck, trying in vain to pry it away. Emiko let her wrist nestle in next to the hollow of the other girl's neck, as her father had taught her. She bent it just enough to drive the base of her thumb against her opponent's carotid artery, stopping the flow of blood to her brain and putting her to sleep almost instantly.

Emiko dropped the unconscious Chiyo like a piece of garbage, then raised her hands above her head and gave a bloodcurdling scream. Victory meant money, which meant food—and maybe even a little sake.

Her peroxide-red hair was chopped as if with a pair of garden shears and stood out at different lengths in all directions. In a country that valued conformity, such a haircut on a young woman was the equivalent of spitting in the face of her elders. It did not matter to her. Emiko had no elders to spit on.

She'd cut away the neckline of her pink Hello Kitty sweatshirt in order to expose a budding cleavage. Kenichi hated for other boys to look at her that way but didn't mind taking a peek himself. Besides, it gave him a reason to be jealous. Emiko enjoyed the feeling of being fought over, especially if muscular Kenichi with his James Dean pompadour, tight white T-shirt, and black leather jacket was the one doing the fighting.

Life had been hard enough after her father died in debt, but then her mother had taken up house with the filthy yakuza underboss, Sato, who seemed to be a lot more interested in Emiko than he was her mother.

Looking back, Emiko should have killed him, but she knew little of such things at the time.

At first she'd stayed with girlfriends from school, but when their parents discovered that she was the daughter of a dead yakuza lieutenant, they politely but firmly told her it would be best if she found somewhere else to lay her head. She'd slept in a park the first night—almost five months before—next to a crazy homeless woman who thought Emiko was a pet goat. The fact that she'd abandoned life, coupled with her ability to fight, made the *bosozoku* street tribes a natural place for the young girl to eventually land.

Now gaunt from malnutrition, too little sleep, and too much alcohol, her collarbones stretched against pale skin as if they wanted to escape. Her fingernails were dirty and broken. Grime ringed the cuffs of her pink sweatshirt.

Kenichi urged her to eat more, begged her to quit fighting, even promising to clean up his act and get a job as a mechanic so they could get married.

Marriage. Emiko scoffed, looking at the muscular boy across the unconscious body of her latest opponent. Marriage was too big a word to comprehend for a girl who didn't expect to live to see her fourteenth birthday. Apart from her feelings for Kenichi, she didn't even care.

The greasy bookie who'd set up the fight with the new girl handed Emiko her money, a measly five thousand yen—roughly twenty-five American dollars—to risk a broken neck.

"Sagara wants to see you," the bookie grunted. He stuffed a wad of bills into the pocket of his canvas trousers that looked to have been doused in motor oil.

Kenichi's strong arm snaked around Emiko's shoulders, drawing her close. "Tell him she is busy tonight," he said. "Come on, Emi-chan. I got the motorcycle fixed. Let's go for a ride across the riv—"

The bookie gave Kenichi a hard cuff to the ear. "Idiot!" he spat. "No one tells Sagara they are busy. He will tell you if you are busy or not."

Kenichi shucked off his leather jacket, always spoiling for a fight. Emiko had been his girlfriend long enough to know that no one could hit him in the head and get away without a beating, least of all a greasy old man.

Sagara's acid voice barked from across the tracks, stopping the boy in midswing. He was a thick man, nearly as wide as he was tall, with a big belly and fat cheeks that pushed his eyes closed from the bottom when he smiled, which was usually at the expense of someone else's misfortune.

"Oi!" He grunted, nodding to the slouching man at his left who held a black pistol, half hidden in the darkness. "Can I buy you two a hot meal or should I have Tomiyuki-kun put a bullet in your worthless brains?"

Kenichi spun at the new threat. Fists doubled, he stood on the balls of his feet. Emiko's father had taught her about men like Sagara. She knew it would be bad strategy to fight such a person in face-to-face combat. He was yakuza, like her father had been—too powerful, too connected for mere teenagers to beat in an open fight.

She patted Kenichi's arm to calm him and then put

on her helpless-child voice. It was another strategy taught to her by her late father.

"Why would a powerful man such as Sagara-sama want to feed two worthless brains like ours?" She bowed low.

"Because I do not want you for your brains," Sagara growled. "Come. I have curry rice. You can eat in the car on the way."

It was generally easy to bribe a starving soul with meat, but Emiko stood her ground. Sagara reeked of evil. She could smell it even from across the tracks.

"If not for our brains, what then?" Emiko said. "I am no prostitute."

Sagara roared with laughter, elbowing his man, Tomiyuki. "As if anyone would want to take your scrawny body." He rubbed his eyes. "There are those in my organization who have noticed you when you fight. We believe it may be time to see if you are ready to move up to bigger things."

Emiko had heard of such yakuza-sponsored events. They were still underground, but the money was said to be better—and sometimes they even arranged an apartment for their fighters to live in—so long as they kept winning.

She shot a wary glance at Kenichi, who shrugged. Curry rice was his favorite. He pitched the keys for his customized Honda to a boy named Tsuchiya, asking him to watch the bike while they were gone, then turned back to Emiko.

"What can it hurt to talk to them?" Kenichi said.

Two minutes later, Emiko was crammed in the back of the dark sedan, squeezed in between Kenichi and the leering Sagara. Streetlights flashed red and amber as they thumped along the main road going south, out of town. The lights grew more infrequent as they left the city, throwing the interior of the car into near darkness, illuminated only by the green glow of the dashboard and the red ember at the end of Sagara's stinking cigar.

The inside of the Toyota Crown smelled like cheap aftershave and tobacco smoke. Kenichi, always looking for sources of protein so he could grow muscles like his hero Arnold Schwarzenegger, wolfed down all his curry and much of Emiko's when she said she was finished. A familiar gnawing at her stomach pushed away hunger. Her father had called the feeling *haragei*, the *art of the belly*, and told her she should pay attention to it. These feelings would, he said, warn her of danger.

As they sped up on a long section of highway out of the city, the gnawing in her stomach grew so strong she almost cried out. In the front seat, Tomiyuki smoked one cigarette after the other while he drove. Even in the darkness of the sedan, Emiko could see the young lieutenant was missing the last joints on the pinky and ring fingers of his left hand—evidence of two fairly significant misdeeds he'd had to atone for. Sagara folded his stubby arms across a great belly and looked down at her with a squinty, condescending grin.

Emiko closed her eyes to escape the man and tried to go to sleep. She should never have gotten in that car.

She woke up sometime later to a slowing motion of the car. Her head was resting on Sagara's shoulder. It took a moment for her to realize where she was, but as the smells and sounds came back to her, she gave a startled shudder and sat straight up. Sagara smiled down at her as if he'd never moved his squinting eyes. Kenichi was still asleep, a line of drool running from his mouth to his T-shirt. She nudged him with her foot. He woke up blinking wildly, just as startled as she had been at finding himself in an unfamiliar place.

The low rays of a morning sun crawled across the pavement in front of them, chasing a thick blanket of mist back into the tall pines that lined the road.

A stone wall, like the ones Emiko had seen around feudal castles, stood on either side of the road ahead of them. Tomiyuki slowed the Toyota as two massive wooden gates yawned open. The gates shut behind them as soon as they drove through, and Emiko found herself surrounded by manicured gardens, koi ponds, and squat stone lanterns. Arched Shinto torii gates straddled well-groomed gravel paths. Huge stone monoliths rose here and there at least fifteen feet into the air. She could see several buildings tucked back in the trees, but their dark wooden architecture made them blend in to become part of their natural surroundings.

Tomiyuki stopped the sedan and turned to his boss with a subservient nod.

Outside, a smiling man wearing a white judo gi under dark blue *hakama*—a type of loose, flowing pant worn by ancient samurai—waited on the newly mown grass with folded arms. A rich head of dark hair was conservatively short, like that of a Japanese businessman. Though he smiled at the new arrivals, the man's dark eyes held the flint-hard air of one accustomed to being in complete control of his surroundings.

The man bowed deeply when Sagara approached, both hands flat against the sides of his *hakama*.

The yakuza boss returned the bow, rising quickly to motion Emiko forward with a flick of his thick wrist.

"Come, come," he grunted, commanding her in low tones, as if she were a dog.

Tomiyuki gave her a rough shove from behind to hurry her up. She turned to glare at him and saw that he carried a wooden case like the one her father had used to transport his cutting swords. She shot a worried glance at Kenichi, who stretched his muscular arms skyward and yawned, still not comprehending exactly where he was.

Sagara gestured toward the man in the *hakama* with an open hand. "Like I told you," he said, "you have been noticed as a possible fighter. Oda sensei is going to see what you are made of."

Emiko found herself bowing before she realized what she was doing, transfixed by the man's dark eyes. The other bosozoku would have laughed her out of the gang.

The man called Oda looked at her, seeming to gaze past her eyes to study the back of her skull. She squirmed awkwardly at the intrusion, feeling as if she was being physically touched.

"Are we to stay here?" she asked.

"Not so fast." Sagara laughed. "Oda-san doesn't just take on any student who comes along. You must be tested first." He snapped his sausage-like fingers, summoning Tomiyuki up with the case. The yakuza soldier set the case on the ground and clicked the latches, folding it open to reveal two gleaming *wakizashi*, shorter versions of a samurai sword. Each was two feet long and finely appointed with intricate guards and stingray-skin handle wrappings.

Tomiyuki handed one of the swords to Sagara with both hands, holding it out in front of him as if it might bite.

The yakuza boss took the blade and passed it to Emiko. "What do you think?" he asked, giving her time to peruse the glinting steel.

"It is beautiful," she said, her voice hushed. Indeed the sword looked to be hundreds of years old and still hummed with a life force that could not be denied.

"Good," Sagara said, stepping back slightly. He nodded behind her. "Let's see what you and your friend are made of."

Emiko recoiled, lowering the blade. A rush of adrenaline surged through her and she saw a wan-faced Kenichi holding the other sword. He stood directly behind her, less than five feet away.

"I cannot fight Kenichi with a live blade." Her words dripped with disdain. "One of us could be killed." She made no mention of the fact that with the training she'd received at the hand of her father, the one killed would most certainly be Kenichi.

The man in the hakama watched silently, motionless.

"You have no choice," Sagara said. He licked his lips, excited at the prospect of blood. "The two of you must fight and show us what you can do."

"And what if I say no?" Brave, sweet Kenichi let his sword fall to the grass. "I will not fight my girlfriend."

Sagara nodded to Tomoyuki, who stepped in behind Kenichi and put a pistol to the boy's head.

"I am Sagara Hiroya, underboss of the Taniguchi yakuza family," he growled. "People do not tell me no!"

Emiko moved before she thought, spinning with the sword extended at the end of an outstretched arm. The last six inches of the razor-sharp blade caught the yakuza boss under the left ear and opened his neck, throwing his fat head back like an oversized PEZ candy dispenser. A fountain of blood arced upward, painting Emiko, who was still spinning, swinging the blade toward Tomoyuki. She heard the report of the pistol that killed Kenichi but brought the wakizashi around a split second later to take Tomoyuki's hand and then his head in the fluid motion. Drenched in blood, she took the sword in both hands and turned to face the still gurgling Sagara.

"No!" she spat, a heartbeat before something heavy struck the back of her head and her world went black.

CHAPTER 20

Virginia

For a time the only sound in Miyagi's bath was the tick of expanding metal on the woodstove. Quinn didn't speak. Revelations like this called for silent support, not talk. The longer he looked at the tattoo, the more scars he noticed on Miyagi's body. And the more he listened to her story, the more he realized there were some scars that went much deeper than her skin.

"I knew I could not save Kenichi." Miyagi's reflection rippled on the surface as she continued her story. Her tattoo seemed to dance and sway, visible in the clear water. "But I had to kill Sagara as my last act of defiance. As it happened, unbeknownst to the fat yakuza boss, that was the test that Oda had planned all along. When I awoke a few hours later, I found myself as if transported back in time. I lay covered with luxurious silk quilts with my head on a pillow filled with buckwheat chaff. Oda knelt beside me, mopping my forehead tenderly with a cool cloth. He told me he was sorry Kenichi had died but said I had done the right thing, which is to say the thing he would have done. I was to stay with him and become his student. I told him I did not want to be his student, but he explained that the choice was not mine to make. When I asked him what he would do if I told him no as I had told the fool Sagara, he merely laughed and said he fully expected me to try to kill him many times before I understood the value of my training with the *Kuroi Kiri*—the Black Mist."

Miyagi rolled her lips, gathering her arms to her chest in sudden embarrassment. "The stories of an old woman are certainly a bore," she said. "I am sorry to burden you with them, Quinn-san, but I do have my reasons."

"First of all," Jericho said, "I have never considered you anything close to old." He wiped the sweat from his forehead with the back of his hand. "And this conversation is far from boring."

"The bath is hot," she said. "Perhaps you need to get out of the tub for a time." She swished the water so it disrupted the multihued reflection that lapped at her chest. Quinn found it incredible that he and Thibodaux had spent so many days wondering about the mysterious tattoo that was now displayed so openly before him. It was something he'd likely never be able to mention to the big Cajun—something too sacred to speak of outside the confines of the bath.

"I'm fine," he said. "But I understand if you need to get out."

She shook her head, apparently happy he was able to stay for a time.

Quinn nodded. "Please go on."

"Very well." She took a long breath, her chest rising in the water. "At first, Oda was a marvelous teacher.

The Garden, as I came to call the compound in which I was being held, was much like stepping back to feudal Japan. Entire families seemed to live within the walls—gardeners, tailors, teachers, sword smiths, and artists. All sorts to keep a society running smoothly, or at least it seemed that way to a teenage girl, snatched out of the real world. Apart from the tradesmen, there were the fighters, those of us in training. We all dressed in traditional clothing—kimono, pantaloons, and woven grass slippers—and were never to be caught without our weapons. Oda sensei assured us that we were a samurai class and he was our firm but patient lord. I began to grow into a healthier weight and gained social confidence under his guiding hand. When I first arrived, Oda spent his time in the company of several different girls. His favorite, it seemed, was Takako. She was much older than I was and very beautiful. Since she was the oldest, she saw it as her duty to take care of all the girls like a kind auntie—several times causing her much sorrow and pain at the hand of Oda. The fact that he spent time with each of us did not appear to bother her, but when he began to pay particular attention to me alone Takako began to bully me during practice. She was much taller and at first had no trouble beating me. Worse than the beatings, I felt that I had lost a friend. Oda ordered her to leave me alone, and I believe she came to forgive me in her own way.

"We all knew Oda was insatiable in his lust. But the moment he had any girl alone, he had a way of making us believe there would never be anyone else." Miyagi's shoulders rolled forward, as if to protect her heart. She sighed. "Still, there was always a favorite, a number one, so to speak. That position had belonged to Takako until I arrived. At first, he took me. I pretended it was against my will, but I did not fight back. By the time I had been in the Garden for three months, I sought him out in the soft grass behind the shrine and gave myself to him completely. Though I knew firsthand how to kill a man and by then had done so many times, I was still young and uneducated about sex and the attendant consequences of such things." Miyagi blushed, something Quinn had never before seen her do. "Eventually, I became pregnant. Two months before I turned sixteen, I bore him a daughter." She shivered in spite of the steaming water, wrapping her arms around her bare chest as if suddenly aware that she had exposed more than just her physical body to Quinn. "At the time, our relationship seemed completely natural, though looking back, what he did to me could only be defined as a rape. Oda was almost thirty and I was but fourteen when he first took me. In a way, I suppose, it was just another aspect of the brutal training I received at the hand of the Black Mist.

"There were other children born in the Garden, but I wanted my daughter to be the favorite. I redoubled my efforts, working day and night to make the father of my baby proud of me. I entertained no more thoughts of leaving, and only wanted to please this man who had such a mental and physical hold over me. It was about this time that he suggested I begin my *irezumi*."

She stood to display the tattoo, holding an open hand over her groin. It made Quinn smile inside that for all her toughness and martial skill, Emiko Miyagi retained a certain degree of modesty.

She used the other hand to give him a tour of the

brilliantly inked tattoo, letting her fingers glide over her skin. She turned slowly, careful not to splash, displaying the dark coat of ink that covered her delicate skin like black and green armor scales. Even the backs of her knees, which must have been excruciatingly painful, were completely covered, the ink stopping just above midthigh. "I was special, he said, and should mark myself as such. He helped me pick the design. The koi fish swimming upstream signifies struggle in life. Kwannon is the goddess of mercy. The woman is a concubine from our ancient stories, transformed by an encounter with a Zen monk. It took nearly five years to get this far. Five years of agony while the *tebori* master stabbed me over and over again with tiny needles. Oda sensei insisted that the act of getting the tattoo in the traditional way was more important than the tattoo itself. When someone from the outside world saw it, they would know without a doubt that I was capable of enduring endless suffering." She ran a fingertip up the curve of her left hip. The concubine was a beautiful woman. Clutching a dagger, she was dressed in the flowing gowns of a courtesan. But work on the tattoo had ceased, leaving only the concubine's face completed. Her other features and kimono were empty black outlines, like a child's unfinished coloring book. "It remains undone," Emiko said, detached as if looking at a museum painting and not the brilliant ink covering her own body. "A constant reminder that my struggles are not over, and, unlike the courtesan, I am not yet myself transformed into enlightenment."

She sank into the water with a weary sigh. "The training in the Garden was brutal—fighting at least once and sometimes three times a day. There was hardly any time for rest, but I did not care. I was as happy as I had ever been."

Emiko looked up at Quinn and smoothed a lock of hair out of her face. Beads of sweat poised on her quivering upper lip. Tears welled in her eyes. Quinn had seen this woman endure all manner of pain, watched her reset her own dislocated finger, but he'd never before seen her cry.

"As I said, the training was intense, so my daughter spent much of her day with her father. She was an incredibly intelligent child but, as I came to learn, also extremely cruel. One evening as I returned from the dojo I saw her attack the little boy of our cleaning woman because he had broken her favorite mirror. When I moved to stop her, Oda sensei held me back, saying the training would benefit both children. Our daughter beat the poor boy until he lay senseless on our floor. Then, before I could stop her, she took a piece of the broken mirror and sliced his face. She was five years old . . ."

Emiko swallowed. Tendons knotted along her neck. Other than that, she maintained complete composure. "I watched as she treated the other children in the Garden with utter cruelty and disdain. But I was weak, and even that I overlooked because Oda sensei said she would soon grow to control herself. Then, one night, I returned from the bath earlier than usual. I heard Oda's voice as I approached and, for some reason, stopped to listen. 'You are a special girl,' he told our daughter. 'You have your mother's gifts but none of her flaws.' I heard her tell him she wanted a tattoo like his someday. She said I was weak and had to be destroyed. I stood outside our home, stunned to hear Oda tell our daughter that I would soon be out of the way. 'Your mother is not like you and your papa,' he told her, 'she is imperfect. I assure you, her death will be quick and merciful.' And then, my little girl clapped her hands as if her papa had just given her a present."

Miyagi's chest heaved in the water as if she'd arrested a violent sob. "I was completely undone. Everything after that has melted into blurs and shadows in my memory.

"Later that night, I swallowed my disgust and made love to Oda, for I knew that he slept deepest after such things. I tried to take our daughter with me, to get her away from this horrible man before he poisoned her against me completely and turned her into a monster. She awoke when we were outside. I will never forget her face when she looked at me in the darkness of the woods beyond our home. It was as if she'd seen something that sickened her. She screamed for the guards to stop me before I could take her, then tore at my flesh with her little teeth like a wild animal. I am certain she hoped to kill me."

Miyagi pulled back the hair from her neck and leaned forward to reveal the faint white outline of a half-moon scar below her right ear.

"I pushed the child away and she ran, screaming for her papa. For six years I had known nothing but constant battle, allowing me to hack my way through the guards and escape with little trouble—but I was already so wounded inside there was nothing worse they could have done to me with bullet or blade. I had left in my nightgown, thinking to change after we got away so as not to awaken Oda. My clothes were lost during the escape and the gown was torn away during my flight over the wall. I wondered aimlessly through the countryside, naked and covered with blood of the guards I'd killed. Lacking the will to even end my own misery, I sat down and waited to die from exposure.

"I had no idea I was even near a road. When I heard an approaching car, I got up, thinking I would run. Weakened and lost in sorrow, I could do nothing but stand there." She laughed softly. "My hair was ratted and I was bathed in blood. Certainly, I must have looked like some mountain she-demon as the headlights of the passing car threw me into a blinding light. As it turned out, a young U.S. Army officer named Winfield Palmer was driving the car. Of all the people that could have driven by, I was blessed to have the one man at that time who would be so foolish as to pick up a naked, blood-covered, and crazed Japanese woman and put her in his car."

She shrugged. "And the rest, as they say, is history. Eventually, Palmer-san thought he would woo me. He was young and full of virility and goodness, so I tried, I really did. But in the end, I knew such a relationship was impossible. He had seen me completely undone, emotionally exposed. There must be some intrigue in every relationship, and after he rescued me I held nothing that he did not already know. There is no possibility of mystery between the two of us. I swore never to marry anyone, especially him, who had seen beneath my skin."

"But your name?" Quinn said, prodding her for the rest of the story she seemed to want to tell.

"Palmer-san made it possible for me to come to the

U.S. He moved up in the military and in political position. I was able to use my martial skills working for him. He allowed me to take the family name of my murdered boyfriend—Kenichi Miyagi—so that everyone would assume that I was married and I would have that memory."

"You said there was something I needed to hear in all this," Quinn said, still trying to make the connection.

"Oda-san surely relocated his Garden to some new location after I escaped. Still, I believe the answers to your questions are in Japan," Miyagi said. "Palmer-san may not condone it, but I will secure you a passport under a cover identity. It will be ready tomorrow along with a credit card and Virginia driver's license. I have already arranged a contact for you once you arrive."

"So," Quinn said as he nodded, working through her logic, "you believe the man who trained you is behind all this?"

"Our daughter—my daughter . . . her name is *Ran*," Miyagi said, rhyming it with the American name Ron, but with a hard R so it sounded closer to *Lon*. She used the tip of her index finger to trace the lines of a Chinese character on her opposite hand. A drop of bathwater ran down her palm like a tear. "It means orchid."

"That's a beautiful name," Quinn said, still baffled as to where all this was going.

"I wanted her only to have a good and peaceful life, but many times, even as a tiny girl, she told me she wished to have a tattoo identical to that of her father—a *komainu*."

Miyagi reached for a small towel on the wooden shelf and covered herself as she rose from the bath.

Rivulets of water traced silver lines against the rippling blacks and vibrant greens and pinks on the otherworldly designs of her tattoo.

"*Komainu?*" Quinn wasn't familiar with the word.

"A foo dog," Miyagi explained. "I believe it was my daughter who shot your wife."

CHAPTER 21

Kanab, Utah

The phone didn't have a chance to finish the first ring before Doctor Elton snatched it up.

"Kane County Clinic."

Brandy stood with her back to the door, as if to bar entry to any of the infected patients who crowded the lobby and exam rooms.

Elton talked little and listened much, nodding, then scribbling a few notes. His chest grew tighter with each word spoken by the woman on the other end.

His eyes stopped on Brandy and he sat up straighter in the chair. "Pardon me? . . . Yes, I understand."

He hung up, staring at the phone. The conversation had lasted no more than two minutes, but he felt as if he'd been run over by an ore truck.

"What?" Brandy prodded, wringing chubby hands in front of her purple scrubs. "What did they—"

A soft, but persistent knock interrupted the conversation and caused Brandy, who hated mysteries, to throw back her head in a long groan. Donita peeked tentatively through the door again.

"Doctor," she said. "I am really, really sorry to bother you, but I think you should come out here. Your sister-in-law just came in the back way. It looks like her husband is getting worse."

"I'd better go check on this," Elton said, rising from his chair. Rick Bedford was a good man, a hero in Elton's book.

Marta met him in the hallway outside the office. Rick's arm was draped over her shoulder. "Hey, Todd. Sorry about not going through the receptionist," she said. "We didn't want to scare any of your other patients."

Elton was an educated and rational man, but one look at his brother-in-law sent him into a near panic. He swallowed hard, willing himself to stay calm before showing them into the X-ray lab, the only open room.

Bedford's army buddy had been bad, but most of his boils had been confined to his torso, arms, and hands. Rick's face was dotted, distorted, and swollen with the awful pustulent things. His shirt hung open to the waist, revealing more of the same as if he'd been attacked by a hive of angry bees. Some of the boils had begun to weep, bringing the foul smell of infection— and that wasn't the worst of it. Even from five feet away, it was evident that Bedford wasn't getting enough oxygen. His normally tan face was pale and drawn. His lungs rattled as if he was breathing through wadded paper.

Though Bedford swayed on his feet, ready to pass out at any moment, he remained standing, unable to sit without pain from the boils that surely covered his buttocks and thighs. Brandy rolled in an oxygen monitor and clipped the lead to his finger. She shook her head and frowned at the results.

Elton donned a surgical mask, then pressed his

stethoscope to Rick's back. An aid was hardly necessary to hear the horrific crackling noise at each breath. He stepped to the sink, scrubbing his hands, then slathering them with alcohol gel. "I'm calling over to get you a bed next door in the hospital," he said. "Wait right here."

Marta held her husband's hand. It seemed to be the only part of his body unaffected by boils.

"What is wrong with him, Todd?" she pleaded, glancing away as if she had something to say but didn't want Brandy to hear it.

"I'm not sure. But his buddy R.J. has it as well." Elton had known his sister-in-law for a long time, longer even than he'd known his wife. The look in her eyes said she wasn't telling him everything. "What is it, kiddo?"

"Whatever it is, I've got it, too . . ." She raised the hem of her shirt so he could see the boils on her armpit.

"Looks like it's going around all right." Elton's voice was much too strained to console her. He pitied poor Marta but couldn't help feeling a sense of dread that he was doomed to this same fate, just from treating so many infected people. A flash of anger jumped up in his chest, but he tamped it down. It wasn't Marta's fault.

"Sore throat?" he asked, bringing his focus away from his fears and back to her pain.

"Like acid." She grimaced.

"Okay," he said, trying to sound more sure than he truly was. "Sit tight in here for just a minute. I'll call up to the hospital and get you a room with two beds."

Brandy followed him out, glaring as Elton shut the

door behind him. Back in his office he collapsed in the desk chair and leaned back, clenching his eyes shut. Fatigue and frustration made him want to rub them, but he stopped short, thinking of the bacteria or virus or whatever this was that might somehow have found its way to his fingertips.

Brandy stood with her broad backside to the door again, staring down at him. "You do realize that your brother-in-law is in the early stages of respiratory distress. If all these people have the same thing, they're all going to need ventilators."

"I know." Elton groaned.

"There's a good chance a ventilator won't be enough. He's going to need ECMO."

"I said I know."

ECMO was Extracorporeal Membrane Oxygenation—a heart-lung bypass. There were risks, but in acute cases of respiratory distress, putting a patient on ECMO while the causal disease ran its course was sometimes the only option.

"Well," Brandy chided, "if you know, then why aren't we sending him to Salt Lake?"

Elton groaned, throwing up his hands. "CDC says we have to lock the clinic doors."

Brandy drew back as if she'd been punched, frowning. "We can't just kick these people out, Doctor. They're sick."

"Nobody's saying to kick them out," Elton said, his voice a tense whisper. "As of fifteen minutes ago, this clinic is under quarantine. I've been ordered to lock everyone in."

CHAPTER 22

Twenty-one minutes later
The Oval Office

Winfield Palmer chewed on his bottom lip, his normally ruddy face more flushed than usual as he stood beside the Resolute Desk to the left of the president. It was no small matter being the best friend and confidant to the most powerful man on earth, and the National Security Advisor did not take such a calling lightly.

President Chris Clark tapped a fat Mont Blanc pen against the edge of a black leather folio, his head bowed in thought. With his chiseled good looks and Midwestern schoolboy grin, he looked as if he'd been born to the part of commander in chief.

"We're certain we have it contained?"

"Mr. President," Palmer said. "We are not even certain what it is. We hope we have it contained. So far, it looks as though Afton, Wyoming, and Cedar City and Kanab in Utah are the only hot spots."

"So," Clark said at length, looking up at his friend. "My signature effectively imprisons these people?"

"The Public Health Service Act gives the CDC authority to detain for listed illnesses and diseases," Palmer said. "Unfortunately, boils—or whatever this happens to be—isn't on that list."

"Until I say it is."

"That would be correct, Mr. President."

Even after three years as part of the Cabinet, it sounded odd in Palmer's ears to call his friend Mr. President. They'd roomed together at West Point and both had gone back there to teach among the unconventional thinkers of the Department of Social Sciences—Sosh, they called it. Somehow, even then, Palmer had known Chris Clark would someday be the president. He had an easygoing but self-assured air that made people want to hitch their wagons to his—walk through fire for him.

Their thirty-five-year friendship allowed them to banter easily, even argue over the finer points, and each trusted the other more than a brother. One of them just happened to be the most powerful man on the planet.

"Sorry about this, you poor schmucks." President Clark sighed, scrawling his signature across the document with the Mont Blanc. "Boils." He replaced the lid on the pen and dropped it on top of the folio, shuddering. "Sounds like some kind of biblical plague. We have National Guard troops en route?"

Palmer looked at his watch, nodding. "Out of Salt Lake. Lieutenant Colonel Toby Miller is in command in Wyoming. He's got all of Star Valley cordoned off. The location makes it fairly easy and the people are cooperating so far. Colonel Rob Huber will run the show in Utah. Cedar City is right on Interstate 15, so access for us is a little easier. It's still in the middle of nowhere.

The sheriffs in both Iron and Kane Counties are being completely cooperative. Kanab—in Kane County—seems to have the most cases so far at fifteen. It is pretty small, less than seventy-five hundred. A peaceful little burg, farmland and high desert mountains, so it won't take many. Geography helps, with only three main roads and a handful of secondaries out of town. Colonel Huber is in constant contact with the sheriff—a solid guy named Monte Young. He's been the sheriff there for five terms, always running unopposed. His constituents trust him. Latest reports say his son-in-law is one of the sick ones."

"That sucks," Clark said.

"That it does, sir. But Sheriff Young appears to be up to the task. His men are on their public address system now advising citizens to practice social distancing, keeping away from each other, not going to stores, basically just staying home. Biggest problem will be foreign tourists coming and going to Zion National Park and Lake Powell, which are both nearby. Some are bound to be trapped within the perimeter, so they might have issues."

The president leaned back in his soft leather chair. "The last thing we need is some poor kid with the Guard having to use force to keep a group of Austrian hikers under quarantine." He shot an accusing eye at his National Security Advisor. "How was Miss's mood this morning?"

Miss was Melissa Ryan, the fifty-two-year-old brunette bombshell who saw Palmer romantically at least three times a week—and also happened to be the Secretary of State. They were together so often, their security details often melded into one at public events, though his was Secret Service and hers was Department of State, Diplomatic Security. An incredibly savvy diplomat and media darling, Ryan was considered a favorite for president once Clark's run was over.

"I'm sure she's fine, Mr. President," Palmer said, trying to look innocent. "But she's in Mexico at the free trade summit."

"Get her back here as soon as you can," Clark said. "This thing has the potential to turn ugly in a heartbeat. We have any idea how it started?"

Palmer shook his head and gave the answer he most hated giving his boss. "We don't know yet. CDC has a specialist en route from Salt Lake. So far, I'm hearing of just a few isolated cases worldwide. England has three with two university students near Bradford and a housewife in Harrogate. Italy reports one case, and there are two in Germany. The Ministry of Health in Japan says they had five cases near Kyoto several months ago. In fact, it looks like Japan had the earliest appearance of the disease. All were fatal, but they appear to have it contained with no further outbreak."

"Have they talked border closure?"

"It's being discussed, I'm sure," Palmer said. "But so far, everyone is just increasing screening at immigration points."

"Let's pray it doesn't come to that." Clark's eyes narrowed. "Shutting borders means stopping trade, and that would knock the legs out from under world markets. With the present economy we might not recover. Seems an odd coincidence that all the affected countries are friends of ours. Have we ruled out bioterrorism?"

"We have not," Palmer said.

"I guarantee you, Win," Clark mused, "Andrew Filson will have his ass here inside the hour, screaming at me to carpet bomb Europe, Japan, and the entire state of Utah."

Palmer would have chuckled but for the seriousness of the situation. Secretary of Defense Andrew Filson saw a terrorist behind every tree both at home and abroad. Sadly, his hawkish fears often turned out to be warranted. The Sec Def invoked a sort of broad-target spray-and-pray strategy when it came to counter-terrorism. Clark appreciated diverse thought, even encouraging healthy arguments among his Cabinet. Thankfully, he was prone to listen to more tempered ideas than Filson's and allowed Palmer to use certain assets to handle things with a more surgical precision than carpet bombing.

"I wish I could disagree with—" Palmer's cell phone rang. He looked at the president before answering it.

"Go ahead," Clark said.

Palmer picked up. It was his secretary, Millie. His face blanched at her news.

"I understand," he said, feeling the need to sit down. "Of course. Bring it all in if you don't mind."

He hung up, wheels turning in his head, looking for the next move.

Clark dropped the Mont Blanc on the desk blotter and held up both hands. "So?" he asked. "Are you going to make me guess?"

"Twenty-two more plague cases have been reported to the CDC. Nine in Henderson, Nevada, and five in Mesquite, just over the border from Utah."

"That's fourteen." The president frowned, obviously sensing more bad news. "What about the other eight?"

Palmer held his phone ready to dial, knowing full well who he had to call next. "The other cases are in Afghanistan, Mr. President. All of them at Bagram."

"Shit!" Clark said, slamming the flat of his hand on the desk. "Okay, you see what's going on with CDC and the new U.S. locations. I'll try and keep Andrew from nuking everything in Afghanistan that's not Bagram."

"Very well, sir," Palmer said. "Considering what we're seeing over here, I suggest you give the order to quarantine the base."

"Noted." President Clark rubbed his eyes with a thumb and forefinger. "This is really something," he said. "Just days until I address Congress and the nation. What am I supposed to say? 'Ladies and gentlemen, the state of the union is . . . infected.' "

"There may be one bright spot on the horizon," Palmer said. "Japan was well ahead of us in their out-break. Ambassador Pennington says a pharmaceutical company over there appears to be making potential in-roads on a vaccine."

CHAPTER 23

Yanagi Pharmaceutical Company
Fukuoka, Japan

More than almost anything in the world, Isamu Watanabe wanted to be in charge. Slender and baby-faced, he went out of his way to dress in conservative suits, kept his hair short and businesslike—combed up in front, just like the boss. But it didn't matter, none of those senior to him ever thought of him as an adult. He was tired of groveling to men like Masamoto—men who had no more good sense than a ginko nut but who had risen through the ranks simply because they had not been killed. The same age as Watanabe at thirty-two, Masamoto was still *sempai*—senior man. There was nothing to be done about it but be patient and hope the boss saw everyone for what they really had to offer rather than just seniority.

"You wait outside by the door while I go in," Masamoto said, half barking the command as if he was already the boss himself. If the stubby, thickheaded yakuza was good for anything, it was as an example of what not to be.

"As you wish, but I think it would be better if we went in together," Watanabe said, keeping his voice even, slightly subservient. "There is strength in numbers. The entire board will be present. It might not be a bad idea if there were at least two of us."

"Maybe." Masamoto began to rethink his plan.

Watanabe set his jaw, struggling to keep from saying what was on his mind. Yanagi Pharmaceuticals was a powerful enterprise, well established and respected. Such companies considered their honor and dignity to be sacrosanct. Anything that might prove damaging to a clean reputation could mar public confidence and hurt the bottom line. Loss of company face was to be avoided at all costs.

New national laws had made it illegal for anyone to do business with the yakuza and rendered many of their operations defunct or teetering on bankruptcy. This, however, was a tried-and-true yakuza scheme. Present the damning evidence to the board and offer them silence for a position in the company and protection money in the form of dividends. Still, it required finesse to pull such a thing off, finesse that Masamoto did not possess.

"Okay," the senior man said. "You can come inside but wait by the door and let me do the talking."

A petite young woman in a conservative gray skirt and matching jacket opened the door to the boardroom at precisely fifteen minutes past ten. Her hair was pulled back in a pink plastic clip. A white silk blouse was conservative and alluring at the same time.

Watanabe entered behind Masamoto and took a standing position to the left of the door as ordered. Eleven men, none under the age of fifty, sat in high-backed leather chairs around a long oak table. It was highly polished, and their dour expressions could be seen in their reflected faces on the surface of the wood. A tall man with thick white hair sat at the far end of the room, commanding the head of the table. He wore a tailored blue wool suit that accented his athletic build and a shockingly red power tie.

The man looked up from an open folder, both hands flat on the table. Dark eyes, kind and soft as those of a favorite uncle, met the gaze of the two yakuza men. Watanabe could not help chuckling to himself. This would be easier than he had thought.

Masamoto would, no doubt, assume this to be Yanagi, the owner and chairman of the company, since he sat at the head of the table. But Watanabe knew better. He'd taken the time to research Yanagi Pharmaceuticals on the Internet. The man at the head of this table was perhaps in his early sixties, but nowhere close to the company owner's seventy-four years.

Masamoto gave his introduction, invoking the name of the boss and his organization. He kept his tone civil and his words humble, but the inference was clear. His boss had come into possession of certain photographs of a senior vice president from Yanagi Pharma engaged in a delicate situation with an underage girl in Thailand. In truth, the boss had followed the man on a business trip, gotten him drunk, and set him up. But that didn't matter. What was important now was company reputation. Masamoto assured everyone at the table that with a seat on the board, he could keep this volatile information away from the media and stockholders.

All the men stared down at their respective stacks of paperwork, avoiding eye contact or even admission that a problem existed. The young woman in the gray business suit stood dutifully on the other side of the door, hands folded in front of her, face passive. Watanabe could not be certain, but he thought he could smell peppermint.

The man with white hair at the head of the table was anything but passive. The picture of polite behavior, he sat ramrod straight, nodding every now and again to show he was paying attention. In the middle of Masamoto's presentation and proposal, the man took a fat tortoiseshell fountain pen from the pocket of his white shirt and made a note, as if to record some special bit of knowledge that was too precious to forget. His face appeared to glow with genuine happiness that the yakuza men and come to pay him a visit. Watanabe felt himself leaning forward, wanting to be closer to the man, to bask in his kindness.

At length, Masamoto reached the end of his practiced speech. He bowed, pushing the incriminating photos toward the head of the table.

The white-haired man sat still for a long moment, smiling and blinking kind eyes. Then, in the space of one of those blinks, the eyes grew flint-hard. One instant he was a kindly gray-haired uncle, the next, a seething, anger-filled mountain devil.

Focusing on Masamoto as if to set him on fire, the man snatched up the fountain pen and began to twirl it back and forth on slender fingers. Watanabe marveled at the precise movements. These were not the hands of a business executive.

The white-haired man stuck out his bottom jaw, breathing heavily. Watanabe would not have been surprised if fire had shot from the man's nostrils. The pen flipped back and forth between his fingers, floating almost automatically as if moved on its own accord and not because of anything he did.

"Exactly what is it you would do?" the man asked, challenging.

Watanabe jumped when the man spoke. He glanced at the girl to see if she noticed. She was pretty, in a harsh sort of way, and he worried she might think him less of a man if she had seen him startled. She stared straight ahead like a store mannequin.

Masamoto bowed again, obviously buying time to think. Surely he hadn't expected such a transformation from the dried-up company executive. "What would I do?" He let his eyes flit to each man around the long, polished table, as if one of them might throw him a life raft. "What would I do?" he repeated.

Watanabe had to force himself not to roll his eyes. Surely the boss should have put him in charge.

"Yes," the white-haired man said, kind and smiling again, as if he was Masamoto's uncle and wanted him to give the correct answer. "How do you envision your role in the company?"

"I, well . . . I would . . ." Masamoto stammered. Watanabe could see sweat forming on his *sempai*'s forehead. He knew things were about to go from bad to worse. When Masamoto became nervous, he got mean. Watanabe was no stranger to violence himself. He'd taken part in kidnappings, torture, had even helped dismember a girl and dump the pieces in the ocean on the other side of Shika-no-shima Island—but he had enough sense to know when a more diplomatic approach was warranted. Brute force was the only trick in Masamoto's arsenal.

The man at the head of the table pointed his fountain pen at the stammering yakuza soldier as the good humor bled again from his face. The man's emotions flowed back and forth like waves of the sea. Watanabe felt his stomach lurch at the suddenness of the change.

"It is just as I thought." The man's voice dripped with acid disdain. "You bring nothing to this table but empty threats."

Here it comes, Watanabe thought. It was his duty to support his *sempai,* but he kept his hands locked behind him, hoping it wouldn't come to that.

"I assure you," Masamoto snapped like an angry child, "I bring the protection of our organization."

"Protection from what?" the white-haired man demanded.

"I would offer protection from fear," Masamoto said. He shot a glance at Watanabe, proud that he'd come up with such a fine answer so quickly.

The white-haired man stopped, then nodded as if Masamoto might have actually given a good answer. He removed the cap from his fountain pen and made a few notes in the folder in front of him. When he was finished, he blew gently on the ink, then set the pen on the table. Rising from his seat, he took off his suit jacket and draped it across the back of his leather chair. He picked up the fountain pen and began to twirl it again; this time he left the cap off so the gold tip glinted in the boardroom's fluorescent lighting.

Watanabe's eyes widened at the sight of the man without his suit coat. Long, fluid muscles moved under the white shirt like those of a racehorse under shimmering skin. This was no ordinary old man.

"Fear?" The man stepped around the table to face

Masamoto as if they were gunfighters from an American Western movie. "Tell me. What do *I* have to fear?"

They were still twenty feet apart, but something told Watanabe that was much too close.

Masamoto looked helplessly at Watanabe for an answer. "You . . . We . . . You . . ."

The white-haired man put up a hand, silencing the dumbfounded gangster, moving ever closer as he spoke.

"Sometimes," he said, "it is wise to fear things that are certain do us great harm. Such a notion that we might be injured keeps us safe. Don't you think? Have you ever heard that there are four things to fear in Japan?"

Masamoto's mouth hung open. He shook his head. Though more stoutly built than the older man, he was at least six inches shorter—and, to Watanabe, looked to be growing smaller.

"*Earthquakes*," the white-haired man snapped, halfway across the room now. "*Thunderbolts*." He cocked his head to one side, letting his words sink in. It seemed to Watanabe that he glided across the floor. "*Fire*." The man stopped in front of Masamoto, chest to chest, towering above him. "And perhaps the most fearsome of all . . ." His eyes narrowed. The pen twirled. "*Old men*."

Watanabe knew something bad was about to happen before he saw it. His hand dropped to his waistband to draw his gun, but a sudden crushing pain to his windpipe sent a shower of exploding lights through his head. The girl in the gray business suit struck like a viper, slamming a hammer-fist into his throat. She moved in close, her face just inches from his as she snatched away his pistol. The odor of peppermint on her breath hit him full in the face. She wagged a mani-cured forefinger back and forth as one might do to warn a small child to stop some bad behavior.

Watanabe collapsed to the floor, his back sliding against the wall. He watched helplessly as the white-haired man smiled and then, with the slightest flick of his fingers, drove the fountain pen deep into Masa-moto's left eye.

Screaming, the stubby yakuza dropped to his knees. He tried to draw his pistol, but the white-haired man swatted it out of his hand and sent it skittering across the floor. Blood poured down his cheek, splattering his shirt.

"You will pay!" Masamoto screamed, his voice shat-tered from the excruciating pain.

The white-haired man nodded at the girl in the busi-ness suit. She bowed slightly, eyes going wild as if she'd just been unleashed. Using both hands, she hiked up the gray skirt. The colorful flash of a black and green tattoo covered the taut skin on both her hips above black knee-high stockings. Drawing back, she kicked Masamoto in the face, driving the pen into his brain.

"There," the white-haired man said, bending low to look Watanabe in the eye where he'd still sat helpless, collapsed against the wall. "Please inform Tanaka-san that Yanagi Pharmaceuticals has nothing to fear. There is a new man at the head of the table." He slapped Watanabe's cheek, bringing the taste of blood to his lips. "Did you understand that?"

Watanabe nodded, feeling stupid for being so frightened of an old man. Of course, this particular old man had just stabbed his partner in the eye.

"I understand."

"Good," the white-haired man said. "Tell Tanaka he owes me a new pen." He took his seat at the head of the table, nodding at Masamoto's still twitching body. "He may send his men to pick up the pieces later this evening. I will have him prepared for easier disposal. It is the least I can do."

"I understand." Watanabe's head bobbed quickly. "I will tell him."

The young yakuza stumbled out of the boardroom, leaving behind the body of his dead *sempai*. Perhaps, he thought, being in charge was not as good as he had believed.

CHAPTER 24

Quinn left Emiko Miyagi's home feeling honored that she would confide so many personal details to him and, at the same time, weighed down by the knowledge she had given him. Trying to find a killer was an entirely different thing if that killer happened to be the daughter of a dear friend.

Two miles later he ran into a traffic accident that completely blocked the George Washington Parkway. Gassing the Boxer engine, he leaned the lanky GS into a quick U-turn and backtracked to cut through a neighborhood so he could take Fort Hunt Road into the city. The Bluetooth speaker buzzed inside his helmet shortly after he'd turned onto the quiet two-lane.

"Quinn," he said, half annoyed at the interruption to the solitude of his ride. Were it not for his job, he'd never sully a journey on the back of a motorcycle by connecting himself to any form of electronic communication.

It turned out to be Ronnie Garcia, an ever-welcome distraction. "Hey," she said. "You okay?"

"I am." Quinn slowed a hair, keeping a wary eye for

traffic that might pull out in front of him on the side streets while he talked. "You?"

"On a break from pursuit driving class," she said. "It's fun and all, but nothing like the real thing. I think working with you has ruined me."

You and me both, Quinn thought, but he didn't say it.

"Listen," Garcia continued, "I feel like I should tell you, Palmer is really pissed. He called to ask me if I thought you were cracking up under pressure . . ."

"And what did you tell him?"

"I told him you were the most stable crazy person I knew." She laughed.

"Really?"

"Of course not," she said, sounding hurt. "I know psychs are nothing to screw around with. I said you were fine. He is worried that you're going to go gunning for every Asian female that you think looks out of place."

"Thanks," Quinn said, watching the side mirror as a Fairfax County blue-and-white fell in behind him. ". . . I appreciate it."

The cruiser followed for half a block before the top lights came on.

"Listen, Ronnie," Quinn said, "I'm gonna have to call you back. There's an Asian female police officer about to pull me over . . ."

"Shut up." She laughed.

"Seriously," Quinn said. "But not to worry. She looks harmless. Gotta go."

Used to last-minute interruptions from a man like Quinn, Garcia said good-bye and ended the call.

Quinn pulled the BMW to the curve under a stand of white-barked sycamore along the quiet Fort Hunt neighborhood.

The driver was a slender woman of what Quinn guessed to be Chinese heritage. His conversation with Ronnie Garcia notwithstanding, and considering recent events, he kept a wary eye on everyone, Asian, female, or otherwise.

This one approached in the lead while her partner, a burly blond man, followed a few steps to the rear.

Though he'd never worked traffic, Quinn knew it was one of the more dangerous aspects of patrol. He put the sidestand down but remained on the BMW to ease the approaching officers' nerves. He had his helmet and gloves off by the time they reached him.

"Good afternoon, sir," the female officer said. She had high cheekbones and what his mother would have called laughing eyes. Her name was Officer Chin. "Looks like you have a taillamp out."

"Sorry about that." Quinn held out his driver's license and insurance card.

The big Swede, whose nameplate said he was Larsson, took a half step forward. "You armed?" he said, giving a sideways glare at Chin for not asking.

"Pardon?" This was a first.

"Simple question," Larsson said. "Are you carrying a gun?"

"I'm a federal agent with Air Force OSI," Quinn said. "My creds are in my inside left pocket."

"I don't care who you work for. This is northern Virginia." Larsson smirked. "We got a dozen federal cops per acre. That wasn't my question."

Some federal agent must have run away with this guy's wife or something. "Yes." Quinn lifted the corner of his Transit jacket to reveal the butt of the Kimber.

Larsson gave a low whistle. "Shit, that is a nice pistol. I thought you Air Force boys carried Sigs."

"Most do," Quinn said without further explanation.

"I'll need to take a look at it for a minute," Larsson said.

Both Quinn and Officer Chin looked up in surprise.

"Right here on the side of the road?" Quinn asked.

Larsson held out his hand, palm up. "Yes, right here on the side of the road."

"Come on, Max." Chin shook her head. "We don't have time—"

"Who's the training officer here?" Larsson chided before turning to Quinn. "I don't know how long you been doing this, but there's an old saying in traffic. The guy running the stop is always right—and that would be me. You wanna complain, be my guest—after we're done."

Quinn took a deep breath. It went against everything he knew to hand over a sidearm like this. Still, Larsson was correct. He did have the right to secure the weapon during the stop, even if all he wanted to do was drool over it. Quinn decided not to mention the suppressed Beretta .22 under his arm.

He handed the Kimber to Officer Chin, who passed it back to a gloating Larsson.

"See, that wasn't so hard." The big Swede chuckled, an instant before he flicked off the safety and shot Officer Chin in the face.

Quinn leaped off the motorcycle, moving toward

Larsson rather than away from him. Quinn wasn't the type to hide behind a tree, and there was really nowhere else to run.

Larsson dropped Quinn's Kimber to the pavement after the initial shot and drew his own pistol. Quinn caught the man's arm as the weapon cleared the holster, pinning it against his side and driving him backward all the way to the hood of his patrol car. He was big, but slow, and had relied too much on bullets doing his work for him.

Quinn gave him a vicious head butt, all but destroying the man's nose. The Sig fell out of his hand to thump against the hood of the car before sliding to the pavement with a clatter.

"Who are you working for?" Quinn threw the stunned man to the ground, kicking the weapon out of his reach before dropping a knee into his groin. A ballistic vest protected the downed officer from any body blows, so Quinn grabbed him by the collar, slamming his head against the pavement.

"Who . . . are . . . you . . . working for?!" Quinn yelled, slamming the man's head back at each word. Spit flew from his mouth. He rolled the officer and handcuffed him before he could regain his senses and fight back. With Larsson contained, Quinn turned to check on Officer Chin but found the 10mm round from his Kimber had taken much of her throat and lower jaw. She'd been dead before she hit the ground.

Quinn returned to the fallen Swede, taking some satisfaction in the trickle of blood oozing from the man's ear. "I'm going to ask you one more time." Quinn took deep breaths, working to regain his composure. "Who's calling the shots?"

Larsson clenched his eyes shut and laughed through the pain of his wounds. "You are a dead man, Jericho Quinn."

Sirens wailed from less than two blocks away. Quinn cursed under his breath when he saw the 'man down' radio on Larsson's duty belt. As soon as Quinn had thrown him on the hood of the cruiser, the device had signaled an alert to his dispatcher. When he'd failed to answer, they'd sent the cavalry to assist.

Quinn nodded to the dash camera mounted in the patrol car but Larsson shook his head.

"That? Camera's been tits up for a week now." He winced. "Just my word against yours, cowboy. And I say you killed my partner dead and then tried to do the same to me. These guys will gun you down the second they get the opportunity."

Tires screeched as patrol cars converged from both directions of Fort Hunt Road, sliding to a stop and boxing Quinn in.

Responders saw a grim picture. Officer Chin lay in a pool of blood, half her face torn away. Larsson should have won an Oscar for his performance. Flat on his back against the pavement, he screamed, turning his face as if he was in mortal fear for his life. Quinn stood over him with a gun in his hand.

CHAPTER 25

Secretary of Defense Filson stood fidgeting in the Oval Office thirty-five minutes after Palmer had called to summon him on behalf of the president. Sec State Melissa Ryan was on the speakerphone. Palmer and President Clark were both seated. Filson, however, paced in place, his shirttail half untucked—as if he'd been playing basketball in his suit. Thick black glasses seemed constantly on the verge of jumping off a bulbous nose that should have held them firmly in place.

Lisa Kapoor, the director of Health and Human Services, sat across from Palmer in one of the twin Queen Anne chairs that flanked the Resolute Desk.

Kapoor, a well-respected heart surgeon before she'd been pressed into government service, was near the end of her briefing. It was nothing more than a summary of what they already knew, but at this early stage, that was to be expected. She was a matronly woman of Indian heritage with a keen intellect that matched the fire in her amber eyes. Blessed with the attendant real-world experience that came from being a grandmother of nine, she was not only smart, but just plain pleasant to be around. In her early sixties, she kept her curly gray hair neatly trimmed so it looked as though she was wearing a hairnet. Filson had tried early in the meeting to bully her as he did most people he met, but the fact that she'd raised three sons had rendered her immune to swaggering male bravado.

"It looks as though the only commonality in each affected U.S. city is the fact that they all had at least one soldier returning from Bagram Air Base," she said. "The cases overseas appear to have ties to Afghanistan as well."

Clark rubbed his face in thought. "But we're still unsure how the illness is spread? Airborne, blood?"

Secretary Kapoor shook her head. "We do not know, Mr. President. I have CDC advising local providers to use all universal precautions. The spouse of each returning soldier seems to have contracted the disease as well. Of course, we've yet to determine if the cause is breathing common air, skin contact, or from unprotected sex."

"Phhht," Filson harrumphed. "If you'd been away from your spouse for a year, would you have protected sex?"

"Shut up, Andrew," Clark said. "She's just stating facts. I hate to do this to all those men and women who are scheduled to come home, but I don't see any way around putting an embargo on returning troops to the U.S. from Afghanistan in general until we get a handle on this."

"Understood and agreed," Filson said, pushing his thick glasses back on his nose. "But I don't like it. This whole thing has the smell of biological warfare."

A smooth, feminine voice piped up over the speaker-phone. It was Melissa Ryan, Clark's Secretary of State—and Winfield Palmer's significant other.

"Funny you should bring up bioweapons, Andrew." She was no dove, but her struggle for diplomacy was consistently at odds with Filson's hawkish behavior. "The president of Afghanistan made a statement to the press this morning, accusing the United States of care-lessly releasing a biological weapon we had been plan-ning to use against the Taliban."

"You know that's bullshit," Filson scoffed.

"I do," the Sec State said. "And so does he. Since when does the truth have anything to do with politics? What I'm telling you is that everyone is going to put their own spin on this thing. He's got a country to con-trol. We're on our way out, so we make a likely fall guy."

"It has already hit the major networks," Secretary Kapoor said.

"That's true," Ryan's honeyed voice said over the phone speaker. "Cell phones and the Internet have ren-dered secrets a thing of the past. I am sitting here in Mexico watching your favorite governor beat you to the podium."

Clark cursed under his breath. "McKeon's giving a press conference?"

"As we speak," Melissa Ryan said. "He's urging his good friend, President Clark, to get to the bottom of this outbreak and find our embattled troops some help."

The president threw up his hands. "How long have we known about this, forty-five minutes? Where does this son of a bitch get off telling me about troops . . ." His voice trailed off and he took a deep, thoughtful breath. "Sorry, ladies," he said. "Not very commander-in-chiefly of me. Lee McKeon may support my initiatives, but he can be a ruthless self-promoter in front of the cameras. We'll ignore him as we usually do." Clark turned to Secretary Kapoor again. "Tell me more about this Japanese study."

The HHS secretary picked up her coffee from the side table. The bone-white mug bore the seal of the president.

"I have a team made up of people from CDC, FDA, and the Immunization Safety Office on the way to Fukuoka, Mr. President. If they find the Japanese do have a viable vaccine, they'll start the necessary testing."

"Let's say their science works," Clark said. "How long are we talking for FDA approval?"

Secretary Kapoor took a deep breath. "Approvals, with all the attendant trials and such, can take as long as ten years, sir—but I'm hopeful we can get this done in six months—"

"Six months?" Clark snapped. "That's just not going to work. Didn't we help China get a swine flu vaccine up and running in a couple of months?"

"True," Kapoor said. "But that was a special case."

The president raised a hand to show that he wasn't interested in excuses. "Everyone who has contracted this disease has eventually died. Is that correct?"

"It's still too early yet for us to tell with the cases that have presented in the U.S., sir," Kapoor said. "They're too new. But mortality in Japan was one hundred percent of those affected, yes."

Clark stood with the groan of a much older man. He turned to look out the windows at the Rose Garden as he spoke. "I have to address the American people in four days. By that time, it seems to be an absolute certainty that some of the infected souls in our country will have perished. I am not about to tell their families we have a possible vaccine but need time to run more tests."

"With respect, sir," Kapoor said, "I would urge restraint. My information says the vaccine that Japan has developed is an attenuated virus."

"Speak English, dammit!" Filson grumped.

Kappor sighed. "That means the bugs are weakened but still very much alive. Live-virus vaccines are tricky things. Even if this Japanese company has developed one that works, it will take time to grow it for mass implementation."

"We don't have to immunize everyone right off the bat," Sec Def Filson mused, looking at the president. "Just the military and first responders. That would send a signal—"

"I'm aware of the country's vaccination plan, Andrew," Kapoor said.

"Pompous or not," Clark said, "Secretary Filson is right about one thing. The American people need some sort of hope of a vaccine—even if it's on the horizon. They must be told we are implementing a plan as fast as humanly possible. Neither they nor I have any stomach for bureaucracy—"

Palmer's cell buzzed. Clark nodded for him to take it, then went back to his discussion with the Cabinet secretaries. He believed wholeheartedly that world-saving ideas sprang from a healthy debate.

Millie, Palmer's dutiful secretary, was frantic on the other end of the line. Her excitement was infectious, and Palmer found himself gritting his teeth as she spoke.

Quinn's driver's license and license plate had been flagged as soon as he started working for Palmer, so his office was alerted if anyone ever ran a check. When Fairfax County had stopped Quinn's bike and run the plate, the first flag had pinged the system. Millie had called Fairfax County and gotten the gist of the story as it unfolded, giving it to Palmer moments later.

Palmer cleared his throat.

"What is it, Win?" Clark said. You look like you could use some Maalox." Clark had known him long enough to realize that if he interrupted the president, Winfield Palmer had important information.

"I apologize, sir," Palmer said. "I must ask to be excused."

CHAPTER 26

Virginia

Brakes squealed and tires crunched on gravel as a half dozen patrol cars and two unmarked sedans converged on Quinn from both directions. Doors swung open like a phalanx of Greek shields, and an army of police officers bailed out, bristling with weapons, all of which were pointed at him.

"Hands! Hands! Hands!" a gruff voice shouted.

Crazed barking came from behind Quinn as he let the Sig clatter to the street. A half breath later, he heard the thump of loping paws on pavement and wheeled in time to see a snarling Belgian Malinois leap toward him in a brindle flash of teeth and angry yellow eyes. The dog and officers alike were all hungry for a piece of anyone who would dare to harm one of their own.

Quinn raised his left arm in time to give the dog a viable target, hoping the responding officers' desire to see him mauled outweighed their urge to shoot him. Even through the thick Transit leather, it felt as if a refrigerator had been dropped on his forearm. The dog grabbed a mouthful of leather and pliable crash armor, pinching his arm just below the elbow. It was a solid hold. Quinn kept his tone soft and unthreatening. Saying "good boy" and "good job." The animal shook its head back and forth, but Quinn stayed with it, mimicking the actions of training with a bite sleeve. The last thing he wanted was for the dog to try to establish a different hold that might not be as protected.

After what seemed like an eternity, the handler shouted a command in Dutch. Front paws on his chest, the Malinois eyed Quinn a moment longer, shook him once more for good measure, then disengaged to drop onto the pavement. The handler moved in to take the trailing leash.

An instant later, someone the size of a college linebacker plowed into Quinn from the side, shoving him into the pavement and grinding his face into the gravel. It was all Quinn could do not to fight back, but these first responders were looking at a bloody scene involving someone they knew. Until he was in handcuffs, there was too big a risk one of them would shoot him.

Quinn caught the acid stench of vomit on the air where one of them had already thrown up at the sight of Officer Chin. Head wounds from a large-caliber weapon were not nearly so clean and neat as they were portrayed on the big screen. Amped by the sight of a violent encounter and the death of a friend, there was still the distinct possibility they'd shoot Quinn even after he was in custody.

A muscular young officer with spit-shined boots and a tight uniform shirt cut to accentuate the V of his back put a knee between Quinn's shoulder blades and patted him down for weapons. He shouted "gun!" when he saw the tiny Beretta and "knife!" when he found the CRKT Hissatsu in the scabbard along Quinn's spine.

The Malinois whined on the sidelines, hungry for a second bite.

Another beefy officer, this one older, with short, salt-and-pepper hair walked up and toed Quinn's jaw with a black leather boot. The officer studied him for some time as if trying to decide whether or not to kick out his teeth.

"Mason, get this guy out of my sight," the older officer said. The plate on his uniform said his name was Kincaid. "We'll let CSU get here to secure the scene before we take him in. It'll do him good to sit on his hands a bit." Kincaid let his eyes fall to Officer Chin's body. He shook his head sadly and then planted the toe of his boot squarely in Quinn's ribs.

Quinn tried to roll with the kick, but handcuffed and on his belly there was nowhere to go. He groaned, bracing himself for another.

"I'm not going to waste my time," the officer said, and walked away.

The streets had rained law enforcement shortly after the first police officers on scene threw Quinn in the back of their patrol car. Everyone that walked by gave him a glare that said they'd be all too happy to carve out his liver. He couldn't blame them. Their friend, a fellow officer, had been murdered in an extremely violent way. Her dead body remained in the middle of the street, just as she had fallen, uncovered and vulnerable until crime scene investigators could get there to gather evidence.

Larsson sat in the open door of an ambulance with a bandaged skull, telling trumped-up lies and turning Quinn into the devil incarnate.

Inside the patrol car, Jericho began to work on the handcuffs as soon as Officer Mason slammed the door. Popping the stitching in his khakis over the small of his back with a fingernail, he kept his upper body as motionless as possible while he slid the thin metal shim out of his waistband. He worked as fast as he could, knowing it wouldn't be long before sitting on his wrists caused him to lose the dexterity he needed to manipulate the tiny piece of metal. Officer Mason had been charged with adrenaline and anger during the arrest and had been none too gentle with the cuffs. They were already cutting off the circulation in Quinn's hands.

Thankfully, the handcuffs hadn't been double locked, letting Quinn click them one notch tighter as he inserted the shim farther into the mechanism. It was painful but allowed easier access to the teeth that actually locked the cuffs so he could push them out of the way. Once the left cuff was off and circulation restored to his hand, it was relatively simple to shim the other side.

He tucked the shim back in his waistband just as young Officer Mason got in the front seat. Kincaid flopped down in the passenger seat, then turned to glare at Quinn through the Plexiglas screen. His eyes burned with righteous hatred.

"I wouldn't want to be you, son." The officer dripped with unmasked contempt. "Jenny Chin worked at Fairfax Detention before she came over to the PD. She still has a lot of friends there, and they are going to turn your life into a living hell. It wouldn't surprise me if you don't survive the night."

Kincaid turned to face forward, motioning for the junior officer to drive with a flick of his wrist.

Mason nosed the patrol car around two more units that had cordoned off Fort Hunt Road, working his way northwest.

Quinn took a deep breath and settled back in his seat. As a rule, a prisoner's tension grew as the jail loomed closer. Law enforcement officers' anxiety levels were highest at the point of arrest and tended to relax as more time passed. Angry and victorious, the closer they got to the safety and security of the jail, the sloppier they were likely to become.

Quinn was counting on it.

Ten minutes away from the scene, he started.

"Hey," he said, kicking the back of the passenger seat. He got no response, so he kicked again.

Kincaid turned and slid the two-foot Plexiglas divider open so he could be heard.

"So help me," he said through a clenched jaw, "I'm just looking for a reason to stop this car and beat the shit out of you."

"How well do you know that Larsson guy?" Quinn said.

"Do yourself a favor and remain silent," Kincaid said, slamming the divider.

"Hey!" Quinn kicked the seat again.

The officers ignored him. They were professional enough not to pull over and beat him. That was going to make things substantially more difficult.

"I want to confess!" He yelled so they could hear him through the screen—feeding them what they wanted. "Right now. I'll give you a slam-dunk case. Tell you exactly why I shot that girl. You guys can be the heroes and I'll get my time on TV."

Quinn waited for a moment to let his offer sink in.

He'd rehearsed the plan completely through twice in his head, choreographing it like an intricate, perfectly timed dance. Mason was right-handed. He carried his weapon in a leather security holster that required the activation of a button with his index finger when he drew. He was new on the job and likely depended heavily on the security design of the holster to retain the pistol—a grave tactical error. Kincaid was left-handed and carried his pistol in a simple leather holster with a thumb-break snap. It would be easier to grab, but as an old salt, he'd surely been in more fights where he'd had to hang on to his weapon.

Where possible, Quinn made it a point never to screw with the old bull when a youngster was present—someone who didn't know yet what he didn't know.

The moment Kincaid opened the divider, Quinn screamed as if someone had just run out in front of the car.

"Look out!" he yelled as he moved.

The officers' attention was momentarily drawn forward. Mason stomped the brake instinctively, throwing them both off balance. Quinn snaked an arm through the open divider, pushing in all the way to his shoulder in order to reach the rookie's pistol. Defeating the security button with his thumb, he drew the pistol with his left hand and used it to smack Kincaid in the side of the head.

Still not comprehending what had happened to their handcuffed prisoner, the older officer raised a hand to ward off the blow. Quinn grabbed a wrist with his free hand and hauled back, drawing the older officer's hand into the backseat with him, bending it into an arm bar against the sharp lip of the steel divider.

A deafening boom shook the inside of the vehicle as he shot two rounds at the radio.

"Pull over or I'll kill him!" Quinn yelled, hauling back on Kincaid's arm.

He felt the older officer move his right hand and shot another round through the divider, between the two men. "Leave the gun alone," he said. "I don't want to kill you. I just want out."

Mason looked at Kincaid but kept the car moving.

"Look at it this way, kid," Quinn yelled above the ringing in his ears. "If you let me go, you'll have a chance to catch me all over again."

Kincaid nodded, cursing like a sailor.

"Good job," Quinn said when Mason had stopped the car. He directed the younger officer to open the back door and put his face against the windshield while Kincaid ditched his pistol in the front seat. A half a minute later and both officers stood handcuffed to each other, hugging a street sign. It was a quiet neighborhood and someone had surely called the police the moment they saw two patrol officers forced out of their marked cruiser at gunpoint.

Quinn leaned in close to the older officer.

"I didn't kill your friend," he said. "Larsson did."

"Shut your mouth," Kincaid hissed.

"Give it time, and you'll realize you don't know him as well as you thought you did. Notice how you're handcuffed to a pole and I'm not shooting you?" He turned to leave, then spun, kneeing Kincaid hard in the ribs. It drove the wind from the man's lungs even with the ballistic vest. "That's for kicking me when I was down."

CHAPTER 27

Back in the cruiser, Quinn turned down a quiet residential street, listening to converging units on the handheld radios. By the time help got to the stranded officers he was ten blocks away. He pulled up next to two boys sitting on the hood of a late-model Corolla and commandeered their car with little trouble. He sped away in the Toyota, leaving the boys minus their cell phones but with a war story about the time a wanted cop-killer stole their car.

Quinn ditched the Corolla a block from the Franconia Springfield Metro station but skipped the train in favor of a cab. The subway would be crawling with cops and bristling with security cameras. He told the cabbie to take him to the Comfort Inn in Chantilly, Virginia.

Palmer kept a room rented near Dulles where both Quinn and Thibodaux kept bug-out bags with cash, extra weapons, and burner cell phones. Quinn knew his photograph would be flashing through the blogosphere and over every news program in the country in a matter of minutes. Authorities were not likely to find out about his connection to Palmer anytime soon, so the hotel room and bug-out bag would be safe for the time being. He didn't plan on stopping there for any length of time. Just long enough for Miyagi to meet him with the new ID and passport.

He still had to go to Japan. Being wanted for murder would make it more difficult—but all the more necessary.

He told the desk clerk he'd rented a room earlier but had forgotten the key and ID in the room. She sent security up and they found an ID in the side table drawer with Quinn's photo under the name Irving Walstrom. She made him another key and slid it across the counter.

Once inside the hotel room, he sat on the edge of the bed, staring at one of the burner phones. He'd lost all his weapons during the arrest. Pressing Thibodaux's number, he lay back, closing his eyes to try to relax.

The gunny wouldn't recognize the number, so Quinn wasn't surprised when he didn't answer. He hit REDIAL. Two calls in quick succession meant something was up.

"Hallo." The big Cajun's guarded voice was a welcome sound on the other end of the line.

"Jacques," Quinn said, "it's me."

"Hey, beb," Thibodaux said. A baby squalled in the background. "You okay?"

"Not really," Quinn said. "Listen, there will be some folks coming around to look for me, FBI maybe. I'm not sure."

"Tell me where you are, l'ami, and I'll come get you. Palmer will work this out."

"Maybe," Quinn said, "maybe not. You'll see what I mean very soon."

"Whatever," the Cajun said. "Let me come and get you. We'll handle this. I been to handlin' school."

"I have to get out of town, Jacques."

"You're breakin' my heart, l'ami," Thibodaux said. His voice fell stern as if he was talking to one of his sons. "Meet me and let me help you out."

"Listen, Jacques," Quinn said, "it's against the law to lie to a federal agent. Helping me out could seriously screw up your security clearance—if it doesn't get you thrown in jail."

"Are you shittin' me?" Thibodaux seethed with frustration. "You're in trouble, and you think I'd give a rat's ass about my career!"

Quinn was sorry for even calling now. "I'm not dragging you into this."

"After all you already dragged me into?" the Cajun scoffed. "You wanta be a turd, go lay in the yard—but you know better than that . . . you truly do."

"This is too dangerous—"

"Easy now, Superman," Thibodaux cut him off. "That's your biggest problem. You know that? It honestly ain't your job to take care of the whole damn universe. In case you haven't noticed, I'm a pretty fair hand at takin' care of my own self."

"Jacques, you have to listen to me. This is bad." Quinn swung his feet off the bed. "They'll be monitoring your phone, watching you, questioning your family, whatever it takes to find me."

"I don't give a shit if they crawl up our collective orifices, there ain't a Thibodaux among us who'd give you up."

"It's safer this way," Quinn groaned. "Do me a favor and let Ronnie know I'm laying low for a while."

"Man, oh, man!" Thibodaux whistled. "You gotta reconsider not callin' her yourself. Badass babe or not, the girl's feelin' sort of fragile about your relationship at the moment."

"I can't," Quinn said. "It's too dangerous."

"There you go again, puttin' on the big red S."

"Will you call her for me or not?"

"Whatever." Jacques sighed, still not happy. "Anything special you want me to tell her?"

Quinn paused for a moment. "Tell her to be careful."

"Seriously, beb? You're on the run for your life and all you can think to say to your sweetheart is 'be careful'? Son, remind me to pass you a slap when you come in from the cold. 'Be careful' . . . I swear . . ."

"Well," Quinn said, not knowing what else to say. "*You* be careful."

"I love you, too, l'ami." Thibodaux gave a dismissive laugh. "I love you, too."

CHAPTER 28

Qasim Ranjhani stood at the window of his small apartment in the peaceful area of Lahore known as Johar Town, south of the medical college where he'd done postgraduate work. He gazed over the top of McDonald's and Boston Pizza while he listened to the phone at Yanagi Pharmaceutical ring for the fifth time. Heavy traffic thumped past on Canal Bank Highway. Things were changing in Pakistan, and not for the better.

And now, no one was answering his calls.

With the four-hour time difference, it was just after 1:00 p.m. in Japan, and Ranjhani could not comprehend why no one would be on hand to pick up the phone. He was about to hang up, when a familiar male voice came on the line.

"*Moshi moshi*." The voice gave the traditional Japanese greeting, assuming the call came from inside the country.

"Oda-san," Ranjhani said, still tense with agitation that he'd been made to wait for someone to answer. He spoke English rather than his native Punjabi dialect of Majhi. His mother had seen to it he'd learned to speak English correctly, and his father, though a proud Pakistani, had felt it important he learn Arabic to better understand the Koran as it had been dictated to Muhammad by Allah Himself.

"Ahh, peace be unto you, Doctor," Oda said, switching to English. "To what do I owe the pleasure of this call?" Ranjhani thought of him as a smiling viper. For a merciless killer, the man was always extremely polite.

"I am checking on my investment," Ranjhani said, taking a long breath through his nose to calm his nerves. It did no good to let such a man know you were angry. He was not intimidated and prone to violent outbursts himself. "I have to say, I grow tired of speaking with your subordinate. I understand there was a problem with your project in Virginia. I wanted to hear about it from you personally."

"Everything is fine. I assure you," Oda said, a smile in his voice. "A minor inconvenience."

Ranjhani sniffed, holding back his emotions. "I am sure I do not need to remind you what this minor inconvenience has done in the past."

"No." Oda's voice turned ice cold. "You do not need to remind me. You pay my organization extremely well because we have certain skills—skills at which we excel. Our honor depends on it."

"Honor?" Ranjhani gave a nervous chuckle in spite of himself. "I have always understood there was no honor among thieves."

There was deadly silence on the line, so long that Ranjhani feared the man might have hung up and come to kill him.

At length, Oda spoke. "Then you are fortunate that I

am a killer and not a thief. The whole of American law enforcement will help us put an end to our problem in Virginia once and for all. Do not concern yourself with trivial things. I have good news."

"Good news would be welcome," Ranjhani said, unconvinced.

"The American scientists have arrived. We have demonstrated our process and made them to feel quite at home. I am confident all four will be pleased with the results of our tests this afternoon."

"That is good news," Ranjhani said. "So, you believe we will remain on schedule?"

"I not only believe it, Doctor," Oda said. Ranjhani could again envision the man smiling. "I am certain of it. That is what you pay me for. The first batch of two hundred fifty thousand doses of your . . . vaccine is ready now. The gun is loaded. The tests will allow us to pull the trigger. In the meantime, the Americans grow complacent. The time has come to, as they say, turn up the heat."

One call ended, Ranjhani punched another number and walked to his bureau on the other side of the room while he waited for the phone to ring. Two polished wooden boxes, each roughly the size of a brick, sat beside his billfold and wristwatch. The sight of them added another jolt of excitement.

"Hello?" Lee McKeon picked up.

"Things in Asia are moving forward."

"That is good," the governor said, his voice noncommittal. He was with someone.

"I know you are uncomfortable with a meeting," Ranjhani said, looking at the boxes. "But it has become a necessity."

"Is that so?"

"Indeed," Rahjhani said. "I have something for you that I must deliver with my own hands."

PART TWO

*And when it was morning, the East Wind
brought the locusts*

—EXODUS 10:13

CHAPTER 29

Alexandria, Virginia

"**N**o doubt in my mind. I could do it." Deputy U.S. Marshal August Bowen drummed strong fingers against the two extra Glock magazines on his ballistic vest and watched for a reaction from the tall blonde in the seat in front of him. He rubbed a dark goatee with the other hand, as if amused. Oakley Half Jacket shades covered his eyes in the backseat of the Ford SUV.

"I'm gonna call bullshit on that," Deputy Mitch Lucas said from behind the wheel. He had a voice like a blender grinding ice. Overworking his upper body in the gym and neglecting his tiny legs had earned Lucas the nickname Chicken Hawk in the squad room. It was no secret that he didn't care much for Bowen. "You're saying you could proposition her on duty and not get arrested?"

Born and raised in Florida, Samantha "Sammy" Willson had come to seek her fortune in D.C. when she got out of college, and worked with the Metropolitan Police vice unit for a time before she'd joined the Marshals Service. Her previous life made her a perfect fit for the Sex Offender Investigations Coordinator, or SOIC, for the office. In particular U.S. Marshal fashion, SOICs hunted down unregistered sex offenders before they could offend again.

She pointed a knife-hand up the road as if calling in an airstrike. "It's another half mile. Donaldson's house is the gray clapboard on the right. He has dogs but the informant says the're friendly." She glanced over her shoulder at Bowen. "No way, Gus," she said, her Florida drawl rolling off her tongue. "Cute turns creepy when you hit on me while I'm working vice. Oh, yeah, you'd go to jail."

All three deputies were similarly dressed in khaki cargo pants, dark polos, and heavy ballistic vests that were outfitted with all manner of pouch and pocket to hold extra pistol magazines, Taser, radio, flashlight, and plastic flex cuffs. They were military-looking, olive-green things with more MOLLE webbing than any of them had gear to fill. In addition to their basic load of weapons and ammo, each carried an oblong trauma kit the size of a fat sub sandwich. A tab bearing the deputies' blood type was affixed to each vest over the right shoulder.

"I'm telling you, I could do it, Sammy." Bowen grinned. He was just under six feet tall and big enough the backseat felt cramped with all the tactical gear. Eight months trudging through the Hindu Kush with his Recon Scout team had hardened his physique and weathered his skin. The experience had also turned his muddy-river hair prematurely silver gray at the age of thirty-six.

"Okay," Willson said. "Imagine I'm on the street wearing my spandex shorts and a halter top—"

"I do that all the time." Lucas licked his lips.

"Shut up, Mitch," she said, then focused on Bowen, fluttering her eyes to get into character. She popped her gum and heaved her chest. Her sex appeal was strong enough to punch straight through the heavy ballistic vest. "Hey, sugar," she said. "You want a date?"

"You know," Bowen said, "I think I would love a date."

"Gotcha!" Lucas said, leering sideways at Willson. He had the eyes of a man who kept someone tied up in his basement.

"Hang on." Bowen raised his hand. "We haven't talked about anything illegal yet."

"Okay, sugar." Willson nodded, resuming her character. "I don't date for free, you know."

"I know." Bowen peered over the top of his Oakleys, shrugging as if he was a little embarrassed. "To tell you the truth, I'm doing a series of figure drawings and I need a model for an hour or so—"

Willson's mouth fell open.

"Wait, wait, wait." Lucas tapped the steering wheel with the flat of his hand. "You want to draw her naked?"

"Come on, Sammy." Bowen grinned. "What would you say?"

"In reality," Willson said, nodding, "I'd say shove off, you weirdo."

"And, you owe me lunch," Bowen said, hand on the door as they neared the target house. "It's a tried-and-true technique."

"Seriously?" Willson turned half around in her seat to stare at Bowen. "You mean to tell me you've hired a hooker?"

Bowen nodded.

"Jeez Louise," Willson scoffed, grabbing her seat belt. "I thought we did backgrounds to weed out guys like that." The deep red of her fingernails stood out in stark contrast to her tactical gear.

Bowen grinned, as if such a thing made perfect sense. "Sitting on her butt eating bonbons while I did a few sketches was a heck of a lot better than her normal routine. An undercover cop would just tell me to get lost. They wouldn't sit for a nude drawing."

Willson looked at him for a long moment, then raised an eyebrow to make a face like she just might consider it. She shook away the thought and put her game face back on.

"Donaldson's house is right up there before the intersection." She faced forward in her seat again. "We got over ten thousand images of explicit child porn the last time—some of them of kids as young as four. But remember, he's not only a pervert, he's a runner—and a fast one at that."

A haggard blond woman in a green Hawaiian muumuu stood by a group of mailboxes at the corner fifty meters ahead, watching the Ford approach.

Willson pointed at the driveway past the woman and on the other side of the road. "That's Donaldson's place there."

"Keep driving." Bowen tapped the headrest behind Lucas. His cell phone began to buzz in the pocket inside his vest. He ignored it.

"What?" Chicken Hawk Lucas shot a glance in the rearview mirror.

"Trust me," Bowen said, looking intently at the road. "Just drive on by."

"Go ahead, Mitch." Willson shrugged as the SUV passed the row of mailboxes and the staring woman. "It can't hur—"

Bowen flung open his door, smacking it into the haggard blond and sending her flying in a blossom of arms, hairy legs, and flowered Hawaiian patterns. He bailed out before the SUV came to a screeching stop.

Bowen grabbed a handful of dress and a flailing arm to haul Frank Donaldson to his feet. The bright green muumuu hung off a hairy shoulder. Blood poured from a gaping split in his forehead where the doorpost had impacted him.

"How'd you know?" the addled man asked, kicking at the ratty blond wig that lay like roadkill in the gravel.

Bowen ratcheted the handcuffs tight and pushed the prisoner against the side of the SUV to pat him down.

"Uncle Sam's all-expense-paid trips to the Middle East," he said. "I've seen a lot of guys in man-dresses."

Bowen's cell phone rang for the fourth time in as many minutes. Convinced Donaldson wasn't hiding anything but a black bra and a pair of matching lacy panties, he handed him off to Lucas and Willson before answering. He recognized the number.

"Yes, Chief?"

"Bowen," Chief James Ragsdale said, as if he was speaking around the stub of one of his favorite cigars. "Director wants to see you at fifteen hundred hours. Anything I should know about?"

Bowen shot a wary glance at the wounded prisoner. "No," he said. "I don't think she would be aware of anything."

"Good," Ragsdale barked. "Do me a favor and put on a suit before you head over."

* * *

August Bowen snugged a red-and-blue-striped power tie against the top button of a starched white shirt and popped his neck from side to side.

Sammy Willson sat at her desk, situated so it butted up to his, and stared at him with a little more than awe. "The director of the United States Marshals Service doesn't just call in PODs to chat," Willson said.

They'd dropped Donaldson off at the jail and returned so Bowen could get changed for his meeting.

A POD was a *plain old deputy*—no rank, just a simple silver star. And that was just where Deputy Bowen wanted to be. His mother, who ran the Republican Party in Flathead County, had asked him if he wanted the presidential appointment so he could carry a gold badge as the U.S. Marshal of Montana rather than be a lowly deputy. He'd told her thanks but no thanks, giving the age-old reply of deputy marshals, content with their lot in life—"a gold badge is given, a silver badge is earned." So, he'd gone to Glynco for training, done his time in Billings, and had recently transferred to the Eastern District of Virginia five months before to get a feel for life in a bigger office—and to be near his doctor girlfriend.

Bowen looked at his watch and sat down.

"Whatever it is," he said, picking up the drawing pad on his desk. "She doesn't want to see me until three. I have a few minutes to clear my head."

Bowen's pencil whispered across the paper as he put the finishing touches on a sketch of a court clerk named Roslyn. After his last Reserve deployment as a Scout to Afghanistan, the Army shrink had told him to use his art when he was working things out in his head. An audience with the director was certainly something he needed to work out.

"Maybe she's giving you a Director's Award for something you did overseas," Willson said. Out of her tactical gear it was easier to see that she was not only tall but extremely fit, with a quick smile and curvy build that made prisoners turn flirty when she moved them to court. At first blush bad guys on the street thought she might be a pushover. Half a second into any confrontation and she showed them the error of such thinking. There was a no-nonsense air that Bowen found . . . comfortable—like a favorite kid sister.

"Pleeeease." Mitch Lucas scoffed from three desks over, tucked into the back corner of the squad room, farthest from the supervisory deputy's office door. "They don't give you a Director's Award for being a hero in the military. That's the Army's job."

Bowen smiled, half-entertained, half-disgusted. The little Chicken Hawk was a decent enough deputy. He worked his shift in court, hooked and hauled prisoners without too much whining, and did a fair job of finding fugitives with his computer. But Lucas let it be known at every turn that he felt sidelined by Bowen's presence. Bowen got the good details. Bowen got the good warrants. Bowen got the girls.

Everyone else suffered for not being Bowen.

Lucas turned back to his computer. "What exactly were you decorated for anyway?"

"You know, Mitch," Bowen groaned, tossing his pencil on the desk. He leaned back in his chair in an effort to pop his back. "Heroic shit."

"Who you drawing now?" Lucas pecked away, apparently feeling it was his duty to harass the new guy. "Another court clerk with big ti—"

"Hey now!" Bowen cut him off, eyes still closed in midstretch. "You're about to cross the line, Mitch."

Sammy Willson backed away. She turned to Lucas, shaking her head in warning. Lucas sat still, thinking things over. Both deputies had seen what Bowen did to people on the street when they, as he put it, "crossed the line." It wasn't pretty.

"How about you go f—"

"That'd be crossing the same line," Bowen said, cutting him off.

Lucas's hands slipped away from the keyboard. "Who gets to decide where this line is that you're always talking about?"

"I do," Bowen said. "And I draw it close so I don't have to reach very far to slap the shit out of a bully." He stood to leave, shrugged on a dark gray suit jacket, and winked at Willson. "And when, not if, I do, I might get days off, but I doubt they'd fire me. Hell, maybe they'd give me the Director's Award. Apparently, being a half bubble off from the war earns me a fair bit of leeway."

Sammy Willson frowned. "You're an idiot, Mitch."

"He thinks he's God's gift to the Marshals Service," Lucas said.

"My daddy had a dog like you when I was little." Willson sighed. "He was a pretty good dog, too, chasing away panthers and keeping snakes out of the yard. Trouble was, he kept trying to bite everybody that came to visit."

"What happened?" Lucas smirked, but still half interested.

"He bit the wrong guy one day and got himself shot." She nodded at Bowen as he disappeared through the front door of the office. "I'm tellin' you, Mitchell. That's the wrong guy."

CHAPTER 30

Bowen swiped his pass card and drove his black government-issue Dodge Charger into the underground parking lot beneath the Crystal City mall off Jeff Davis Highway. He was old enough to realize he was at the top end of his physical prime but still young enough to try to maximize it. He knew his way around the gym and had boxed during ROTC in college. He'd lost only one fight that mattered and still flushed with anger at the judges and himself when he thought about it for too long.

His girlfriend was a doctor at GW University Hospital, which for all practical purposes meant he lived alone. Though he loved to cook, there was rarely any reason to do much but eat canned soup while he stood at his sink. He kept his prematurely gray hair on the longish side so he could be reminded every morning when he trimmed his goatee that he was no longer in the Army.

Bowen parked the Charger in a vacant visitor space against the concrete wall and checked his tie in the rearview mirror before he went upstairs. Since coming aboard with the agency it had always bugged him that

TIME OF ATTACK   217

the FBI had the Hoover Building, the ATF had their bunker-like fortress near Gallaudet College. ICE, Interior, DEA, all had their own buildings worthy of Washington, D.C., architecture. But the United States Marshals Service, the nation's oldest federal law enforcement agency, rented space in a mall.

Bowen took the elevator up to the shopping level, then hung a right in the underground to work his way through the afternoon crowds of government employees and military brass from the nearby Pentagon. The guard beside the nondescript glass doors across from Morton's Steakhouse checked his Headquarters ID and let him by.

Bowen nodded to a group of black women from Human Resources on their way out for lunch. Being stationed in Virginia meant he'd come to headquarters a few times, so he knew people by face if not by name. They smiled back, chatting happily among themselves, apparently not recognizing him. He jumped in the elevator they'd come out of and pushed the button to the twelfth floor.

Miles Nelson, the Assistant Director for Investigative Operations, was waiting for him in the common area of the director's suite. A South Carolina native, Nelson gave him an earnest handshake and welcome.

"Thanks for coming," he said.

"I didn't know I had a choice, sir." Bowen forced a grin.

Nelson laughed, his Southern charm coming through. "You didn't. Come on. She's waiting for you." Accustomed to spending time in the lofty realms of the twelfth floor, the AD put a hand on Bowen's back and ushered him into the director's office.

The office was spacious, at least thirty feet across with a separate sitting area and centered coffee table that she must have decided was too intimate for this particular meeting. Rich blue and gold carpeting glowed in the light from the windows along the north wall that offered a panoramic view of Reagan National Airport, the Potomac River, and downtown Washington, D.C. He wondered if people like this had big offices to make visitors feel small. It was sure working with him, a POD with a cubicle and a gun locker.

Director Carroll stayed seated when they walked in, flanked by her chief of staff and the deputy director. She was in her mid-fifties, with a full mane of frosted blond hair that lay perfectly on her padded shoulders. A high-collared wool suit and fist-size gold brooch accented her stern demeanor. The pinched look on her face made Bowen think she might spring from her seat at any moment and shout "Off with his head!" He'd seen few Taliban fighters that looked as fierce.

The chief of staff, a female former chief deputy from somewhere in the Midwest—Bowen couldn't remember where—smiled, as if to set his nerves at ease. The DD was busy talking on his cell. "Go ahead and have a seat, Deputy Bowen," the director said, not sounding as ferocious as she looked. "You are wondering, no doubt, why I called you in." Bowen started to answer but she kept talking.

"AD Nelson tells me you grew up in Montana," she said, with more of a nasal tone than he would have guessed from her photograph that hung in the Alexandria squad room. "Am I right on that?"

"You are correct," Bowen said. "Flathead County."

"He says you're an avid bow hunter."

"I am," the deputy said, eyes looking to Nelson for any sign of an explanation.

"I suppose," the director went on, fiddling with the brooch on her shoulder as she spoke, "hunting with a bow and arrow requires a good deal of patience and skill . . . Good qualities to have in a deputy marshal."

"I suppose so." Bowen gave an obedient nod, wondering where this was going.

"Well." The director looked him over one last time, as if she hadn't quite made up her mind until that very moment. "Fairfax County has given us a remarkable opportunity in the form of a fugitive warrant for Officer Chin's shooter."

Everyone within five hundred miles of D.C. had heard about some nut job murdering the young police officer. Bowen was sure the D.C. Area Regional Fugitive Task Force had boots on the ground helping find the shooter, but he'd not been involved. So far, they'd kept the identity of the fugitive off the news.

The director went on. "The Bureau has been going round and round with Fairfax County and Main Justice trying to grab this one." She leaned forward, staring, nodding as if only she held some great secret to the universe. "But I told the attorney general it had to be us." She pounded the desk. "You want to know why?"

"Yes, ma'am."

"Because we have you, Deputy August Bowen." She smiled. "And the FBI, thankfully, does not."

Bowen opened his mouth to speak, but an almost imperceptible headshake from the chief of staff stopped him.

"Does the name Jericho Quinn mean anything to you?"

"Yes, ma'am," Bowen said. "We worked together a couple of times on some cases in Montana. I believe he's still in OSI."

"I understand you lost a boxing match to him in college."

Bowen's neck burned at the memory. He groaned. "Indeed I did, ma'am."

"So you know him pretty well."

"I suppose so," Bowen said. "He's an Air Force Academy grad. I was Army ROTC, so there was always a certain amount of rivalry. But I'd have no trouble working with him again, if that's what you mean. That fight thing was a long time ago."

"I don't want you to work with him." Director Carroll leaned back in her chair. "I want you to hunt him down and arrest him."

She didn't say "off with his head," but the nuance was crystal clear.

Dismissed with his marching orders, Bowen accompanied Nelson back to his division in the adjacent office tower, with the AD insisting they stop for coffee at a Starbucks across from the barbecue joint in the underground mall along the way.

"Can you tell me what we have on him, sir?" Bowen asked five minutes later when he sank down into Nelson's plush leather couch. The notion of Jericho Quinn murdering a police officer popped back and forth inside his head, refusing to settle. Still, people did weird things. He knew that from experience.

The Assistant Director for Investigative Operations

had a view similar to the director's. Bowen would have thought the office was huge had he not just been to Carroll's palatial digs.

Nelson slid an open Bible to one side of his desk and took a folder from the lap drawer. "Well, to tell the truth, we don't have very much," he said. "The Air Force seems to have misplaced Quinn's entire file."

"Family?" Bowen offered. "Friends?"

"There is that." Nelson nodded. "Turns out somebody shot his ex-wife at a wedding in Colorado a couple of days ago. She lost her leg. Looks like the shooter may have been going for his daughter."

That was too big a detail to be unrelated. "Anyone arrested?"

Nelson shook his head. "Nope. But at least OSI still had that incident report. There are a couple of names. One's a Marine, I believe. That should get you started."

Bowen took that as an indication he should get right to work.

"But wait." Nelson grinned. "There's more." It was impossible not to like this guy. For one of the top managers in the Service, he was amazingly down to earth, kicked back at his desk and talking with a POD. Bowen couldn't help thinking he'd like to work for the man someday, if only that didn't mean being assigned to headquarters.

Nelson held up a clear plastic bag like a trophy. "We have his phone."

That was good news. People kept all sorts of data on their phones, usually trusting a simple passcode to safeguard their secrets—appointments, e-mails, photographs, and most important to Bowen, friends and contacts. With the information from the phone, he should be able to build a pretty clear map of Jericho Quinn's recent life.

"It's encrypted," Nelson said, sliding it across the desk and moving his Bible back to the center.

"No problem." Bowen nodded. "I'll take it to Geoff. He could get a call history off two tin cans and a string. We'll find him, sir."

"You'd better," Nelson said. "Because the way I hear it, there are a lot of folks out there who don't plan to work very hard to bring him in alive."

CHAPTER 31

Quinn met Emiko Miyagi at an Exxon station east of Chantilly, not far from Dulles, where she gave him an envelope containing three fat rolls of twenty- and hundred- dollar bills, two credit cards, a passport, a Virginia driver's license, and an airline ticket, all under the name of John Hackman. It was a fitting name, she pointed out, considering his penchant for using a blade.

Since Narita Airport's entry procedures required a photograph and two fingerprints from each entering passenger, Quinn opted to take a less direct route into the country, flying out of Dulles to Seoul, then taking a domestic hop to Buson before boarding a ferry for the three-hour ride across the Sea of Japan to Fukuoka, where he was to meet Miyagi's contact.

There were a great many variables, but the passport and other documents were genuine, so they, at least, would not trip him up. One-way plane reservations, purchased the same day of travel, triggered more scrutiny than Quinn wanted and would surely provide a red flag to anyone looking for him after the shooting. Miyagi purchased round-trip tickets and had been able to manipulate the system to make it appear as though she'd purchased them a month before.

"I can't tell you how much I appreciate this," Quinn said, taking the documents. "I realize you're risking your career, and even your freedom. Palmer must be beside himself."

Miyagi looked at the ground, looking almost girlish.

"He directed me to tell you to call in if I saw you," she said when she handed over the envelope. "But I would advise against such a thing."

"Thank you, Miyagi-san," Quinn said, slipping the documents in his pockets.

"You know my secrets," she said. "I believe you should call me Emiko. I should also mention something about your contact, my friend, Ayako-chan. She is . . . how should I say this? Given to the wild side."

"Wild enough to help a wanted fugitive?"

Miyagi smiled, for the first time since before she'd told him her story. "Wild enough that she will likely try to become intimate with you moments after you meet. But I beg you not to judge her. She has been through much."

"I'm not one to judge anybody." Quinn scoffed.

"Thank you," Miyagi said. "Now, I must warn you. If my daugh . . . if Ran continued to progress as she was when I left, she will be an incredibly strong adversary."

"But I have had you as my teacher." Quinn shrugged off the warning. "She has missed out on that."

Miyagi held her breath for a moment, choosing her words carefully. "You are extremely good at what you do. But Oda is . . . very close to perfect in his fighting skill."

"It's been a long time." Quinn shrugged. "He's older. Maybe he's slowed down."

"Perhaps." Miyagi nodded. "But he was always more skilled than me." She rolled her lips. "And I am more skilled than you."

CHAPTER 32

Deputy August Bowen read over what little information he had in the file while Geoff Barker tinkered with Quinn's phone, which was now attached to his laptop computer.

Seating at the Federal Law Enforcement Training Academy in Glynco was alphabetical, and Barker had sat next to Bowen during Marshals Basic eight years earlier. He was generally quiet, strong as a bull, and had a tiny Superman curl that hung down across his forehead. All smiles and Georgia charm, he was the kind of kid Bowen would have wanted dating his daughter, if he had a daughter.

He was also one of the smartest people Bowen had ever come across. His small office was crammed with telephone lineman gear, maps of cell towers, and stacks of black plastic Pelican cases containing all sorts of sensitive and secret equipment Barker used to do his job. The screen on some kind of oscilloscope blipped on the table behind him, like something out of a science fiction movie.

"This wasn't a random shooting." Bowen shut the thin folder and closed his eyes to think out loud. "You gotta wonder why a sniper would go after somebody's family. Witnesses say they think the shooter in Colorado was an Asian female. According to this OSI agent's report, Quinn suspects her of being Japanese."

"Maybe Quinn went after her," Geoff said without looking up from his computer. A lifelong resident of Atlanta, his drawl could make him appear slow at first blush, but Bowen had never seen anyone who knew their way around phones and electronic surveillance as well as Geoff Barker. Even in Marshals Basic he'd shown a bent in that direction.

"That's what I would do," Bowen said. He tipped his head toward the phone. "So, what do you think? You gonna be able to get in?"

"Dude," Barker said, still not looking up. "This is high-level government encryption."

Bowen's heart fell. "So, you can't get in?"

"Of course I can." Barker scoffed. "I write high-level government encryption." He tapped a few more keys, waited a beat, then looked up with a wide grin. "I'm in," he said.

"Why would an OSI agent need an encrypted phone?" Bowen mused, half to himself.

Barker's eyes darted back and forth across the computer screen, studying the contents of the phone.

"The most frequently called number comes back to a V. Garcia . . ." He kept scanning. "Japanese shooter, you say?"

Bowen nodded. "That's what Quinn thinks, at least."

"Hmmm," Barker mused, hitting PRINT so Bowen would have a copy of what he was looking at. "There's an Emiko Miyagi in here. I'll go up on her number and see what I can find. Meantime, I got contacts with

Japan National Police. Work up a BOLO, and I'll get it over to them." BOLO was Be On the Look Out—a locater notice, like a wanted poster but with less need for controlled distribution.

"We should make it wide," Bowen said. "Plaster his photo all over the news over there." He got up from his seat with a long groan. This whole thing made him feel tired.

"Where you going first?" Barker asked, still futzing with the computer.

"I came here first," Bowen said. "But now, I'm going to swing by and take a look at that crime scene, get a feel for it, so to speak. I got no love lost for the guy, but this just doesn't sound like him."

"Shitty deal, hunting someone who's supposed to be one of the good guys," Barker offered, handing Bowen the paper from his printer tray.

"Jericho Quinn's not a bad guy," Bowen said. "But I'm pretty sure *good* doesn't describe him, either."

CHAPTER 33

The Korea Air flight from Dulles to Seoul took fourteen hours. Miyagi had booked Quinn a seat in Business Class so he could lean back and try to get some sleep. He would, she'd reminded him, need all his wits about him if he wanted to locate Oda and her daughter while avoiding capture himself.

The brutal training regimen and long months of Air Force Special Operations training had taught Quinn to grab sleep when the opportunity arose. But being hunted by his own government was new territory, and he tossed and turned for most of the flight. At length, he gave up and found a Japanese channel on the video player at his seat. If he couldn't sleep, at least he could get his brush-up on the language by watching inane comedy shows with lots of whipped cream and water gags.

An hour before they landed at Incheon International, the flight attendants went on high alert. There was a curt announcement in Korean and English asking everyone to stay in their seats. Quinn watched as one attendant, a slender Korean woman in her forties, hustled up the aisle to answer a call on the bulkhead phone. He couldn't be certain, but it looked as though her eyes kept darting to him and then away, as if she was trying not to stare.

All the attendants, including the gray-haired Korean purser who had remained unflappable during the agonizingly long flight, bounced around the aircraft as if on ball bearings.

Quinn craned his head around to look behind him, but the aircraft was too big to see much without getting out of his seat. He thought about defying orders and getting up to go to the restroom, but the look on the purser's animated face said that might get him sent out on the wing at thirty thousand feet.

There was another announcement as the plane squawked onto the tarmac at Incheon, asking . . . no, ordering, everyone to keep their seats for a few minutes after the plane arrived at the gate.

Whispers of indignation and curiosity spread among the passengers like paper burning. Some worried they would miss connecting flights. Others had to go to the bathroom. Quinn was in a center bank of seats so couldn't see out the window, but the flashing strobes of approaching emergency vehicles were impossible to miss.

He unbuckled his seat belt and slid the leather satchel, his only baggage, from under the seat in front of him. There was a slim chance he could make it past them and disappear if he bolted. No one would expect that.

CHAPTER 34

Bowen parked the black Charger on the grassy shoulder a half block away from the spot where Officer Chin had been murdered. He'd heard someone on news radio say she'd been killed, but he couldn't get his head wrapped around that term. Spiders were *killed* when you stepped on them. Cancer *killed* you. Soldiers *killed* the enemy in battle. But when someone looked a pretty young officer like Jenny Chin in the eye and then shot away most of her face, you couldn't call that anything but murder.

Bowen had arrested a fair number of murderers in his career. Most were hopped up on something—drugs or emotions. It took a brazen killer to do this, and those were few and far between.

A ribbon of yellow crime scene tape still fluttered from the smooth bark of a slender redbud tree along the street ahead, muted in the early evening gray. Bowen sniffed the chilly air and walked toward it, unsure of what he might find, or what he was even looking for. Hunting—tracking of any kind—required an open mind. If you looked for one thing too hard, you skimmed over a half dozen more tidbits that were just as important, maybe more so.

Bowen found the tracks left by Quinn's knobby-tired BMW and the divot in the grassy shoulder left by the bike's side stand. Squatting low at the edge of the pavement, he studied the brown stains in the gravel that would be Officer Chin's blood. He found a small, white fragment of bone in the stones, still shiny with a film of dried blood and fluid. Marshals were manhunters, not evidence gatherers, so he didn't have any bags with him. He used his handkerchief to pick it up, then dropped it into an open latex glove. He tied a knot in the glove and stuffed it into his pocket. Every piece of Jenny Chin deserved a decent burial.

From the position of the blood, Chin had been standing by the motorcycle when she was shot. The case report said her partner, a veteran officer named Larsson, had been standing behind her while she made the approach. According to him, Quinn had been distraught and when he saw the officer was Asian, he just drew his gun and tried to kill both of them. That certainly wasn't the Jericho Quinn that Bowen knew.

He could still see the man's eyes from their fight all those years ago—focused, intense. There was a cold science in the way he fought, the precision of a fine machine—but no malice. Though Bowen liked to blame the judges, Quinn had knocked him down twice and handily won the fight. Afterward, he'd come up to shake hands, pointing out that Bowen had broken his nose. There was a grace in Quinn's win, a certain humility that said he could do it again with no trouble at all, but he didn't want to rub your face in it.

Bowen ran his fingertips across the surface of the road, thinking. From this close range, Jericho Quinn didn't *try* to shoot anything. He shot it or he didn't.

Bowen looked up to watch a woman about his age walk down a nearby driveway to join him. She wore tight jeans and a wool sweater with the design of a llama on the front. Her arms were folded, her chin to her chest as if she was praying.

Bowen didn't get up but fished his badge out of his jacket pocket and held it up.

"U.S. Marshals," he said.

"Hmm." The woman scuffed the toe of a white tennis shoe on the dead grass.

"You see what happened?"

"Nope." She nodded to the row of tightly spaced cottonwood trees growing like a giant hedge between her house and the road. "As far as I know, nobody did. This is the perfect spot to murder someone so nobody who lives along here could see it."

"I noticed that," Bowen said, tapping his credential case against his open hand.

"I have some coffee on if you need a place to write your report or anything." She was flirting and cute enough, but he ignored her.

Bowen looked up and down the street, thinking. This was too perfect. If it had happened like Larsson said, Quinn hadn't planned on shooting anyone until he saw Jenny Chin was Asian, after they'd pulled him over. It was too coincidental that he'd stopped in the perfect spot to commit a murder.

"U.S. Marshals? I didn't know y'all solved homicides. I thought you chased bad guys. You know, Tommy Lee Jones and all."

"You're right." Bowen smiled. "Sometimes, though, you have to do one before you can do the other."

CHAPTER 35

Seconds before he jumped from his seat, Quinn heard the agonized scream of a woman in the back of the plane. The exit door hissed open and four Korean paramedics in blue jumpsuits poured onto the plane, rushing past Quinn with medical bags and a slender stretcher used to evacuate people from aircraft.

The paramedics rolled back by with the woman a few moments later. She was obviously in the final stages of labor and likely to have the baby before she left the airport.

Quinn let out a long breath, willing his body to calm. He'd not survive long on this kind of emotion. Sooner or later he'd overreact, make a mess of things. If he intended to find Ran and Oda, he had to calm down, get a good night's sleep—or as close to one as he could—and start fresh. He'd not lied when he told Miyagi that he did not fear death. He did fear getting captured and stopped from doing his job. He feared failure above most other things in the world.

Breathing easier once he was off the plane and moving in a crowd again, Quinn bought a large SLR camera and the bulkiest telephoto lens he could find at the airport store, then hopped the subway to Seoul Station in order to make his connection.

Less than three hours after he'd arrived in Korea, Quinn was standing on the docks in Buson. The sun was going down over the hills behind him, casting long shadows over stacked containers, loading cranes, and superstructures of row after row of cargo vessels.

There were several fast ferries that made the trip to Fukuoka, Japan, in less than three hours. But those passengers would be required to undergo the same scrutiny they would at Narita Airport upon entering Japan: a photo and two index fingerprints.

Instead, Quinn opted to try for a slower, commercial ship that would cross during the night. He looped the camera and long telephoto lens around his neck and approached the captain of a car hauler, heading over with a shipment of new Daewoo sedans and likely picking up a load of high-mileage vehicles to bring back for resale in China or Russia.

Quinn stuck a wad of cash in his passport and held it up to the squat Korean man who smoked a cigarette along the flaking rail of his ship. He pointed to the east, held up the camera, and said "Japan."

The captain spoke no English beyond "Hello," which he said over and over again with a slight, ducking bow of his head and shoulders, but the cash spoke loudly enough to get the point across. He didn't care about the passport, but the fact that Quinn had offered it to him was enough to show he wasn't trying to hide anything. The bulky camera put a finishing touch on his cover. Standing out was often the best way to blend in.

The ship cast off a half hour later, and Quinn spent the next forty-five minutes walking up and down the deck, snapping photos of anything and everything. The captain said hello each time they passed.

Eventually, the sun set and the lights of Buson disappeared from view. Quinn found the captain again, returned his fiftieth "hello," and made the universal sign for sleep by tilting his head against an open palm.

The captain lit another cigarette and gave a vigorous nod, ecstatic at being able to communicate with his new guest. He motioned for Quinn to follow him to the foredeck and the captain's quarters. He gave a sweeping motion of his arms and pointed inside, repeating Quinn's sleep gesture. Quinn said thank you and ducked inside.

Surely the nicest accommodations on the ship, they smelled of fishy mildew and whiskey—but Quinn didn't care. He fell into the hard berth, pulling his jacket tight around his neck for warmth against the cold metal bulkhead inches from his back. Resting his face against the leather satchel to protect it from the greasy blanket, he let the rhythmic slap of waves against the hull push him into a welcome unconsciousness.

CHAPTER 36

Lee McKeon walked his Bichon Frise puppy in the backyard of the governor's estate as he talked. His advisors had told him he needed a dog to help him look all-American. It seemed to him that a freakishly tall Pakistani man dragging a fluffy dog along the grass looked anything but American. But his approval rating had gone up when the photos were leaked to the press.

"I haven't heard anything yet," the governor said, trying not to trip over the leash as the stupid animal ran around him in circles. "There have been no reports."

"Be patient, my friend," Qasim Ranjhani said on the other end of the line. He paused as if checking a clock. "A few hours at the most. It will be in the news by then. I assure you."

CHAPTER 37

August Bowen left the meeting with Veronica Garcia with more questions than he had answers. For starters, he couldn't understand why a man with a woman like the strong and curvaceous Latina would still be bothering with his ex-wife.

There was little doubt that Garcia would have lied to protect Quinn if she'd had any information, he but felt pretty certain Quinn hadn't contacted her since the shooting. She had an ache of betrayal in her eyes that was hard to fake, but Bowen recognized Quinn's recent lack of communications was his way of shielding her.

Gunnery Sergeant Thibodaux had been tougher to read, answering most every question with another question. He was good natured and congenial enough but as impenetrable as a concrete wall.

By the time Bowen pulled off the quiet, tree-lined residential street into Emiko Miyagi's long circular driveway, he knew only that Quinn's friends cared little about what aiding a wanted fugitive would do to their respective careers. They had all, no doubt, spilled blood together. Bowen could see it in their eyes. It was a look he knew all too well.

He left the file in the car, keeping both hands free as he walked up to the front door of the colonial red brick home that was supposed to be Emiko Miyagi's address. A chilly wind had kicked up from the north, swaying the high crowns of the big sycamores along the driveway and whistling through the boxwood shrubs that surrounded the house. Bowen shivered, as much from the feeling in his gut as from the cold.

Years in federal law enforcement and two deployments on active duty with the Army had given him the ability to smell spy games—and this whole deal reeked of it. So far, he had an unknown Asian sniper shooting at an OSI agent who had an encrypted phone—whose personnel file had vanished—teamed up with a decorated Marine and a beautiful Latina who had wanted to meet near the CIA's training facility at Camp Peary. Oh, yeah, this was definitely spy games. He preferred head-on, out-in-the-open law enforcement to all the sneaking around and intrigue.

Bowen rang the doorbell, counted to ten, and listened for footsteps. He rang it again. Still nothing. The backyard, which looked to be the size of some British castle estate, had a ten-foot stone wall running all the way around it. He rattled the gate. Locked.

He was just about to give in to the thought of climbing over, when the BlackBerry buzzed in his pocket.

"This is August," he said, stepping back to consider what it would take to leap up on the fence. He hadn't quite given up on the idea.

"Gus," Geoff Barker said. His voice was antsy, as if about to pop with news. "You're not gonna believe what I've found."

"Let me have it," Bowen said, trying a nearby ash

tree to see if it would bend enough to get him on top of the wall.

"Dude, this phone has some seriously good tech," Barker said. "Real cutting-edge shit. They don't just hand this out to everyone, if you know what I mean."

"Funny," Bowen said. "I've come to the same conclusion."

"Well, considering that is the case," Barker continued, "I figured if this Miyagi woman is involved in the same line of work, she's too smart to leave much in the way of a call record on her number. I checked it out anyway and was right. There was nothing outgoing. I mean she doesn't even order pizza unencrypted."

Bowen peered through a tiny crack between the curtain and frame of a side window. The inside hall was bare polished pine, orderly and clean. There were few decorations but for a wooden stand on which sat a Japanese sword.

"This lady doesn't seem like the pizza ordering kind," Bowen mumbled into the phone, half to himself.

"You know she had to make some calls," Barker said. "But she was smart enough, or at least had the right tech to wipe them."

"Okay," Bowen groaned. He paced the fence line, looking for some way through.

"But get this," Barker said. "I figured her friends may not be so savvy in tradecraft so I went back three years. In all that time, there's a record of only one incoming call from Japan."

"Can you get subscriber info?"

"Dude." Barker scoffed. "Have faith. I told you I had contacts with the Japanese National Police. It's already done. Number comes back to Ayako Shimizu in

Fukuoka, Japan. According to my buddy, Ms. Shimizu is a fairly successful hooker who plies her wares near Hakata Harbor."

"That's where he's going," Bowen said. "A prostitute would hear everything that was going on in her area. If Quinn's looking for information in Japan, Shimizu would be a good place to start."

"That's where I'd be," the other deputy said.

"You think you can get your friend to arrange a contact for me with the police over there? I'll call AD Nelson and see if he'll let me take a road trip."

"Sure," Baker said. "I'm on it. You speak Japanese?"

"Yeah, right." Bowen laughed. "There's a big need for Asian languages in Kalispell, Montana. I'll do what I always do when I book someone in who doesn't speak English. I'll speak louder and slooowwwwer." He matched his volume and speed to the words.

"Yeah," Baker said. "Tell me how that works out for you."

"Come on," Bowen said, turning to go back to his car. "We'll be brother lawmen. We should all speak the same language. Right?"

"Hmmm," Baker groaned. "I'll see if they can find you someone who speaks English."

"We have a photo of Shimizu anywhere?"

"Coming your way, brother," Baker said. "Be careful, though. She looks like she could carve out your liver and fry your cojones up as a side dish."

CHAPTER 38

Quinn woke to the sound of feet running back and forth on deck. Large winches fore and aft groaned and squealed, playing out heavy line as big as a man's wrist as they made ready to offload and load cargo. Gruff voices barked orders in Japanese and Korean.

Quinn swung his feet off the edge of the cramped berth and sat up, rubbing the effects of exhausted sleep from his eyes. He was angry with himself for sleeping so deeply for so long. His plan had been to be ready to step off the boat as it came even with the pier. There was no way to know when Customs might pay a visit— and he wanted to be gone when they did.

The sun was still a pink line below the clouds on the eastern horizon when he stuck his head out of the captain's cabin. Land lay off the port side of the vessel, but Quinn realized they were coming around the long barrier peninsula that protected the port from the more open waters of the Korean Strait. It was still dark enough for a covert arrival.

Quinn stepped out of the cramped cabin and popped his neck from side to side, breathing in the moist sea air. Standing along the rail, he could just make out the red outline of Hakata Tower looming ghostlike through the heavy mist, still two miles away.

Japan. He could smell the mystery of the place.

Though he spoke flawless Arabic and excellent Chinese, Japan's culture had bitten Jericho more deeply than any he'd ever experienced. He'd taken immersion language classes in junior high and high school in Alaska, surrounding himself with all things samurai from food to martial arts. The Anchorage Rotary Club had sponsored him for a semester of high school in the Roppongi area of Tokyo his sophomore year.

That had been well before Kim came into the picture, and he'd met a girl there. Her name was Sayuri, and at sixteen, she seemed to him to be the embodiment of all that was feminine. Wise beyond her years, she had warned him that Japan had a way of getting into a person's blood. He would return to Alaska, and, though memories of her would surely fade, he would forever be tugged back toward her country.

He smiled when he thought about it, ocean spray stinging his face. He was on a mission, sure to be deadly for someone, but in truth, he couldn't wait to step onto Japanese soil merely for the thrill of being back.

A shuddering rumble from deep within the Korean ship drew him out of his reminiscing. Deckhands moved to the rail opposite Quinn, standing ready with boat hooks. The captain came out of the wheelhouse carrying a plastic tote heavily wrapped in duct tape. He whistled Quinn over as another boat, much smaller than the Korean ship, materialized out of the mist and pulled up alongside. Rigged for squid fishing, a long, overhead line with dozens of clear glass lamps like basketball-size Christmas ornaments ran down the center length of the smaller boat. Neither vessel came to a full stop, but matched speed and course at what Quinn guessed to be less than five or six knots.

The captain dropped the plastic tote to the waiting hands of two men on the squid boat and then pantomimed for Quinn to climb over and jump down with it.

Quinn nodded, understanding immediately what the captain wanted. The Korean ship would dock at the commercial pier—behind what would surely be a very tall fence and subject to search by Japan Customs. The squid boat, being a local vessel, would simply dock in Fukuoka harbor with all the other fishing boats. Both Quinn and whatever was in the plastic tote could quietly enter Japan without notice from any authorities.

Quinn gave the smiling Korean captain five more twenty-dollar bills and slipped over the edge with his leather satchel to drop down next to the pilothouse on the spray-soaked deck of the smaller boat.

The squid boat skipper was a short man with a wide, unsmiling face weathered by the sea and tension of smuggling contraband. A blue bandanna, tied at all four corners, dropped over his head in a functional but comical hat to keep water from dripping in his eyes. He obviously spoke Japanese, but since he was now carrying an illegal immigrant and tote full of what was probably illicit Chinese Ecstasy, the man kept his thoughts to himself.

Quinn spent the next half hour while the boat slogged toward Fukuoka Harbor standing under a blue-tarp bimini soaking up the spindrift from the breaking waves and the uneasy stares of the three-man crew.

The wind picked up as they chugged up next to the

pier. Heavy spray washed across the concrete docks, blown by a steady wind from the east and open water. The crew deployed bumper tires and threw ropes to two waiting dockhands. Two Japanese Coast Guard cutters bobbed with the tide at their berths. Across the quay, a man in a blue uniform braved the elements and scrubbed the deck of a forty-foot police boat.

Quinn softened the squid boat captain's glare with a series of polite bows and a wad of twenties—a good sum for a quarter hour ride. Then, slinging the leather bag over his shoulder, he stepped over the gunnel and into Japan.

Apart from a handful of stevedores smoking cigarettes while they waited on the other side of the Customs fence for the early morning arrival of the Korean car hauler, the docks were all but deserted. Spotlights chased back the shadows around two ships already at berth, glinting off car glass and chrome. There were no agents to greet him, no swarm of police—and so far, no assassin's bullet. Light poles bristled with surveillance cameras, but most were pointed toward the other direction. For the time being at least, Quinn's only company as he walked toward the quiet parking lot seemed to be a lonely seagull wheeling above in the wind and spray.

A shrill whistle turned his attention toward the narrow byway that ran along the commercial docks, adjacent to the blocky white building that contained the Fukuoka Port government offices. Twenty yards away, in the parking lot on the far side of a well-groomed hedgerow, a woman straddled a small yellow motorbike. A cigarette hung from her lips, glowing brightly against the gray of early morning. She tossed her head when Quinn looked at her, letting him know she'd meant the whistle for him.

The woman wore a shorty helmet that left her chin exposed. Painted rally-style, it was canary yellow to match the bike with a white stripe down the center. Wide goggles protected her eyes from the rain. It was difficult to tell much about her face. It did not smile, but Quinn thought that might be a function of her lips holding the cigarette. Despite the wet weather she wore a stylish denim jacket, darkened by rain at the shoulders. A black dress that stopped at midthigh and gray tights revealed strong legs. Flat-heeled leather boots that came halfway up stout calves rounded out her outfit.

White cotton gloves on the handlebars, she tossed her head again, beckoning him to hurry before looking back and forth over her shoulder.

"Welcome to Japan, Mr. Quinn," she said in English when he got close enough to hear.

"Hai," he said in Japanese. *Yes*. He was surprised Miyagi hadn't told her friend to use Hackman, the name on his passport.

"I am Ayako," she said. "Get on." Her voice held the honeyed purr of a heavy drinker. She handed him a battered black helmet and white cloth mask worn by so many in Asia during flu and hay fever season. "The police would certainly stop us if you do not wear the helmet," she said. "With the mask, people will have to look closely to see you are not Japanese. Americans are usually too vain to wear them, even if it would keep them from getting sick."

"Sounds reasonable." Quinn slung the leather bag over his shoulder and fastened the helmet under his chin. He pulled the elastic straps of the mask over each ear, concealing his face.

"I don't want to stay here longer than we have to." Ayako craned her head around to look at him, revving the little engine. It sounded more like a lawnmower than a bike. Dark eyes stared from behind the large goggles, making her look at once adventurous and comical. As with Emiko, it was difficult to tell this one's age. Her damp hair and amber skin softened in the diffuse light of early morning, she could have been a college coed. But if she was a friend from Miyagi's childhood, Ayako had to be at least in her late thirties.

Quinn climbed on behind her, scooting as close as he dared to keep from falling off the back of the little bike.

"I am not a clay doll," Ayako said over her shoulder. "Please hold on."

Quinn situated the leather satchel so it hung behind him and wrapped his arms around the woman's waist. After sleeping with his face next to the Korean captain's greasy pillow, he found the smell of strawberry shampoo and cigarettes that clung to Ayako's damp clothes pleasantly intoxicating.

Quinn couldn't remember the last time he'd ridden as a passenger behind a female rider. Anatomy made for any number of problems in such an arrangement. Though far from fat, Ayako was a girl with plenty of roundness. It was difficult to know whether he should keep his arms high, under her heavy bust, or low and risk brushing the lap of her skirt. She was a short-coupled woman, leaving little margin for error. She planted both feet on the ground to steady the bike and solved the problem by positioning his arms high, around her ribs, so her breasts rested on his forearms.

She chuckled out loud, giving the bike gas. "I don't meet many men who worry about where they touch me."

"Nice scooter," Quinn said as she got under way, hoping to move the conversation away from the subject of his manners.

Ayako slammed on the brakes, stopping so abruptly she threw Quinn's weight forward, shoving her against the gas tank on the little bike. Her chest heaved against his arms.

"This is not a scooter," she corrected, using informal, almost confrontational Japanese. He could hear her teeth grating as she spoke. "It is a motorbike."

Quinn grimaced. "Sorry, I didn't mean—"

"One straddles a motorbike. On a scooter, one keeps their legs together . . ." Softening immediately, she looked over her shoulder to give Quinn a coy wink. "I have never been so good at that."

She laughed out loud at her own joke and gave the little motorbike enough gas that is sounded as if it might fly apart as they melded into the honk and grind of the morning traffic of Fukuoka City.

CHAPTER 39

Bagram Air Base
Afghanistan

Lieutenant Colonel Paul Hunt shut the screen to his laptop computer and leaned back in his chair with a long sigh. He still wore his surgical scrubs. They were more comfortable than anything else in the up-and-down heat and cold of this miserable country.

In a fit of patriotism, he'd signed up for military service after 9/11. That also happened to be after he'd accumulated what his wife called roughly a bajillion dollars in medical school debt. The Air Force was happy to get a qualified doctor and, though they paid him with some parity to what a doc made in the civilian world, the school debts were still his. Frankly, until he'd been trapped in Afghanistan by this quarantine, the money he owed caused him more stress than the possibility of mortar attack or getting his foot blown off by a land mine if he stepped off the pavement on base.

He'd come into the military with an adventurous heart, thinking there was nowhere on earth that he wouldn't want to visit on some level. One could learn something from every culture in every land. He still believed that, though the things one learned might just be to stay the hell away. Russia, the British Empire, Hannibal, Alexander the Great, had all tried and failed to conquer Afghanistan. America hadn't really tried to conquer the place, just drive the Taliban out and rebuild it. But you had to *want* progress. You had to allow yourself to be rebuilt.

Hunt often thought how impossible it was to bomb a place back to the Stone Age when they were already there. Still, he had a job while he was here, and he did it well.

Behind him, two senior airmen stood over their lab duties, sterilizing hospital instruments and making certain crash carts were stocked with necessary supplies at the end of their shift.

Hunt didn't know if the Skype chats with his wife made the time away from her easier or more difficult. In truth, it didn't matter. The months ticked by, the kids passed milestones he'd never get to see, and the war dragged on—whether he missed his wife or not.

And now, they were telling him and everyone else in the godforsaken place that they had to stay indefinitely, at least until someone could figure out what was causing this new plague of boils. The young troops who'd been raised on video games had taken to calling the disease Epic Egypt or Pharaoh 2.0 and chanting "Let my people go" as they walked between their basic duties and the chow hall.

There had been three deaths on base so far—one soldier and two Afghan nationals who helped with road maintenance. The boils had been horrific enough, causing a near panic among the Afghani workforce, who saw it as a sign from Allah of some great sin. They'd been extra pissed when local mullahs banished them from their communities and sent them packing back to Bagram at the pointy end of a Kalashnikov.

At the insistence of the Afghan government, the base commander had put a hiatus on all traffic going outside the wire, leaving frontline troops not only denied their rotation home, but without a job of patrol while stuck in theater. Boredom had always been an issue at Bagram, but now, with fuses shortened by the lack of relief and this surprise imprisonment, tensions bordered on deadly. It was only a matter of time before someone—military, contractor, or Afghan—broke under pressure. Even the Kyrgyz barbers and massage girls were beginning to show signs of stress, wearing less makeup and not bothering to flirt for business.

In a show of sheer genius, the base commander had ordered photographs of the infected men, complete with their terrifying boils, to be placed in strategic locations so they could be seen by the maximum number of people. Instead of causing panic, as some feared the posters would, the grisly photographs served as reminders of why the dire orders were in place.

Though the sight of the boils was enough to induce another plague of chronic diarrhea and stomach tension, in the end, the pustules were only a symptom. All the deaths had been from respiratory distress. So far, the remaining infected were soldiers. One was on a ventilator and another was attached to a full-blown ECMO for heart-lung bypass. The other three sounded as if they had pneumonia. He only had one more ECMO unit, meaning the next person to get sickest was the one most likely to live the longest. Unless the military did some magic and brought him more units, the others would simply drown as fluid filled their lungs.

Hunt had gone over each patient's chart a dozen times. The infected who'd made it stateside had all come from the 405th Civil Affairs Battalion based at Nellis. There had to be a connection there—but the sick who remained in Afghanistan appeared to be a hodgepodge of random units.

"There has to be something you all have in common," Hunt said out loud. "Some little thing you share."

"Colonel," the older of the two Senior Airmen said from behind him. "Everything is in place. With your permission, we'd like to knock off in time to get a haircut."

"You're free to go," Hunt said, smiling. The kid reminded him of his oldest son. "But your hair looks fine."

"I know. But the girls are pretty." The senior airman shrugged. "And it gives us something to do."

Hunt tossed the last file on his desk and ran a hand through his own hair. He could do with a trim as well.

CHAPTER 40

Kanab, Utah

Todd Elton sat on the hood of his black Chevy Silverado at the edge of the runway and watched the gray-green C-130 Hercules from the Nevada Air Guard's 152 Airlift Wing come in low across the east desert. It continued north as if the pilots might have decided against stopping in such a plague-infested land, then, at the last minute, executed a lumbering turn to final approach nearly over the top of the hospital at the north end of town.

The arrival of a military aircraft in a place cut off from society—if only for two days—tended to draw a crowd. By the time the C-130 had touched down and rolled to a stop, a convoy of twenty pickups and three motorcycles had arrived at the airport.

Colonel Huber with the Utah National Guard had his men dressed in black biohazard suits, standing ready to accept the new cargo—and keep anyone in the twenty pickups from stealing it.

Monte Young, Elton's father-in-law and the only sheriff Kane County had known for twenty-four years, stood at the front of a white Dodge Durango with a six-pointed badge on the door.

The rear of the C-130 yawned open and the National Guardsmen began the work of unloading palletized food and medical supplies.

The crew on the arriving transport was careful not to go beyond the confines of the ramp. None of them would dare leave the plane. If they did, they would find themselves calling Kanab home for the foreseeable future.

Though most of the valley was predominately Mormon and taught to prepare for disasters with extra food, it was amazing how fast the shelves of the local grocery had been stripped bare once news of the quarantine was broadcast.

Neighbor stopped visiting neighbor and a personally enforced approach boundary of at least fifteen feet became the norm. If someone had a cold or sneezed, the nonapproach area was raised to a bubble of thirty feet or more. As a doctor, and one mandated to deal directly with those already infected, Elton was placed even farther out in what he called a yell-zone—where he had to raise his voice just to be heard in normal conversations.

The guy who'd brought pizza to the clinic the night before had left the food at the curb, yelling at him to leave his money on the sidewalk. Elton didn't have the heart to tell the poor kid that if he was infected, his money would be the last thing anyone should touch.

Last to be unloaded were the sets of large Pelican hard cases that Elton knew contained ECMO units. His heart fell when only two were lowered onto the tarmac.

An armed soldier ordered him to halt when he tried to walk closer.

"I thought we were getting a dozen ventilators and at least six ECMO machines," he yelled to the guy who looked like he might be in charge.

"Realigned," the soldier said.

"What does that mean?"

"Means the hospitals need the units for themselves. New cases are popping up in Salt Lake City, Las Vegas, Seattle, and Los Angeles. Everyone's holding on to what they have in case they need it."

Elton's shoulders fell, stunned.

"Sorry, Doc," the soldier said. "There's talk of bringing some over from the East Coast. Maybe next trip."

Elton knew better. If the disease was spreading, no hospital administrator was going to give up a piece of equipment they might need for their own patients.

He looked at the two Pelican cases. They wouldn't be enough—and with all the information and conspiracy theories flying around the Internet, everyone in town already knew it.

A barrel-chested man wearing jeans and a faded tan Carhartt jacket stood beside a KLR motorcycle off the side of the runway. A curly head of black hair moved in the noon breeze. Brody Teeples was a known hothead and sometimes drunk. A talented cabinetmaker, he was ever spoiling for a fight. He had a mouth like a sailor and the eye of an artist. And though he was quick to crack another man's skull for looking at him wrong, one word from his wife would cow him immediately. He loved her more than life.

And she was one of the sick.

Teeples strode over to face Elton, not caring to keep

the distance of any yell-zone. His eyes, red from crying, stared holes in the doc. He hadn't shaved in days.

"My Stephanie better get every bit of the care your family gets." Teeples's hands clenched in tight fists at his side. His lip quivered as he spoke.

"We don't even know what—"

"I'm not askin' you what it is!" Brody screamed, showing his teeth. "I'm telling you my wife had better get the care she deserves. The way I see it, your brother-in-law, who happens to also be related to the sheriff, is getting the best treatment while the rest suffer."

Elton clenched his teeth at the accusation. He knew it would only incite things, but he slid down from his pickup to face the fuming Teeples, who had him by two inches and at least sixty pounds.

"And I'm telling you that we're doing all we can," Elton said.

Monte Young's jovial voice drew Teeples's attention away and saved Elton from the imminent beat-down.

Though nearing sixty, the sheriff was a wide, squarely built man with a strong jaw. He had a bit of a belly, but big arms and shoulders to go with it. Certainly past his prime fighting days, Young gave the impression that he would have no qualms against throwing out his back while he used his last bit of good health to give a ne'er-do-well a whipping.

"You boys didn't hear about the whole social distancing thing?"

"I don't give a damn about me getting sick," Teeples said. "I just want to make sure your son-in-law takes care of somebody besides people related to you."

"And you know he will," Young said.

"I don't know shit anymore, Sheriff." Teeples shook

his head, sniffing back angry tears. "The news says everyone that gets this stuff dies. They're saying the only chance anyone has is to be on a heart-lung machine—and any fool can see they didn't bring enough of those on that plane."

Elton took a deep breath. "I'm going to do everything I can—"

Teeples spun, cutting him off. "Don't you go making promises you don't intend to keep."

Sheriff Young moved a half step closer. "And you might consider not making threats that will get you hurt."

"Take it like you want, Sheriff," Teeples snapped. "But if my wife dies because your family gets better treatment, there's gonna be hell to pay. You can count on that. And I'm starting with the little doctor man here."

Young nodded his head as if chewing over the words. "You know," he said at length, "they've given these poor National Guard boys live ammo to enforce the orders of this quarantine—and protect the hospital."

"I'm not scared of no National Guard troops."

"I guess I wouldn't be, either, if I was you." The sheriff shrugged. "They might pause before they shoot you, thinking you're just a poor, misguided soul who's upset over his sick wife. But they don't know you like I do, Brody." Young's eyes suddenly narrowed and his voice grew stern. "I won't make that mistake."

"You threatening me?"

"Take it like you want," Young said, hand on his sidearm.

A shout from the colonel drew everyone's attention away and gave Elton a chance to move away from the stare-down and toward his truck. He drove away, leaving the sheriff and Brody Teeples posturing on the tarmac. His main concern was to lead the National Guardsmen back to the hospital with a truck full of medical supplies and the ECMO machines. There were fifteen people there with an unknown illness. No one knew how contagious it was, or how it even spread—but, for now, the hospital seemed to be the safest place in town.

CHAPTER 41

Quinn slipped out of his boots in the entry of Ayako's studio apartment and watched as she used her fingers to fluff the moisture from her hair. Without the helmet and oversized goggles, it was easier to get a look at her. She hung the denim jacket on a hook along the wall and mopped her brow with her forearm. A white wooden bowling pin with a little black bow tie stood on the shelf just inside the door.

Quinn nearly knocked it over when he took off his jacket. "You are a bowler?" He pushed the heavy pin back a little, making sure it stayed upright.

"Not really." Ayako gave a pensive sigh. "I once shared an apartment with another girl. If I came home and saw the bowling pin in the window I would know she was . . . busy with a client. It is all I have left to remind me of her."

Quinn decided not to ask more about the girl. Instead, he took the time to study Ayako.

The short skirt, white blouse, and kneesocks were meant to replicate the look of a Japanese schoolgirl—a popular fantasy for Japanese men who hired prostitutes. Quinn couldn't help noticing that the socks were a little too large for her tiny feet and the baggy heels hung out of the back of her slippers. She was still able to carry off the costume, but Quinn could make out the tiniest of lines around her smallish mouth. Wide, chocolate eyes, though attractive in their own way, held a weary look that liner and makeup could not hide.

"I am sure you are tired, Quinn-san," she said in English. "Would you like something to drink?"

"Some water would be nice."

She opened the fridge to give a look at what she could offer. "How about orange juice and toast? I doubt you got breakfast on your way across from Korea."

"I would not turn down something to eat," Quinn said.

Ayako moved two graphic novels and a pile of mail off the table so he'd have a place to sit. She made him toast and a poached egg to go with his juice, bantering about the Japanese intricacies of sorting recyclable trash while bustling around the small kitchen. A dish-towel hung cavalierly over her shoulder, and she spoke easily, as if she'd known Quinn all her life.

The TAG Aquaracer on Quinn's wrist said it had been nearly twenty hours since he'd eaten anything—a long time for someone with his gaunt frame and high metabolism. Ayako sat across from him with her hands in her lap, watching intently while he ate.

"Emiko-chan says you have great skill at violent things." Ayako rolled pink lips as if she should not have let that slip out. "She says you are the best."

"There is no best." Quinn smiled over the glass of juice. "Some are better on one day, others are better on the next."

"Still," Ayako said, fingering a little photo charm

that hung from her cell phone. "I can see from the way you move that you are the man for this job."

Quinn frowned. "What job?"

Ayako raised a penciled brow, surprised at his reaction. "Emi-chan said you were coming to help me."

"Interesting," Quinn said. "I was under the impression that you were going to help me."

"She only told me you had some questions that I could answer." Ayako shrugged. "And that you could help me sort out a problem with your particular skills."

"She didn't mention Oda or the girl with the foo dog tattoo?"

Ayako recoiled as if she'd been slapped. Standing quickly, she turned to a stack of dishes in the metal sink, throwing more around for effect than she actually washed.

"I am sorry if I have upset you," Quinn said. "But I need to find this man, Oda. I believe he put this girl up to shooting someone."

Ayako spun to face him, a dripping dishcloth in her hand. One dark kneesock puddled around a tiny ankle. Her chest heaved under the translucent cotton blouse, unbuttoned far enough to expose a little black bow at the center of her bra. Had it not been for the stricken look in her eyes, Quinn would have thought she was flirting. "Oda is . . ." She swallowed hard, then turned to vomit in the sink.

Quinn jumped out of his chair to steady her, but she put up her hand, shrugging him off.

"Do not touch me!"

He backed away. Emiko's description hadn't prepared him for this.

Slowly, her breathing calmed. She took a paper towel from a roll by the sink and dabbed at her mouth.

"I am sorry. It is only that . . . Oda has this effect on people. Emiko probably told you as much." She closed her eyes as she spoke, swallowing, working to focus her thoughts.

"So you know where to find him?"

Ayako said nothing for a long time, her hands trembling as she tried to dry a clay teacup. At length, she looked up, leaning against the edge of the kitchen counter, batting her eyes. "I was never allowed to know exactly where he stays. Perhaps if you help me with my problem, you will find the answers you are after."

"Okay . . ." Quinn groaned. He took his seat back at the table, skeptical. He needed this woman's cooperation and hoped his particular skills would not get him in trouble.

Ayako folded her arms across her chest. "There are several yakuza families operating here in Fukuoka, the weakest of which is the Taniguchi clan. They are also the most dangerous, always trying to claw their way up the ladder. The second in command is a lieutenant named Sato. Emiko may have mentioned him."

"No." Quinn shook his head.

"That is interesting." Ayako wrinkled her nose and pursed her lips, as if discussing the man made her want to spit. "Sato is the yakuza soldier who forced Emiko's mother to be his concubine when her father died. Of course he tossed her to the side like a piece of trash when he was tired of her—as he does with all his women. Frankly, I believe he was more interested in Emiko, as his tastes run toward younger girls. A longtime client of mine who works for Sato told me the Taniguchi clan had some kind of issue with Oda recently. Such 'issues' usually mean someone has been killed in a particularly bad way. Sato will know more."

"That's all I can ask." Quinn leaned back in his chair, ready to listen. "What's this problem that you need sorted out?"

Visibly calmer now that Quinn had agreed to help, Ayako padded across the small apartment and plopped down on a love seat along the block wall. Her unmade bed was just a few feet away. Well practiced at playing an innocent schoolgirl, she draped her legs over the arm of the love seat and hugged a pillow to her chest while she stared at the ceiling. It took Quinn a moment to notice there was a poster of some Korean boy-toy heartthrob tacked up there, staring back down.

Quinn waited for her to think through her scheme. One of her kneesocks had a hole on the bottom. In fact, on closer inspection, all her clothes were frayed or worn in some way or another—just like her.

"My niece is missing," Ayako said after a thoughtful silence. "I need you to help me get her back."

"Kidnapped?"

"Without a doubt she is being held against her will, and I know by who," Ayako said, still gazing up at the poster of the Korean singer who was no more than half her age.

"Sounds like a problem you should take to the police."

"That would not turn out well." Ayako gave a strained laugh. "The police are fully aware of what I do for a living. They would never believe any niece of mine is only an innocent university student. She would be judged by association." Still on her back, Ayako turned her head to look at Quinn under heavy eyelids. "Do you know what they call prostitutes in Japan?"

"I know the Japanese word, if that's what you mean."

"There are lots of names for us," Ayako said, giving a resigned shrug. She let her gaze return to the Korean teenager on the ceiling. "*Iero kiyabu,* for instance . . ."

Quinn shook his head, not recognizing the term. It sounded Japanese, but he'd never heard it.

"*I-e-ro ki-ya-bu* . . . yellow cab," she said, sighing. "I supposed it is because we give rides to strangers . . . Miyu-chan is no *iero kiyabu*, no matter what they think, but since she came to visit me, the police would assume."

"How long has she been missing and who has her?" Quinn cut to the chase, preferring not to dwell on the plight of girls in the yellow cab profession. Prostitutes made for perfect informants, and he'd dealt with many over the years in his own line of work. No two were exactly the same but most shared the common qualities of desperation and a sort of penned-up sadness that made Quinn want to beat to death the men who used them.

"Two days." Ayako swung her legs to the floor and sat up, facing Quinn. "But she is still safe, if that's what you are wondering. Sato is a pig but, luckily, he's been away from the country. He prefers girls who are unsullied, so his men will keep her that way. He returns from Guam tonight. We must get to her before then. So, you see? We have a common cause."

"And you have some idea of a plan?" Quinn asked.

"I do, now that you are here." Ayako smiled, nodding as if it was all so clear to her. "That is the most excellent part. If Emiko says you are the best, then you are surely the best. I want you to walk into Sato's office and say, 'Mr. Yakuza Boss, Miyu-chan is not a prostitute. She is my friend. You must give her to me or I will cut off your genitals' . . . or something like that."

It was Quinn's turn to laugh. "And if he doesn't give her to me?"

"Then you must keep your word and cut off his genitals."

"Or something like that."

"Emiko-chan would agree with me," Ayako said. "This one deserves it."

Quinn rubbed the stubble on his chin, thinking things through. Fatigue from the long flight and the ocean crossing was beginning to catch up with him. "Why not ask this longtime client of yours about Miyu?" He asked. "If he works for Sato, then he should know where she's being held."

"Watanabe stinks of urine." Ayako scoffed. "He has moved up the ranks in the underworld, but he still acts like a *chinpira*."

Quinn chuckled, almost feeling sorry for this Watanabe guy. For a woman to describe a man as Ayako had, she had to have a pretty low opinion of him. To "smell of urine" was another way of calling someone immature in Japanese. *Chinpira* were low-level yakuza thugs who bullied people when they thought they could get away with it but groveled to their senior bosses. Quinn had met with a few such young hoodlums during his visits to Japan. The three *bozozoku* thugs he'd killed in Virginia had been perfect examples of such punks. Unless they happened to be on business from a higher authority, one look that said he meant business was usually enough to send them walking the other direction—as long as they could do so with their honor intact.

"In any case," Ayako said, "Watanabe pays me well because it makes him feel like a big man. He asks for my complete loyalty but has none for me—only his boss. Sometimes he cries in his rice wine over how sad and thankless his life is in the Japanese mafia—and then falls asleep in the hotel bed all night, keeping me from seeing other customers. It is a hazard of my chosen occupation, I suppose." She shrugged. "No use in clenching the buttocks when the gas has already passed . . ."

Quinn smiled. It was the colorful Japanese equivalent to not crying over spilled milk.

"Exactly where would I find this Sato?"

"Watanabe let it slip he will attend a boxing match in Fukuoka tonight, shortly after his flight arrives from Guam."

"So, Miyu will be with him?" Quinn asked, thinking through his options.

"I do not know," Ayako said. "But if she is not, we can follow Sato from the fights. He is sure to go straight to her afterward. He will not want to put off partaking of such a young treasure."

Ayako looked at her watch, suddenly springing to her feet. "*Shimata!*" she snapped. Dammit! "I am late. My client will be disappointed if I am not there before he leaves for work."

She rummaged through a pile of clothes on her bed, snatching up a frilly pink blouse and matching lace apron. She put on the denim jacket and shoved the new clothes inside it, next to her body to protect them from the rain during her bike ride.

Ayako tipped her head toward the bed while she gazed in the small vanity mirror to apply pink gloss to puckered lips. "Please, get some sleep. I will be out for some time."

Quinn looked at the pile of tangled sheets and pillows, nodding slowly.

"Do not worry," Ayako smiled with her freshly glossed lips. "This apartment is my sanctuary. You will be the first man to ever sleep here. Now please, get some rest before we go and visit Sato tonight. You will need it if you are forced to cut off his genitals."

Chapter 42

Kanab, Utah

The five local doctors and the nine additional docs and nurses CDC had sent in had their hands full seeing the rapidly weakening patients. News reports said stores in virtually every city west of the Rocky Mountains had run out of food and flashlight batteries. At first, students were sent home from school if they sneezed more than once. By the second day, the schools closed altogether. Thriving communities turned into ghost towns overnight as residents opted to stay inside and fill their minds with the endless supply of conspiracy theories and fearmongering on radio, television, and social media.

The disease manifested itself in such a horrific way that the media began to show seemingly nonstop footage of boil-infested bodies, heaping on to the already hysterical fear. Grassroots groups who had once fought the government for the right not to vaccinate their children clamored for action, demanding that same government do something to stop the spread of this "biblical plague of boils."

The number of plague victims in Kanab appeared to have leveled off at twenty-one with no new cases in the last few hours, but in a town of 4,500, half of them Mormons, there were bound to be births. Broken arms, an emergency appendectomy, and a thumb cut off in a fight with a table saw all kept hospital and clinic personnel hopping.

CDC personnel took over as soon as they were on the ground—and Elton was happy to let them. They set up a triage unit in the clinic, sealing off the connected hospital with sheets of clear plastic and duct tape. Anyone going in had to don an orange chem-bio suit complete with hood and filter. FEMA engineers had arrived shortly after the CDC, landing in a squadron of dark helicopters that were certain to raise the blood pressure of more than just the conspiracy theorists in the little southern Utah burg.

Todd Elton pulled on one of the hoods and made his way past a knot of CDC staff gathered around a quaking Mrs. Johnson as she sat on the edge of a gurney in the hallway. The poor old woman's white hair was still in perfect order, though her frail body had been overwhelmed with red sores. She deserved her own room, but there just weren't any left, so she joined the others in a row of rolling beds in the hallway beside the nurse's station.

The CDC docs had consulted with him at first, but after they felt they had the lay of the land, all but pushed him to the side. He'd been in close contact with the infected, so they saw him as a potential patient. As a scientist, he couldn't really disagree.

Elton reached the room he was looking for, knocked on the door, and pushed it open.

The man on the bed groaned, turning his head to look up. "Hey, Doc," he whispered, licking cracked lips. His lungs rattled and wheezed. "How you holding up?"

Elton picked up the chart hanging beside the monitor. He had only known R. J. Howard a few days, but it was impossible not to like him.

"You're a strong guy, R.J.," he said. "If news reports are correct, you and several others in your unit picked this up overseas."

"Yeah, the CCD guys had me answer a whole list of questions about what we did over there." Howard grinned. "I think they figured we were running around with the massage girls or something and caught it that way. But Bedford was a hundred percent loyal." He turned away, sighing. "I was too, a lotta good it did me . . ."

"I'm sure you were," Elton said.

"Can I ask you something, Doc?" Howard kept his face toward the window, keeping the pressure off a scabby red boil behind his right ear.

"Sure."

"I heard some of the CDC guys talking. They said that this stuff was one hundred percent fatal in Japan. Is that right?"

Elton made a mental note to talk to the lab rats about their bedside manner and patient outlook. Still, as a physician, he'd made it a policy to be direct and honest when someone asked him a question.

"I heard the same thing about the cases in Japan," he said. "But I will tell you what I do know. Whatever this is, you and Bedford have had it longer than anyone here."

"Hey," Howard interrupted, licking his lips again. "How is Rick doing?"

"We've had to put him on a heart-lung bypass—but that's keeping him alive. Your body is doing a much better job of fighting it than some people who have had it for less time."

"I feel sorry for them, then, because this stuff is kicking my ass—" Howard broke into a violent coughing fit, his face dark as it struggled to get his breath before finally calming back down. He started to finish his thought, but Elton held up a hand to stop him.

"I get the picture, R.J.," he said. "You just rest. I'll be back to check on you in a little while."

Elton forced a smile as he turned to leave. R. J. Howard was getting worse before his eyes. It wouldn't be long before he'd need ECMO treatment just like Rick Bedford. And it was a sure bet the townspeople would revolt if he put the people who made them sick on the only two units available that had any chance of saving their lives.

CHAPTER 43

Quinn bought a ticket to the fights six rows from ringside for ten thousand yen—roughly the equivalent of a hundred dollars. He followed the flow of the crowd into the squat tan building known as the Kyuden Memorial Gymnasium. Aging posters from previous boxing matches, WWF wrestling, and long-ago concerts by Journey and Queen hung framed on corridor walls.

Tables set up just inside the lobby sold programs as well as bouquets of flowers fans could give the fighters. Vending machines along the wall sold Pocari Sweat and vitamin drinks. Beer, assorted brands of sake, hot dogs, and rice balls were available outside the door to the main hall.

Apart from the slight odor of seaweed from the rice balls, the smell was much like the fights Quinn went to in the States. The difference being that when he attended fights, he was usually the one wearing trunks and gloves. He had the crooked nose to prove it.

Inside the main hall, the buzz of the crowd and sight of the canvas itself flooded Quinn with a sense of nostalgia. There was a particular energy in a group that came to watch people hit each other that wasn't found anywhere else. Boxing had a referee, judges, and plenty of rules—but it was a fight, and those who came to watch were not truly happy until they saw blood.

Quinn couldn't blame them. He felt the same but was happiest when he was the one in the ring, drawing the blood and doing the bleeding. Still, it was a young man's game. Every fight, in or out of the ring, took something from him—maybe not years, but definitely something. He wondered if he would have chosen to be a fighter if he had it to do over again—or if there had ever really been a choice at all. Maybe his life had chosen him.

Ayako was already in place. She ignored him when he walked by, looking for his seat number. She had gone in first and sat at the end of the bleachers, three rows up from where the scantily clad Filipina ring girls waited with their cards to number the individual rounds. The main event on this evening was an All-Asia lightweight title between a local favorite named Uta and a thick-necked boxer from the Philippines named Ortega. A sizable number of fans from the Philippines crowded the floor seating around their champion's corner.

Ayako sat directly above them with a clear view of the ringside seating where Sato would sit. One of Uta's major sponsors, the yakuza underboss of Taniguchi clan would get the best seats in the house, right beside the judges.

Quinn had just taken his seat beside an older Japanese man when Sato walked in surrounded by a cadre of younger subordinates. A stout man, he wore a camelhair sport coat over a black turtleneck and black slacks. His black hair was neatly trimmed and combed back to reveal a prominent widow's peak. Wire-frame glasses gave him a studious look for a gangster.

When he reached his seat, Sato handed his overcoat to a skinny subordinate with wavy hair and a black turtleneck that matched his boss's. From Ayako's description, this one was likely Watanabe.

The younger man took the coat while another held the chair for Sato as he sat down. The crowd around him, including the judges already at ringside, gave the yakuza underboss deferential nods when he looked at them. He folded his arms across his belly and waited for the fight to start, apparently tired from his flight in from Guam.

Quinn studied the four subordinate gangsters. None of them was very tall, with Watanabe the tallest if not the biggest, at about five-nine. What they lacked in height, they all made up for in intensity. Each man scanned the crowd for signs of threat against their boss. All four carried themselves like bullies, men used to forcing their way in the world. They were all too happy to do the dirty work so Sato could keep his hands relatively clean.

The heaviest one—Quinn thought of him as Pig Face because of his wide, flat mug—was the apparent second in command. He stayed within arm's reach of Sato and the others deferred to him when he spoke or even looked in their direction—especially Watanabe, who looked several times like he might wet himself when the bigger man said something to him. Pig Face weighed in at around 220, heavy for a man just over five and a half feet tall. The size of his belly caused him to have to hitch up his slacks every few seconds, exposing the slight bulge of a handgun against his black leather jacket each time.

The other two looked enough alike they could have been brothers. Both were in their mid-twenties, and while followers, had no problem staring down anyone who got near their boss. All of them, including—no, especially—Watanabe, would be armed. He didn't look the type to do much fighting unless he had what he thought was a clear advantage.

When confronting multiple opponents, Quinn preferred to take on the toughest one first. Pig Face would earn that honor. The twins would be next. If they were brothers, they would fight for each other as much as for Sato. That would make them dangerous. Watanabe, last on the list, was not quite a pushover but definitely someone Quinn could handle—as long as he made it through all the others. One good pop in the nose would likely render the man inoperable.

Of course, there would be others where they were holding Miyu prisoner, but Quinn supposed Sato would want his best men with him and leave underlings to guard a mere girl.

A shout went up as the announcer introduced Ortega, a 134-pound bruiser at the heavy end of lightweight class. A crowd of women, some older grandma types and others busty, dark-complexioned women in tight jeans and T-shirts, shouted "Viva Philippines!" over and over as their favorite son climbed into the ring. He wore black shorts with a bright orange belt and matching boots.

A commotion arose on the near side of the ring. Drowning Pool's "Let the Bodies Hit the Floor" began to build over the overhead loudspeaker, buzzing the cardboard program in Quinn's hand. A small army of high school boys, still in their black uniforms, marched in from the dressing room carrying tall purple banners, like those a samurai army might have carried into battle. Each wore a white headband with the Japanese characters for *Hisshou* emblazoned on the front on either side of a rising sun—*Must Win*.

The entire gymnasium broke into raucous cheering as Uta strutted out with his entourage packed around him. He wore black shorts embroidered with a line of pink cherry blossoms.

Only in Japan, Quinn thought, would a boxer allow pink flowers on his trunks.

The crowd went wild after one of the high school boys stepped to the microphone and sang *Kimigayo*, Japan's national anthem.

After a quick introduction of all the judges, the announcer stepped from the ring with his microphone, giving the exaggerated signal for the start as his feet hit ground level.

"Roundo One!"

The first four rounds of the eight-round fight easily went to Ortega. Uta, though a talented enough boxer, was badly outgunned by the taller Filipino and did a mighty job just not falling down.

Quinn let his eyes play around the crowd during the early rounds—scouting, planning. He paid special attention to Sato and the way he worked. A flick of the yakuza boss's wrist sent Watanabe scuttling to a man who sat with his back to the wall, high in the bleachers. He was obviously a bookie. The skinny soldier handed over a long envelope, listened for a moment, then bowed deeply before scuttling back down the bleachers to whisper something to Pig Nose, who in turn whispered the information to Sato.

Up in the bleachers beside the bookie, an attractive middle-aged woman in designer jeans and a fuzzy white angora sweater leaned in to listen for instructions before standing to move ringside. She sat in a vacant seat behind the three judges. She waited for the bell, then leaned forward to whisper something to the man in the middle.

Though the yakuza underboss sat only three chairs away from the cooperative judge, by using a cutout, he was able to communicate his wishes—and thus control the outcome of the fight—without speaking to anyone directly.

By the eighth round Uta had landed some decent body blows, but all the smart money was on Ortega. Sato's smile flickered only briefly during the last ninety seconds of the fight when Uta went down and it looked like he might have a hard time getting up. At the screaming insistence of his coach, the boy crawled to his feet and held up his gloves, nodding to the referee that he was okay to continue.

Sato's smile returned. A minute and a half later, the fight was judged a draw. Even the Filipinos seemed resigned to the decision.

Sato and his men filed out with Watanabe bringing up the rear to collect Sato's winnings from the bookie.

Ayako moved up beside Quinn as soon as they'd gone.

"A draw?" Quinn said, chuckling. "Does anyone really believe that?"

"Uta is Japanese." She shrugged. "And we are in Japan. Come, they're getting away."

* * *

A heavy rain fell outside Kyuden Gymnasium. Car lights bounced off wet pavement, turning the streets into shining rivers of red and white light. Umbrellas blossomed everywhere like black flowers in the night.

Traffic was heavy, and it was a fairly easy task for Ayako's Honda Super Cub to keep up with the two black yakuza Toyota sedans. At first, she insisted that she be the one to drive. It was her bike. Quinn suspected it was because she liked him grabbing her around the waist. The wet roads and Quinn's added weight finally convinced her that she could have just as much fun holding on behind him.

Quinn stayed at least two cars back as the sedans cut through the narrow streets of a residential area, presumably watching for a tail. Looking for other yakuza families after revenge, they didn't appear to notice the angry little prostitute and the American agent looking for answers on the yellow motorbike.

Or, Quinn thought, the yakuza underboss was drawing him into a trap.

"They're going to Nakasu," Ayako shouted over his shoulder, loud so he could hear her above the hissing spray of rain and din of traffic.

"Nakasu?" Quinn repeated. The word meant nothing to him.

"Have you been to Kabukicho?"

"I have," Quinn said. Her helmet bumped against his as he stopped abruptly for traffic. "Crazy place."

Kabukicho was the world-famous red light district of Tokyo, crammed full of hostess bars, massage parlors, prostitutes—and the criminal gangs that ran them. It was not an uncommon occurrence for a drunk salaryman to wake up without his wallet—or worse—after his drink had been spiked.

"Nakasu is like Kabukicho," Ayako said, scrunching in close. "Only more dangerous . . ."

Ten minutes later, Quinn followed the black sedans across the Naka River and onto the island known as Nakasu. Pay-by-the-hour love hotels, clamoring Pachinko parlors, and brightly lit soap-bath establishments lined the twisting streets. Set apart from the rest of Fukuoka, Nakasu was exactly what its name implied, an island in the middle of two rivers.

Men in white tuxedo shirts and snappy black ties stood outside curtained storefronts, hawking the young and tender merchandise they had inside. Girls dressed in abbreviated schoolgirl uniforms stood under umbrellas. Petite costumed maids stood in open overcoats exposing short skirts and laced bustier tops while they handed out brochures among crowds of pedestrians. Flashing neon reflected off their smiling faces and heaving chests, giving the place the frenetic, strobe-light feeling of an entire neighborhood caught in a rave.

"You see something you like?" Ayako chuckled. Her chest bounced against his back as he maneuvered the little bike through the crowds.

"I guess maids are a big deal here in Nakasu," Quinn said, shaking his head.

"Most of those girls will not actually touch you," Ayako said. "Oh, they will call you master and charge you a great deal of money to serve you drinks. I, on the other hand, will touch all you want for a price, but I refuse to call anyone master."

Quinn stopped suddenly, planting both feet to keep the bike upright. He watched as the sedans slowed, then turned to park in an alley behind a two-story wooden structure jammed in among a Lawson convenience store and a shop that sold graphic novels. Rainwater poured off the tile roof, splashing the grimy pavement. The sign out front said the place was a buckwheat noodle shop.

"Of course," Ayoko said, her voice tense. "They would keep her here."

"What is this place?" Quinn asked. He was pretty sure "noodle shop" only scratched the surface.

"If Sato catches any of his men using drugs he requires them to cut off a finger as penance," Ayoko said. "But he has no problem selling such poison to make a profit. I have heard Watanabe talk of shipments from Korea—most likely things like *yao tou*."

Chinese for "head shaking," *yao tou* was the street name for Ecstasy in many parts of Asia.

Down the block, two yakuza wannabes wearing dark tracksuits hustled out with umbrellas to meet their boss and senior leaders in the arriving sedans. Both were boys, Quinn suspected high school dropouts in their late teens.

"This is sort of a middle place for the drugs," Ayako said. "Sato will hold them here before they go out to the dealers." Her eyes narrowed behind the round goggles. "We must be careful. If he keeps his drugs here, he will also have weapons."

"That's a good thing," Quinn said. "I was starting to feel naked."

CHAPTER 44

Five minutes later saw Quinn and Ayako standing beside the sliding wooden door in the alley alongside Sato's noodle shop. The bike was parked safely behind a broken vending machine three buildings away.

"Once this door opens," Quinn said, "we can't slow down. Stay close, but not too close."

The rain had abated some, falling now in a light mist. Ayako took a deep breath, amazingly calm for what they were about to do.

"Sato would have Miyu downstairs where he could keep her quiet," she said. "They will surely send up an alarm as we pass through the noodle shop."

Quinn nodded. "That is why we have to be fast. Your job is to go straight to your niece and protect her. I'll take care of the others. Got that?"

"Got it," Ayako said, her hand pausing at the door. Helmet and goggles abandoned with the bike, her round face shone with the rain. Wet hair clung to her skin. "I counted six plus Sato. That is a great many people to fight your way through."

"It is." Quinn nodded.

If there was a positive side of fighting a large group

of people, it was that they tended to be overconfident. The younger, less experienced ones relied on others to look for threats, while the older hands focused on training their juniors rather than looking outbound as they should.

Pig Face, the man who had been closest to Sato at the fights, would be a different story. There was a reason a man like Sato had survived as long as he had—and Pig Face was in all likelihood that reason. Quinn would fight his way to that one. Incapacitate him and the rest would fall in place, particularly Sato.

"I need Sato alive," Quinn said as Ayako began to slide the door open.

"For a time," she whispered.

A bell tinkled as Quinn stepped through the door and shouldered his way past a set of hanging curtains. The sea-salt smell of warm fish stock and boiled noodles hung heavy on the humid air. A bald man wearing a white apron shouted the traditional Japanese greeting of "*irashaimase!*" Please come in!

The two youngsters in tracksuits stood behind a long, waist-high wooden counter talking to the man in the apron. Trays in hand, they were getting Sato his dinner. Quinn vaulted the counter, hitting the nearest kid in the nose as he moved past. The kid yowled as an entire bowl of steaming noodle soup spilled onto his chest.

The second kid dropped his tray and went for a butcher knife on the counter. His strategy was good but his tactics were slow, and Quinn was able to trap his wrist before he could bring the knife into play.

Quinn had decided before he went in that there would be no talking to anyone but Sato. The overwhelming odds of seven against one made no room for error—or compassion.

He turned the boy's wrist back on itself, snapping the bones and allowing him to grab the blade before it fell. Quinn's attack was brutal, striking the young gangster repeatedly with the knife in the chest and neck, then letting him fall as he turned on his partner.

Half blinded by the pain from a bath in scalding soup, the other man didn't notice Quinn had focused on him until it was too late.

Both men lay dead on the kitchen floor half a heartbeat later, their bodies facedown in a bloody mixture of noodle soup and gore. Quinn looked up at the cook and put a finger to his lips.

"Shhh," he spoke in Japanese. "I will not waste words on men who would keep an innocent girl prisoner for someone else to rape." He turned the knife so the long blade glinted in the stark light of the kitchen. "Are you such a man?"

The cook shook his head, lips clenched into a tight line. "No, no . . . I am but a noodle cook."

"Where is Sato," Quinn hissed, still turning the blade.

The cook glanced toward the back of the restaurant. "Downstairs." He gulped. "There are four others with him."

"And the girl?"

The cook clenched his eyes together, bowing his head. "Yes," he whispered, gulping as if he knew the information would get him killed. "She is down there as well, in a small bedroom directly under the kitchen." He blinked tearful eyes. "Please, show mercy, I beg you. Sato is a violent man. He makes me pay him a percentage of my income for the privilege of having him do business in my shop."

"Leave," Quinn hissed in guttural Japanese. "Leave now and don't look back."

The addled cook was moving before Quinn finished the sentence. He left the sliding door open, exposing the curtains to a torrent of wind and rain.

Ayako stood at the counter, staring down at the two dead teenagers on the floor. "They were bad boys," she whispered. "And would have grown into evil men."

Neither of the dead had a gun, so Quinn kept the butcher knife.

"You would go against four of Sato's men with a kitchen blade?" Ayako gave a smiling nod of approval. "Emiko told me you were such a man."

"It does the job." Quinn shrugged as he made his way to the back of the restaurant. "Remember, your job is to find Miyu."

The stairs leading down to the basement were made of dark, well-worn wood and likely dated back to before World War II. Quinn moved down them with purpose, knowing the creaking steps would take away any chance at surprise.

Years of hunting animals in Alaska had taught him that tentative movement drew attention to itself. Sato and, more important, Pig Face expected the two underlings to bring down noodle soup at any moment. Although they were sure to look up at the approach, they were not likely to arm themselves right away.

An impatient voice came from around the corner as the last stair creaked under Quinn's weight. "Hurry up, you two," the voice snapped, growing closer. It was low, as one might speak to a dog. "The boss is getting impatient—"

Quinn met one of the twins with the point of the butcher knife, driving it deep into the V of his collarbone at the base of the windpipe. He stepped past as the sputtering man sank to his knees. Unable to cry out or do anything more than gurgle, the man's fingers clutched his neck, vainly trying to stanch the spray of blood.

The second twin drew his pistol and did enough shouting for himself and his downed partner. Quinn caught a flash of movement in the corner of his eye. He turned a fraction of a second too late to stop the crashing blow of a glass beer mug as it impacted the back of his head.

Stunned and reeling, he let the knife slip from his hand. He staggered forward, knowing he had to close the distance before the second twin brought the pistol into play. He hit the man with all his force, driving him backward and grabbing the wrist that held the pistol.

Someone hit him again, this time low in the kidney with a series of potent fists that sent waves of nausea through his gut and took him to his knees. The twin with the pistol wrenched away, cursing from nerves and disgust. Strong hands grabbed Quinn by either arm, hauling him to the desk where Sato sat smugly watching the encounter as if he was used to such things happening virtually in his lap. A trembling girl cowered on a cushion behind him, eyes red from nonstop crying. She wore a T-shirt and cutoff jeans, likely the same clothes she'd been wearing at the time she was abducted.

A fist thudded into Quinn's kidney again to get his attention. Unseen hands bent him forward to rub his face against the desk as if trying to smear him into the polished wood. Quinn swallowed hard, trying not to vomit from the excruciating pain in his back.

"Who are you?" Sato said. An air of smug superiority hung over him like a dark cloud. "And more importantly, where are my noodles?"

The man to Quinn's right cackled with laughter at his boss's joke. This must have been the groveling Watanabe whom Ayako had told him about.

Sato gave him an amused grin.

"Really now. Who are you?" He nodded toward Ayako. The surviving twin had both her arms pulled behind her back. "You are with the whore, so I must suppose you have come for my young prize." He wagged a bony finger back and forth. "An unwise move, I can assure you . . ."

A short dagger, not unlike Quinn's blade, Gentle Hand, rested on a small maple stand to the yakuza boss's right. It was mere inches from Quinn's face.

"Trade . . ." Quinn mumbled. He eyed the dagger with his teeth pressed against the desk. His words were slurred, but he could tell from the half grin on Sato's face that he'd gotten the point across.

"What did you say?" The yakuza lieutenant smirked at the fact that his prisoner would even speak, let alone try to bargain with him. He flicked his fingers at the two captors, motioning for them to ease up enough so that Quinn could be understood.

"You are correct, Sato-san." Quinn moved his aching jaw back and forth. He bent in a modified half bow once he was allowed to stand, still wincing from the blows to his back. "We have come to retrieve Miyu-chan. She is not what you believe her to be."

"Oh, I doubt that." Sato smirked. "I believe her to be pure and unsullied by other men—nothing like her filthy tramp of an auntie."

Quinn let out a long, panting sigh. "Then I suppose she is exactly what you believe her to be," he said. "But that does not change the fact that I have come to get her back."

Rough hands still held on tight to his arms. He'd been right about Pig Face; the man held his left arm like a vise. It threatened to cut off all circulation from the elbows down. Watanabe put on a good show but was without a doubt the weak link of Sato's lackeys.

Quinn shot a quick glance at Ayako. She fluttered long lashes and gave him an almost imperceptible nod. He hoped it meant she had control of her own situation and was just waiting for his move.

"Shall we take him to the boat?" Watanabe offered. Quinn could feel a trembling surge of emotion run through the man's hands each time he spoke directly to his boss.

"There is always time to resort to more violent mea-sures," Sato said. He peered at Quinn. "I find myself interested to hear exactly what you believe you have to trade."

"This is a matter of honor." Quinn stood up straighter. "You will return the girl unharmed—and I will cut off a little finger."

CHAPTER 45

Sato leaned back in his chair, arms folded across his chest. On his left hand, he wore a gold ring with a milky white stone. It looked like a human tooth—likely that of some past enemy, Quinn thought. The yakuza underboss looked him up and down.

"Your Japanese is excellent," he said. "Are you European?"

"I am serious," Quinn said, earning another jab to the kidney. He swayed on his feet, waiting for the sickening waves to pass.

"The boss asked you a question," Pig Face said, hitting him again for good measure.

Quinn sagged on his ankles, forcing the two men to work harder to hold him up in front of Sato. He was certain another punch like that would knock him out—and probably send him to the hospital.

"I . . . I . . . am not European," he panted. "Forgive me . . . I knew it was a breach of etiquette to barge into your place, but please understand, Miyu-chan is the niece of my friend. I mean what I say. I will give you a little finger to atone."

"That would be a very interesting thing to witness,"

Sato mused. "You are aware that in my world, one has to make the finger fly himself."

"I understand." Quinn let his head hang down in humility.

"I must admit that we would all enjoy such entertainment." Sato slid the maple stand along with the dagger across the desk. He nodded at Watanabe.

The yakuza soldier released his grip on Quinn and stepped tentatively away. Then, as if he'd done this many times before, he took a white handkerchief from the pocket of his jacket and placed it flat on the corner of the desk. He drew a pistol from his waistband, then slid the dagger so it lay against the edge of the cloth.

Quinn waited for the reassuring pressure of the gun's muzzle against his neck as Watanabe stepped behind him. The closer the weapon was to the target, the easier it was for that target to move out of the line of fire. And, more important, if Watanabe was close enough to touch Quinn, he was close enough for Quinn to touch him back. It was a rookie mistake—and it would cost the man dearly.

Quinn placed his right hand flat on the cloth, fingers spread. He took a deep breath, settling his thoughts— and then slowly picked up the blade with his left. Pig Face followed his movement, continuing to hold his upper arm like he might fly away if released.

"I have seen this done before," Sato said. "Take it from me, you cannot simply saw off a finger. The bone, though small, gets in the way. It must be more of a . . . chop." He turned to Pig Face. "Did not Tanda-kun use a chisel?"

Quinn made his move while Pig Face was busy answering his boss.

Turning his head just enough to get out of the line of fire, he let Watanabe's first round fly past. Quinn lowered his center, stepping back so Watanabe's gun hand extended well over his shoulder before grabbing the wrist and bringing it down in an arm bar, using his own collarbone as a fulcrum. Trapping Watanabe's pistol in his right hand, Quinn brought the dagger in his left hand backward, arcing the flashing blade across the tender flesh of Pig Face's throat. Tendons at Watanabe's elbow crunched. His finger convulsed on the trigger, firing a round into the wall just inches over Sato's head. Pig Face's grip fell away and he sagged to his knees, unable to believe the man he'd just pounded had killed him so quickly.

Quinn wrenched Watanabe's wrist sideways. The pistol clattered to the floor and the man's fingers splayed open. In the same breath, Quinn reached up and hacked off the screaming soldier's extended little finger, letting it thud neatly to the white cloth. Blood arced from the wound, spraying the desk and Sato's face along with it.

Still unsure of what was going on behind him, Quinn stepped under Watanabe's outstretched arm, reversing his wrist and flipping the squalling man over on his head, all the while retaining his grip on the trapped, and now mutilated, hand.

Quinn ducked to grab the pistol before Sato could retrieve a weapon from his desk. A broad smile crossed his lips as he leveled the gun at the yakuza boss. "I never said the offer was for *my* finger."

With both Sato and Ayako now in view, he was able to see that she had stabbed her captor in the side of his neck with a small blade she'd produced from her bra.

The screaming man lay on the floor clutching himself and writhing in a rapidly growing pool of his own blood.

Miyu flung herself toward the safety of Ayako.

"Which one took you?" Ayako asked, brushing a lock of hair out of Miyu's face.

The girl shot a frightened glance at Watanabe, nodding at him.

"You?" Ayako stared wide-eyed at the bleeding yakuza soldier. He leaned against the wall, leg's splayed, clutching his mutilated hand. Without another word, she stepped over and kicked him twice in the groin before he could roll into a tight ball. Head hanging toward the floor in pain and shame, he alternated between whimpers and dry heaves.

Sato set his jaw and clapped his hands in mock applause. "Well played," he said. "But surely a man of your skill did not just come for the girl."

"Perceptive," Quinn said, speaking low Japanese as if he was speaking to a dog, or worse yet, as Sato might speak to a woman. "It is easy to see why you are in charge." Considering the man's past history with Emiko's mother, Quinn wondered what Emiko would do to him now, if she were there.

Ayako removed the thin leather belts from two of the dead yakuza and tied Sato's hands to the arms of his heavy desk chair.

The gangster looked on with detached interest. He must have assumed that if they were going to kill him, they would have done so already. In truth, Quinn hadn't made up his mind.

"I understand you have information about Oda."

Sato blanched white as if his throat and not Pig

Face's had just been cut. Beads of sweat formed on his upper lip at the mention of the man's name.

"You are the underboss of a powerful yakuza family," Quinn said. "Surely you are not frightened of this man."

Sato shook his head. Face was everything to a yakuza chief. Loss of it meant giving up control, and lack of control in his world meant certain death. He breathed deeply as he weighed his options.

Quinn kept the handgun pointed at Sato's chest. "You know where he is?"

"I do not," Sato said.

"Then you are no good to me." Quinn's finger tightened on the trigger.

"Wait!" Sato screamed. "Tanaka is the boss. He would know where Oda is."

"I see." Quinn nodded. "And where do I find this boss of yours?"

"I would have to set up the meeting." Sato's face twitched.

Quinn shot a glance at Ayako, who'd been whispering in the corner with her niece. She shook her head, then stood to stride purposefully to the desk.

Staring down at Sato with a molten hatred unique to tormented women, she leaned in, her lips brushing his ear.

"We saved Miyu," she hissed. "But you will just find another girl and do the same thing to her."

"I—"

"Shut up!" Ayako pressed the point of her dagger to his shoulder. "You take whatever you want with no thought to the suffering you cause. Let me tell you what it feels like to be on the receiving end of such treatment . . ."

Sato's lips pulled back in a tight line, revealing his teeth.

"Such violation is a slow arrow through the heart," Ayako whispered. "First there is a terror, then helplessness—then pain . . ." She pressed the blade home, slowly at first, using the flat of her hand to drive it deep into the fleshy part of Sato's upper arm.

Sato jerked hard against the belts holding his wrists, arching his back as the blade severed nerve and muscle.

Quinn wondered how many helpless young women he'd terrorized, sending them into such spasms as they tried in vain to get away. He touched Ayako's hand when she withdrew the knife and moved to stab Sato again. She wilted immediately. Hand trembling, she let the bloodstained blade clatter to the desk.

Killing a man was no small thing. She'd already done it once tonight, and Quinn wanted to save her from the added memory of another. Sato's black eyes flicked back and forth as he watched the exchange, his body collapsing against the chair when he realized Ayako wasn't going to end him right there.

He should not have relaxed so soon.

Quinn turned to a whimpering Watanabe, who had come to his senses enough to stare wide-eyed at his thrashing superior's treatment at the hands of a woman he paid for sex. Up to now, he'd been so absorbed in his own injuries that he'd paid no attention to what was going on.

Quinn gave him a nod. "I'm assuming you can take us to Tanaka."

"Yes, yes, yes!" Watanabe nodded his head so hard it looked as if he might break his own neck.

"I told you he smelled of urine," Ayako said, looking up from where she comforted Miyu-chan.

Quinn rubbed his chin with the rear sight of the pistol. It was an H&K P30 and fit his hand perfectly.

"Here's the deal," he said. "Go tell Tanaka exactly what happened here. Make sure you tell him we killed six of his guys and whacked your pinkie off with relative ease. Then, tell him I've got his shipment of Ecstasy."

Watanabe looked up, kneeling, both hands flat on the ground in front of him, subservient.

Quinn was tempted to prod him with a foot but didn't want to make the mistake of getting too close unnecessarily. "You understand?"

"Yes, yes," he said. Blood pooled on the floor around his mutilated hand. "I understand."

"You have Ayako-chan's cell number?"

"Yes."

"Then get out of here." Quinn pitched the man his severed finger. "And tell Tanaka he doesn't have forever to get back in touch."

Watanabe flailed to his feet and disappeared up the stairs as if being chased by a ghost.

Suddenly exhausted, Quinn looked around the room at the blood and devastation. The cloying smell of blood and urine filled the basement room.

"Take Miyu-chan ahead." He waved Ayako out the door but kept his eyes focused on a quaking Sato. A picture of Emiko Miyagi as a motherless child flashed across his mind. "I have one more thing I have to do."

CHAPTER 46

Kanab, Utah

Dr. Todd Elton filled a syringe and set the glass ampule on the shelf. A commotion of voices drew him out to the hallway just as Brody Teeples pushed open the door and barged through the clinic like a snowplow. A look of barely contained anger boiled under a heavy, furrowed brow. Huge hands, calloused and used to working outside in the weather, clenched into white-knuckled fists.

Elton considered running, but there was nowhere to go. Three pregnant women took up all the exam rooms, and a guy with a compound fracture in his wrist was sacked out on the table in the X-ray lab. With all the rooms full, patients lined the hallway—a guy who'd been in a fight with a table saw held a piece of his thumb in a wadded paper towel, a man with the perfect imprint of a horse hoof over his collarbone, and a seventeen-year-old high school girl who'd stepped on a rusty nail while going out to bottle-feed her calf. A half dozen more Elton hadn't spoken with yet sat, stood, and slumped up and down the narrow hall.

"I want to see my wife!" Teeples bellowed, ignoring all the other patients. "Where is she?"

Elton put up a hand, forcing himself not to back-pedal. He swam, jogged, skipped rope, and even did a little CrossFit to stay in shape—all good, honest exercises that didn't involve bashing his fists into other people's faces. In a time like this, clean blood work and an excellent body mass index was bound to work against him.

Teeples outweighed him by at least eighty pounds and, judging from his nose, got in a knockdown drag-out fight at the bars nearby at least once a week just for the fun of it.

"I don't even know if she's still alive!" Teeples said, coming to a stop two feet away. "You are gonna take me to her right damn now!" He jabbed the doctor in the chest with a thick index finger at each word.

Elton took a reflexive step back, rubbing his chest. It occurred to him that he'd never really been hit in the face before. Judging by how painful the chest pokes were, he'd be lucky if a full-blown punch with a fist didn't knock him out cold.

Brandy stepped out of one of the exam rooms and moved to help. Elton motioned her to stay back.

"Your wife's over in the hospital, Brody." He raised both hands, hoping it looked conciliatory. "I'm not going to lie to you. She's very sick. It's too dangerous for you to see her right now. Anyway, the CDC is in charge of who comes and goes. Not me."

"I'm going to see for myself." Teeples strode forward, raising his fist and brandishing it like a hammer to make a point. "I don't give a shit what you or the CDC—"

Elton realized he was still holding the syringe. Without thinking, he jabbed it into the man's bicep, giving him the full injection.

Teeples lashed out, but it was fearful instead of vindictive and more of a glancing blow. Still, it caught Elton on the chin and sent him staggering back against the wall. He had to catch himself to keep from falling on the guy holding the severed thumb.

"What the hell was in that?" Teeples bellowed.

"Okay." Elton held up his hands again to ward off any further attack. He worked his jaw back and forth. It wasn't as bad as he'd thought it would be. "Just stay calm. We can fix this."

Teeples's face darkened. "What are you talking about? What did you give me?"

"You'll be fine," Elton said. "As long as we get you treated right away."

"What do you mean treated?" Teeples rubbed his arm. He'd knocked the syringe to the floor and now stared at the bent thing where it lay empty on the carpet. "Treated for what?"

Elton turned to Brandy, gambling that Teeples spent his time fighting in bars rather than watching reruns of *House* and *Chicago Hope*. "I need you to get me ten milligrams of midazolam right away."

Brandy was a good PA and a smart lady, but the stress of the situation had her a little slow on the uptake. "But Doc—"

Elton cut her off. "Just do it before this man goes into anaphylactic shock."

Teeples nodded his big head. "Just do it," he parroted.

"I'm sorry, Brody," Elton said. "You startled me, so I defended myself with what I had in my hand."

"If you made me sick I'm gonna kick your ass!"

"Let's get you treated first," Elton said, struggling to keep his voice steady. "Then we can talk about ass kicking."

"Here you go, Doctor," Brandy said. She handed him the syringe. "This should do the trick."

Ten minutes later, they had Brody Teeples strapped to a wheelchair in the waiting room with an oxygen mask over his face. His head lolled, but he was a big man and it would take a lot of any drug to put him under completely.

Sheriff Monte Young had come to take him into custody for criminal trespass once his breathing had stabilized.

"What'd you use to knock him out?" The sheriff asked.

"Versed." Elton sighed. "We use it during colonoscopies . . ."

"Fittin' "—Young chuckled—"considering the patient."

"I feel all weird," Teeples said, blinking as if he couldn't quite get anything to focus. "I think that doc gave me some bad stuff."

"Hmmm." The sheriff chuckled. "You know when your last tetanus shot was?"

Teeples shook his big head. "Nope," he said.

"About fifteen minutes ago . . ."

CHAPTER 47

Japan

By one in the morning Quinn and Ayako had put an exhausted Miyu on the first train they could find going back to her parents north of Tokyo. Quinn was soaked with rain and limping badly by the time they returned to the apartment. A sickening ache crawled up his spine from his left kidney.

"I insist you take the bed," Ayako said, using the screen of her cell phone to illuminate the door so she could find the lock with the key.

A familiar but almost imperceptible flutter hit Quinn low in the gut. Without taking time to process, he grabbed Emiko's shoulder, stopping her in her tracks. Index finger to his lips, he forgot about the pain and stepped to the side of the door. He took Ayako's hand and pointed the light from her phone at the threshold below. Flecks of mud and grime from the street formed the partial outline of a footprint on the scuffed metal. The yakuza boss had not wasted any time sending someone for his drugs once Watanabe had passed on the message. Ayako had thought no one knew where she lived, but there were too many eyes in a country as crowded as Japan. Information was easy to find, particularly for an organized crime boss with Tanaka's reach.

Quinn eased the pistol out of his waistband, pulling Ayako away from the door as he spoke.

"No, I'll take the couch," he said, keeping up appearances. "I couldn't sleep if I knew I'd kicked you out of your own bed." He leaned in close to whisper something in Ayako's ear. She nodded in the dim light, understanding. Behind her, over the rail of the balcony, a heavy rain fell through the blackness like silver bullets under the bright glow of a streetlamp.

Rather than walk straight into an ambush, Quinn pushed the door open and counted to three. He'd returned the pistol to his waistband so he'd have both hands free. Ayako stood beside him. On three, he gave her a pat on the small of her back.

"Something is wrong," she said at the signal, loud enough anyone inside would be able to hear. Quinn nodded and she ran as fast as she could, passing in front of the open door with a scrambling shuffle of feet on wet concrete. Quinn stood fast, just outside in the darkness.

He didn't have long to wait before three men poured out of the door like bees from a bothered hive, hot on Ayako's trail. The first in line was an older, broad-shouldered man in a red leather blazer. Quinn had seen him earlier at the boxing match, sitting up beside the bookie. The other two were young heavies, probably from the same gym, in need of a little street cred with the local yakuza boss.

"Hey!" Quinn yelled, getting the men's attention.

Lightning flashed, illuminating his face for a split second before he ducked into the open apartment.

All three pulled up short, piling into each other like a Japanese version of Keystone Cops before turning back.

Once inside the door, Quinn grabbed Ayako's bowling pin off the shelf—a tool of opportunity—and sidestepped like a matador. He gave the lead boxer a snoot full of the wooden pin as he barged in, dislocating his jaw and pulling him past to make room for his friends. Quinn caught the next man under the chin with the heavy pin, snapping his head up, then bringing the pin back down to drive him to the floor. It was a devastating blow, and the guy would be lucky if it didn't kill him. Quinn didn't have time to care. It was better than what the men had planned for him.

Finally, the older man with the red jacket charged through the door with his pistol out and ready to shoot. Quinn knocked the weapon to the side with a swipe of the bowling pin, but the man kept coming, shouldering his way inside Quinn's swing before he could hit him again.

The man bellowed a bone-chilling cry. A wicked left hook came out of nowhere, sending a fountain of stars exploding behind Quinn's eyes. His elbow ached from the police dog attack, and the earlier pounding to his kidneys slowed him down. He stumbled, crashing into the coatrack before he caught himself.

The guy in the red jacket hit him when he spun, this time with two straight jabs to the chin. Quinn let his head snap back, blocking the second jab and countering with a right uppercut to the guy's jaw. It was a glancing blow and Quinn's fist slid by with little effect.

Not worried about any Marquess of Queensberry rules, Quinn brought his forearm across his opponent's face on the backswing, snapping his head sideways and stunning the man long enough for Quinn to send an elbow strike into the bridge of the bad guy's nose, pushing him toward the bed.

Rather than fight, the man pedaled backward, reaching behind him for what Quinn supposed was a second gun. Quinn rolled, grabbing the large pillow from Ayako's love seat. He shoved it against the other man's chest as he drew his own pistol, pressing it in tight and pulling the trigger twice in rapid succession. The shots were muffled by the thick foam of the pillow.

Ayako's voice was breathless behind him.

"Oh my . . ." she said softly. "Tanaka-san will soon run out of men."

Quinn let the dead man slump to the ground.

"We can't stay here. He's sure to send more thugs once these don't report back."

Ayako knelt beside her bed and began to stuff clothes into a small duffel. Satisfied she had what she needed, she stood and grabbed a soft-sided guitar case that leaned against the wall.

"A guitar?" Quinn looked at the case.

"You'll see." She slung the case over her shoulder.

Quinn nodded, gritting his teeth. The rush of the fight subsiding, he had to lean against the wall to steady himself amid waves of nausea and pain.

"Come." Ayako touched his shoulder, helping him toward the door. "You need to stop fighting for a few hours. I know a place. It will be drafty, but it is safe."

CHAPTER 48

An old and bent man with a shaved head and the dark robes of a Buddhist monk stood in the shadows under a black umbrella, framed by a heavy timber gate. It was the only apparent opening in a white stone wall that ran in either direction to disappear in the sheets of rain. Weak yellow light from a rusty oil lantern pooled at the old man's feet. A game of Angry Birds on a smartphone illuminated his face as Ayako rode up with Quinn on the little yellow motorbike.

"Kobo-san," Ayako called out. "Thank you for meeting us."

The old man shook his head. He slipped the cell phone inside his robes as Ayako brought the little bike to a crunching stop on the gravel.

"I do not know about enlightenment." Kobo chuckled. "But I feel certain I could achieve a sense of no-thought if I played that silly game long enough." He bowed to Ayako and pulled the gate open, waving them inside.

The sharp odor of burning incense hung on the moist air, hitting Quinn's nose and rousing his tired senses. Tall Japanese cedars stood close together like ranks of towering soldiers in the night. The thin sliver of orange light from the old monk's lantern did little to push back the inky darkness. A steady rain dripped from the high branches in pattering staccato along the wood and stucco wall surrounding the grounds.

Bone-tired and stooped in pain, Quinn trudged behind Ayako as she pushed the little bike through the gate. They followed the crunch of the old man's footfalls in the gravel, down the silver ribbon of gravel toward a small wooden house nestled among the shadowed trees.

"There are quilts and futons inside," Kobo said, shining his lamp toward the dark cottage. Rain poured off the tile roof in a steady stream, hissing to the gravel below. "You may take your rest here."

Ayako began to explain their situation, but Kobo put up his hand.

"Please," he said. "Rest. Reasons do not matter to me, nor should they matter to you. Each of us is in need of a safe haven from time to time."

The monk left the lantern with them and crunched away in the darkness under his umbrella, his path lit only by the Angry Birds launching across his phone.

The cottage, originally meant for itinerant monks, was set well off the main path behind the small Buddhist temple and surrounded by drooping cedars. Towering obelisks of black granite, situated on either side, looked like tall black holes cut out of the night. There was no electricity, and the lamp cast only a hazy orange shadow on the heavy ceiling beams and rough-hewn floor. The place was seldom used, and dust puffed up at every movement. Even Quinn, who was frightened by little in the world, found it impossible not to think of spiders.

Ayako dragged the futon mats from a closet at the far side of the fifteen-by-fifteen room.

"Quinn-san, please," she said, unfolding the futons and situating two hard buckwheat pillows side by side. "You do not look well. I think you should get off your feet."

In truth, Quinn felt as though he might pass out at any moment. The constant optempo since Kim's shooting, coupled with a steady stream of adrenaline, the dog bite, and one savage beating after another, had stacked up to drive him to his knees.

A soft rapping at the door caused him to draw the H&K pistol. Kobo said something Quinn couldn't hear, and Ayako opened the door to retrieve two small sandwich bags of crushed ice.

She closed the door and turned the flimsy lock.

"He saw you are hurt," she said, "and thought some ice might help with the pain."

Quinn stripped off his leather jacket and set the pistol on top of it next to the pillow.

"Ice is probably a good idea."

He sank to the mattress with a long, low groan. The futon was clammy, laden with dust, and filled with lumpy cotton stuffing. Each mattress was roughly six feet long and three feet wide. Barely a few inches thick, they were meant for a springy tatami-mat floor instead of the hard wood of the temple house. Quinn was too exhausted to care.

Ayako knelt beside him. "Please," she said softly, "roll over on your stomach."

The old lamp's tiny orange flame did little to light the room, and Quinn blinked up at her in the darkness.

"What?"

"You are skilled at killing," she whispered. "I am skilled at taking care of the pains of a man. Besides, do you not know the saying 'cold as the heart of a whore'?"

"Your back is badly bruised." She held up the plastic bags, smiling softly. "Kobo has brought us two bags of ice and I offer my cold heart to help heal you."

The intense cold of the ice over his kidney pushed back the worst of the pain almost as soon as Ayako put the bag on Quinn's back. She moved it expertly every few minutes, never allowing any one place to get uncomfortably cold, yet still allowing for the ice to do its job.

"You spoke of a girl who works for Oda," she said, the flat of her hand gently on the bare skin over his kidney, warming it slightly between applications of ice.

"She is supposed to have a tattoo," Quinn said. "A foo dog . . . a komainu, like Oda."

Quinn didn't know how much Ayako knew, so he didn't mention anything about Ran being Emiko Miyagi's daughter.

"I see," Ayako said, her hand trembling at the talk of Oda. Quinn thought of probing a little deeper but decided he didn't have the energy at the moment for such a discussion.

She leaned back, kicking her legs out to one side so her knees were only inches from Quinn's face where he lay against the buckwheat pillow.

She held her ankle with one hand as she spoke. "I believe we each have a moment that we live for. Something very important toward which our entire life is aimed."

Quinn nodded, fighting sleep.

"I am convinced that this is but a detour in your life, Quinn-san." She bit her lip as if she did not want to continue, but felt she must. "My meeting you, to help you in what you and I are doing . . . I believe this may be my one moment . . ."

Quinn reached out to touch the back of her hand that held her ankle. It seemed cruel to leave her sitting there alone in the dark. A tear fell from above and landed on his wrist.

"We have a saying here in Japan," she whispered. "All married women are not wives."

Quinn nodded but said nothing.

"If I had not decided to become a prostitute . . . do you think I would have made a good wife?"

"Of course," Quinn said, blinking back sleep.

She rubbed away the tear on his hand. "I do as well," she said.

Exhaustion crept in like a drug as the ice and Ayako's touch chased away more pain. Quinn jerked, catching himself as he fell asleep.

He was vaguely aware of the warmth of Ayako's body as she crawled in beside him and pulled the musty quilt over them both. His last memory before he drifted off was the smell of cigarettes and the candy scent of her strawberry shampoo. She said something to him, her voice soft and whiskeyed, but he was asleep before it registered as tender.

* * *

Quinn woke six hours later to the sound of the sliding door rattling in the wooden track. Hand on the H&K, he sat up, blinking, working to clear his head. A sickening ache low in his back brought the memories of the night before flooding back to him. Still, the ice and sleep had helped and he was feeling somewhat better.

The door clacked open and Ayako appeared, carrying a pink cloth grocery bag in one hand and her striped helmet in the other. She dropped her keys on the rough timber table and ducked her head toward Quinn in a polite bow.

"You are awake," she said. "I have had no calls yet from that devil Watanabe."

"Tanaka is zero for nine." Quinn yawned, trying to work the kinks out of his spine. "He can't let us continue to kill his men without addressing the problem. Besides, he'll want his *tao tou* back." Quinn returned the pistol to the Transit jacket and fell back onto the futon to stare up at a cobweb on the ceiling beams. "He'll call."

"In any case," Ayako said, "you need to eat. The kitchen here is rudimentary at best. But please forgive my clumsiness. Before you arrived, it was many years since I prepared anything more than a mixed drink for a man." She held up a small wooden box containing four pink skeins of tiny fish eggs. Each skein was about six inches long and the diameter of a small squash. "Emiko said you like Japanese food."

"I do." Quinn nodded, his mouth suddenly watering at the thought of a meal.

"I got *mentaiko*," she said. "Spiced cod roe. We are known for it here in Fukuoka."

"Sounds delicious." Quinn couldn't help smiling as he watched Ayako putter around the simple wooden counter that served as a kitchen in the small cottage. Her hair still hung in damp locks from her shopping trip in the morning rain. She'd slipped off her wet sweatpants and jacket to reveal a pink Hello Kitty T-shirt and loose violet gym shorts that matched the slippers she'd brought in the duffel from her apartment.

The softness of the colors reminded Quinn of an Easter egg. He wondered if she realized that though she worked each day to make herself alluring with costumes and makeup, it was now, fresh from the rain and dressed in plain T-shirt and shorts, that her natural beauty shone through.

Perhaps, Quinn thought, she knew exactly what she was doing and had expertly dialed in on what Quinn found attractive.

"There is a tub in the room behind that screen there." She pointed to the back wall of the cottage, beside the closet where the mattresses had been stored. "I lit the heater earlier, so the water should be hot. Please, go ahead and have a bath. Breakfast will be ready by the time you are finished."

The comforting smell of miso soup filled the cottage as Quinn removed the planks that covered the wooden tub and lowered himself into the water. It was small, thankfully with only room for one, but deep enough to soak all the way to his shoulders. Like most Japanese he'd met, Ayako apparently liked her baths somewhere just south of a rolling boil. Quinn knew he really needed more ice but hurt too bad to care. He kept his movement to a minimum and was soon used to the heat. His ribs were certainly cracked from the boot treatment he'd received from the Fairfax County officer. The beer mug at Sato's had given him a knot the size of a golf ball behind his ear, and his left kidney felt swollen to twice its normal size.

Breathing in the heady aroma of miso and the hint of Ayako, who must have already bathed, Quinn leaned his head back and marveled that he'd lived through yet another day. He was stiff, bruised, and pissing blood, but he was alive. He took a quick look at the H&K pistol within easy reach on the folded towel, then closed his eyes to consider his situation.

He'd been in Japan for less than forty-eight hours and was already beginning to lose count of the casualties he'd left in his wake. Some were a blur, some stood out in vibrant detail. It had taken him five full minutes of scrubbing to get the blood from the night before out from under his fingernails. Someday, there would be a mental reckoning for the things he'd done, the way he lived. Even with good intentions and the weight of the government behind him, repeated violence came with a high price, and he was living on credit. But he'd decided long ago to do his job and let the shrinks worry over him when the time came.

For now, he had bigger things to fret about than any mental collapse on the horizon. He was a fugitive, wanted for murder and escape. They'd probably pile kidnapping on since he'd handcuffed the officers to the signpost. He was hiding out with a Japanese prostitute he hardly knew, was in possession of a pistol he'd stolen from an organized crime boss who wanted him dead, and sitting on a shipment of illicit Korean Ecstasy—not to mention a couple of other items that would be sure to get him five days in the electric chair if the Fukuoka police happened to walk in.

"Ahhh, Veronica," he said under his breath. "If you could see me now." He chuckled and felt the searing heat of the water from even that small movement. Of course Ronnie would be the first person to his mind. He fretted over Kim and agonized over Mattie's safety— but thoughts of Ronnie Garcia were always in front of all else.

Thibodaux was right. It would be a woman that did him in. Thibodaux was right about a lot of things.

Ayako set out a simple spread of rice balls wrapped in seaweed and pickled radish to go with the miso soup and spicy cod roe. Had it not been for the hot bath, Quinn wouldn't have been able to fold himself into position on the cushion at the low wooden table. As it was, he had to move the table to one side of the room so he could lean his back against the wall.

Ayako used the points of her chopsticks to tear a bite-size piece of the red, pepper-flecked *mentaiko* and popped it into her mouth. Quinn followed her example and found it delicious—like the eggs on the outside of a California roll but with more substance.

"I cannot remember the last time I had breakfast with a nice man," she said, waving her chopsticks in small circles as she spoke around a mouthful of food. "Or any man at all for that matter. The men I am with rarely take time with me for the simple pleasures of eating a good meal."

"Maybe you're looking in the wrong places," Quinn

said. He was still exhausted, and probably shouldn't have been so forward, but Ayako seemed to appreciate such direct talk.

"Maybe so." She ate another bite of rice, chewing while she thought. "How about you?"

Quinn took a sip of miso soup, then peered at her over the raised bowl. "What do you mean?"

"Do you ever have breakfast with any nice girls, or just other killers?"

At first, Quinn thought she was joking, or maybe trying to get back at him for what he'd said. But she continued to look at him, eating her rice and blinking dark lashes in earnest curiosity.

"I guess," he said. "Yes, of course I do."

Ayako raised her eyebrows as if she didn't quite believe him. "You and I are a little bit the same, I think." She popped another bite of cod roe into her mouth. "Perhaps we do what we do because we are not much good at anything else."

Quinn laughed. "That could be it."

He supposed Ayako spent a lot of time on her back, pondering the mystery and vagaries of life. Positional prostitutional philosophy, Jacques would have called it.

Ayako pushed away from the small table, rising quickly as if an idea had just occurred to her. She retrieved the canvas guitar case from her side of the sleeping mats and carried it reverently to the table.

She cleared away the dishes and carefully unzipped the case.

"This was my father's," she said, pulling back the lid to reveal a *wakizashi*—the shorter companion sword to a traditional Japanese *katana*. "And his father's before him." She lifted it out, one hand on the black-lacquered sheath, the other cradling the cotton-wrapped ray skin of the handle. "According to the inscription on the handle, this sword was crafted by Mitsunokami Tameyasu over three hundred years ago." She nodded toward the hilt. "The writing on the guard says '*Fujin*'—the Japanese god of the wind."

"Please." She offered the weapon to Quinn, humbly bowing her head when he took it in both hands. "It is somewhat plain. Not as beautifully decorated as more modern *wakizashi*. I suppose my ancestors were austere men."

Quinn grasped the handle and unsheathed the shining blade. Eighteen inches from tip to iron handguard, it sang in his hand as living steel should. There was something about a three-centuries-old weapon that pierced the soul as surely as it cut flesh and bone.

"I wish you to have it, Quinn-san," Ayako said, her head still bowed.

"Oh, no." Quinn slid it back in the sheath with a solid click. He pushed it toward her with both hands. "I couldn't."

"I have no husband," Ayako said. "Who else would take it? The fool Watanabe?" She sniffed. A tear fell on her thigh and she brushed it away with the heel of her hand. "Please. I would like it to go to a good man."

Her cell phone rang, playing a snippet of the pop song by her Korean heartthrob and rescuing Quinn for the moment.

Ayako listened intently, making "emm" and "ehh" noises every few seconds to let the person on the other end know she was still on the line. She'd regained her composure by the time she hung up.

"That was Watanabe," she said. "You were right.

Tanaka has agreed to meet us. He has a warehouse on the harbor, near the commercial docks. We are to meet him there in an hour." Ayako brushed a lock of black hair out of her eyes that were still red from crying. "Something is not quite right. Watanabe sounded too happy. They must be planning something."

"Of course they are," Quinn said. "But so are we."

He moved to return the sword, but she turned away.

"It is yours now." She raised an open hand, showing her palm and refusing any further discussion. Moving to her duffel at the head of her futon, she peeled the pink T-shirt over her head and stepped out of her shorts as if Quinn wasn't leaning against the wall ten feet away. He didn't have time to look away before he caught the telltale shadow of a scar. White against the honey color of her skin, it ran diagonally across her belly, canted from the right of her navel to her panty line. Quinn had plenty of scars of his own and recognized this one as old and too jagged to have been made during a surgery. Turning, he couldn't help wondering if the story behind that scar had something to do with her visceral reaction toward the mere mention of Oda's name.

"I am dressed," she said softly. He heard the sound of creaking wood as she sat back on the futon to put on her socks.

She looked fresh and beautiful in a pair of faded jeans and a loose, gray turtleneck sweater.

"Less . . . whore-like?" She shrugged.

"Stop that," he chided.

"Do you know what a woman wants, Quinn-san?"

"I'm not the man to ask." He wished Thibodaux was there. The big Cajun had barrels of philosophy about women.

"I think most men believe we want to be ravished—swept off our feet." She sat on the end of the bed, one sock on, the other in her hand. "And perhaps some of us do when we are young. But what we really want is to feel safe. Every day I feel excitement, fear, sadness, anger, and sometimes, believe it or not, even desire . . . but safety is something I have not felt in a very long time—until now."

Quinn did not know what to say, so he said nothing.

Tears ran down her cheeks. She sat on the futon and hugged her knees to her chest, giving a tiny nod toward Quinn's hands. "Please, I beg you to accept the sword. Its value is far less than the gift you have given me."

Quinn held it up in both hands, bowing at the waist, thanking her.

"In fact"—she leaned over to tug her other sock over a tiny foot—"bring it with us. Where we are going, the ferocious god of wind may be welcome assistance."

CHAPTER 49

Quinn was surprised to see a metallic red Honda Blackbird parked on the gravel pad in front of the temple cottage beside Ayako's yellow bike.

"We would never have been able to get away from Tanaka on my little bike." She smiled. "And this is more suited to your riding style."

Quinn stepped up to the motorcycle. It was enough to make him momentarily forget how bad he hurt. "Where did you get this so early in the morning?"

"I stopped to see a client before he left for work," she said. "He has allowed us to borrow it for a while."

"Now we're talkin'," Quinn said in English.

Ayako gave him a quizzical look.

"My brother had one of these when we were younger." Quinn fell back into Japanese. "It brings back memories."

"I thought you would approve," Ayako said.

He ran a hand down the Honda's aggressive fairing and across the smooth arc of the fuel tank. If his BMW GSA was the Hummer of motorcycles, the Honda Blackbird was the stealth fighter. He didn't care for the two side luggage cases on this particular bike, thinking they detracted from the sinister look. But they served a purpose and made a good hiding spot for the two pink shopping bags he'd borrowed from Ayako's kitchen cupboard when they'd cleared out after the altercation with Tanaka's men.

Carrying the short sword in the soft-sided guitar case would keep them from getting stopped by any curious patrol officers. For a country steeped in a history of warfare and weaponry, Japanese police got twitchy if they thought someone was riding around with a sword slung over their back.

Once everything was stowed, Quinn swung a leg over the big bike and planted both feet to steady it. He wore the borrowed helmet and his leather jacket against the weather and any possible crash.

Ayako climbed on behind him and scrunched up closer than she probably had to. Her thighs ran tight alongside his, arms wrapped around him, body pressed flat to his back.

"All set?" he asked over his shoulder.

"All set." She gave his belly a playful pat.

Quinn pushed the ignition button and brought the Blackbird's 1100 CC engine to growling life. The throaty purr begged him to roll on the throttle.

"You know what I love about this bike?" he asked.

"I do not." She shook her head, letting her helmet bump the back of his.

"It runs as good as it looks," he said.

"The same could be said of you, Quinn-san." Ayako gave him another squeeze.

Quinn groaned within himself. She might very well feel safe, but this girl was as dangerous as any yakuza gangster.

* * *

Tanaka's dockside warehouse was a perfect location to be chopped into pieces and carried out to sea in a fishing vessel. To avoid a soupy end, Quinn made a short detour to a small Shinto shrine on a wooded hill a little over two miles away. He left one of the pink grocery bags there, tucked safely behind a flat granite monolith in a thick stand of bamboo.

The last thing he planned to do was meet Tanaka in his space, on his terms. Instead, he used a favorite technique he'd learned from an old salt when he'd first joined OSI and was assigned to the Crim unit—criminal investigations.

Thieves stuck with thieves, drug dealers hung with other drug dealers. Informants were, more often than not, steeped in the criminal culture. Good guys rarely had information on bad guys. That was the nature of the beast. Meetings with people on the other side of the law were ticklish at best and could turn deadly in the blink of an eye.

It was an inviolable rule that Quinn would pick the location of any meet with an informant. If a snitch called him for a meeting, Quinn would send him to a second location. Then, if things didn't smell right on his arrival, Quinn might drive by and have the snitch follow him to a third—in a sort of rolling meet.

Quinn's only chance of finding the woman who shot Kim appeared to be a heart-to-heart with Tanaka. Aborting this meeting was out of the question. It might get tricky, but he could move the location to make it more likely they would survive.

A flock of gulls fought over trash among a flotilla of boats to Quinn's right as the red sport bike thumped along the heavy timber pier and onto the frontage road that led along the water's edge. The smell of salted fish, diesel, and a hint of soy from some galley blew in on a stiff sea breeze. It was the smell of the Orient, and Quinn imagined that on some days it would be possible to smell Korea on that wind—or even China.

Ayako gave him a nervous squeeze when they neared a boxy metal warehouse bearing Tanaka's name and his lotus leaf insignia. Quinn felt her squirm behind him, as if she had to go to the bathroom. Two Toyota Crown sedans, glossy black against the gray mist, sat outside the yawning bay doors of the huge building.

Ayako's grip grew tighter. Quinn flinched, gritting his teeth as she squeezed his ribs and kidneys. Thankfully, the nausea ebbed quickly. He imagined broken blood vessels leaking inside his body in tiny spurts each time he breathed or took a step. He needed to see a doctor, but calling in sick wasn't really an option at the moment—so he rode on.

Ten of Tanaka's men lined the short driveway in front of the Toyota Crowns. Five on either side, they stood shoulder to shoulder, roughly three feet apart, in a modified parade rest. Their hands were clasped in front of dark business suits. Watanabe stood far back, nearest to the warehouse doors. He had apparently delivered the message just as Quinn had directed. Tanaka had put his heavy hitters out front to set the tone. Every man was fit and thickly built, like tree trunks and boulders in neckties. Pistols bulged under their coats. All wore dark glasses, despite the overcast sky.

Quinn passed the yakuza soldier nearest the road at the mouth of the driveway, then leaned the Blackbird into a quick U-turn—so he ended up facing the way he'd come. He toed the transmission into first gear on the way down, planting both feet on the rain-slick pavement. He flipped up the visor on his helmet. Ayako carried the H&K, and he could feel the gun's comforting imprint where she held it sideways between them against his spine, tucked out of sight.

"You have Tanaka-san's property?" the nearest man barked. He looked to be a cardboard cutout of what a yakuza gangster was supposed to be. Short hair, stern, slender with an impeccable dark suit. Raindrops spattered his sunglasses. His face hardly moved as he spoke.

"Of course not," Quinn answered in the same, rough Japanese. "I am not foolish."

The yakuza grunted as if he'd thought as much, then motioned toward the open twin doors of the warehouse, beyond the gauntlet of toughs.

"Tanaka-san is expecting you."

Quinn reached over his shoulder with his right hand to grab the remaining pink shopping bag from Ayako.

"Give him this." Quinn extended his hand.

The yakuza soldier took a half step back, then caught himself. All the men along the drive perked up at the unknown contents of the bag. Hand grenade attacks among warring families were not unheard of in this part of Japan.

"Relax," Quinn said. "I want to talk to him, not kill him. But I don't want him to kill us, either, so I'm not meeting him here."

"What then?" The man gave a worried frown. It would be his fault if something happened to mess up the meeting at his post.

"Have him meet me at the shrine two miles up this road," Quinn said. "He has five minutes to get there or I'm gone."

"Tanaka-san does not take orders!"

"Consider it an invitation, then." Quinn shrugged. "Tell him he can bring two of you with him for protection if he wants."

"Ha!" The gangster scoffed. "Protection from who?" Stifled laughter went up and down the lines of suited men.

"Me." Quinn dumped Sato's severed head out of the pink bag. It hit the wet asphalt, thudding like a green melon. The nearest yakuza soldier retched as the awful thing rolled across his shoe, wrinkled mouth open in a dead man's yawn.

"He has five minutes." Quinn snapped his visor shut and revved the throttle.

Before any of Tanaka's men could react, he poured on the gas. One hundred and forty horses spun the Blackbird's rear tire on the pavement, sending up a plume of white smoke. He leaned forward to keep the bike from rising into a wheelie as it shot down the road like a low-flying jet.

She was surely aware of the danger, but Ayako snuggled in tight behind him, squealing in his ear like a child on a carnival ride.

CHAPTER 50

Deputy Bowen woke up to the scream of landing gear on the tarmac and a three-year-old Vietnamese boy kicking the back of his seat like he was trying to stomp a snake.

Bowen rubbed the sleep from his eyes and moved his neck from side to side in a vain attempt to work out the inevitable kinks brought on by the fourteen-hour flight between Dulles and Tokyo. He was still astounded that he'd been allowed to even make the trip. Normal protocol was to send a written lead to investigators in the country where a fugitive was suspected to be. But evidently, Director Carroll realized someone like Jericho Quinn required measures beyond normal protocol if they intended to capture him.

Bowen opened the sketch pad in the seat pocket and looked it over while the plane taxied to the gate. There was a pencil study of Quinn, boxing, the way Bowen remembered him. A quick figure study of Ronnie Garcia—he couldn't help that—and a faceless sniper hiding in some weeds. Drawing helped him work through things—and the good Lord knew he had plenty to work through.

Bowen grabbed his tan BLACKHAWK! daypack—his only luggage—from the overhead compartment and shuffled off the plane with the other passengers.

A willow-thin Delta attendant he'd chatted with during the flight met him at the door. She'd ducked into the bathroom just before landing to straighten her hair and apply a fresh coat of lipstick that matched a bright red uniform dress. Extending her hand, she passed him a cocktail napkin with her cell number, thanking him sweetly as she did all the passengers when they walked by.

She'd invited him over to try his hand at drawing her, but she was far too needy to be his type. He smiled though, knowing the chances of her being on the return flight were good enough that he didn't want to make her mad.

He had plenty of other things to worry about without getting tangled up with some flight attendant first rattle out of the box—like navigating his way in a country that didn't use the alphabet.

Thankfully, all the signs leading him through the arrival process were in English as well as the unintelligible chicken scratches that were Japanese. With all the fearmongering in the news lately about plagues and zombie viruses, the medical screening queue was the first obstacle for entry.

What looked like a large tripod-mounted camera faced newcomers as they passed through a small turnstile just outside the jetway. A sign above advised that authorities were checking the temperature of all arrivals and apologized for the intrusion.

Immigration was next, where a fatigued-looking but overly polite woman with a Buster Brown haircut checked Bowen's passport and inserted an entry visa stamp. She took a photo and he had both index fingers printed before the lady dismissed him to move on toward baggage claim.

Since all he had was a carry-on, Bowen made it to the Customs counter quickly. He gave the most innocent smile he could muster and handed over the declaration form he'd filled out on the plane, promising he wasn't a drug mule or an international money launderer.

An express train from Narita took him on the one-hour ride to yet another airport in downtown Tokyo, where he stood with his ticket long enough a half dozen people came up to offer him help. He came to the conclusion that navigating in Japan wasn't that difficult if you didn't mind standing around a few minutes looking hopelessly lost.

Roughly twenty-four hours after he'd left his home in Alexandria and three hours after touching down in Japan, Bowen walked through the exit gates at Fukuoka-Hakata Airport. He'd never seen a photograph of the man he was supposed to meet but recognized him instantly by the unwavering look of challenge, common to those who carried a badge for a living. *I'm a cop*, the look said. *And you're not.*

"Agent Bowen?" the Japanese policeman said, cocking his head to one side. He wore dark slacks, a white shirt and tie, and a light tan golf jacket. His hair was cut in a longish flattop, as if Bowen had commandeered him on his normal day to go to the barber.

"*Deputy* Bowen," he said, remembering to bow like Geoff Barker had taught him. "U.S. Marshals, Eastern District of Virginia."

"I am Hase," the man said. He pronounced it Hah-say.

"Pleased to meet you," Bowen said. Barker had tried to teach him some phrases, but languages had never been his thing so he didn't hazard a try. He'd been told there were long drawn-out meeting rituals in Japan. If that was the case, Detective Hase must have taken pity on him.

"You have no other bags?"

Bowen held the daypack aloft. "Nope," he said. "This is it."

Detective Hase gave another deep bow, then extended a hand toward the door. "Very good. I understand you want to speak with Shimizu Ayako."

"I do," Bowen said, stifling a yawn.

Hase looked at the Seiko dive watch on his wrist. "It is five past nine. It will be somewhat difficult to check into your hotel this early, but if you would like to stop by—"

Just then, a woman shoved her way past, marching toward the automatic doors. She looked to be in her late twenties and wore tight, stylish jeans, a flimsy chiffon blouse that hung off one shoulder, and black stiletto heels. A crying boy who looked no older than six tromped along behind her, tears streaming down a pudgy face. He wore little blue short pants and a white polo shirt. A black leather school pack, weighed down with books, hung over his back.

Bowen had no idea what she was saying, but the woman, presumably the kid's mother, berated him at every step. She flung her arms for effect, oblivious to the embarrassed looks and sidelong glances of everyone else in the terminal at such un-Japanese behavior.

The boy tried to make his case through his tears. Whatever he said infuriated his mother, causing her to turn on him like an angry bear. She marched back to where he stood, jabbing him in the heaving chest with a manicured finger.

Bowen's chest tightened. "What's her problem?"

"I do not know." Hase shook his head. "She is a very rude woman."

"What is she saying?" Bowen's eyes locked on to her. So far, she'd not noticed.

"The boy missed his train for school, making her late to meet someone here," Hase said. "He says it wasn't his fault but she doesn't believe him. I'd like to intervene, but she has not struck the child so my superiors would not approve . . ."

Bowen stepped deliberately between the ranting woman and the boy while Hase was still talking, stooping to rub away the tears with his thumb. The kid's eyes flew wide at the sight of a big American with a goatee. His lips trembled until Bowen handed him a little silver lapel pin shaped like a Marshal badge.

"Tell him I'm a policeman from the United States," Bowen said.

Hase translated, obviously happy to do something to stop the woman's tirade.

The little boy spoke through his sniffles.

"He says thank you," Hase translated.

"You tell him that his mother will probably whip him because we stepped in," Bowen said. "But he will always know that there were two people here today who knew the way she was treating him was wrong." He looked up at Hase. "Can you translate that exactly?"

The detective grinned. "If she complains to my

bosses, I'm blaming this on the crazy marshal, you know."

"Fine by me," Bowen said. "Just tell him."

By now a crowd of Japanese women had gathered to publicly chastise the woman. Hase spoke to her for some time, even raising his own voice before sending her on her way. The boy turned to wave at Bowen as he walked out the terminal doors. He had already pinned the little badge to the collar of his shirt.

"That is the most fun I have had in some time," Detective Hase said, following the woman with a hard gaze. "I think I like you, Deputy Marshal August Bowen. Are you this way at all times?"

"Pretty much." Bowen shrugged. "It's a problem I have."

"How do you ever get anything done if you stop to help everyone you see?"

"Like I said," Bowen said with a sigh, "it's a problem."

"It is a good problem, I think," Hase said. "So, we were speaking of your hotel."

"I'm fine," Bowen said. "My brain's just not sure what time it is. If you know where Shimizu is right now, I'd rather go see her. To tell you the truth, I haven't even gotten reservations at a hotel yet."

"I can assist you with that." Detective Hase smiled. "Please." He bowed again, looking at Bowen as if he was still trying to figure the deputy out. "My car is outside. Ayako Shimizu's apartment is nearby."

CHAPTER 51

Quinn was off the bike and running moments after the side stand hit the ground, the H&K pistol in one hand, the guitar case containing the short sword in the other. Ayako followed close behind, bounding up the wide gravel path.

Rising on square terraces of rough-hewn timber filled with gravel that were spaced just far enough apart to keep them from reaching a full sprint, the path ran from the small parking lot through the Shinto torii gates that resembled a red wooden pi symbol with two horizontals, then wound through the thick cypress woods and bamboo forests that protected the temple itself from the hubbub of the nearby city.

Ground fog flowed like bony fingers between moss-covered logs and boulders the size of small cars, reaching out from the tumbledown forest. Rain dripped from every tree and bush. Engraved stone monoliths, some over fifteen feet tall, rose on either side of the path, shining in the wet air as if polished. Pungent smoke from burning incense hung in a hazy layer among the trees.

Quinn had always thought Japan took on an ancient

look when wet with rain. It was a surreal and beautiful place, but thankfully, the weather was inclement enough that the grounds were deserted.

Quinn sent Ayako with the pistol to stand at the edge of the bamboo thicket twenty feet away from where he would make his stand. She assured him that she knew how to shoot, so he took her at her word. It calmed him some when she grabbed the slide and press-checked the chamber, assuring herself a round was in the tube. Finger alongside the trigger guard, she trotted away toward the bamboo holding the pistol as if she'd been born with it in her hand.

Quinn leaned the unzipped guitar case against the monolith and positioned the short sword so it would be easy to retrieve, then took a position with his back to the flat surface. The weatherworn inscription on the smooth stone was fitting.

Duty is heavy as a mountain—death, light as a feather.

Tanaka Isanagi arrived three and a half minutes later.

The yakuza boss didn't so much walk up the gravel path as he materialized through the swirling fog and incense smoke. Well into his sixties, he was slender with a long face and wild, untrimmed black eyebrows that stood in stark contrast to the gleaming skin of his bald head. He'd removed his suit coat, demonstrating to Quinn that he was unarmed—and unafraid.

Two of the gangsters from the warehouse walked a few steps behind, spread out to make themselves more difficult targets. Both wore dark Ray-Ban sunglasses, despite the overcast sky. Watanabe slouched along behind the trio, limping along in the rear as he nursed a bandaged hand.

"I told your man you could bring *two* bodyguards," Quinn said as the yakuza boss drew closer.

"Surely you do not count Watanabe-kun?" Tanaka scoffed. "If he is a burden I will order him to kill himself immediately."

Watanabe stopped in his tracks, eyes terror-stricken.

"That won't be necessary," Quinn said.

Tanaka stopped, but the two guards kept walking toward Quinn, closing the distance fast.

Quinn shot a glance at Ayako, shaking his head. It was important to keep the upper hand, but he didn't want to kill anyone until he had some answers.

"Seriously," he said. "These are the best two you have?" One of the men was the hulking bruiser he'd already met when Sato's head rolled across his shoe. The other was a taller man with dark, seventies-style sideburns and a thick, black mustache. Quinn guessed he probably had some Russian in his ancestry.

"They need to search you," Tanaka said. "For my safety."

Quinn raised his hands as if to comply, then kicked the big bruiser in the crotch. The two men were close, and Quinn was able to pivot slightly and slam the arch of his foot against Sideburns's knee, driving him into a screaming heap on the ground. Quinn crouched to avoid a flailing roundhouse from the bruiser, snatching the sheathed short sword from the case.

Quinn brought the tip of the lacquer scabbard straight up, letting it slam against the bruiser's chin, driving his gaping mouth shut with a satisfying crack of tooth and jaw.

The man's eyes rolled back in his skull, showing their whites.

Sideburns reached under his suit for a pistol, but Quinn ripped the scabbard from the sword and stepped in, letting the razor-sharp point hover just above the knot of the man's tie.

Quinn glanced up at Tanaka. "How about if I just tell you what weapons I have?"

Tanaka flicked his hands toward his defeated men, motioning them back behind him. A bemused look crossed his long face.

"Do you know why I came to see you," the gangster said, looking Quinn up and down.

"Because I have your shipment of *yao tou*?"

Tanaka flicked his hand again, dismissing the notion. "Though I will appreciate the safe return of my property, there is plenty more where that came from. I did not follow you here for that. I came because you are the most interesting thing that has happened to me in twenty years. You Americans say the pen is mightier than the sword. We Japanese say *bunbu ichi—pen and sword in accord*. When I began this life it was filled with acts of courage and violence. Now, my world has become that of a common businessman." Tanaka leaned in as if to confide a secret. "Too much pen and not nearly enough sword for me—until now."

"I'm glad I could help you out."

"Oh, make no mistake"—Tanaka wagged his finger back and forth—"we are not friends. Much of what will make my life interesting will be deciding how I am to kill you without losing too many more men. I do not, of course, count Watanabe as any loss."

The yakuza underling hung his head in shame.

"Too bad for your men," Quinn said, smiling sweetly.

"Your Japanese is excellent," Tanaka said.

Quinn glared at the man, losing patience. "How about we get this over with? You tell me what I need to know and I tell you where to find your drugs."

"Very well." Tanaka opened both hands in front of him, book-like, ready to talk.

"I am looking for the woman who shot my wife."

Tanaka scoffed. "A high-minded endeavor for a husband who keeps company with this whore . . ."

Quinn let the comment slide off. He had more important things to do than bandy words with an organized crime boss.

"I believe her name is *Ran*," Quinn said.

Tanaka's eyes flashed momentarily, then settled again, a dark pool disturbed by a stone. He knew her.

"Long hair," Quinn added. "Attractive, but very dangerous. Probably tattooed—"

"I know that girl!" Watanabe nodded vigorously. "She punched me in the throat."

"Somehow"—Tanaka shook his head in disgust as he glared at his quivering thug—"I find such a thing easy to believe." He turned to Quinn. "I was informed you are looking for Oda."

"I believe this woman works for him," Quinn said. "I find one, I find the other."

"Perhaps." Tanaka sniffed, quickly, lips pursed and pointed on his long face, like a bald rat. "But perhaps it is not so easy. Do you know anything about this man?"

"Not enough, I'm afraid," Quinn said. He was looking for information, so he might as well be honest.

"He leads an organization he calls *Kuroi Kiri*." Tanaka raised a bushy eyebrow. "Do you know the term?"

"Black Mist," Quinn said. "Dark deeds . . ."

"Precisely," Tanaka said. "Extremely dark deeds. He

is like something out of an old samurai movie. The men and women who work for him are *ronin*, hired blades who sell their services to the highest bidder. Few people know exactly where Oda lays his head. Otherwise, he would not have kept it on his shoulders for so long."

"But you know?"

Tanaka shook his head. "I would tell you if I did. A short time ago, he murdered one of my men during some business dealings. At that time he had taken the position on the governing board of Yanagi Chemical here in Fukuoka—"

"What?" Watanabe's mouth hung open. "That is the man you are looking for? I could have told you this and saved us much trouble."

Tanaka shot a withering stare toward the interruption. "I have a suspicion that trouble would find you no matter what." He half turned, looking directly at Quinn and conspicuously ignoring the whimpering stooge. "I must tell you, Oda is like lightning—rarely in the same place twice, and surely not for very long. But perhaps Yanagi Chemical would be a good place to begin."

Quinn nodded slowly. "And how do I know you have not set up a trap for me at Yanagi?"

"I suppose you do not." Tanaka clasped his hands in front of him. "But, I have no great love for Oda. As you can imagine, my organization might often find itself at odds with such a man. I would consider it a great favor indeed if you would kill him for me. If not, then he will kill you for me."

CHAPTER 52

Oda shoved the trembling girl aside at the interruption of the ringing telephone. Barely thirteen, she was a new addition to his stable. She was attractive in her own way—sturdy shoulders and strong cheekbones—but looks had deceived him. He remembered when females didn't melt to mush at a little physical pain. There was a time when girls like this were tough, able to withstand a bit of correction and stand up to the rigors of the life he demanded. Such a young and vibrant woman would have been putty in his hands, moldable into whatever he wanted her to be. Now, it seemed, the entire gender were no more than chalk, crumbling to dust at the slightest cuff or kick. This one had wept like a baby at the mere sight of his tattoo.

"Get out!" he growled before picking up the phone. Naked, the whelp whimpered pathetically as she opened the sliding paper door and limped out, dragging her robes with her.

Oda snatched up the phone, looking at the number.

"What is it?" He kept his voice dismissive. With the idiot Tanaka it was important to set a standard from the beginning of any conversation. He had no time for second-rate gangsters who held to old ways that were fast getting them marginalized by virtually ever facet of Japanese society.

"Ah, Oda-san," Tanaka said, "thank you for taking my call."

"You are either calling to apologize or to threaten me. I am interested to hear which, for it will dictate what I do once we are finished."

"It is neither, I'm afraid."

"Very well," Oda said, "that may also dictate certain actions."

"I only wish to be of assistance." Tanaka spoke quickly, risking interruption in order to keep Oda from giving any edicts he'd feel obliged to keep. "A man came to see me looking for you. I believe he will pay you a visit as well."

"And how would he know where to look?"

There was a long silence—a liar's pause—before Tanaka answered. "I fear one of my men may have given him some information before this man killed him."

"How very convenient that the man who betrayed me is dead," Oda said, his voice cold, snakelike.

"As soon as it came to my attention, I called to warn you," Tanaka said.

"Describe this man." Oda knew who it was before the yakuza boss told him.

"An American, I think," Tanaka said. "Dark—both in features and demeanor. He has killed before. I am certain of that."

"Thank you for the notice, Tanaka-san," Oda said. "I will look forward to his visit with much pleasure."

Oda ended the call and tossed the phone on his desk. He was not frightened of Jericho Quinn. But it was a mark of failure in his organization that the man was still alive and had gotten this far.

Certainly as head of the organization it was his fault that Quinn had been left alive for so long. His fault because he had left the job to others. Failure was one thing he would not tolerate. Someone would have to atone for this—and since he did not feel like punishing himself, he knew exactly where to begin.

CHAPTER 53

Governor Lee McKeon paced in front of the window of the cheap motel. It was impossible to sit still while he discussed weighty matters.

Qasim Ranjhani sat on the bed, leaning against the far wall. In contrast to McKeon's nerves, Ranjhani's hands were folded serenely in his lap. The governor had big ideas and the will to see them through, but for the most part, it was Ranjhani who worked the trenches. It was he who got his hands dirty while McKeon played the concerned politician. Years before, and under another name, McKeon had gotten his hands dirty as well.

The motel was located on Portland's east side, off 82nd Avenue, well off the beaten path. The desk clerk stunk of cheap bourbon and was unlikely to even know there was a governor of Oregon, let alone what he looked like. McKeon was fairly certain someone from his Oregon State Police protective detail had followed him discreetly, but that could not be helped. This particular motel was known as a place for illicit affairs, particularly with other men. All the entries were from an inside hall, and several people had arrived at roughly the same time as McKeon. Unless they booted his door, anyone who had defied his order and followed him anyway would have no idea who he happened to be meeting with. Rumors of an affair he could weather, even an affair with another man—but if they'd known what he was actually planning, the men protecting him would have shot him on the spot.

"So," McKeon said, fairly giddy with the possibilities. "We are actually going to do this?"

"So it seems, my friend. So it seems." Ranjhani was cool and matter-of-fact. To talk of killing thousands to this man was to talk of killing a common fly.

"Do you believe they will all leave at once?"

"That depends on U.S. military response," Ranjhani said. "The illness takes a week or so to develop. Most will think any initial symptoms are merely a reaction to the live virus vaccine."

"Brilliant." McKeon nodded.

"Oda has forty thousand units of vaccine for the American soldiers in Afghanistan and another fifteen thousand for Kuwait." Ranjhani paused. "At your request, we have orchestrated a small outbreak to stir up emotion in South Korea. Roughly a hundred ninety-five thousand units are waiting in cold storage for shipment to the United States, but I suspect officials will rob some of those for their twenty-eight thousand troops in Seoul."

Ranjhani was quiet for a time, allowing the governor to do the math.

"And what of Oda?" McKeon gave a long, thoughtful sigh. "I was under the impression he undertook this task in order to get American troops out of Japan."

"There is a particular beauty in the domino effect of

all this," Ranjhani said. "When thousands of their emergency personnel begin to sicken and die, the U.S. government will have no choice but to recall overseas troops. It is difficult to be the world's policeman if your own home is on fire."

McKeon smiled. In a matter of hours, eighty thousand U.S. soldiers, sailors, airmen, and Marines and over 160,000 Americans—mainly medical and law enforcement personnel—would be vaccinated as "first responders." Soon afterward, they would find that they were dying. South Korea would be left alone. American citizens would realize that their own government had spread the deadly virus. Conspiracy theorists would, at long last, be proven correct. The Middle East would be purged of infidel invaders as remaining troops rushed home to take care of a collapsing nation.

The governor held his breath, thinking through the details.

"It hinges on the tests." McKeon's voice clicked with tension.

"It does." Ranjhani shrugged. "But the American officials are under tremendous pressure to approve a cure. The woman the CDC sent to Japan has already received two calls Oda believes came from the White House. Photographs of the sick flood the Internet, but just to push things along we have seeded several forums with the idea that the U.S. administration is conspiring with Japan to hold back the new vaccine in order to tamp down population growth."

"Brilliant," McKeon said, laughing, running a hand over his long face.

"Oda has given me assurances," Ranjhani went on. "The tests will go as we have planned. Japan, after all, is no enemy. Why would they produce anything to hurt the United States?"

McKeon took a deep breath, addressing the elephant neither man had mentioned. "And what of our American agent? It sounds to me as though he could still pose a major problem."

"Ah." Ranjhani sighed. "I suppose Quinn proved useful in establishing Drake's credibility. He is apparently in Japan looking for Oda and the girl who shot his ex-wife. He knows nothing of the vaccine, and, in any case, Oda assures me Quinn will be sorted out within hours."

"That is welcome news." An infectious grin spread across McKeon's face. "It is all happening as my father predicted. Allah willing, in a very short time, the world we live in will be a very different place."

"Ahh," Ranjhani said. "That it will, my friend, *insh'Allah*." He popped the latches on a scuffed aluminum briefcase that sat on the table before him. Inside were two simple boxes of polished wood, each a little smaller than a brick. "And that brings me to my real reason for coming to this country of infidels."

CHAPTER 54

Bowen and Hase were greeted by two men carrying a heavy roll of carpet down the stairs from Ayako Shimizu's apartment. Each wore a light blue tracksuit and Ray-Ban sunglasses. The lead man, slightly older than his partner, had a ponderous belly, and the sagging load caused him to grunt and sweat as he shuffled along. When he saw Detective Hase, he dropped his end and ran. Unsupported, the carpet fell out of the second man's hands and unfurled on the damp pavement, revealing the body of a man in a red leather jacket.

"You want me to go after the runner?" Bowen asked. There was no hurry. The fat guy was running slow enough Bowen could have stopped for a cheeseburger and still caught him before he got out of sight.

"Do not bother." Hase sighed. "I know him. I am much more interested in what is upstairs."

Hase ordered the second man, a young yakuza soldier named Kono, to sit on the curb. Amazingly, he complied, hanging his head between his knees, waiting obediently to be carted off to jail.

There was another body in the apartment, another

yakuza soldier, according to Hase. This one displayed a cracked skull, apparently caused by a sudden collision with the bloody bowling pin that lay on the floor beside the body.

Three distinct pools of blood stained the wooden floor. One next to the dead man's ear, another beside a pillow with the stuffing blown out of it, and third, just inside the door. Either there had been a third body or someone had survived.

Bowen looked around the apartment—a neatly folded towel next to a pile of crumpled laundry, a blanket and sheet in perfect order amid a chaos of bedclothes, a set of dishes sorted and stacked beside the sink full of crusted bowls and pots—all but screamed the obsessive-compulsive behavior of an Air Force Academy cadet.

"He was here all right," Bowen said. "We find the woman, we'll find Quinn."

Detective Hase looked up from his cell phone. "I concur," he said. "Crime scene investigators will be here any moment. Ayako-san has a certain client who, I believe, will tell us where to find her."

CHAPTER 55

Munakata

Shimoyama Takako sensed his presence as she approached her front door. She was dressed traditionally as she always was in a lavender kimono with a foam green belt and a darker green coat. The neighbors in her upscale suburban neighborhood believed she dressed this way because she taught flower arrangement or the tea ceremony. They could never know it was because her employer—the man she loved and so desperately wanted to please—required it.

She knew she should turn and run. But what good would that do? He would only catch her and she would look a mess. One did not run from Oda any more than a bee flew away from honey. Though he was surely there to chastise her—or even worse—Takako's heart swelled at the fact that he waited for her inside. She longed for his presence, the sight and smell of him close to her. Even if he was angry, he was there, in her home, and that was something.

She closed the door behind her and set her keys in a red lacquer tray on the stained pine shelf to the right of he entryway. A pair of black shoes, his shoes, sat neatly below the shelf, toes facing outward as if ready for a quick exit. She touched them, feeling the warmth of his body lingering in the rich leather. He hadn't been here long.

A flight of stairs, deeply stained to match the exposed ceiling beams, rose up in front of her toward the second floor—where she kept her pistol.

Her toilet was to her immediate right, but the door was open. One look told her he wasn't there. Her bedroom lay to the left. It was too much to hope that he waited for her there, ready to forgive her imperfections.

The ceiling creaked as someone walked on the floor above.

"I am up here, my darling." Oda's voice rolled down the stairs like a gentle breeze.

Shimoyama kicked off her shoes. She padded quickly up the stairs, holding up the hem of her kimono with both hands. Her socks were startlingly white and split at the toe—traditional, as Oda liked everything to be.

She stopped cold when she reached the top.

Oda stood at the far corner of the room, naked but for a twisted white loincloth. A long sword, her father's, hung loosely in his right hand. The black sheath lay on the floor, discarded as he surely intended to discard her.

Shimoyama knew there could be only one reason he'd removed his clothes. He didn't want to soil them with her blood.

Diffuse light sifted in from the paper window shade behind him, framing the garish red of the two long-nosed mountain demons tattooed on either side of his hairless chest. Riots of black and green swirled on the sinewed muscles of his thighs and arms. Ink melded with dark wood and shadow, giving the impression that he sprang from the walls of the house.

"You look lovely as ever." Oda turned the blade back and forth as he spoke so it caught the scant light from the stairwell.

"Thank you," she said. "It is good to see you, Oda-san."

"Is it?"

Shimoyama's eyes flashed around her room. She could not just let him kill her. He would lose what little respect he had for her if she merely gave up. Perhaps, if she put up a good fight, he would remember their past, the tender moments they'd shared together, and show some mercy.

Her Beretta pistol was still on the low table, where she'd left it. She licked her lips. Her mouth had gone dry and it was difficult to swallow. Perhaps this was a test. Perhaps he did not intend to kill her after all. Oda would never leave a weapon like that in the open if he intended to cut her down. He was too good at what he did.

He spoke, drawing her from thoughts of possible salvation. "I suppose you know why I am here."

She bowed her head. She and Oda had killed many men while fighting side by side, stripped of their clothing in order to escape the bloody consequences of using a sword for such intimate work.

"Because Quinn is still alive."

"Because he is in Japan."

"We will find him."

Oda all but exploded in a furious scream. He stomped

forward, planting his leading foot as he struck downward with the *katana*.

Shimoyama rolled out of instinct. She felt the whisper of wind as the blade hissed past her face. The foam green obi fell away, cut neatly into two pieces on the tatami floor, leaving her kimono hanging open to reveal her white undergarment. He was toying with her. She had seen him use the same cut to cleave a man from shoulder to hip.

The Beretta was still two meters away.

"I want him dead today!" Spittle flew from Oda's lips. He had never been able to control himself for long with Shimoyama, not when she was young and beautiful, and certainly not now that she was old. "I want him dead before nightfall. Within the hour."

"I understand." Shimoyama took a step backward, angling closer to the table—and the pistol.

"I am quite certain that you do not understand," Oda snapped. "If you truly knew what it means for this American agent to be here in Japan you would have followed through and killed him before."

"I will see to—"

"I fully expected you would see to it before he left the United States."

"I understand." There was little more she could say.

"There will be no atonement for you if he discovers our project. Do you understand that?"

"I do." Shimoyama's lips trembled. "I have no excuse—"

"Shut up," Oda said, his voice dropped to a whisper. "Foolish, foolish woman. I will handle this myself. But that leaves me the problem of what I should do with you . . ." He turned the sword back and forth, admiring it in the light. "Do you know how many men your father killed with this sword?"

"I do not," she said, turning her head slightly and stepping back again. Three feet from the table, she rolled again, coming up with the pistol in both hands. She pointed it directly at Oda.

He sighed softly, the way he'd done so many times in the past when she'd performed in an extraordinary way. Could it be that he was proud of her? She beamed, thinking she'd done well. A lock of hair had come loose from a lacquer comb and fallen across her eyes during her aerobatics. She pushed it back, not wanting him to see her unkempt.

Suddenly dizzy, she held the Beretta in one hand and attempted to steady herself with the other. She winced when her palm touched the table. It burned as if on fire.

Oda stooped to pick up the polished sheath and slid the blade in before setting it gently on the table in front of her. He stepped away and methodically began to put on his clothes.

Shimoyama swayed, feeling a white heat crawl up her arms. The heat turned to unbearable pain as it moved past her elbows as if she was being attacked by a swarm of wasps. Her mouth hung open, too confused to even scream.

"What . . . is . . . happening?" Her words came in breathy gasps.

Oda fastened the buttons of his starched white shirt one by one, head tilted, eyes now glued to her.

"None of this is actually your fault, you know." He

looped a red necktie around his upturned collar. "I do not blame you for Jericho Quinn."

The Beretta fell from Shimoyama's hand, thudding to the wooden floor. Red blisters bulged with fluid on her palms wherever she had touched the pistol—as if she'd been branded. He'd put something on the grips before she'd arrived, then driven her to pick it up with the threat of her own sword.

"I . . . I . . ." The pain enveloped her shoulders. Tendons in her neck tightened and cramped like steel cables, jerking open her jaw. An enormous pressure began to build in her chest. It seemed her heart would break out of her ribs.

"It is a form of fungus." Oda smiled as he continued to dress. "A mycotoxin—grown from bat guano I think—but somewhat similar to the Yellow Rain used in Laos. My friends have been able to make this even more potent. A lethal dose can be absorbed through minimal skin contact. Can you imagine the uses for such an incredible poison?"

"You cared for me once . . ." Shimoyama pitched forward, destroying the harmony of her ivory pen and papers. Cheek pressed against the open pages of her journal, she blinked up at him. "If I am not to blame . . . why do this to me?"

"I needed to conduct a test, my darling." Oda pulled the silk tie snug against his collar and shrugged. "And, because you remind me that I am growing old."

He took his coat from the kitchen chair and disappeared down the stairs without looking back.

Shimoyama felt her throat constrict, like a sob she couldn't quite finish or control. Unable to move her head from where it lay against the book, she flailed with her right hand, the only part of her that she still felt under her will. Searching blindly, her fingers brushed the cell phone. She gritted her teeth through the acid pain and punched in a number by feel alone—a number that she had not called for a very long time. A trembling finger pressed SEND.

Her heart raced wildly, out of control. Her body tensed, racked with spasms that felt as though they would break her back. A moment later, she fell slack, splayed across the table, completely still. A drop of blood trickled from her nose, creasing the white powder of her cheek to fall with a tiny plop against the pages of the open book.

CHAPTER 56

Each week, with few exceptions, the tattooed woman had at least one new wound. The newest one, a thin scar that ran in a diagonal line from the base of her perfect chin through her lower lip, was just one of many.

Goro had seen them all.

The wound that caused it had bisected her pouting lower lip, leaving it almost, but not quite, aligned. Much like the woman's soul, Goro thought. It had likely been caused by a sword. He had seen many such wounds tattooing young yakuza soldiers. They grew too familiar with the blade of their forefathers and hit something that sent the weapon bouncing back to bite them. To some, the scars were disfiguring. The woman's only added a dangerous layer to her beauty.

Some of her wounds were tiny nicks on her otherwise perfect skin. Others were deeper and should have been stitched—but they rarely were. Some were in places that must have been excruciatingly painful, the sort of injury that went well beyond physical wounds.

The stooped old man known as Horiguchi Goro III peered at the young woman's hip through thick glasses.

He sat cross-legged on a flat cushion, leaning over her body in rapt, Zen-like concentration.

Goro was small and bent, with the tiniest wisp of a mustache that was white as an egret feather. Horiguchi had not been his name at birth, but it had been his master's name, and the master of his master before that. After years of apprenticeship, he was able to take the name himself.

Goro's thumb and forefinger of his left hand stretched the almost translucent flesh just below the fall of the waist where the body rose again over the wing of the pelvis. The skin was close to the bone here, thin, with little muscle and full of nerves. It was an extremely painful area of the body in which to receive a traditional tattoo, but the woman remained motionless. Their sessions lasted for two hours with Goro piercing her tender skin over and over again with the bundled needles. Never, in the five years since he'd started her tattoo, had the woman flinched or even made a sound.

Goro had placed a small white towel over the young woman's nakedness. She didn't care to bother with it, content to lay back on the tatami mats staring up at the ceiling, completely nude while he worked.

He supposed that since he was an old man, she believed him to be immune to such things, but a man too old to be affected by this would be a dead man indeed. She was exceptional in her beauty, and the intricacies of her tattoo required a depth of concentration such a full and inviting vision would not allow. So he covered her when he could, and when he could not because of the tattoo's location, he thought of each little inch of skin as if it were not connected to any other part of this lovely creature. Had he done otherwise, he was certain she would have killed him.

The traditional Japanese art of hand tattooing was known as *tebori*—from *te*, meaning hand, and *hori*, meaning to carve. In his left hand, Goro held the bamboo *tebori* stick, twenty centimeters long and roughly the diameter of a wooden pencil. At the end of this stick he had tied a bundle of seven stainless-steel needles in which to hold the ink. They were fanned slightly so the middle three points stuck out a tiny bit farther than the two on either side.

Resting the bamboo *tebori* over his left thumb, the tattoo master held it with his right hand like a small pool cue, controlling the application by angling the needles this way and that as he inserted them over and over with expert precision. After every centimeter of work, he dipped them again in black ink, a mixture of soot and cooking oil. Lost in the artistic moment, he worked the rich tint under the skin. It did not portray, as much as it became, the gnarled black branches of a blossom-laden cherry tree, snaking down the young woman's ribs and over the flare of her hip.

His method was the same, whether he was shading a broad area or drawing a thin line—dipping the bundle of needles in thick black ink, working a centimeter of the design, then dipping again. He used a cotton cloth to wipe the flesh free of ink and blood every few seconds so he could check his work.

The needles whispered softly as they always did when he found his rhythm, piercing and pulling out of the skin with a soft *sha, sha, sha, sha.*

Goro knew that to be a great tattoo artist one not only had to possess an artistic heart, but a deep knowledge of the canvas where that art appeared—the human body. He had been tattooing for nearly forty years and had the nasty black practice scars on his thighs and ankles to prove it. He was very good at what he did, known for allowing the subject's skin to dictate the form and flow of the design.

If someone wanted a mountain goblin, that was their business. He would do as they wished. But the customer was told from the beginning that the way that particular goblin would look was up to Goro and the intricacies of the wearer's body, not the subject's personal whim.

The young woman had been specific in her wishes for the subject and general style of her tattoo but had left the artistic license of application and background to him. As long as the primary image on her lithe back was that of a foo dog that resembled one in a photograph she had brought with her, the supporting art and shading was left to him.

Goro stopped the bamboo *tebori* in midstroke at the chime of the young woman's cell phone. It was the mournful sound of Buddhist temple bells. He peered down at her over the top of his thick glasses, waiting to see if she wanted to answer. She came up on one elbow, head thrown back so tresses of long hair fell across her neck and shoulders in an exquisite black cascade that complemented the vibrant pink and green hues of cherry blossom. The cotton cloth fell away as she rolled across the tatami mats toward the impatient phone.

In the five years since she'd been coming to see him,

he young woman had remained completely silent during the horribly painful tattooing process. But the sound of temple bells on her ringtone caused her to groan, deeply and with a sorrow that Goro could feel in his bones.

CHAPTER 57

Kanab, Utah

Todd Elton lay on his cot and stared up at his iPad watching tiny airplanes zip around a world map. The red planes carried infected passengers. Blue planes transported medical teams researching a cure. The game was called Plague Inc. One of the CDC docs had told him about it. The macabre goal was to kill off everyone in the world with an illness you invented before a cure could be developed. It was brilliant really, with options for using garnered points to mutate the plague and make it more resistant to cold or easier to spread.

He'd learned to beat the game by making his virus, which he called *"Teeples Brodiosis,"* extremely contagious but with few symptoms at first. After he had much of the world infected, he used his garnered points to evolve the symptoms and make them more fatal. In the beginning stages, the stuff had to be contagious or it didn't spread fast enough. But, if there were too many symptoms people freaked, working on a cure too quickly and even shutting down their borders before he could infect every country.

As it turned out, it took a certain amount of finesse to kill off the entire human race.

Brandy poked her head in the half-open door.

"You should be getting some rest while you can," she said. "Mrs. Christenson is going to pop by midnight."

Elton rubbed his face. "Glad I paid attention during my OB GYN rotation in med school . . ." He looked at the iPad again, then back up at Brandy. "You wonder why we're not getting sick?"

"A lot of prayer and hand sanitizer?"

"Think about it," Elton said. "If Bedford and R.J. got back into town on Sunday and made everyone else sick by Tuesday, that means someone else inside the hospital or clinic should be showing symptoms by now. You and I were up close and personal with every one of these patients before we knew it was bad enough we should use more than regular precautions. No other spouses besides my sister-in-law . . ."

Brandy frowned. "You sound like you want someone else to get sick."

"It just doesn't make sense, that's all." Elton rubbed his face. He really should have been sleeping instead of playing that stupid game.

"Well," Brandy said, turning to leave. "If you're not going to get some rest before Mrs. Christenson has her baby, you should probably go up and see your brother-in-law's friend. The ventilator isn't doing much for him. I understand he's failing fast."

Elton got up and staggered down the hall to the hospital wing. He pulled on the bulky orange biohazard suit and hood before the FEMA guard—who was similarly dressed but for his submachine gun—allowed him through the door.

One of the CDC docs, a big-boned guy with a kind eye and quiet demeanor, turned and shook his head inside his clear hood when Elton walked into R. J. Howard's room.

"Hey, Doc," R.J. whispered, already struggling for breath behind a clear oxygen mask. His face was so swollen with boils that if his name hadn't been taped at the foot of his bed, Elton never would have recognized him. The ventilator hissed and droned beside the bed, forcing oxygen into his lungs. It wasn't enough. "Glad . . . you . . . stopped by," he said into the mask.

"Shhh," Elton said, panic rising in his chest. The man was dying before his eyes, and there was little he could do about it. "We already have Rick Bedford on ECMO treatment. We'll get you on a machine right away."

Howard's head moved back and forth on the pillow. He pulled the mask away with trembling fingers so he could be heard. "No," he groaned, croaking out each word. "Ms. Teeples . . . is over . . . there . . . right?"

"She is," Elton said, looking at the poor young woman across the room. She wasn't much better than Howard.

"You should . . . put her on . . . the machine," he said. "She deserves it . . . for being . . . married . . . to that guy . . ."

Considering the man's vitals, he was unlikely to survive even with a heart-lung bypass.

"I don't see a number listed for your wife in Cedar City," Elton said.

"Don't . . . know it," he whispered.

"Maybe we can send someone else from your unit by to talk to her."

"Nobody else . . . in my unit . . . from there," Howard groaned. "Anyway . . . she . . . left me . . . before I came . . . home," he whispered.

Elton stood closer so he could be certain he heard correctly. "Did you say you were the only member of the 405th from Cedar City?"

Exhausted, Howard could do nothing but nod.

"And you stopped off here before you ever made it back there when you came home from Afghanistan?"

"Right," Howard said, eyes fluttering closed.

"Get some rest," Elton said, all but jumping to his feet.

Ten minutes later Elton had peeled off the clammy suit and, after passing through two negative pressure barriers, was allowed into the trailer that served as the CDC inner sanctum.

The lead CDC physician was a short Indian man with thick glasses and wavy black hair. His name was Krishnamurti but rather than making everyone pronounce it each time they addressed him, he went by Doctor K.

"Tell me what you are trying to say," Krishnamurti said from behind his Ikea wooden desk.

Elton ran a hand over a map of the United States projected on the office wall.

"Look at this," he said. "The 405th returned home from Afghanistan last Sunday." Elton consulted a list Doctor K had just given him. "Specialist Dean Fortuna is from Afton, Wyoming, where his wife is among the ill. First Sergeant Richard Bedford is from here in Kanab. His wife is also infected. Sergeant R. J. Howard is from Cedar City."

"That is correct," Krishnamurti said. "So what is your point?"

"Sergeant Howard never made it to Cedar City." Elton stabbed his finger at the map for effect. "He's been here in Kanab since he out-processed. If he's the vector from Afghanistan, how come people in Cedar City are getting sick?"

"Another soldier perhaps," Doctor K said, flicking his hand as if to ward off a mosquito.

"No one else from the 405th lists Cedar City as their home. But here's the kicker." Elton leaned in closer, both hands on Doctor K's desk. "Howard just told me his wife left him before he even got home from Afghanistan."

Krishnamurti shrugged. "What difference does that make?"

"She's on the infected list in Cedar City." Elton slapped the flat of his hand against the clipboard. "Something else is making these people sick. I say you get on the horn to your people in . . . wherever your people are . . . and have them get to the bottom of this."

CHAPTER 58

The tattooed woman flicked her fingers dismissively at Goro, ignoring the cotton towel that had fallen away when she'd rolled toward her cell phone. The little man sat leering at her over his ugly glasses. He jumped as if he'd been shot when he realized she'd caught him looking and scuttled out of the room, tripping over his own feet. She was certain he covered her with small towels while he worked in order to get a better look. It did not matter. If he wanted to ogle, she didn't care. He was small and ugly and probably never got within ten meters of a woman unless he had a tattoo needle in his hand. To be such a gifted artist, she would have thought he'd be more at ease with the sight of a female body.

Sitting naked on the cool tatami mat, she clutched her knees to her chest and let the phone chime in her hand. The doleful temple bells stopped for a moment. She held her breath, waiting, hoping, but it started again almost immediately.

Oda knew she had failed. Not once, but twice. There would be consequences for that.

She reached down to touch the warmth of blood that

oozed from the tender skin over her hipbone. It was barely visible against the shining black ink. She wiped it away with the palm of her free hand, oblivious to the fact that her flesh was raw from thousands of jabs with Goro's inked needles. Pain, she'd learned, was a most natural thing. It was something she could feed on, whether it was someone else's or her own.

The temple chimes began again. She transferred the phone to her blood-smeared hand and pressed it to her ear.

"Hello, Father," she said. "You have a job for me?"

CHAPTER 59

Deputy Bowen still knew very little about Detective Susumu Hase of the Fukuoka Police Organized Crime Squad. He was a careful driver, consistently keeping his hands at ten and two o'clock on the wheel of his unmarked blue Nissan sedan as if he were taking a driving test. He seemed content to travel in silence, staring intently ahead as he drove, keeping any thoughts to himself and happy to let the miles roll by without a word.

Bowen was no lover of mindless chatter, but he liked to learn a little about the people he worked with, especially if that person would be watching his back when he went up against a killer with Jericho Quinn's skill set. Whatever his reasons, there was a substantial body count piling up in Quinn's wake.

"How long have you been on the job?" Bowen asked, looking out the passenger window at the needle-like Fukuoka Tower building as they passed through the city.

"On the job?" Hase mused, trying to work out the translation in his mind.

"Sorry," Bowen said. "How long have you been with the police department?"

"Ah," Hase said, understanding. "Fourteen years. I was at Munakata Precinct before I became a detective. It is a little to the northeast of here, on the water." He took his eyes off traffic long enough to shoot a glance at Bowen. "And you? How long have you been . . . on the job?"

"I was in the Army for four years after college. I've been with the Marshals Service for ten years now."

Hase nodded slowly, looking at least informed if not impressed.

"I wasn't allowed to bring my sidearm into Japan," Bowen said, making sure Hase knew he wouldn't be much help in a gunfight.

"Guns are not as much of an issue in Japan." Detective Hase shrugged. "Our society is much less violent than America, I suppose."

"Mind if I ask what you carry?"

"Guns are not as prominent here in Japan as they are in the U.S." The detective shoulder-checked as he spoke, then took a left lane. "On patrol I carried a New Nambu five-shot revolver. As a detective who deals with yakuza and other organized crime groups on a regular basis I am allowed to carry a Sig Sauer."

"Good weapon," Bowen said. "Which one?"

"The P230 in .32 ACP." Hase shot a glance toward the passenger seat, gauging the American lawman's reaction. "As I said, guns are not as prevalent in this country."

"Ah." Bowen smiled politely, but he couldn't help thinking that with that tiny caliber, for all practical purposes they were both unarmed.

He grabbed the edge of his seat when Hase made a right-hand turn into what looked to be oncoming traffic, then remembered they drove on the left in Japan. Hase took the on-ramp to some sort of expressway, then crossed a bridge to exit among a tumble of mismatched buildings and random shops that looked like concrete blocks dumped out of a sack. Streets ran at odd angles and disappeared into blind alleys with no apparent reason or order.

Hase had apparently spent plenty of time in the area and knew exactly where he was going. He parked the Nissan in an open space at the end of a narrow block, backing in over some sort of fold-up barrier underneath.

Bowen raised an eyebrow. "The police have to pay to park?"

"Why should we not pay to park?" Detective Hase dropped his keys in his jacket pocket. "I am a policeman, not the emperor."

Bowen took a quick look around, trying to memorize where they'd left the vehicle, but the tangled streets and chicken scratches that comprised Japanese signage provided him little to go by. The sounds, the sights, everything was as foreign as if it had been from another planet. It was like trying to navigate using a map drawn by some impressionist painter. If anything happened to Hase, Bowen realized he would have no idea where they were, or how to contact the cavalry.

By the time he turned around from trying to orient himself, Hase was halfway down the block.

"You know Ayako Shimizu very well?" Bowen asked after trotting to catch up.

"I do," Hase said. "She is my . . ." He turned his head, brow creased. "I am not sure of the word."

"Informant?"

"That is it." Hase nodded, working through the vocabulary. "*Informant* . . . because she informs me about criminal actions."

"She's supposed to have a place around here?"

"In a manner of speaking," Hase said. "She works at several of the hotels in this area. One in particular is her favorite. We will try there first."

"I see," Bowen said. A girl in a short skirt and tall heels rode by on a bicycle, reminding Bowen of an album cover from his youth. She parked the bike in front of a white tile building called the Excalibur and shuffled inside, looking like Bambi on ice in the tall stiletto heels. Bowen nodded at the sign out front as they walked by. REST: 4400 YEN, STAY: 7900 YEN. "These are *that* kind of hotel. Rooms by the hour?"

"Something like that," Hase answered. "They are used by prostitutes like Shimizu to be sure, but these love hotels also fill a certain need. In this country many generations of families often live under the same small roof with very thin walls. Sometimes a couple needs to get away."

"Have you ever been to one?"

Hase gave a noncommittal grin. "I am not married."

Bowen smiled back. "And that's not what I asked."

"Come," Hase said, still avoiding the question. "That is the one, down the street." He pointed to a red brick hotel with a matching privacy wall out front at the end of the crooked block. A life-size statue of Cleopatra reigned in naked glory beside the entrance. The sign above her said this love hotel was called THE LUXOR.

"My sister came to this one once when she was younger," Hase said, his face pensive. "So I have a special relationship with the proprietors. College girls often wear fancy kimono to their graduation ceremony. My sister's boyfriend convinced her to accompany him here . . . and, of course, remove her kimono. She did, but when their three hours of 'rest' was up she realized she did not have the necessary skill to dress herself back in the kimono. The entire process is quite intricate. Lucky for her, the old auntie at the front desk knew how to tie kimono and was able to help her get dressed before she returned home to our family." He looked at Bowen through the narrow eyes of an elder brother. "But I could tell."

"What happened?" Bowen asked as he stopped in front of the Luxor, waiting for Hase to finish his story before they went inside.

The detective winked. "I had a talk with my sister's boyfriend and he is now my brother-in-law. We laugh about it now because I come here for work and talk to that same old lady that helped her out. My sister does not think it is very funny."

He motioned Bowen through the door ahead of him. "Please," he said. "After you. Japanese people are very polite. If someone is going to kill us, it will be in the back."

Bowen stopped to look at him.

The detective grinned, showing a playful side brought out by the family story. "I am joking, Bowen-san."

A bell chimed when they opened the glass door and entered a dim, but surprisingly clean, tile foyer. More nude statuary greeted them beside the front desk. These were plaster renditions of the goddesses Athena and Aphrodite, Greek not Egyptian, but Bowen doubted any of the Luxor's patrons cared even if they happened to know.

"*Irashaimase*," the granny behind the front desk window said. *Please come in.* A curtain with a print of a beautiful geisha hung down so the clerk would have to stoop to see anyone who was checking in. It was an illusion of privacy because there were two cameras facing the door that presumably fed monitors in the back office.

The clerk buzzed a side door open and waved Hase out of the main foyer with a flick of her liver-spotted hand. Bowen didn't understand her words, but it was apparent that having a police officer loitering around check-in would be bad for business.

They were taken to a cramped back room, stacked to waist level with bins full of clean towels, bottles of shampoo, assorted lotions, and complimentary cans of beer. A plastic laundry basket sat just inside the door, filled to the brim with adult magazines and toys Bowen expected to find at such an establishment. If Hase and the old woman were embarrassed, they didn't show it.

The two spoke for a short time, with the detective doing the lion's share of listening while the old woman rattled on about something that Bowen thought was probably her bursitis, the way she kept holding up her elbow.

Finally, Hase turned to explain. "First," he said, "you should know that Mrs. Mori thinks you are very handsome."

Bowen looked at the grinning old woman. She was seventy if she was a day. "You're talking about this woman here?"

"Yes," Hase said. "She said is a shame that all the

rooms are full and wonders if all American law enforcement officers are as good looking as you."

"Not sure I know how to answer that."

"That's okay." Hase laughed. "You don't have to." He nodded at a television monitor mounted on the back wall. A baseball game was playing, but the old woman picked up a remote and began to move through the channels. She clicked through five adult movies, pausing on one that was apparently a favorite of hers, before finally clicking through to a color-coded grid.

She studied the list of room numbers for a moment, then spoke rapidly to Hase.

"He's still here, in Room four-oh-two—the Caesar Suite." The detective pointed to the television screen. "That picture of a small lock below the room number means the door is shut. It will show unlocked if he opens the door to let someone in or leaves his room for any reason. They cannot allow people to walk freely around the halls in a place like this. Men can use one of the free papers from the lobby to pick out a girl and then call and place his order from the room."

"The girl on the bicycle." Bowen mused.

"Yes." Hase nodded. "I am sure she was from one of the free paper advertisements. The man in Room four-oh-two has called to order such a girl, but Mrs. Mori said she has not yet arrived."

"I see." Bowen marveled over the differences between the Japanese and American versions of no-tell motels. "High tech."

"High . . . tekku?"

"Tech," Bowen said. "Technology."

"Ah, yes," Hase said, translating for the woman who smiled at the compliment regarding her system.

"So anyway." Bowen nodded toward the flat screen. "Who is this man waiting in the Caesar Suite and why are we interested in him?"

"His name is Watanabe," Hase said. "A yakuza soldier I have arrested numerous times. He is a regular client of Ayako Shimizu and will know how to find her if we ask the right questions."

"And what type of questions are those?"

Hase turned to walk toward the elevator. "The same type of questions that turned my sister's boyfriend into my brother-in-law."

CHAPTER 60

Quinn and Ayako waited beside a vending machine that sold vitamin drinks in a shadowed alley across the busy four-lane thoroughfare of Sumiyoshi Street. A conservative black sign in large block characters ran between the uppermost row of windows and the flat roofline of the fifteen-story building. It read YANAGI PHARMACEUTICAL.

A steady wind howled, cold enough that periodic raindrops stung when they hit exposed skin. The motorcycle leaned on its side stand a few feet away, hot engine ticking as it cooled.

Ayako sniffed, brushing a wisp of hair out of her cold-pinked cheek. The wind blew it back again, so she gave up after two tries. She hunched over a small notebook, scribbling something while Quinn kept his eyes focused across the street. Whatever it was, she brooded about it for a moment, before tucking the book inside her bra, next to her heart.

Sighing heavily—as if she'd come to some grave decision—she took her phone out of her jacket.

"The website says this pharmaceutical company is a subsidiary of Yanagi Chemical Corporation . . ." She used her thumb to scroll down the page as she read. "What would Oda want with a company that manufactures antibiotics and tetanus vaccine?"

"I don't know," Quinn said, leaning against the bike. "But it can't be good."

He'd watched four women and a man who all looked to be American or European leave together shortly after he'd parked the bike a little before 11:00. Now they walked back up the street, returning with cups of takeout coffee from a nearby café, chattering happily among themselves. Two of the women gave each other a high five as they crossed the street at the end of the block. They were celebrating something.

Quinn fought the urge to strong-arm his way to Oda. He'd come this far looking for answers. It would do little good to blow it all because of impatience. Still, they had to start somewhere—and of all Quinn's good qualities, quietly waiting was not chief among them.

Emiko Miyagi had pointed out this fault early on. She told him of a poem that described the three most prominent shoguns in feudal Japan and their methods of dealing with a bird that refused to sing.

If it doesn't sing, kill it, the first said.

If it doesn't sing, make it sing, was the second's philosophy.

The third, and most successful shogun, Lord Tokugawa had said: *If it doesn't sing, wait for it. It will.*

Quinn had pointed out that Lord Tokugawa was also one of the most ruthless men who ever ruled Japan. "Balance, Quinn-san," Miyagi had said. "It is always about balance."

He smiled at the memory. The man behind the attempted murder of his little girl was very likely across the street. Balance was one thing, but at this point, the scales tipped toward going inside and making someone sing.

The American visitors were nearly to the front door.

Quinn turned to Ayako. Strands of black hair plastered across her face. "How about we get you out of this wind?"

She gave him a little bow. Grinning enough to show the delicate crow's-feet at the corner of her eyes.

"That is an excellent—"

Ayako gave a little jump when the cell phone in her hand began to ring. She looked at the caller ID, frowning.

"*Moshi moshi*," she answered. "Emm . . . Yes . . . yes, of course." She looked up at Quinn, eyes wide. "It is for you. A man named Winfield Palmer."

CHAPTER 61

Mrs. Mori was able to watch Bowen and Hase on the closed-circuit monitors in her office off the lobby of the Luxor love hotel. The detective waved at the hallway camera when they reached Room 402. The door gave a faint click as she opened it remotely.

The king-size bed was turned down, but empty. A pixilated adult movie played on the big-screen television. A single pair of well-worn but highly polished black shoes had been placed in the alcove just inside the door.

Bowen was hit immediately with a face full of steam and the heady odor of scented bath soap. The sound of dripping water to their right said Watanabe was in the bathroom.

Thinking it was his date, the yakuza soldier yelled something through the door.

Hase grinned, putting a finger to his lips. "He says he has the oil," the detective whispered. "He wants us to come in and . . . apply it . . . In so many words."

"This should be rich," Bowen said, and pushed open the door.

He was greeted by the unpleasant sight of the heavily tattooed Isamu Watanabe, who was facedown and naked on a large plastic air mattress that took up all the usable space of the bathroom floor below the tub. The gangster's right hand was wrapped in a bloodstained bandage. He kept it tucked in close to his side to protect it, but that hadn't stopped him from using his other hand to douse himself with cooking oil. It puddled in the small of his back and ran down into the creases of the air mattress.

Facing away, with his cheek pressed against the plastic, he barked a command to who he thought was the girl he'd ordered from the free paper.

"He wants us to rub his back," Hase said out loud. He stomped the end of the mattress, sending the startled yakuza rolling. "I don't think I would care for that, would you?"

Watanabe spun at the male voice, drawing into a ball to cover himself and cowering against the far wall.

Body ink was nothing new to Bowen. Many of his friends in the military had tats. He'd heard of the Japanese mafia's culture of tattooing their entire body, but he'd never actually seen one. Even on this sniveling runt it was an impressive thing to behold—blues, greens, and oranges flowing in surreal lines to form dragons and fire-breathing demons.

In a sudden gust of bravado, the surprised yakuza sprang for a pistol that lay on the counter beside the bathroom sink. He might as well have been reaching for the moon.

Hase gave the air mattress another stomp and sent the yakuza flying backward to bounce off the tile wall.

By the time Watanabe could rebound, the detective produced an expandable metal baton from under his golf jacket and opened it with a flick of his wrist. Swinging the telescoping club with startling accuracy, the detective struck Watanabe twice in the injured hand and knocked out a front tooth before the man even knew he was being hit.

Bowen, who stood closer to the sink, snatched up the pistol and tucked it into his waistband, hoping Hase might forget he had it.

Though he'd appeared all mild manners and good sense from the time they'd met at the airport, Bowen was pleased to note that Detective Hase had an "on" switch. Evidently, Watanabe flipped it.

The yakuza soldier put both hands to his face and sank to his knees on the deflated air mattress. He sobbed as if he was choking to death.

Still clutching the expandable baton, the detective leaned in, launching into a series of spit-filled, rapid-fire questions. He hardly gave the cowering Watanabe time to answer before starting in on the next.

Bowen imagined it would be difficult for anyone to withstand a long interrogation by the screaming Hase, but enduring it with a mutilated hand while naked, slathered with cooking oil, and missing a tooth only added to the humiliation.

A look of amused surprise spread across Hase's face. He turned to Bowen.

"Watanabe tells me that your fugitive cut off his finger last night and killed five members of his yakuza family. Ayako Shimizu killed a sixth."

"So we were right that he is running with Shimizu?"

"Six dead." Hase patted the metal club against an open palm. "And that is not taking into account those we found at Shimizu's apartment. According to Watanabe, this American with a dark beard and cruel eyes cut the head off the gangster underboss and gave it to the top boss—a man called Tanaka."

Bowen whistled. Quinn had really gone into the deep end of the pool.

"Does he say where we can find them?"

Hase began to shout again. The naked man groveled, still kneeling in the pool of oil. The peony flowers surrounding the fanged demons of his tattooed back appeared to ripple as his glistening skin twitched in pain and fear.

"He says he cannot seem to go two days in a row without someone beating him up." Detective Hase half turned, trying to suppress a grin. "I told him you were an American police officer and your rules for interrogation were probably much more lax than ours."

Bowen looked at the froth of blood streaming between Watanabe's broken teeth. "Somehow I doubt that," he said.

"He swears he hasn't seen Ayako Shimizu since she stomped him in the groin . . ."

Watanabe broke in, bowing as he rattled off what sounded like a long excuse for something.

"Wait," Detective Hase said. "He's making a correction. Ayako Shimizu and the American were on a motorcycle the last he saw them, leaving a shrine near Tanaka's warehouse."

Watanabe chattered on, fearful he might leave something out.

"Apparently," Hase said, rolling his eyes, "Watanabe has decided he hates being in the yakuza now."

"Did he say where Shimizu and the American were headed?"

"He did," Hase said. "I know the place. It is not too far from here. Yanagi Pharmaceutical."

CHAPTER 62

Quinn turned his back to the wind that whipped down the alley as he spoke, eyes still glued to the front of Yanagi Pharmaceutical.

"How did you find me?"

On the other end of the phone, Winfield Palmer gave a long, deliberate sigh. Quinn could picture him sitting behind his broad mahogany desk, perusing a computerized map of Japan with a red blip that signified Quinn's location.

"Don't blame Emiko," the national security advisor said. "She would have helped you escape even if I'd not told her to."

"Seriously?" Quinn scoffed. "You have known all the time where I was?"

"Pretty much," Palmer said. "That leather satchel your IDs came with keeps us pretty up to date."

"Can I ask why?" Quinn slowed his breathing, letting this new reality sink in.

"You've proven yourself too many times for me to think you shot Officer Chin." Palmer paused as if he wanted to get his words just right. Such self-awareness was a rarity for him. "You were correct when we talked after Kim was shot. There is definitely something global in the works. That hit team in Vegas was just too neat and tidy. And then someone tries to frame you for the murder. If Oda is behind all this, as Emiko suspects, then there is a larger game in play. Oda is a big gun. It would be overkill to use his organization just to kill a member of someone's family."

"You have a theory?"

"Wish I did," Palmer said. "But I do have another problem. Have you been watching the news?"

"I've been a little busy running from the law," Quinn said.

"But you know about this pandemic?"

"I do," Quinn said. "Looks awful."

"For a time it looked like there might have been a bit of bright news on the horizon. Japan was hit with this same virus months ago. They were able to contain it but started work on a vaccine anyway. Our folks on the ground there say they have developed a live virus vaccine that produces antibodies in humans. The president wants it pushed through ASAP." Palmer groaned. "A couple of wrinkles over here though have made me second-guess our celebrations."

"Let me guess," Quinn said, still watching the building across the street. "Yanagi Pharmaceutical is involved."

"That's correct." Palmer sighed. "How did you know?"

"I'm sitting across from their front doors right now, waiting for Oda to show up."

"Dammit!" Palmer hissed. "I knew a vaccine this soon was a fantasy. Can you get inside?"

"I can now," Quinn said. "Has anyone tested the vaccine?"

"Supposedly," Palmer groaned. "We have CDC and HHS personnel there now, but they're under tremendous pressure to stop this virus."

"Yeah," Quinn said. "I just saw them come back from a break. Looks like the tests went well. They may as well have been toasting each other with champagne."

"It wouldn't be that difficult for someone to doctor the results enough for them to accept a bogus test."

"Okay," Quinn said. "I'll go check it out. But do me a favor and tell Miyagi I forgive her."

"She'll be glad to hear that," Palmer said. "Don't quote me, but for some reason, I think she has a little teacher crush on you . . ." He chuckled. "Anyway, wish me luck. I have to go tell the president I'm taking away the good news for his State of the Union address tonight."

Quinn ended the call and peered over at Ayako, who stood so the vending machine blocked some of the wind.

"Did you know about this?"

She shook her head. "I am beginning to believe Emiko-chan does not tell me anything. I can guess from your half of the conversation that the authorities know where you are?"

"They do," Quinn said, dark eyes narrowing as an idea formed in his head. "Would you mind if I make another quick call?"

Veronica Garcia answered on the second ring.

"Hello?"

Her honey-soft voice caused Quinn to catch his breath.

"It's me," he said, feeling a little dizzy at the sound of her.

"Jericho?"

"Yep."

"Oh . . . a . . . hi." Her voice was hollow, distant.

"I'm sorry I didn't call before I left."

"Okay," she said, her voice noncommittal. "Jacques gave me your message."

"Yeah," Quinn said, picturing her. "But I still should have called."

"That's true," she said. "Turns out you were right about the feds. A deputy U.S. marshal came by looking for you. I was able to tell him you were too big a jerk to call me before you ran."

"You'll probably be mad at me for asking this," Quinn said. "But do you know how Kim is doing?"

There was silence on the line. Quinn felt like an idiot. You didn't ask your girlfriend to check on the status of your ex-wife.

Garcia rescued him. "She's doing better every day. OSI still has her under protection. Mattie, too."

"Thanks." He wanted to say more, but Ayako stood too close, arms crossed and a jealous pout pinching her face. "Listen, I have to go. I'll call you again soon. I . . ."

"I know," Garcia said, and hung up.

Garcia slipped the cell phone into the pocket of a black Massif Nomex jacket, then looked up at Thibodaux and Miyagi with a tear in her eye.

The big Cajun gave her shoulder a squeeze in an attempt to console her.

"You okay, cher?"

She sniffed. "I'm fine."

Thibodaux turned so he could see her with his good eye. "He asked you about Kim?"

"He did." A broad smile spread over Ronnie's full lips as a realization dawned on her. "But do you know what that means? It means he called me first."

Quinn handed the phone back to Ayako and grabbed the helmet from where it hung on the handlebar of the Blackbird.

"Was that your girlfriend?" Ayako frowned.

Quinn pulled on the helmet and fastened the strap. "She is." He threw a leg over the bike and pushed the starter. "Or she was. To tell you the truth, I'm not sure anymore."

"Hmmm," Ayako said, climbing on behind him. She snaked her arms around him as if she didn't want him to get away.

Quinn released the clutch and pulled out of the alley to wait at the curb for traffic. Remembering he was in Japan and not the United States, he looked right first, then left for oncoming traffic. Jetting across when he had an opening, he leaned the Blackbird into a tight U-turn on the narrow street that ran alongside the Yanagi building. Ayako scrambled off and he kicked the side stand down next to the curb, facing the main thoroughfare again but from the opposite direction.

Still straddling the bike, he watched as a silver gray Suzuki Hayabusa roared down Sumiyoshi to park directly in front of the building. The big motorcycle dwarfed the rider, but she handled it as if she'd been born on the back of one.

Quinn's gut tightened as she shook her long black hair free of a matte black helmet. It was the woman from the gondola canals at the Venetian—the woman who shot Kim.

If Miyagi had been right, this was her daughter, *Ran*. Ayako gave a pitiful groan.

The young woman glanced up and down the street, paying particular attention to the way she'd come and the roofline of the buildings above her. An assassin herself, she knew where she would hide and considered those the danger areas she needed to watch.

The Blackbird was parked behind a concrete pillar and difficult to see from her vantage point.

Apparently satisfied that she hadn't been followed and wasn't about to be shot by a sniper, the woman bounded up the long stairway to the Yanagi building and opened the front door.

Without thinking, Quinn abandoned his helmet on the handlebar of the Blackbird, breaking into a trot for the door. He'd been focused on finding Oda so he would lead him to this girl. Now, he could go straight to her. Oda may have ordered the hit, but she had pulled the trigger and deserved a little something extra for that.

He was vaguely aware of Ayako running beside him with the guitar case strapped over her shoulder as he jerked open the glass door.

He caught a glimpse of the young woman's gray motorcycle jacket starting up an open flight of stairs at the far end of the expansive lobby, across fifty feet of pink granite tile. The entire ground floor was a perfect example of minimalist style with little more than a few

imple calligraphies, an oval reception desk, and a half
dozen uniformed security guards.

The nearest guard called out in challenge as soon as
Quinn entered the lobby. The young woman turned, saw
Quinn coming for her, and ran for the cover of the
stairs. All six guards converged on Quinn as he closed
the distance.

He was vaguely aware of hitting the first one under
the chin, snapping the man's head back and driving
him to the tile like he was spiking a volleyball. He
swatted the next two out of his way like spiderwebs on
a trail—annoyance more than anything. Ayako met one,
grabbing the poor man around the neck and pulling
him to her to give him three rapid-fire knees to the
groin before shoving him to the side.

The next two were in the process of a coordinated
attack when gunfire opened up from the stairs above.
Nothing more than hired security, these two fled toward the front doors, realizing that Quinn was the target and wanting to get as far away from him as they
could.

Quinn drew the H&K and sent the young assassin
scuttling with two well-placed shots. He raced up the
stairs after her, pistol trained on the balcony where
she'd disappeared. A set of wooden doors, like those
found in a hospital, were still swinging when he rounded
the corner.

Not wanting to give the woman time to set up an
ambush, Quinn pressed on with Ayako right behind.

Ahead, a Japanese lab tech in a long white coat pushed
a metal rack taller than his head across the hallway intersection, blocking the young woman's escape. Quinn

paused to take a shot, but Ayako slid into him from behind, spoiling his aim and allowing his target to slip
away. The fleeing woman yanked the rack sideways as
she went around, sending twenty-four hundred eggs
crashing to the polished laboratory floor.

Quinn ducked as two more rounds zinged off a
stainless-steel lab shelf behind him. Struggling to keep
his feet in the slippery mess of eggs and crushed shell,
he shoved the surprised lab tech out of the way and
moved to the corner where the woman had disappeared.

Two men in suits met him head-on as he did a quick-
peek around the corner. These were much more devoted
to their jobs than the uniformed guards downstairs.

"Kill them," the young woman yelled from the far
end of the hall, twenty feet away.

The lead man, a bruiser built for power over speed,
hit Quinn hard between the eyes.

The blow felt like a brick, but Quinn had been hit
before and rolled with it, stepping back against the wall.
He was not in the habit of shooting innocent security
guards who were just doing their jobs, but this guy
went for a pistol, apparently happy to carry out the kill
order. Quinn beat him to the punch, firing the H&K
from tight against his waist. His first round connected—
there was nowhere else for it to go with the wide man
standing in front of him—but to little effect.

Quinn swatted the guard's pistol out of the way, then
angled the barrel of the H&K upward, firing again as
the man battered him with left hooks, trying to bring
his gun into play. He was amazingly agile to be as big
as he was and carrying two bullets. Quinn's third shot
took him under the chin, stopping him in his tracks. He

wayed, falling forward, dead weight smearing Quinn into the wall on his way to the floor.

When he finally shook himself free, Quinn looked up in time to see Ayako withdraw the blade of her father's short sword from the belly of the second security man. He'd seen this one before, even snapped a photo when he'd caught the guy following him at Reagan National Airport two months earlier.

Before he could move again, two pistol rounds slapped Quinn in the chest. The ballistic armor under his leather Transit jacket stopped them from penetrating, but the blunt trauma felt like he'd been kicked by a horse. He stepped sideways, returning fire as he pulled Ayako out of the way.

The young woman shot again, then ducked around a corner where the hall jogged to the right.

Quinn dropped the magazine on the H&K during the momentary lull.

"Four rounds plus one in the tube," he whispered.

Ayako nodded, bloody sword at her side.

Quinn advanced quickly down the hall behind the pistol, hugging the wall so he could use any doorway for cover. Ayako stayed behind him. Well back from the corner he began to step sideways, inch by inch, to broaden his field of view. It was called *cutting the pie*.

The hallway was empty and footfalls echoed down the stairs at the far end.

She was running, circling back to the lobby, probably aiming for the front door.

CHAPTER 63

Quinn and Ayako shoved their way through two more sets of uniformed Yanagi security before making it back to the exit.

Already straddling her bike, the woman began to shoot as they ran for the Blackbird. They were only twenty yards apart. She'd been half again that far away when she shot the Pakistani in Vegas. This time, with the possibility of Quinn shooting back, her shots went wide.

Quinn jumped aboard the waiting bike and hit the start button. "Get on!" he yelled at Ayako.

She stood frozen, a few paces ahead of the Blackbird's front wheel, staring at the shooter as if in a trance.

He gunned the throttle, scooting the bike up adjacent to Ayako, bumping her with his elbow to get her attention.

"I said get on!" he barked, passing the pistol back behind him. "I can't ride and shoot at the same time."

She snapped out of the trance as pistol rounds zinged past their heads and slapped the concrete pillar behind them. A window shattered in the convenience store across the street. Passersby screamed and ran for cover.

Facing the silver Hayabusa, Quinn rolled on the throttle as soon as he felt Ayako take the H&K and jump aboard behind him. Tugging upward on the handlebars, he brought the bike into a low wheelie to put as much of it as possible between them and oncoming gunfire.

The woman kept shooting as the Blackbird sped past. Thankfully, she was unable to hit anything vital on the rapidly approaching target. They were thirty meters down the road when Quinn heard the Hayabusa roar to life behind him. The last thing he wanted was for this woman to be on his tail.

He slowed just enough to keep from pitching them both off the bike in a high-side crash, locking up the Honda's rear brake so it lost traction. Looking back over his shoulder, he leaned, dumping the clutch and pouring on the throttle to turn the bike into a smooth 180 in a near perfect foot-down drift. He and his brother both had the scars to prove they'd practiced such moves hundreds of times in the high school parking lot growing up.

Smoke poured from the Hayabusa's rear tire as it grabbed for traction on the chilly pavement. Firing the pistol left-handed, she was unable to shift gears. The bike screamed to redline, still in second as she sped by against traffic. Cabs and delivery vans peeled off in either direction to avoid the oncoming motorcycle. Horns blared. A black sedan careened into a fire hydrant, sending a geyser of spray into the winter air.

Quinn slowed again, drifting the back tire through another 180-degree turn. Ayako craned her head around to keep her eye on the fleeing Suzuki. Centrifugal force threw her sideways on the tiny passenger seat. Flailing, she clutched at Quinn's jacket in mid-lean. The rear tire bucked as it caught traction. Quinn poured on more throttle, breaking the tire loose and narrowly avoiding a wreck.

"Sorry," Ayako screamed over the sound of wind and whining gears—so Japanese to apologize in the middle of a bike chase and shoot-out.

Thankfully, the Hayabusa took care of splitting the lion's share of oncoming traffic, so Quinn could just keep the Blackbird pointing down the centerline. Ten seconds after turning around, he passed a blue Nissan with the slender antennas of an undercover police car. The American riding in the passenger seat caught his eye, head snapping around as they shot by.

Quinn could hardly believe it. August Bowen had come all the way to Japan to find him. The thought of a deputy U.S. Marshal always getting his man sounded all well and good—until you happened to be that man.

A near miss with two uniformed high school girls on bicycles pushed thoughts of manhunters and felony arrest out of Quinn's mind. There was nothing he could do about it now. This woman had shot Kim and tried to kill his little girl. She would not get away again.

Bitter cold wind whipped at Quinn's face as he dipped in and out of traffic. Blocky buildings rose up on either side of the street, making it seem as though they were riding through a canyon of concrete and glass. White lines, metal poles, and slippery steel manhole covers flew by in a deadly blur. Both he and Ayako had dropped their helmets when the chase began. She rode with her body tucked in tight against his back, pressed against his leather jacket. Leaning forward over

he handlebars of the bike, Quinn had no such protec-
ion.

There was always the chance that he'd spill, and
offer up his brains to the asphalt gods—but the main
problem with riding at such speeds with no helmet or
goggles was the inability to see. An amazing amount of
debris floated in the city air. Bits of trash, flecks of
dust, gravel thrown up by passing trucks—all scoured
his face like a sandblaster, putting grit in his teeth and
threatening to blind him. Squinting through it, he took
the Blackbird to its limits. He waited to shift until the
tach touched redline, and let off the gas only when absolutely necessary to keep from crashing the bike or
running off the road.

Hayabusa was the Japanese word for peregrine fal-
con. Capable of speeds over two hundred miles an
hour, one of this sleek raptor's favorite meals happened
to be blackbirds. Suzuki had purpose-built the Hayabusa to chase down and eat Honda's sport bike. There
was no question that the Busa was a faster motorcycle.
But city streets didn't give the woman space to really
open it up, and Quinn stayed tucked in behind her as if
tied on with a cable, rarely falling back more than fifty
meters.

A bright red concrete truck changed lanes without
warning. The woman was able to steer out of it, leaning
the Busa into a knee-dragging turn worthy of any race-
track as she followed the curve of Sumiyoshi Street
through its arc in front of the main train station.

"She's running toward the docks!" Ayako yelled in
Quinn's ear as he took the Blackbird into the same
turn. Quinn gave her thigh a pat with his clutch hand, a

warning to hang on as he leaned into the same corner. The fiberglass fairing groaned, scraping against the asphalt, but he rolled on speed smoothly, popping back up on the straightaway.

Ignoring every red light, the Hayabusa shot through the intersections as if she didn't care if she lived or died. Quinn stayed close, but slowed enough to keep from being eaten by any oncoming trucks. Thankfully, most of the lights were green and in their favor.

The Busa took a hard left where the road T'd in front of the sweeping white architecture of the Fukuoka Sun Palace Hotel. The woman missed her lane, shooting again into oncoming traffic. So far, she'd not looked back once. If she knew Quinn was gaining on her, now less than fifteen meters behind, it did not change the way she rode.

Ayako squeezed so tightly Quinn thought she might crack one of his remaining good ribs.

Almost close enough to reach out and touch now, the silver Busa cut right. The red metal girders of the Hakata Port Tower rose up in the distance.

"There is nowhere else to go," Ayako whispered in his ear. "She is trapped." The words were torn away by speed and wind, but Quinn heard them—and they sounded a little sad.

"Get the pistol ready," he yelled over his shoulder.

"I am sorry, Quinn-san," Ayako yelled. "I must have dropped it when we sped away so quickly."

Quinn clenched his jaw. He'd been chasing an armed assassin for the last five minutes with little more than good intentions. A new plan began to take shape in his mind.

"I am truly sorry," she yelled again, wanting to be sure he heard her over the wind and engine noise. "I do not know what happened—"

"Can't be helped," Quinn said as the end of the road loomed in front of them. "Be ready to hand me the sword."

CHAPTER 64

Though plenty fast, Detective Hase's Nissan Skyline was no match for two of the fastest street motorcycles in the world. It wasn't long before the bikes were nearly out of sight.

Bowen was astonished at the detective's unflappable nature. He kept his hands on the wheel at ten and two o'clock, even during a pursuit, weaving in and out of traffic so hard the deputy had to brace himself to keep from falling over on top of him during the slide-over-baby turns.

Several times in the middle of a sharp corner, Bowen was certain they were both about to be killed by an oncoming truck or bus, only to remember at the last minute that Japanese people drove on the left side of the road.

Hase's unmarked car had lights in the dash and the rear window. The siren blared, but few drivers recognized it as a police vehicle.

Police chatter in unintelligible Japanese poured out of the radio. Bowen hung on to the side handle with one hand while he banged on the dash with the other, urging him around a goggled old man in flip-flops putting down the middle of the road on a smoking scooter.

The ring of a phone over the radio speaker interrupted the chatter and the deputy's rant.

Hase moved his hands long enough to tap the hands-free button on his steering wheel, then moved them back to ten and two, machinelike.

"*Hase desu*," he answered with an abrupt grunt. His head swiveled right, then left before crossing an intersection choked with cars, piled in a hopelessly tangled wreck from avoiding the fleeing motorcycles.

"Hmm . . . Hmmm . . . Ehhh . . ." Hase said, in between what sounded to Bowen to be long strings of clicky, garbled nonsense.

Hase tapped the wheel again and ended the call. Eyes on the road, he translated for Bowen. The corners of his normally pensive mouth turned up in a tight smile.

"There is a police helicopter ahead. It looks like your fugitive will not be a fugitive for long. They are heading for the docks beside Hakata Tower. They have nowhere else to go."

CHAPTER 65

A bus full of Korean tourists pulled out of the ferry terminal parking lot and directly into the Hayabusa's path as the woman shot past the red steel latticework of the Hakata Port Tower. Fresh from the trip across the sea, the Koreans pressed animated faces against the window as the woman horsed the big bike to the right in an attempt to avoid a collision.

They were too close and the streets were too wet.

Rather than slam into the side of the bus, the woman laid down the bike, throwing herself into a low-side skid so that it slid in front of her. Metal groaned and ground against pavement, sending up a shower of sparks. The bus driver slammed on his brakes, throwing the faces in the windows forward in their seats. The woman skidded on her back, body tense to keep from tumbling until she bled off speed. Like Quinn, she'd dropped her helmet before the chase began, so she kept her neck up to protect her head.

Flat on her back, the woman was able to slide directly under the bus as her bike struck a tire and jumped through the air, slamming into the fender with a horrific, shattering crunch.

Quinn watched her pistol fall and saw it spinning like a top on the sidewalk. The slide was locked to the rear, empty. It would do him little good, but at least she wouldn't have it to reload.

He goosed the gas to squirt the Blackbird up a delivery ramp at the end of the dockside storefront, working through a crowd of over a hundred junior high students in dark, conservative uniforms who appeared to be on a field trip to the port. When he finally made it around the bus, he saw the woman running toward a group of schoolgirls. She held a short blade of her own and hacked her way through the terrified children. Two girls, neither over twelve, fell before the flashing blade. The others scattered, screaming at the sight of so much blood.

Quinn longed for a gun. Ayako, who'd been looking over his shoulder, shrank at the sight of such cruelty, pressing her face to his back.

The woman kept moving toward the water, a curtain of black hair hanging down over her eyes, swishing back and forth in her frenzied hacking.

Quinn crouched low over the handlebars, urging the bike through the milling crowd on the broad promenade along the pier. His first thought was to run into the murderous woman, but he realized he'd likely kill more kids with the heavy bike than she would with the blade. Five meters away, he abandoned the Blackbird and jumped to the ground, taking the short sword with him. Ayako fell in behind, close, but giving him enough space to work.

First attack was a tricky thing. It was all too easy to give up too much strategy by showing your hand early in the game. If the woman knew how badly he was injured, she'd know exactly where to attack him. But the adrenaline of the chase smoothed the ache in his bones and masked the pain in his back.

He gave a vicious war cry as he crashed in, extending the short sword over his head. Unlike the longer *katana*, the *wakizashi* was generally a one-handed weapon. What it lost in power, it gained in maneuverability.

Quinn brought the blade down almost, but not quite on top of the woman's head. She countered, blocking his sword and bringing her own in a tight arc, slicing the air where his arms would have been had he fully committed to the strike.

The fighters parted as if pushed away from each other by some unseen force, circled slowly, and then came together in a clash of blades, repeating the action over and over in an attempt to gain the upper hand.

At length, their blades locked at the guards at belt level between the two fighters. It was an odd thing, Quinn thought, to look into the face of this young woman who had come so close to killing his little girl, to smell the odor of peppermint on her breath, and to see the map of practice scars that nicked her face and hands. Had he not been locked in battle, it would have been easy to feel pity for this girl who was barely old enough to be called a woman. He'd often feel pity for those he'd killed—after the fact.

Locked together, each pushed against the other, standing their ground. The first to pull away would be exposed to a rapid and surely fatal cut.

Grunting, the woman gave a toss of her head to get the hair out of her eyes. "You are better than I expected you to be."

"I watched a lot of *The Princess Bride*." Quinn smiled.

"What?"

Never in his life had he wanted so badly to cut someone down. In order to do that, he had to stay alive. In an unspoken, mutually agreed momentary truce, the fighters pushed apart, circling again for another attack.

Feinting, the woman drew Quinn out to block a blow from his left, forcing him to twist toward his injured kidney. He blocked the attack but stumbled slightly, allowing her blade to slice through the shoulder of his leather jacket.

A smile perked the corners of the woman's lips. She circled, moving easily like a shark at the scent of blood.

"You are hurt." She tipped her head toward his waist.

Quinn brushed the words aside as he would a blade, changing the subject while he caught his breath. In truth, the intense pain brought on by that simple twisting movement had nearly taken him to his knees.

He kept the tip of his sword high. "You've been after me since Colorado."

The woman's lips pulled back into a scornful laugh. Black eyes glared. "I watched you long before that, Jericho Quinn."

"Did your father send you after me . . . *Ran*?" He used her given name, the one Miyagi had told him. It sounded more like *Lon* when he said it in Japanese.

The girl laughed, wagging her head derisively in spite of the situation. "Ohhh, you think you know so much."

"I know your mother is named Emiko." He circled, letting the tip of his blade drop so it pointed at her cold heart.

She rolled her eyes, stomping forward in a flurry of cuts that opened a flap of thick leather along his arm.

She stepped back to survey the damage. "You know nothing."

"If your father is so great and powerful, why does he send females to do his heavy work?" Quinn's words dripped with scorn but dizziness tugged at his brain. At any moment he would stumble an inch in the wrong direction. When he did, she would cut him down without a second thought.

"Do not flatter yourself." The woman eyed him as if she had already won. "You are a passable warrior, Jericho Quinn." She feinted right, then left, drawing him out again before her blade flashed in a diagonal line across the front of his jacket. The blade cut all the way through, slicing leather, armor, and then skin. Quinn felt the acid burn as the razor edge scraped a rib, but the jacket took the worst of the attack and he was able to step offline, keeping his feet—for the moment.

She backed up a half step, circling, preparing to strike again. "To you, the blade is only a pastime. The way of the sword has been my life."

Badly wounded now, Quinn was vaguely aware of a flashing blur to his right. Knocked violently sideways, he heard Ayako's anguished scream as she rushed past him, impaling her belly on the startled woman's blade.

Ayako drove forward, grabbing the hilt with both hands and pushing the woman backward. Gasping, she whispered something that Quinn couldn't make out before falling to the concrete, the stingray skin handle of the short sword sticking from her bleeding stomach.

The young woman's face went pale at the sudden attack. Stunned by Ayako's heroics, she backpedaled, scowling and cursing under her breath. Quinn raised his sword and advanced, but she turned and ran toward the pier to dive over the edge and disappear with a splash below.

Quinn fell to his knees beside a gasping Ayako. She lay on her side. Blood seeped through clenched fingers where they closed around the hilt. The blade had pierced her all the way through and the tip protruded out her back, tenting the cloth of her jacket.

"I am sorry, Quinn-san," she whispered. A sheen of pink blood covered her teeth. Her lungs rattled with each labored breath.

"Shhh." Quinn put a finger to her lips. "Listen," he said. "Hear the sirens? Help is on the way."

Tears pressed through the heavy makeup of Ayako's clenched lashes. Wincing, she reached inside her shirt and retrieved the pink notebook. "Please," she gasped, her voice barely audible. "Take . . . this."

Her fingers left a red trail on the cover as she pressed it into his hand.

"I would have made a good wife," she whispered.

"Yes, you would have," Quinn said.

"I think this was my moment." She coughed, beginning to shiver from shock and blood loss. She nodded toward the water. "Be careful of that one . . ." Ayako swallowed hard, gasping for air. "She is fierce, like her mother . . ."

Her face went slack and her hands fell away from her belly.

Police and medical support squealed onto the scene. Quinn returned Fujin to the scabbard and shoved it down the back of the collar of his jacket so it ran along his spine. There were already people tending to the wounded children, so Quinn got on the Blackbird and rode to the edge of the pier, scanning for any sign of the woman.

"Hey!" A voice called out in English behind him.

Quinn looked over his shoulder and felt his heart sink as he saw a familiar man approach.

"What brings you to Japan, Gus Bowen?"

"You know, looking for killers," the deputy said, a raw edge to his voice. "Shit like that." His hand was under his sport coat. If he had a gun, he didn't show it.

"Maybe you came for a rematch on that fight." Quinn turned, ignoring Bowen to keep his eyes on the line of squid boats that bobbed in the mist along the two sets of docks nearest the pier.

"No sport in that." Bowen whistled. "You can barely stand up. We need to get you to a hospital."

"I got things to do," Quinn said.

"I saw what your friend did to save you." Bowen's voice was full of reverence. "Incredibly brave."

Quinn shook his head, preferring not to discuss someone like Ayako Shimizu with anyone who didn't know her.

"Come on, Jericho. You're hurt. What do you say we let the Japanese deal with their own mess?"

"That's the problem, Gus," Quinn said. "This is my mess."

Two piers over, the engine of a speedboat burbled to life. There had been an escape plan all along.

Bowen finally showed the pistol but he let it hang

down by his side instead of aiming in. He stood, staring, mulling something over in his mind.

"Let's go sort this all out," he finally said, sounding flat and fatigued.

Quinn kept a hand on the throttle, ready to move. He'd seen Bowen shoot and didn't want to try his hand at being a target. "Can you remember a telephone number?"

Bowen nodded, drilling holes with his eyes.

Quinn gave him Win Palmer's personal line.

"Jericho." Bowen frowned. "Don't make me chase you. You know I will if I have to."

"I'm not making you do anything." Quinn revved the engine. "In fact, I'd just as soon you didn't. Don't forget that number."

Quinn sped down the dock on the Blackbird, leaving Bowen, Hase, and the other responding law enforcement to take care of the wounded and terrified children.

August Bowen was about justice—not just the law. Had it been otherwise, he would have never let Quinn leave alive.

Sticky blood from the wound across his ribs matted his shirt to his chest. His head and back throbbed with a sickening ache that went well beyond his bones. But above all the cuts, breaks, and bruises, the deepest wound came from watching Ayako die.

Quinn poured on the gas, weaving in and out of traffic. With all the local authorities at the port, there was no one to try to stop him. He had no idea where he was going. It didn't matter as long as it was far away. He'd never considered himself an emotional man. But now, physically broken and mentally exhausted to the point he could hardly keep the bike going in a straight line, he thought of what Ayako had done for him and sniffed back a tear. Never before had he felt so hopeless. Never had he been so close to giving up.

And then, he remembered her book.

CHAPTER 66

Kanab, Utah

Marta Bedford coughed. It took Herculean effort to lift her leg and try to move it so it didn't press on the worst of her boils along the back of her knee. Grunting and hacking like an invalid woman twice her age, she grabbed the metal railing on the narrow hospital bed and maneuvered onto her right side.

Kane County Hospital had never been intended to house this many patients. Green military beds like something out of *M*A*S*H* crammed each room and lined the halls. Todd had made certain that the Bedfords had a room together, but Mrs. Johnson's bed ran along the wall inside the door so there were three in a row, leaving just enough room between each of the patients for medical staff to tend them.

Had Rick not been so heavily sedated for the ECMO heart-lung bypass, Marta could have held his hand. As it was, every few minutes she rolled up on her side and bore the pressure on her boils as long as she could so she could watch him sleep.

Todd had told her there was still a chance the bypass

would save Rick's life. That he might be able to fight off whatever caused the boils as long as they could keep his lungs functioning.

From the time she was a little girl, tears had come easy to Marta Bedford. Her father could simply look sternly at her and bring what he called a geyser of repentance. But now, since Rick had gotten sick, she had long since cried herself out. First, she was angry with God for letting such an illness fall on her good husband. Then, she cried from the horrible pain caused by her own boils. Finally, her tears had been from the despair of knowing that she would not live to see her daughters graduate from high school, go to college, marry, or have children of their own.

In the end, she had forgiven God and come to grips with the fact that she'd never see her grandbabies. Though the pain never slackened, and was barely dented by medication, at least it reminded Marta that she was alive. In a macabre sense of competition, she and Mrs. Johnson had taken to counting the number of new boils on their arms. So far, Marta was "winning" but, as Mrs. Johnson pointed out between phlegm-laced bouts of her hacking cough, it wasn't really fair because Marta was taller and thus had longer arms and more opportunities for boils to grow.

Gripping the bed rail to watch Rick, Marta found a new sore on the inside of her wrist. It was red and swollen with a translucent white dot in the center. They could not be counted until the white appeared.

"Got a new one, Mrs. Johnson," Marta said. Her voice rattled when she spoke.

She got no response.

Marta began the laborious process of rolling back

over to her left side so she could look at her competition.

"That's twenty-seven to twenty," Bedford said as she lifted the sheet and worked her way over. "Mrs. Johnson . . . ?"

Snow-white hair lay across the old woman's pillow. Wrinkled hands folded across her chest. Her jaw hung open, lifeless.

Marta Bedford collapsed back against her sheets. She had a few tears left after all.

CHAPTER 67

Quinn needed a doctor, but he didn't care. He pointed the Blackbird east. Fifteen miles out of Fukuoka he found a small side road in the mountains that took him another half mile back to a secluded gravel pullout. Giant cryptomeria stood like sentries around the gravel pad. The earth underneath their broad evergreen canopies was at once landscaped and pristine, as if it had been swept by a scouring wind and not by human hands.

Quinn all but collapsed under the tent-like awning of one of the Japanese cedars. He leaned against rough bark and closed his eyes. He tried not to think—to clear his mind and let it rest. Ayako deserved more than a passing thought crammed somewhere in between strategy and battle plan. Though she'd ended up in a vocation that put her at odds with social and even moral norms, there was no way for anyone else to know what had driven her there. She'd said it herself— she wanted to be someone's wife and feel safe. Prostitute, whore, yellow cab, woman of the floating world . . . just a woman, pushed by some secret demons—demons that led back to Oda.

Quinn sat in the shadow of the big tree and thought about her for a long time, regretting the lost opportunities and the things he might have said to give her just a little bit more happiness. He wished Thibodaux were there so he could listen to the big Cajun philosophize about womanhood and the fragility of life.

Pressing his injured back against the tree as if the pain might focus his tattered thoughts, Quinn opened his eyes and began to read Ayako's book.

The first two pages contained the lyrics to some Korean pop song—likely by the young boy band from the poster in her apartment. They were written phonetically and decorated with hearts and flower doodles. Over the next several pages, Ayako had noted various appointments using a sort of code to describe her clients with names like Mr. Octopus, The Jelly Fish, and Sir Badger Dog. Grocery lists, more doodle drawings of kittens, and an incredibly realistic pencil study of a young geisha took up the first third of the little book.

Then, in bold ink was the entry—"*Pick up Emiko's friend at Hakata Port.*" Followed by "*He would do nicely*" on a rain-spattered page.

Quinn turned the page and found a letter, written in her artistic, girlish hand. It was addressed to him.

Quinn-san,

If you are reading this, something has happened to me, for I would never let you see it if I were alive. I am sorry that I have not written on a more beautiful piece of paper befitting a good man like you. But, in our present circumstance, if I wait, I might not complete the letter at all. I hope to make this brief, but short letters take a long time to write, and I fear that I do not have so much of that. So, please forgive my clumsy attempt.

You sleep as I write this. I watch you softly breathe and my heart aches because I have lied to you. The thought brings so much pain that confessing to you is an impossible task, even in this letter. So, I must beg your forgiveness and pray that what I have done moves you toward your moment, whatever that may be.

We say in Japan that those who travel for love find a thousand miles not longer than one. Though our journey together has been erratic and full of peril, it has to me, been all too short.

That is all for now.

Ayako

Quinn sniffed back a tear in spite of himself, wondering what lies she'd told to cause her such a heavy burden. She must have written the letter while they were in the temple cottage. It was the only time she would have been able to watch him sleep.

Quinn turned the page, hoping to find another entry— not quite ready to say good-bye to this sweet little woman. His breath caught in his throat when he saw the map.

There was a short note, hastily scrawled in pencil as she'd stood there beside him in the alley watching Yanagi Pharmaceutical, a cold wind whipping her hair across her face.

Please forgive me. All woman have secrets.
I do not wish mine to cause your death.
Remember, when you kill a snake, do it once
and for all.

Below the note was a map, captioned with a single
word: *Oda*.

CHAPTER 68

Governor Lee McKeon stood in front of the bathroom mirror of the Hay Adams Hotel and slipped a pair of beige latex gloves over slender fingers.

He had already showered and shaved. The French cuffs on his starched white shirt were folded but open. Gold cuff links sat in a small leather case on the white marble sink next to his wife's makeup. He wore a conservative burgundy silk tie that his wife said would suit his Asian complexion. This was, after all, an extremely big night for him and he needed to look his best.

The wooden box Qasim Ranjhani had given him lay open beside the cuff links, dark and polished in stark contrast to the white marble. Inside, resting on a small velvet pillow, was a Rolex Sea Dweller, its second hand sweeping around the face in a smooth, fluid movement.

McKeon retrieved a roll of beige athletic tape from his shaving kit and took a half dozen wraps around his wrist, making a sort of gauntlet. Ripping the tape with his teeth, he smoothed the edge on the end nearer his hand so it wouldn't be seen past the cuff of his dress shirt. Next, he tore open a large four-by-four plastic bandage and applied it to the underside of his left wrist over the tape, pressing it tight to make certain the edges didn't roll up. He added one more for safety's sake, placing it halfway up his wrist, overlapping the other so he had a protected piece of skin roughly four by six inches as well as the gauntlet of tape.

McKeon held his wrist up and examined it in the mirror. Satisfied that he was well protected, but inconspicuous, he lifted the Rolex from the wooden case. Careful not to touch the sapphire crystal, even with his gloves, he slipped the watch over his hand so the face was on the inside of his wrist, toward his body, and snapped the clasp. It fit snugly; Ranjhani had made certain of that. The consequences would be dire if it was allowed to slide around and possibly come in contact with his skin.

He removed the latex gloves and had just finished putting on the cuff links when his wife's voice buzzed through the bathroom door.

"Are you ready?" She was a fanatic about many things; early arrival to meetings was at the top of the list.

"Just putting on the finishing touches, my dear." McKeon took his dark blue suit jacket out of the plastic bag hanging on the back of the door and slipped it over narrow shoulders. He tugged the cuff down so it covered the watch. It wouldn't do to accidentally brush the thing against his wife's skin.

"We must not be late," she said again, prodding.

"It's okay. They have assigned seating." Looking in

the mirror one last time, he gave the burgundy tie a final adjustment. "Do not worry." He put a hand on the door, heart pounding in his chest at the thought of what lay before him. "I'm a friend of the President of the United States. I get a seat on the House floor."

CHAPTER 69

Quinn sat on the bike with the engine off, perched on the crest of a hill half a mile away from Oda's compound. The rain had stopped and a weak winter sun showed between the low clouds and the rolling mist-choked mountains to the west. Dark forests ran along the snaking valleys, populated by deer and wild boar. Large houses with tile roofs ran in meandering lines on another foothill to the south. Step-terraced tea plantations, groves of orange trees, and thick stands of bamboo created a glistening wet patchwork of green in the low sunlight. It was singularly beautiful and uniquely Japanese.

He'd briefly considered riding back through town to find August Bowen and ask for help, but in the end decided against it. Not because he didn't want the help, but because he couldn't trust that the deputy would believe him, much less follow him into the mountains to fight some mysterious assassin.

Ayako's map was excellent, and Quinn was able to work his way deep into the mountains to Oda's sanctuary in less than two hours. She'd gone so far as to warn him of sentries and direct him in the best avenue of ap-

proach. For a woman who made her living in the float
ing quarter, she was a brilliant tactician.

Oda's secluded garden compound was itself located
on a hill, but by coming in on a forest trail on an adjacent hill Quinn was able to get a good look at the front
gate and the three sentries that guarded it, if not the
compound itself.

He could make out the dark shapes of several buildings through the thick woods on the other side of the
fence. One, presumably the main house, rose like a
smaller version of a feudal lord's castle, high parapets
and curling green tile roof visible over the treetops. It
was the way he'd imagined it from Miyagi's stories.

Quinn could tell from the insulators that the fence
was electrified. He recognized two of the guards from
Tanaka's warehouse. Still dressed in business suits, the
men paced outside a tall wrought-iron gate. One of the
men smoked an entire cigarette while Quinn watched.
The other, less nervous, periodically aimed his submachine gun at some bird in a nearby tree pretending
to shoot. Inside the fence, a third man, dressed as a
groundskeeper in baggy canvas pants and a denim
shirt, stood post next to a small security booth—presumably with the controls for the gate. All carried
short-barrel Uzi machine pistols on single-point slings
around their necks.

He not only had to take care of the two out front,
he'd have to somehow get through the electrified fence
and dispatch the third man before he could bring the
Uzi into play. Quinn had no real plan beyond that other
than fighting his way forward until he found Oda or the
woman. He really didn't care which. It was certain to
rain guards as soon as the fence was breached. Some

would call that overwhelming odds. He thought of it as a target-rich environment.

Foot on the brake, Quinn tested his arms, moving them back and forth and feeling the wound open up along his ribs. He flexed his hands. His left still worked, albeit a little slower than normal. He still had a full range of motion in his right arm, and though his back was sore, adrenaline, brought on in anticipation of battle, loosened his muscles and dampened the pain. He was not in optimum shape, but he was as ready as he would ever be. And for the sake of Kim, Mattie, Miyagi, and Ayako—he could not stop now.

Holding the sheathed sword in his right hand so it ran along the top of the handlebars, he released the clutch and let the bike roll.

The two yakuza guards jumped back when Quinn and the silent Blackbird burst from the trees ten yards to their left. The nearest tried to raise his weapon, but Quinn hit him across the face with the sheathed sword as he rolled past, moving well over twenty miles an hour. The blow shattered the man's nose and sent him stumbling backward into the electrified fence with a hiss and a puff of acrid smoke.

Rolling from the moving bike, Quinn shook the sword from its scabbard and came up on his feet directly in front of the second guard just as the five-hundred-pound Blackbird crashed through the gate. He swatted the Uzi aside and cut up obliquely, severing the single-point sling and the man's jugular in one motion.

Quinn grabbed for the falling machine gun, but the sling caught on the dying man and jerked it out of his hand. With no time to waste fumbling with the tangled weapon, he sprinted toward the fence, clearing the demolished gate at the same moment the third guard stepped around the shack and raised his weapon. Still five meters out, Quinn knew he was too far away to do any good with the sword. A claxon alarm began to blare beyond the trees, but that didn't matter. In less than a second the guard would send a volley of bullets into him that the torn armor of his Transit jacket would not be able to stop.

The *phhhht* of suppressed gunfire caused Quinn's heart to sink. He marveled that he didn't feel more pain or loss of motion—until he watched the guard ahead of him fall like wheat before a sickle.

Quinn pulled up short, touching his stomach where he assumed the bullets would have hit him. The guard's weapon lay at his feet, carrying no suppressor.

A crunch of gravel behind caused Quinn to wheel, bringing the sword around in a fluid arc.

Jacques Thibodaux's Cajun drawl stopped him cold.

"I know, I know, this boogerman is too dangerous for the likes of us. We should let you do this all by yourself." The gunny trotted up with a suppressed MP5 in his shovel-size hands. He scanned the trees ahead. "But come on, Chair Force, did you really think Palmer would know where you were and not send us to give you a hand?"

Emiko Miyagi and Ronnie Garcia fanned out behind the Marine. Both women carried MP5s identical to Thibodaux's, but Miyagi also carried a sheathed samurai *katana* slung diagonally over her back.

Quinn let the short sword hang by his side.

"I don't know what to say."

" 'Thanks for saving my myopic ass' would seem

appropriate." Thibodaux scoffed. "A body would think you might actually be glad to see us."

Quinn felt as if he might cry.

Ronnie ran to him, lowering her weapon long enough to give him a hard kiss on the mouth.

Thibodaux pressed a small microphone at his throat. "Tell me what you got, kid." He motioned the group forward toward the cover of thick-trunked Japanese cedar, nodding as he listened to the information coming across his earpiece.

Quinn retrieved Fujin's scabbard and stuck the sword down the back of his jacket, before scooping up the dead sentry's Uzi and following at a trot.

Miyagi scanned the woods, saying nothing. She had yet to meet Quinn's gaze. Considering the mission that lay ahead, it was easy to understand why.

Garcia had her hair pulled back in a thick ponytail, and Quinn found himself amazed that someone could fill out a set of khakis as well as she did.

She pointed skyward with her thumb when they slid up next to the trees, explaining Thibodaux's conversation.

"Guttman's got Damocles loitering above us."

Quinn smiled at the news.

Damocles was an off-the-books stealth drone. Developed by Lockheed Martin's infamous Skunkworks, it was extreme high-side technology, "over-the-top" secret. Few in the government, and certainly no members of Congress, knew of its existence. Hanging overhead like the sword on a single hair from the Greek story, the drone could be armed with Tomahawk missiles and, more important to Quinn, a Gorgon Starepod with an array of cameras capable of counting the fuzz on a dandelion blossom from the nether regions of the atmosphere.

"Here's the deal, kids," Thibodaux said at length. "Our young Sergeant Guttman says we have five guys heading our way. There's a female coming around the north side of the main building and another squad of four spilling out of some barracks straight up the middle. According to the kid, some old guy appears to be directing things from on top of the main building."

"That would be Oda," Miyagi hissed. "Where on top of the building?"

Thibodaux consulted with Guttman for more information from the loitering drone.

"Northwest corner," Thibodaux said. "Looks like he's—"

Miyagi was gone before he could finish.

"Damn," he muttered. "I was gonna say looks like he's got four other guys up there with him."

Quinn watched Miyagi meld into the shadows with the sword across her back. "I almost feel sorry for them."

Approaching voices sifted through the trees, yelling commands and demanding answers from the dead gate sentries.

"I don't think these guys know that there is anyone here but you." Thibodaux winked his good eye, nodding toward the white building that was barely visible through the forest. "How about you pretend for a minute you're not a lowly Chair Force officer but an honest-to-goodness Marine and help me charge this castle."

The high likelihood of imminent death aside, Quinn couldn't help grinning like a schoolboy as he ran into the trees alongside his friends.

CHAPTER 70

Washington, D.C.

"**M**ister Speaker!" the House Sergeant at Arms shouted as he stepped through the heavy oak door and stopped. "The President of the United States!"

Thunderous applause rose from the House Chamber.

Governor Lee McKeon was lucky to have a seat among the shoulder-to-shoulder crowd. House and senate members took up most of the floor. Vice President Hughes and the Speaker of the House, Hartman Drake, faced the hall above the lectern under a large American flag. Drake wore a sling over his left shoulder, cradling his wounded arm and reminding the American public that terrorism could strike all too close to home. His bright red bow tie looked like a second smile as he tapped the desk in front of him in polite, one-handed applause. Cabinet members and justices of the Supreme Court occupied the front row near the raised dais. Secretary of State Melissa Ryan, close friend and protégé to the president, was conspicuously absent. Since September the eleventh, one member of the Cabinet was customarily asked to wait in an undisclosed location so the entire line of succession to the presidency could not be wiped out in one fell swoop.

President Chris Clark began to work the crowd the moment he entered the chamber, kissing women, shaking hands, and smiling as though his dimpled cheeks might shatter. McKeon nodded cordially to Jack Blackmore, Clark's lead Secret Service Agent. The two knew each other from the governor's recent meetings with the president. Blackmore stepped aside as McKeon extended both hands, taking Clark in a firm, brotherly shake with both hands so the Rolex Sea Dweller's crystal face rubbed the skin on the back of the president's hand. It was little more than a passing touch, but, according to Ranjhani, it would be enough.

"Good to see you, Lee," Clark said, pumping the man's hand in an earnest handshake of friendship. Laughably, he thought they were allies.

McKeon released his grip and slid away. "Good to see you as well, Mr. President."

Up on the dais, Vice President Hughes and Hartman Drake clapped politely as they watched Clark work his way down the imperial blue carpet toward the podium, shaking more hands along the way.

He couldn't see it, but McKeon knew that on the desk in front of Hughes was a brand-new fountain pen, a gift from the Speaker of the House, who, in turn, had received it from Qasim Ranjhani.

Clark stepped up to the podium and handed an envelope containing a copy of his speech to the vice president and another to the Speaker. Turning, the president stood at the lectern, grinning while Drake introduced him.

"My fellow Americans," he said. "Though recent horrific events may lead you to believe otherwise, the state of the union is . . ."

The president paused, scratching the back of his hand. He looked down at his copy of the speech as if he'd lost place.

"My fellow Americans . . ." The ever-present smile vanished from his lips. He clutched his arm and stared out into the chamber, eyes unfocused, his mouth agape in a silent cry of pain.

Special Agent Blackmore, ever attentive to the needs of his charge, rushed to the president's side the moment before he collapsed, guiding him to the ground. Secret Service personnel rushed from the sidelines, forming an instant perimeter around the fallen leader.

From the back of the chamber, Governor Lee McKeon watched four other agents bound up to the vice president while Capitol Police officers moved to Hartman Drake, ready to usher the men toward the Speaker's Entrance, away from any threat as dictated by protocol.

Bob Hughes turned to look back at the flurry of activity around the president, the heavy weight of responsibility certainly bearing down on him.

McKeon suppressed a smile. The vice president needn't have worried. In a few short seconds, any possibility of him stepping into the presidency would be gone forever.

CHAPTER 71

Thibodaux and Garcia engaged Oda's responding troops with a withering fusillade of gunfire as Quinn skirted to the north side of the palatial home. Two sentries rounded the corner of a covered pavilion beside a koi pond, nearly running headlong into Quinn. The Uzi burped in his hands, killing both of them before they realized they'd found him.

A flash of movement caught his eye from above and he watched Miyagi scuttle along the outer edge of the parapet that ran lengthwise down the top of the roofline. Oda had indeed modeled the place after a feudal castle. Each corner had a raised tower with a metal railing that allowed a commander or defenders to look down on anyone trying to mount a siege from below.

Quinn heard a twig snap behind him and spun, moving to the cover of a nearby cedar. A volley of gunfire rattled from the shadows. He raised the Uzi to return fire, but when he pulled the trigger nothing happened.

Tap-rack-bang, failure-to-feed, failure-to-fire drills had been ingrained into his brain from the time he'd first started to carry a gun for a living. *Tap*—he slammed his hand into the base of the magazine to make certain it was seated. *Rack*—he worked the Uzi's open bolt to clear any possible misfeed, then aimed again and pulled the trigger.

No *bang*.

His back pressed flat against the tree, he lifted the weapon to check in more closely. A round had impacted the stamped metal frame, denting the action and rendering it inoperable.

"We did not get to finish our contest," a woman's voice said from the other side of the tree. "The foolish whore prolonged your miserable life."

Quinn dropped the Uzi to the ground. "So," he yelled, "you want to finish what you started?"

"Pitiful Mr. Quinn," the woman said, "that is exactly what I plan to do."

He stepped around the tree, short sword in his hand. He half expected her to shoot him but only breathed a hair easier when he saw the long sword held before her in two hands. She'd beaten him before with the shorter wakizashi. Now she had another foot and a half of razor-sharp reach and the leverage of a two-handed grip.

The woman cocked her head to one side, hair hanging in a sullen flap across her eyes as she studied him. Absent the heavy motorcycle jacket, she was even smaller than Quinn had realized. She was dressed in tight black spandex pants—like Miyagi wore during their workouts—and a loose cotton blouse, open but for the bottom two buttons to reveal the swirling colors of the tattoo that covered her chest like an undershirt. Unlike Miyagi, there was no un-inked line running up the center of her body. She appeared to use the tattoo as some kind of psychological weapon, depending on the sight of it to disarm her opponents.

"What do you think of the design?" She gave a toss of her head.

"I've seen better." Quinn shrugged. His feet slid over the rough ground, matching her pace as she circled.

"That is laughable."

"Seriously," Quinn said. "I have seen your mother's tattoo. It is more skillfully applied."

A flash of panic crossed the girl's eyes. "What do you know of my mother?"

"She is my friend." Quinn suddenly changed directions, closing the distance more quickly than the young woman had anticipated. She blocked his strike and slashed the sleeve of his jacket, toying with him before she stepped back to disengage. She was not quite ready to finish him until he'd satisfied her curiosity.

"I will ask you this only once." She began to circle counterclockwise, forcing Quinn to lead with his left leg, sending waves of agony radiating from his injured kidney. "What do you know of my mother?"

Quinn smiled inside, remembering the words Miyagi had spoken in her garden the last time they'd sparred. *Just because you hold a sword, does not mean it is the only weapon you can use to win the battle.*

Gunfire popped and rattled in pockets below as Miyagi made her way along the rooftop. She'd encountered three sentries and dispatched each of them in turn silently with her dagger. Only one man stood at parade rest beside Oda at the far corner facing the knee-high stone parapet.

"I see you have resorted to bodyguards," Miyagi said when she came up behind them. It had been years since she'd seen him, and yet it still seemed as if a fist gripped her heart.

Both men wheeled. The guard raised a pistol, but Miyagi put three bullets in his chest and a fourth in his forehead in case he happened to be wearing a vest.

Oda's mouth fell open at the sight of her.

"Incredible," he whispered. "You haven't changed at all." He had no weapon and raised both hands as if to embrace her as she advanced.

Miyagi found herself amazed at how much he'd aged. Still, there was a ferocity in his eyes that said he was not some old man to be trifled with. She took a half step back, fighting a rising panic.

He saw it and his face softened at once, drawing her in. A smile spread over rosy cheeks. She'd forgotten how handsome he could make himself.

"Oh, how I have missed you, Emi-chan," he said. "I often wondered if you would ever return home."

"Home . . ." Miyagi mused. "You were never that to me."

Oda shook his head, chiding. "I gave you sanctuary," he said. "And a beautiful daughter."

"It would seem," Miyagi said, swallowing the bile that rose in her throat, "that I gave the daughter to you."

"As you say." Oda shrugged. "But you were always my favorite. You know that, don't you?"

Miyagi struggled to keep her face passive. "Takako-san was once your favorite," she said. "I just came from her home, where I witnessed what you do to former *favorites*."

"That was an unfortunate necessity," he said. "But, she had become slow of wit—unlike you, it appears."

"Is that so?" Miyagi said. She wanted to shoot him,

but the gun felt like it weighed a thousand pounds in her hands. "It might interest you to know she left behind volumes of notebooks detailing her work for you over the past years—including information on your present relationship with a man named Ranjhani. Not so slow of wit, it seems."

"Then I was right to kill her." Oda sighed, but Miyagi caught the tiniest glint of worry in his eyes. "You are strong, Emi-chan, much stronger that she ever was." He flicked his fingers. "Come, put down the gun and let us relive old times."

"And what of Ayako?" Miyagi stared at him. "Was she your favorite as well?"

"No, no." Oda waved away the thought, vain enough to believe Miyagi actually wanted to be his favorite. "Ayako-chan was only a vessel. You are certainly stronger than that foolish whore."

Miyagi leveled the MP5, letting anger chase away her uneasiness. Oda was a monster, but he was merely a man, not a god to be feared.

Miyagi put two rounds in Oda's belly, low so he would feel it. He stumbled backward, teetering at the edge of the roof. He reached out, hands flailing for support, seeking to control her even to the end.

"Emiko . . . help me . . ."

Miyagi let the MP5 fall against her sling and drew her sword, extending it toward the falling man. Groping blindly, he grabbed the blade with both hands, leaving his fingers behind as he tumbled over the parapet.

"Ayako-chan survived when you cut her daughter from the womb," Miyagi whispered, peering over the edge at Oda's shattered body below. "She was the strongest woman I have ever known."

* * *

Quinn feinted left, offering his injured side to draw the tattooed woman out.

Believing he was beaten, she struck again, slicing the sleeve of his Transit jacket. This time he was ready and took the cut on the crash armor, sliding by so he was inside her guard. Crashing in, he gave her a vicious head butt, shattering the bridge of her nose and sending her staggering backward.

Quinn kept coming, punching her over and over in the face with his left hand. She raised the sword to fend him off. It was a blind reaction but caused him to side-step to keep from getting cut. Far from beaten, she held the sword with her left hand and brought her right around in a brutal punch to his kidney.

Fighting through the pain, Quinn pressed closer so he was chest to chest with the young woman, rendering her long sword useless.

"Get off me, you fool!" she spat. The odor of peppermint hit him full in the face.

A torrent of white-hot fury flowed through his body. He stepped to the side, stomping laterally at her knee, hearing the satisfying crunch as cartilage tore and the joint gave way. She screamed, twisting to the side to relieve the sudden pain. Quinn stepped behind her, grabbing the flap of sullen hair and jerking her head backward as he snaked his arm over the top of her throat, catching her head under his arm so her body was arched in front of him, her neck bent backward with nowhere to go. Hauling upward and back, he felt a dull snap.

The sword fell from her grasp, but he held her there a full minute longer, panting, squeezing, his entire body shaking from shock and relief. Finally satisfied that she was dead, Quinn let her body fall to the ground. He wasn't far behind her, collapsing to his knees on the gravel.

Thibodaux and Garcia came up moments later. Ronnie fell beside him, supporting him with strong arms. Jacques let out a mournful sigh. "I wonder if we're ever gonna run out of folks to kill . . ."

"Oda?" Quinn whispered.

"Miyagi took a gun to his knife fight," Thibodaux said.

Still panting, Quinn found the strength to roll the dead woman over and raise her shirt so he could check her tattoo on her back. "*Komainu*," he said under his breath.

"What?" Ronnie stayed locked in beside him.

"A foo dog," Quinn said. "This may be difficult for Emiko to see—"

Miyagi's voice came from behind him. "I am sorry to say it is not so difficult for me after all," she said, standing over the body to peruse the tattoo. "This is not my daughter."

"But the tattoo," Quinn said, "it is just as you described.

"So it is," Miyagi said. "But I was a fool not to remember that *komainu* come in pairs. One most always has his mouth open; on the other, the mouth is closed, as it is here." She used the tip of her sword to point to the dead woman's back. The ferocious temple dog did indeed stare at them over a closed mouth.

"Then who?" Quinn closed his eyes, knowing the answer before she told him.

"Her name is *Hiromi*. Ayako-chan had a difficult

pregnancy," Miyagi said. "She feared that she would lose the child and tried to sneak away, but Oda caught her. He cut out the baby with a dagger and left Ayako to die. Even Shimoyama, who had to that point looked down on the younger girls, took pity on the poor thing and helped her get medical attention. She saved Ayako's life but gave up a little finger in return—and the trust of Oda."

"Of course," Quinn said, remembering the signs he should have seen—the visceral way Ayako had reacted when he mentioned Oda's name, the way she'd gone pale when he told her he was looking for a girl with a *komainu* tattooed on her back. Though Hiromi would have no memory of her real mother, Ayako would have kept up with her. Hiromi was the reason she'd kept disrupting his aim during the chase through Yanagi Pharmaceutical. She was the reason Ayako had dropped the pistol during the motorcycle chase.

It was the first time she'd ever seen her daughter since the day Oda cut the child from her belly. No wonder Ayako wanted to protect her—but even the love for a daughter had limits. Something had snapped when she'd seen her damaged daughter cut down the innocent children. Even then, as she lay dying, she'd given Quinn the last clue in her warning.

"She is fierce," Ayako had said. "Just like her mother."

CHAPTER 72

Winfield Palmer answered on the fourth ring. His voice was hollow, preoccupied.

"Oda is dead," Quinn said. He leaned against Ronnie, who sat with her back to a cedar tree supporting him while Thibodaux and Miyagi went to bring up the car.

"Good," Palmer said. "That's good."

"He was up to something at Yanagi," Quinn said. "I'd say everything they manufactured is highly suspect."

"I agree," Palmer said. His voice was a strained whisper, as if he didn't want to wake someone beside him. "All that vaccine has been impounded. The pages from the notebook Miyagi texted me line out pretty well what happened. I've already got some of your OSI friends looking for the Kyrgyz barber at Bagram. There are others, as yet unidentified, that were spreading the infection by anything that would come in contact with the victim's blood—infected razors, fingernail files, scissors—even dental floss. We've arrested a dental assistant in Cedar City and have leads on several others. Not much hope of finding them now, though."

"You okay, boss?" Quinn was having a hard time grasping why Palmer wasn't sharing in his enthusiasm that they had just dodged a very deadly bullet. He sounded like Eeyore.

"Not really," Palmer said. "Chris Clark was pronounced dead an hour ago."

"The president?"

"There's more, Jericho," Palmer went on. "Bob Hughes collapsed as well. It looks like they both succumbed to some kind of poison."

Quinn sat up straight as the ramifications hit him. "That means—"

"Exactly." Palmer spelled it out for him. "Pursuant to the Twenty-fifth Amendment, Speaker of the House Hartman Drake assumed the presidency of the United States. He's already made an impassioned statement to the American people, reminding them that he was himself the victim of not one, but two terrorist attacks. Citing the need for continuity, he has already named Governor Lee McKeon as his vice president. Congressional approval is a foregone conclusion."

"I gotta tell you, Quinn," Palmer went on, "Drake knows who you are now. If you come back here, you're as good as dead. I sure as hell can't protect you."

"Has he fired you?"

"Not yet," Palmer said. "But it's coming—probably by the end of the day."

"Ronnie says the book ties Officer Larsson to this group. Does that put me clear of Jenny Chin's murder?"

"In a word," Palmer said. "But like I said, Drake hates you. And he's the president of the United States, so he'll push for a thorough investigation and your quick execution.

"Anyway, I used what little pull I have left to call off the Marshals. Deputy Bowen should be linking up with you anytime now, so do me a favor and don't shoot him."

"Got it," Quinn said. "You holding up okay?"

"You know, I lost an extremely close friend," Palmer said. "But the nation lost a great president. There are still a few of us left who know what Drake is all about. We'll just have to work on this from the outside." His voice grew distant. "I don't know how long I can keep you and Jacques on the payroll."

"I'm pretty sure I speak for all of us when I say we're not doing this for the money."

"Well," Palmer said, "whatever you do, you have to do it from over there. The others can come home, but you need to sit tight . . . Listen, I have to go. I'll be in touch."

Quinn hung up and turned to Garcia. Thibodaux and Miyagi had come up at the end of the conversation. He relayed the information Palmer had given him.

"Well, l'ami," the big Cajun said with a sigh. "I've done a lot of weird things since we met. I might as well add taking down the president to that list. Any idea where we'll start?"

Quinn draped an arm around Garcia, leaning on her for support. "I have absolutely no idea."

"Shimoyama's book give us some guidance," Miyagi said, her breath amazingly calm for what she'd just been through. "I suggest we begin in Pakistan . . ."

EPILOGUE

Still uncertain about the effects of the plague, CDC personnel kept the quarantines in place. Once word got out that the disease was being spread one person at a time, hospitals in the western United States began to turn loose of their ventilators and ECMO machines. Before long, Todd Elton had more machines than he had sick patients. The only two fatalities were Mrs. Johnson, who was the oldest of those infected, and R. J. Howard, who, Elton thought, had just plain given up because his wife had left him.

Marta Bedford continued to count her boils, even after Mrs. Johnson had passed, but began to notice fewer and fewer every day. Brody Teeples's wife pulled through as well, but he was in jail for riding his ATV drunk when she came off ECMO, so he wasn't there to see her.

Sheriff Young interviewed all the victims and found that each of them had received a "particularly rough" pedicure at the hands of Haifa, Marta Bedford's new employee. Of course, Haifa was nowhere to be found.

Centers for Disease Control and Prevention, in co-ordination with the FBI, seized all the vaccine manufactured at Yanagi Pharmaceutical. Lab tests confirmed that it was not a vaccine at all, but the potent virus itself.

Fairfax County officer Jenny Chin's funeral was attended by over four hundred uniformed representatives from departments all over the United States. Detectives weren't able to make a solid case against Larsson for her shooting, but volunteers kept him busy in interrogation so he was not able to sully her memory with his attendance.

The arrest warrant for Jericho Quinn remained in effect.

Bowen and Hase met up with Quinn at a Buddhist temple cottage in Fukuoka. The monk, Kobo, stood by and played Angry Birds on his cell phone as they talked in his neutral zone.

"I never believed you did it, you know," Bowen said, keeping his eyes flitting between the big Cajun, Garcia, and Emiko Miyagi. Thibodaux was as tough looking as they came, but Bowen somehow knew that if he'd tried to arrest Quinn at that moment, these women would chew him up and spit him out.

"That's comforting," Quinn said. "So what now?"

Bowen blew air into his cheeks, thinking. "To tell you the truth, I'm not sure. It's a damn strange coincidence that both the president and vice president were killed while you're being framed for murder. I'm no superspy like you, but I'd say some things don't add up."

Quinn sat mute, offering no explanation.

"Anyway." Bowen took a piece of white paper from

his inside jacket pocket. It was folded once down the middle. "I did a sketch of you on the way over, you can have—"

Garcia snatched it out of his hand. "I'll take that," she said. "He'd just throw it away."

"So, you're going back to the States?" Miyagi asked. It was more of a suggestion than a question.

"That's what they tell me," Bowen said. "Like I said, I'm not an international person of mystery like you guys are. I'm just a POD."

Quinn extended his hand. "Having someone among the front lines might be handy in the near future."

Hase stood back a bit, looking more at the ground than anyone in particular. "There is the matter of over a dozen deaths of Japanese citizens," he said, still staring at the floor.

Everyone in the room tensed. They couldn't go back to the U.S., and Detective Hase appeared about to make it impossible to stay in Japan.

"What about them?" Quinn asked.

"I was wondering," the detective said, "if you ever hear anything regarding these deaths or who might have perpetrated them, would you be so kind as to let me know?"

Vice President–elect Lee McKeon's wife had returned to the governor's mansion in Salem to make things ready for their move to the Naval Observatory once Bob Hughes's widow moved out. Secret Service agents, not Oregon State Police, now stood outside the door to this suite at the Hay Adams—on high alert considering the state of the nation.

McKeon stood in front of the bathroom mirror and slowly unbuttoned his shirt. As far as his protective detail knew, the pert little staffer in the other room was supposed to be helping him with some correspondence. It would, he hoped, be a very, very long letter.

Putting his hands flat on the counter, he stared at himself and couldn't help smiling. His biological father had envisioned this day, methodically moving aside anything and anyone that got in his way. And then, Jericho Quinn had come along and forced him to kill himself. McKeon knew Quinn was still out there and that he would come for the president. And, McKeon thought, that was all right. For all anyone in the United States knew, he was not the son of Pakistani doctor Nazeer Badeeb and the Chinese Muslim Li Huang, but a natural-born citizen of the United States of America, perfectly capable of assuming the presidency if Hartman Drake happened to be assassinated by a madman.

The pert young staffer walked in and stepped between him and the mirror. In her mid-twenties, she was Japanese, with long black hair and eyes that were more ochre than brown. She wore nothing but a long-sleeve pajama top, deep maroon to match her lipstick.

Round where he was angular, pale where he was dark, she was over a foot shorter than McKeon and had to stand on tiptoe to get her arms around his neck. She pressed against his body and kissed him long and hard.

"You don't need those stupid Secret Service agents," she growled, biting him on the lip.

He jerked away, finger to his mouth, tasting blood.

"Maybe I need them to protect me from you." He grinned.

"Nonsense," the woman said, letting the pajama top slide to the floor.

His hands snaked around her naked waist, pulling her roughly to him.

Her lips nuzzled his neck and his eyes fell on the intricate tattoo inked across her back—a snarling foo dog, mouth open, fangs bared.

Sinking her teeth into the soft flesh of his ear, she once again drew blood. He shuddered at her whisper.

"I *am* your protector."

ACKNOWLEDGMENTS

Until this year, it had been over thirty years since I set foot in Japan. A young lady told me the last time I left that something about the place would forever tug me back. Turns out she was right.

Yukiko Pollard made this trip more than I could have hoped for. She proved to be an excellent interpreter—bridging the gap where my rusty language skills fell off—and the perfect guide, consultant, and traveling companion. Her insight into the culture and people helped developed nuances and backstory for Jericho's adventure that I could never have gotten otherwise.

Lan Yamada offered me a place to stay and write and provided much in the way of background regarding Fukuoka and the surrounding area. I cannot look back on my time there without thinking that I not only gained valuable writing contacts but lifelong friends. A four-hour dinner with several officers from the Fukuoka Police Department, who wish not to be named, provided invaluable assistance with the subtleties of working in Japanese law enforcement—not to mention helping me see that there is a particular kinship shared by police officers wherever they happen to serve.

I also need to thank the proprietor of an unnamed

love hotel in Tokyo for the guided tour. Interesting, to say the least.

Thanks to Brad Husberg and Doctor Dustin H. for their ideas and pointers regarding plagues of biblical proportions. It is indeed a frightening thing to get scientists talking what-ifs over a bowl of curry chicken.

Thanks to Ben for his assistance with Mandarin and the aforementioned Yukiko and Lan for their help with Japanese.

As always, Ty Cunningham, my martial arts instructor and friend, helped walk me through the violence and fight dynamics. I'm still sore from getting my throat "cut" so many times with a silicon spatula.

Thanks to Andy Goldfine of Aerostich riding gear, who helped me work through what it would be like to be on the receiving end of a police dog bite while wearing an armored motorcycle jacket.

Thanks to Scott Ireton, Sonny Caudill, Vic Aye, and my other motorcycle buds for letting me talk through the riding scenarios.

My agent, Robin Rue, and my editor, Gary Goldstein, are great people and a pleasure to work with.

Ryan and Ray at Northern Knives in Anchorage continue to provide insight into all things edged.

My hat goes off to the men and women of the Air Force Office of Special Investigations—and especially, to my friends with the United States Marshals Service—heroes all.

And, most important, thanks to Victoria, my kindest critic and greatest support.